S.A.V.E.

Book Four of the A.L.I.V.E. Series

R.D. BRADY

D1738748

Scottish Seoul Publishing, LLC

BOOKS BY R.D. BRADY

Hominid

The Belial Series (in order)
The Belial Stone
The Belial Library
The Belial Ring
Recruit: A Belial Series Novella
The Belial Children
The Belial Origins
The Belial Search
The Belial Guard
The Belial Warrior
The Belial Plan
The Belial Witches
The Belial War
The Belial Fall
The Belial Sacrifice

The A.L.I.V.E. Series
B.E.G.I.N.
A.L.I.V.E.

D.E.A.D.

R.I.S.E.

S.A.V.E.

The Steve Kane Series

Runs Deep

Runs Deeper

The Unwelcome Series

Protect

Seek

Proxy

The Nola James Series

Surrender the Fear

Escape the Fear

Published as Riley D. Brady

The Key of Apollo

The Curse of Hecate

Be sure to sign up for R.D.'s mailing list to be the first to hear when she has a new release!

CHAPTER ONE

OFF THE COAST OF SEATTLE, WASHINGTON

THE RAIN BEAT A STEADY RHYTHM AGAINST THE ROOF OF THE wheelhouse of the *Destiny*, a seventy-foot rusted blue crabber off the coast of Washington state.

Martin sat in the corner of the wheelhouse, a heavy gray blanket draped over his shoulders. He wrinkled his nose as yet again the smell of fish invaded his nostrils. He'd made the mistake earlier of trying to cover his nose with his hand, but it had only made the smell stronger.

He held out a hand with disgust. His hands were still wrinkled. He'd spent a full day in the water after Garrigan and his cohorts had dumped him out of the plane.

A plane.

From the water, he'd seen the explosion as the bombs hit the factory in Edmonds. The explosion had set off a small tsunami, which had shoved him farther out to sea. It was pure dumb luck that the crabber had found him. He'd managed to pull himself up onto a buoy but only after he'd spent hours floating. Then he'd spent a cold, miserable night clinging to life on the rusted metal.

The door to the wheelhouse opened. It brought with it a gust of cool air and a spray of rain and seawater. A rough man with a black stocking cap on his head, waders, and a thick raincoat stepped into the room. Captain Ernesto Flavigo gave him a bright smile. "Ah, you're still awake. I thought perhaps you might have gone below to catch some shut-eye."

Martin shook his head. "No. Have you had any luck?"

Ernesto nodded his head as he walked to the coffee machine and poured himself a cup. Martin held his tongue with barely concealed anger as Ernesto took a long sip. He let out a deep, contented sigh. "Yes. I've reached the Coast Guard. I told them about finding you. It appears quite a few people have been lost at sea after the events in Edmonds. The Coast Guard has been run ragged. They don't have enough people for the demand."

Martin didn't give a damn about the Coast Guard and its staff shortages. "When will we be back on shore?"

"Another two hours at most. But the seas are getting choppy, so you may want to go below. It will be safer."

Martin reined in his growl. On one level, he knew the man was just trying to be polite to his unexpected guest. He and his crew of four had plucked him from the sea two hours earlier. They'd been far off the coast and had been shocked to find him on the buoy. But they'd done their best to make him comfortable. They'd given him a change of clothes and plied him with food and hot drinks to help warm him up.

But they were slow men. Slow-moving and slow-thinking. They were also stubborn. He could see that in the set of their shoulders and the cadence of their talk. Pushing them would only make them grow suspicious. He was lucky they believed his "I fell off a boat" story.

Besides, he had no leverage here. There was nothing to hold over the man's head, at least not yet. So he bit his tongue. "I'm sure I'll be fine. What about your SAT phone?"

The weather had made the SAT phone unusable. Either that or the missile strike in Edmonds had wiped out communication lines.

He still couldn't believe that Tilda had gone through with it. He hadn't thought she had the spine for it.

She'd shown him, hadn't she?

Of course, he also hadn't thought Chris Garrigan and Adam Watson would kidnap him. He hadn't read their desperation correctly.

Martin didn't understand that kind of desperation, at least not when it was linked around the well-being of another living creature. He wasn't sure what he would do if someone took his daughter. Oh, he'd send people after her and make sure those who dared to harm what was his were destroyed. But he would not be in the state that Chris Garrigan had been in. The man had been beside himself.

As had Nora Tidwell. Nothing in her file indicated that she would become so attached to the Maldek. She'd been just as desperate to get him back.

They were probably all dead in the blast now. He smiled. At least one good thing had come out of this. That and the decimation of the Drago. That scourge should have been wiped from the planet years ago. And if Martin had been in charge, they would have.

He knew that not all of the Drago had been destroyed. There would be pockets of Drago across the globe that escaped the attack. The United States had underestimated the defenses at the Antarctica base as well. That base went extremely deep. Even with a MOAB, they would not be able to reach the farthest depths of the Drago stronghold. Some would survive. And like cockroaches, they would eventually crawl from the rubble.

But the attacks would set them back on their heels. It could be decades, if not longer, before they reemerged.

"Is the SAT phone working?"

"Yes, yes. Do you want to make a call?" Ernesto pulled the phone from his inside jacket pocket.

Martin had to keep himself from snatching the phone from Ernesto's hand. Of course he wanted to make a call. He'd been asking to make a call for the last two hours. Ernesto had assured him that eventually the SAT phone would work. But he seemed in no hurry to make sure that it did.

Martin took the phone and headed for the door.

"Are you sure you want to go out there? The storm is getting worse."

The storm is just beginning, Martin thought but said nothing.

"Hold on a second." Ernesto slipped the rain slicker off of his shoulders and handed it to Martin. "At least take this. It'll keep most of the rain off of you."

Martin nodded his thanks as he slipped the jacket on. It was still warm from Ernesto. Martin was surprised at the amount of comfort he received from that warmth.

Rain slapped him in the face as he stepped outside. He gripped the railing as he made his way to the stairs and down to the main deck. Two of the crewmen were walking along the aft deck, so Martin headed to the foredeck. Dozens of crates lined the deck, most of them empty. A few crabs stuck in traps eyed him as he walked past. He stepped to the back of the boat. Leaning against the wet railing, he dialed.

Stacy Mal, his assistant, answered the phone quickly. "Who is this? How did you get this number?"

"I *gave* you this number," Martin said with a growl.

"Mr. Drummond. My God. Where have you been? I've had people searching everywhere for you, but we've had no luck at all."

"That's because someone tossed me out of a plane." He swallowed down his anger. "What's the status of MAURC?"

The worry and concern disappeared from Stacy's voice as she immediately slipped back into assistant mode. "It's been rescinded. The facilities at both Edmonds and Antarctica were bombed as scheduled. Satellite imagery indicated that there was no movement at either site. With the threat removed, there was no longer a need for MAURC."

Martin grunted. Well, at least Matilda no longer had all the might of the U.S. military at her fingertips. "Has she crawled back into her hole?"

"Um, not exactly."

"*What* does that mean?"

"R.I.S.E. is acknowledged by all branches of the U.S. military now. They have an official seat at the table."

"What about Garrigan and the others?"

"The sat photos indicate that they were able to escape the site at Edmonds moments before the blast. They are believed to still be alive, although no one has been able to find them after they left the airfield in Seattle. Satellites were misbehaving for a while after the blast."

Martin nodded, exhaustion weighing him down. Why couldn't they all just die the way they were supposed to?

"And there was one additional, unexpected passenger with the Garrigan crew."

Martin frowned. Who could they have possibly taken with them? A Drago? Why would they take one? To experiment on? To find its weaknesses? But why bother when they already had Adam? "Who?"

"Sammy."

Martin stilled, his whole body locked in place as fear extended to every single cell in his body. *"What?"*

Stacy's voice came out in a rush. "Apparently the Drago had taken him hostage. The Garrigan crew retrieved him. He looked like he was injured. He was loaded onto the plane with the rest of them and was with them when they took off."

Martin took a deep calming breath. This was too much. Sammy never should've escaped Area 51. He was the one creature that was supposed to have stayed locked away. Martin would've been happier if the Drago had taken him and kept him. At least then he'd know that the creature would be tortured for years to come. But once again, Leander and her people had ruined that possibility.

"I need you to find Maeve Leander and the others. There must be some trace of them."

"I have everybody working on it already. It's only a matter of time."

Martin ignored the empty platitudes. "Send a chopper to my location. I expect it within the hour."

"Yes, sir." Stacy paused before she blurted, "We all thought you were dead, sir."

"Get to work."

Martin disconnected the call. He stared out at the choppy water. Leander and the hybrid were alive. And they now had Sammy with them.

We all thought you were dead.

Martin gripped the railing. He stared out at the water, just able to make out the coast in the distance. No, he wasn't dead. And that was their mistake. That small burst of compassion would be their undoing.

The rain picked up its pace, lashing at him. *But I won't make that mistake. Compassion has never been an issue with me.*

CHAPTER TWO

HALIFAX, CANADA

DR. MAEVE LEANDER WAS TIRED. HER GROUP OF TEN HAD traveled through Canada, mostly by car, for the last seven days. They'd tried to travel mainly at night, switching out drivers in their two-car caravan. The problem had been with Sammy. They couldn't risk anyone checking the back of the truck and seeing him, so they'd traveled at the speed limit.

Today, they'd finally made it to the eastern coast of Canada. There, Jasper had a connection that provided them with the plane for the next leg of the journey. Maeve had been sleeping before they'd arrived at the coast, so she was one of the only ones who was wide awake as the plane took off. Everyone else fell asleep almost immediately after they were in the air. The tension of the trip seemed to drain the energy from all of them.

Maeve walked to the back of the plane where Sammy lay. He was laid out in the cargo hold. At seven feet tall, with a ten-foot wingspan, it was the only place where he could lie comfortably.

He appeared to be sleeping on the stacks of blankets they'd piled up to make a nest.

Maeve moved forward quietly. She crouched down and pressed

two fingers against the side of his throat. His pulse pounded away beneath her touch, speeding along at a faster pace than that of humans. But from what her and Greg could tell, this was his normal rate.

He was sedated to try and keep him from tearing at his bandages. They still weren't sure how exactly to talk to him. He didn't communicate with any of them in any discernible way, although Maeve was pretty sure that he understood them.

Sammy's eyes flickered open, and dark slits watched her. She gave him what she hoped was a reassuring smile. "Looks good. You're healing nicely. Those bandages will be off in another week or so."

Sammy watched for another long moment before he closed his eyes. Maeve let out a breath she hadn't realized she'd been holding. She wasn't sure what the situation with Sammy was. Alvie trusted him. Luke, Iggy, and Snap did as well. But they were all essentially children. She wasn't sure how much stock she should put in their views.

But as Greg pointed out, children were always the best judges of character.

Maeve made her way back into the cabin. Everyone was sprawled out. The blanket over Nora and Iggy had fallen to the ground. Maeve picked it up and tucked it back around them. Iggy opened his eyes and gave a big yawn. His pointed ears wiggled with the motion. "Ig." He closed his eyes again with a sigh.

Maeve smiled at the little Maldek. It was hard not to love him. Nora and Iggy had a bond that was incredibly strong. And absolutely amazing, especially being Nora was a former D.E.A.D. agent.

Falling under the Department of Defense, the D.E.A.D. had been created in the aftermath of the meltdown of the A.L.I.V.E. cases at Area 51. Their mandate was to track down all the A.L.I.V.E. escapees from Area 51, and according to Nora, kill them. But when it came to Iggy, she couldn't pull the trigger, which was what led her to Maeve and the rest of them. And which was also what put her life on the line and her on the run. But

Maeve knew if given the same choice again, she wouldn't change a thing.

Just like Maeve wouldn't.

Maeve continued up to the cabin. Chris was two rows up from Nora with Alvie and Snap snuggled into his sides, one hand resting protectively on each of them.

She was happy to see him sleeping. It had been a rare thing for him this last week. She knew he felt guilty for what had happened to Crackle and Pop. She'd told him over and over again it wasn't his fault. But he couldn't seem to accept it. Now he was hypervigilant when it came to Snap and Alvie.

The last two of their group in the cabin were Jasper Jenkins and Mike Bileris, both R.I.S.E. operatives. Jasper and Mike had risked everything to save Maeve, Greg, Alvie, Snap, and Luke in Washington. And without them and their resourcefulness, Maeve knew they wouldn't have made it this far.

Greg was in the last row, an arm thrown over his head. Sandra and Luke Gillibrand had taken the last two rows and were each sprawled out. Maeve hoped they were all getting a good night's sleep. God knew, they all needed one.

Jasper and Mike sat near the front, engrossed in a chess game. They didn't look up as Maeve passed by. She stepped into the cockpit and closed the door quietly behind her.

Adam Watson glanced over his shoulder at her before turning his attention back to the controls. She didn't let his silence deter her. She'd gotten used to Adam's quietness. He wasn't unfriendly. He just quite simply didn't talk unless he viewed it as necessary.

She took a seat in the copilot seat, careful not to touch anything. "How are you feeling? Are you tired? Should I get you a coffee?"

Shaking his head, Adam adjusted a dial on the control panel. "No. I'm fine. Thank you. Is everyone sleeping?"

"All but Jasper and Mike. They're playing chess again."

Adam made no response, and Maeve felt no need to fill the silence. She just sat with him as she watched the clouds fly by.

When she was a kid, she had never once been on a plane, despite essentially living on Wright-Patterson Air Force Base. With her mom and Alvie, vacations simply weren't an option. She and her mother never left Wright-Pat.

But over the last couple of years, she'd been rushed in and out of planes across the country. And now she was rushing across the globe.

And that was by far the least unusual change the last few years had brought her.

She glanced over the control panel, not knowing what any of the instruments indicated. The only one that was even slightly familiar was the compass. They were heading west.

"Do we have a specific destination in mind, or are we just hoping for the best?"

Adam glanced at her from the corner of his eye. She could tell he was deciding whether or not to trust her with the truth. Sharing secrets was not something Adam did easily, and Maeve wasn't going to push him. Adam was a Drago, yet he had proven his loyalty to the rest of them time and time again. Maeve had lost count of how many times he had saved people's lives. And if he thought keeping their destination secret was the best plan, then she was okay with it too.

"We're going to my home."

Surprise flashed through Maeve. She knew that Adam had been alive for hundreds of years, so "home" could have a variety of interpretations for him. "What does that mean?"

A rare smile crossed Adam's face. "You've heard the story of my time with the Drago?"

Maeve hadn't been on the plane when Adam's nature had been revealed to the rest of the group. Chris had explained it to her shortly after their rescue from Edmonds. Maeve had never discussed it directly with Adam, though.

"You were born among the Drago. And you and your sister fought. You refused to kill her, and so they thought that you did not have a cold enough heart to be the leader of the Drago."

"Yes, that's true. I was beaten. I was chased. I threw myself into a river as a last desperate attempt to escape."

"How old were you?"

"About four or five."

Maeve gasped, picturing a small blond child running desperately in the dark to escape monsters trying to harm him. "That must've been awful."

"It was. But it was also the best thing that ever happened to me. The current took me out to sea. Days later, I landed on the northeastern coast of Norway. My family had been out fishing. It was their annual trip to the coast. They found me and took me with them to their home. I lived with them in the mountains of Norway in the area now known as Geiranger."

He smiled. "It's beautiful country. Rolling hills, houses hidden among the hills. You can go for days without seeing anyone."

"It sounds beautiful."

"It is. And no one knows about it."

"Not even Tilda?"

Adam's mouth flatlined for the barest of seconds before he nodded. "She knows. But she would never reveal it. She would go to her death before she would."

Maeve studied the man next to her. He was, in many ways, an incredibly old-fashioned man in his sense of duty, loyalty, and love. She supposed that was an accurate assessment, being he wasn't from this time.

"What about other members of your family? They must know about the house."

She felt the sadness before he spoke. "No," he said softly. "The last of them passed away in the early twentieth century. It was a plane crash. There are no more of my family left."

"There's one," Maeve said quietly.

Adam looked over at her and gave her a small nod.

"Is there any way for them to tie the house to you?"

Adam shook his head again. "No. It's under my Norwegian name. I've created a false trail of descendants for ownership. The house passed from one generation to the next. No one knows that name anymore. There'd be no reason for them to go looking for it. And it is extremely off grid."

Maeve settled into her seat a little more tightly, suddenly feeling exhausted. "That sounds perfect right now."

"It's okay, Maeve. We're safe for now. Get some sleep. I won't let anything happen to you. Any of you."

Maeve nodded her head, too tired to reply. But she believed with all of her heart that he spoke the truth.

CHAPTER THREE

GEIRANGER, NORWAY

ONE WEEK LATER

MAEVE STEPPED OUT OF THE CONVERTED BARN AND CLOSED THE door softly. Sammy was resting. His injury was healing fast. She knew that he wouldn't stay there much longer, maybe another day or two at most. She could feel his need to get away. She wasn't sure if it was because that was ingrained in him or because he just needed to get away from them.

She hoped it was just part of his nature.

She had to admit, she was fascinated by him. His skin was a light maroon, but she'd noticed that it had lightened considerably since he'd been in their care. She and Greg hypothesized that the color might be a reaction to the sun. And when the sun was removed from the equation, it became less vibrant, more human. The human aspect of the creature was hard to miss. His facial features were definitely human, especially his blue eyes.

In the week that he'd been with them, though, he hadn't said a word. She wasn't even sure if vocalization was part of his communication process. It was entirely possible that he did not speak because no one had ever spoken with him during those critical years speech can develop. Humans who were not spoken to as young children never developed the capability for speech either.

And Maeve had no doubt that he was yet another hybrid from Area 51. He seemed older than the other releasees, but maybe that was just part of his intelligence shining through and making him seem more mature, more intelligent than the other creatures she'd seen.

A light wind ruffled her hair. She wrapped the heavy blue-and-white sweater around her. The air had gotten much cooler, even in the bright sunlight. She knew winter wasn't far off. They were at Adam's family home in Norway. Maeve hadn't known what to expect when Adam said that they were heading to his home. She'd pictured an ancient, decrepit cabin.

She was pleasantly surprised to find an incredibly updated home on a high hill. They were 500, maybe 600, feet above sea level in an incredibly remote location that required ATVs to reach.

Adam told her he and Tilda had been coming here for a few years, setting the place up in case they needed it as a hideout. No one else in R.I.S.E. knew about it.

Electricity was provided via solar panels on the roof and more solar panels that lined a field half a mile away. Heat was provided by geothermal springs. A well and a rainwater containment system met all of their water needs. They were completely off the grid. It had sounded incredibly rustic when Adam had described it. Maeve had held her breath when they finally came around the bend on the ATVs, not sure what to expect.

And her mind had been blown, but in the best of possible ways. The cabin was two stories tall and made of stucco and wood. The doorways and windows were framed by unhewn wood, and inside, all the doorways were made from rounded trees entwined together into an arch. The floor-to-ceiling windows inside offered a breathtaking view of the fjord. It was like living in a fairytale where everything was lush and green.

But most important, there were no other people anywhere around. In the week that they had been there, they hadn't seen another soul. With a population of two hundred, Adam had been right about how isolated Geiranger was. But that would only last for another few months. In the spring, the tourists would arrive. Nearly a million people would visit this part of the world between May and September. But that problem was a few months off.

Now Maeve stared out at the fjord with her arms wrapped around herself and breathed in deep. She could get used to this.

She felt his presence before she saw him. She glanced over her shoulder as Alvie walked toward her. Only three and a half feet tall, with a large wide face that came to a point at his chin and gray skin tone, Alvie would never be mistaken for a human, even though he was part human. But most people wouldn't look beyond the abnormally shaped head and the disproportionately large dark eyes. If they did, they would see a soul that was incredibly kind and incredibly generous. He was the type of human they should all strive to be.

Maeve held out a hand. Alvie gently grasped it with his long thin fingers with their bony knobs. Love wafted through her. Alvie communicated through emotions. He always had. The two of them had grown up together, and Maeve hadn't really known any other way of living, not until she was much older. So she'd accepted Alvie from the moment she'd met him. And that bond had only grown stronger over the years.

But even without that bond, she would be able to tell that something was wrong. And she didn't have to ask what it was.

"We'll find a way to get them back."

Alvie looked up into her face, searching not just her facial expressions but her mind, to see if she was telling the truth or just trying to make him feel better.

Crackle and Pop had been seriously injured in the attack on the

R.I.S.E. base. Agaren had taken them to the Council's base located on the moon. Chris had made the heartbreaking decision to allow them to go. It had been the only way to save their lives. In the weeks since then, they hadn't heard from Agaren.

But Maeve had to believe that Crackle and Pop were alive and well. She did not know the tall alien well. But for some reason, she did trust him. He would not take Pop and Crackle unless he truly believed he could save their lives. And she was holding on to that.

But their recovery was not Maeve's only concern. Even if the Council was able to save Pop and Crackle, would they consider it a priority to return them to Maeve and the others? Would they take the time they had with two of the triplets to examine them or even just hold on to them for a while until they felt they'd learned enough and returned them?

The lifespan of the Council could be hundreds of years. For them, years would be no time at all. Whereas for the triplets, each hour would feel like a day, each day a week, each week a year. Maeve missed them so much her heart ached. And she knew that her pain was nothing compared to Snap's.

Snap, the remaining member of the triplets, was struggling at going from being part of the trio to standing on her own two feet. Her entire short life, she'd had Pop and Crackle by her side. Spending these last two weeks without them had been killing her. She'd become more listless and despondent. They'd all tried to get her to feel better, but nothing really worked. The only one who seemed to be able to get through to her was Sammy.

Snap spent a great deal of her time with Sammy and Iggy. She took comfort in the presence of both of them. And Maeve was just thankful that the two of them were around.

A picture of the moon drifted into Maeve's mind. She squeezed Alvie's hand and nodded. "Yes, there's a full moon tonight. We'll stay outside and watch it, okay?"

Alvie leaned into her with a sigh. Maeve wrapped her arms around him, wishing there was more that she could do to comfort him. She wished there was more she could do to comfort herself. But for now, watching the full moon was as close to Pop and Crackle as they were going to get.

Maeve looked up at the sky. *I'll get you back. Somehow I'll get you back.*

CHAPTER FOUR

A THOUSAND METERS SOUTHEAST OF THE VALKYRIE DOME, ANTARCTICA

It was negative twenty degrees Fahrenheit. No human would be able to survive out here for long. But Tatiana was no human, despite the tanned skin and long blonde hair that would suggest otherwise.

She crossed the arid landscape, her boots crunching through the upper layer of the hard snow. She had stayed in one of her safe houses in northern Canada for two weeks until she was sure that the U.S. government believed her to be dead.

It had been another five days to return home, a long, difficult trek. They could not take any of their normal means. And they could not allow witnesses or a trail. Weather had also worked against them. But finally, her home was only a short distance away.

But she hadn't been idle. She had planned. She had plotted. And soon, her revenge would be made whole.

The wind picked up and blew against her, dropping the temperature by another twenty degrees. Tatiana barely noticed. The Drago were built to withstand extreme temperatures. And Tatiana, as their queen, was built even more resilient.

She strode up the small hill without so much as a change in her breathing. Anger fueled her steps. She crested the rise and then stopped still. A giant crater now sat where the entrance to her base had stood. She bit her tongue, her eyes narrowing to slits.

You bastards. I will see your blood run through my hands.

She pictured Martin Drummond. Somehow that man was responsible for this. Somehow that man had brought this destruction upon them. And she was going to make sure that she returned the favor.

Tatiana made her way down the icy slope. The main entrance was completely blocked. It took them an hour to figure out how to slide through. For hours, they toiled, pulling boulders and giants slabs of ice out of the way.

And with each minute that passed, she affirmed more and more how much destruction she would rain down on this planet. The humans had made a fatal mistake in leaving her alive. *And I will make sure they pay for that miscalculation.*

Tatiana shoved an icy boulder aside from the collapsed hallway ahead of her.

Movement in the dark speared through the opening she'd made. A face, green in color, with a flattened snout and two rows of teeth along with reptilian eyes appeared through the opening.

Tatiana nodded. "Finish clearing the way."

"Yes, my queen."

Tatiana watched as her people cleared out the obstruction from the other side. She felt no joy at knowing they were alive. She felt no happiness realizing that she and the three who had escaped Washington were not the last of their kind. All she felt was cold resolve. "We will rise again. We will take them from—"

An explosion cut off her words. Searing heat burst through Tatiana's skin. *No. No, this cannot happen now. I—*

But the rest of her thoughts disappeared in a ball of fire, along with the remaining Drago.

CHAPTER FIVE

Matilda Watson, head of R.I.S.E., which stood for Research in Intelligent Space Exploration, strode down the hall in the Pentagon the best she could with the aid of her cane. She stepped into the newly acquired R.I.S.E. control room. Monitors lined the back wall. Analysts were furiously working at computers.

She had just received word that there had been movement near the Drago base in Antarctica. It had been three weeks since the bombing of the Drago strongholds. The R.I.S.E. team had locked down the site in Washington almost immediately. But they had been unable to get a team to Antarctica until today. Flyovers of the site, however, had shown a massive crater where the base once stood. It had been under near constant observation.

But Tilda needed to know how deep the base went. She needed to know the Drago threat was gone.

The level of activity and the noise in the room was higher than it normally was. Tilda scanned the room. This level of activity wasn't because their group was heading to the blast site. Something else was going on.

The second-in-command of R.I.S.E., Pearl Huen, caught sight

of her from across the room. She hurried over, her dark hair perfectly straight in its blunt bowl cut. Her dark eyes peered up at Tilda through her glasses.

"Report," Tilda said.

"There was a strike in Antarctica."

Tilda's gaze shot to Pearl. "Where?"

"The Drago base. It was a direct hit. Anyone that survived the first blast would've been completely decimated in the second one."

"What about the team the satellite picked up earlier?"

"We have conformation: It was Tatiana. She survived Washington."

Damn it. Tilda curled her left hand in a fist. She'd known in her gut that the Drago leader would somehow survive the blast. But she'd hoped she was wrong.

"Where was she when the blast hit?"

"Ground zero. She was still outside the base, no protection, no covering. There is no chance she survived."

Tilda hoped Pearl was right. "What about our team?"

"They were twenty minutes away from the site. A few received minor injuries but nothing serious."

Thank God for that. "Who?"

Pearl didn't ask for clarification of the question. She knew exactly what Tilda was asking. "Not sure yet. No allies have admitted to the strike."

"And our enemies?"

"We've had no indication that any of them would have taken this kind of step."

"So, as of right now, we know nothing."

Pearl nodded. "I'm afraid that's true."

"Commander Watson, I have a satellite feed."

Tilda turned and noted the concerned look on the analyst's face. Steeling herself, she made her way over to the analyst's desk. "Up on the screen."

Two seconds later, the giant screen at the back of the room flared to life, and the room went quiet. Tilda stepped forward as the Antarctica landscape came into view. A flaming object appeared from the right of the screen and slammed into the crater already created on the Arctic floor from R.I.S.E.'s bombing campaign.

Tilda turned away from the glare as the object exploded. An audible gasp went up across the room as the light dimmed. The crater, which had been about a hundred yards wide, was now at least double that. Pearl was right. If Tatiana had been exposed during that hit, she couldn't have survived.

It appeared Tatiana was no longer a concern for R.I.S.E. But that did not mean that there wasn't still a concern. "Play it back at half speed."

Tilda stepped forward, watching the replay. "Again. Slower."

The image slowed down even more, allowing Tilda to get a better view of the missile that hit. Next to her, Pearl gasped.

"Freeze it," Tilda ordered.

The image on the screen stopped as if suspended in midair.

Tilda walked slowly toward it, ignoring the new wave of murmurs that erupted across the room. Instead of seeing the cylindrical body of a warhead, she was looking at a large piece of space rock.

"A meteorite? What are the chances?" Pearl asked softly next to her.

Tilda didn't answer. She simply stared up at the screen. An icy cold washed over her. The chances of a meteor strike hitting the Drago base were beyond impossible. Which meant that this was something else. This was something that she'd been working her whole life to avoid.

God help us all.

CHAPTER SIX

GEIRANGER, NORWAY

Norway was beautiful. In the two weeks since they had set up camp here, Chris Garrigan had to admit, the place had grown on him. Right now he and Adam were climbing up the hill to the summit. Each of them took turns climbing with Adam, twice a day, to check on the news from the outside world. It was the only place where they could actually get a signal.

Maeve was supposed to go this morning, but she hadn't slept well last night, so Chris had slipped out of the room, letting her sleep in. Alvie and Snap snuggled under the blankets with her.

Ahead, a squirrel crisscrossed over a cool bubbling stream as it made its way through the rocks. A fox scampered into the trees. A chipmunk pushed through some leaves, darting across their path before disappearing on the other side.

It really was like something out of a Disney fairytale. Chris and his family should be loving every minute of it.

Except that two of them were missing.

Without Pop and Crackle, nothing felt right. Chris agonized over and over about whether or not he'd made the right decision. Was it possible the military doctors could have saved them? But at the time, the military doctors weren't sure if they would've been able to. Chris couldn't have taken the chance.

Could he?

But now they hadn't seen the triplets in over three weeks, nor had they received word from Agaren. They didn't even know if the triplets had survived the trip to the base. And every time Chris closed his eyes, he saw those two tiny little bodies on the stretchers.

He never thought of himself as a father. He honestly thought that the military was going to be his calling for life. He certainly had never seriously considered starting a family. When he'd met Maeve, he knew that she might be someone he wanted, no, needed to get to know better. When he first met Alvie, he had balked at the idea of inserting himself into their lives. But after spending more and more time with Alvie, it was impossible not to love him. It was impossible not to want to look after him.

Meeting the triplets, his reaction had been no different. With the triplets being so young, Chris felt like their father. He knew he looked nothing like them. He knew they weren't even the same species. And yet he knew what he felt was a father's love for three incredibly beautiful little creatures.

And not knowing where two of them were and how they were doing was tearing him up inside.

Adam turned from where he stood farther up the trail. He looked back at Chris, his sunglasses in place. His white-blond hair looked even brighter in the sunlight. And Chris could picture his piercing blue eyes. Adam looked so incredibly human, and yet he was even less human than Alvie or the triplets.

Adam could pass in society as a human. But he was a full-fledged Drago, the species of creature that had attempted to kidnap his children. The Drago had destroyed the R.I.S.E. base and had planned to wreak havoc across the globe.

Chris wasn't a bloodthirsty individual. He'd never been one who went for the kill when a wound would do just as well. But he wanted the Drago dead. He wanted the threat to his family ended.

But he knew deep down it was even more than that. Chris, Jasper Jenkins, Mike Bileris, and Adam were all incredibly well-trained. All of the R.I.S.E. soldiers had been.

And they'd all had trouble taking the Drago down.

Humanity in general would have even less luck. Humanity could not withstand the onslaught of a full-frontal Drago attack. They would run roughshod over all countries of the world. The only way to destroy them would be a nuclear attack. Chris was sure that was exactly what it would come to if the Drago got a foothold in the human world and decided to expand their base.

Chris couldn't imagine a world where that happened. So he prayed that the attacks in Washington and Antarctica had done their job and annihilated the Drago threat.

At the same time, he recoiled from the idea that he was supporting the full genocide of a race of beings. But some beings simply couldn't exist in this world. They looked to dominate. They looked to take over. They looked to destroy. There would be no living in peace with the Drago. They'd lain in wait for centuries to make their move. And Chris knew without a doubt they would not wait much longer to take their next step if they hadn't been destroyed.

The news channels that reported on the attack in Washington called it a gas leak. People had bought it. Chris wasn't surprised. He'd learned that people wanted the world to be safe and predictable. They wanted easy answers to complex problems. And a gas leak was a much better explanation than the United States government destroying an alien target on U.S. soil. Some of the conspiracy websites had made the case that it was a missile attack. But they had little to no credibility, and people easily wrote them off.

Chris shook his head. The government counted on the disinformation campaign they'd started decades ago to keep people from wanting to look foolish by believing what was actually true. The U.S. government had done an incredible job of convincing the general public that aliens did not exist. Or if they did exist, that they were far, far, far away from Earth.

The truth was, aliens had been living on this planet for centuries. The U.S. government had samples of alien DNA in its labs. And they'd created hybrids and purebreds of dozens of types of alien creatures.

Alvie was the first in that long line of discoveries. Iggy was another one. Not all were as warm and fuzzy as those two, however. There were some that were straight out of someone's nightmares. And others that were beyond a nightmare.

Adam reached the summit and stood waiting for Chris. Pushing aside his thoughts, Chris focused on the task at hand. The sooner they checked the news and the reports, the sooner they would know whether or not they had anything to be concerned about. So far the world was blissfully unaware of the attack in Antarctica. No knowledge of the Drago had escaped the government information net. So for now, it looked like they were safe.

There was also no hint that anyone knew where they were. They were so far off the grid that Chris had a glimmer of hope that maybe, just maybe, they might be safe for a little while. Chris stepped up next to Adam and caught his breath.

It wasn't the exertion of the trail that caused the gasp but the view. Chris had seen it before, but it simply never got old. He'd never been to Norway before, and now he was wondering how it was possible that landscapes like this weren't plastered across every tourism site in the world. Ice-capped mountains lounged in the background, leading to rolling green hills with houses dotted here and there, all ending at the crystal-blue fjord.

It was simply stunning.

It looked like a place out of time. It wasn't marred by highways or big-box stores. It was living simply, and Chris felt an ache in his chest to provide his kids with this kind of existence.

Adam knelt down and pulled his backpack off. He pulled out the old laptop, attaching the battery, and began logging in while Chris went over and pulled the tape off the large array. Adam had set the communications system up years ago, and they had all been very glad to find it in working order when they arrived. It was their only way of communicating with the outside world. They had no phones, no computers, and no neighbors for miles.

It was a good hiding spot. During the entire time they'd been here, they had not seen or heard another soul. Not even a plane had flown overhead. But Chris didn't let down his guard. They could not take any chances.

He knelt down next to Adam as the laptop screen came to life. They skimmed the major news headlines but didn't see anything critical. It seemed the world was continuing to turn, no one the wiser about what had happened and how close they had come to a serious alien invasion.

Adam was about to move on to another news site when Chris put out a hand. "Hold on."

Adam paused his scrolling. There in the bottom-right corner was an article about a meteor strike in Antarctica. Adam zoomed in.

Chris stared at the story. He thought for a moment that maybe it was a report about the missile attack on the Antarctica Drago base, but it was dated this morning. This was a second attack. "Is this the same spot as the first missile attack?"

Adam shook his head. "I don't know. But the crater's massive."

Chris felt a tingling of fear. Maybe R.I.S.E. had just done a follow-up attack and created a cover story about a meteorite. He supposed that was possible, but he didn't like it. They finished searching the rest of the news sites, but there was no mention of anything else of concern. The international security sites indicated that D.E.A.D. wasn't any closer to finding them either. So it looked like for now, they were in the clear.

Adam broke down the system as Chris stood, looking around. A meteor strike in Antarctica. Dread welled up in his chest.

This is not good.

CHAPTER SEVEN

THE AIR HAD STARTED TO TURN COOL AS GRAY CLOUDS COVERED the sun. Maeve glanced up toward the summit as she stepped out of the house. Chris and Adam had left a little less than three hours ago. They should be back soon.

Unless they found something.

She shoved away the thought. The daily checks were part of their routine. An hour up, an hour to check everything, and an hour back. So far, everything had been fine, but Maeve still felt tense until Adam and whoever went with him returned.

So she liked to keep busy. For the evening check, she usually worked with the kids on schoolwork. But in the mornings, she used the time to check in on Sammy. So she pulled her gaze from the summit, straightened her shoulders, and headed for the barn.

She paused in front of the large barn door. Then, taking a breath, she pulled it open. "Barn" wasn't really the most accurate term to describe the space. It had been renovated into a living space. There was heat, electricity, and plumbing. Wooden floors covered the open space, and there was a bed up in the loft above as well as a few bunk beds on the first floor. It looked like a great place to hang out on a ski weekend.

But the current occupants would not be skiing anytime soon.

As the door opened, Luke looked up from his spot in the corner of the room. He sat on a pile of blankets, trying to sketch something into the pad that they'd given him when he arrived. Snap, as usual, was sitting next to Sammy's bed. She was playing with the animal figures that Jasper had whittled for her when they'd arrived.

Sammy lay with his eyes closed, and Maeve could have sworn she could detect the smallest of smiles on his face.

Snap looked up and then ran over to Maeve, giving her a hug. An image of Pop and Crackle wafted through her mind.

Maeve ran a hand over Snap's head. "I know, baby. I miss them too."

Sadness fell over Maeve. She hugged Snap to her. "I'm sad too. But remember, wherever they are, they're thinking of us just as much as we're thinking of them."

Snap nodded against Maeve's chest, and Maeve was content to just hold her there for a few moments.

On the bed, Sammy's eyes opened, and he watched her from his prone position. Maeve tapped Snap on the back. Snap looked over her shoulder and hurried over to Sammy's side as Maeve went around to the other side of the bed. "I just want to check on your wound. I think if all goes well, I can leave the bandages off."

Maeve leaned over and carefully peeled back the tape. She hated removing surgical tape. It always adhered a little too tightly, and most patients winced as she removed it. But no expression of pain or discomfort crossed Sammy's face.

Maeve pulled the bandage off, and surprise filtered through her. "Wow. That looks great."

She'd put in dissolvable stitches, which meant she didn't have to remove them. She was very grateful for that. But right now it looked as if the wound was barely there. She could hardly see the outline of the injury.

She looked at Sammy and smiled. "This looks good. You should get up and walk around a little more than you have been. Maybe even take a short flight. I think you're ready for that. But maybe take it easy with the flying to make sure there's no pain."

Sammy sat up slowly, and then his legs swung over the side of the bed near Snap. He wore a pair of jeans that Adam had found for him. Maeve stepped back as Sammy rolled his shoulders, his wings stretching out with the effort. She marveled at them. The fact that they could keep him afloat astounded her. He was really something out of a fantasy novel.

Luke looked up from his drawing for the first time. "Sammy."

Sammy turned his head and gave the small boy a nod before walking toward the door.

Snap followed after him, and Maeve did the same. Sammy stepped out into the bright sunlight and looked up at the sky. He closed his eyes. His skin, which had begun to look more and more human, immediately began to darken. At first Maeve was worried that maybe it was some sort of reaction, something akin to a sunburn. But Sammy did not look uncomfortable. And then she realized that he was taking energy from the sun. Storing it up. He reminded her for a moment of Superman getting his powers from the yellow sun.

Sammy glanced behind him and then stepped a few feet into the clearing. Maeve held out a hand, holding Snap back so that she didn't follow him. Sammy snapped out his wings.

Maeve let out a gasp. They were simply stunning. His wingspan had to be at least fifteen feet across, not the ten they had thought. She had inspected them a little bit while he'd been sedated, but she hadn't done a full examination. It felt wrong to take advantage of his vulnerable state.

She glanced over at the house. She couldn't help but wish Greg was here to see this. She and Greg had spent hours discussing Sammy's physiology. He was truly a marvel of nature.

Sammy gave his wings a little test push and then hovered in the air.

Maeve's chest tightened, and her gaze immediately went to his wound. But there was no change in it. She let out a breath. "That's good. That's really good."

Then Sammy went a little higher, and higher still. Maeve stood with Snap, looking up as he soared high above them to the clouds.

Snap stood next to her, wiggling with excitement. Iggy followed Sammy through the trees, looking up and doing somersaults. Maeve couldn't help but let out a little laugh. It was good to see all of the kids looking so happy for a change. And she was grateful to Sammy for giving them that.

A dark thought pulled her up short. Now that he could fly, would he leave them? Her gaze immediately darted to the kids looking up at him with rapturous joy on their faces.

Oh, Sammy, please don't just fly away. I don't think they could take losing one more person.

CHAPTER EIGHT

SEATTLE, WASHINGTON

Martin stepped out of the bathroom of his apartment, a towel wrapped around his shoulders. He wrinkled his nose. He could still smell the fish. It had been three weeks since he'd finally gotten off that godforsaken boat. He'd lost track of how many showers he'd taken, and yet the smell of fish was still stuck in his nostrils.

He owed Joseph and Garrigan a great deal of payback for what they put him through. And as soon as he found them, he would make sure that he got his retribution.

Of course, finding them had proven to be almost impossible. They were absolutely nowhere to be seen. He had facial-recognition systems running constantly, and yet not a trace of Maeve, Garrigan, Jasper, Joseph, or any of them had popped up on a single screen. There'd been a few false leads, but none of them had so much as peeked their heads out of whatever hole they were hiding in.

The only one who he could find was Matilda. She was back at the helm of R.I.S.E. And now R.I.S.E. was being welcomed in as a fully acknowledged branch of the United States military. The public didn't know about it yet, but all the other branches of the government did. And there was a great deal of respect being bestowed upon Matilda and what she'd accomplished.

Martin scoffed at the idea. He'd been the one who'd pushed her into the final confrontation with the Drago. If Matilda had listened to him, the Drago threat never would have even evolved to this point. But now she was being held up as the leader of the resistance rather than the obstacle that she'd been to removing the Drago all these years.

Martin seethed at the injustice of it all. He was still hidden in the shadows while Matilda bathed in the spotlight of adulation. She too would get hers. Now, though, even he recognized it wasn't the time. The spotlight on her was too bright. Any attempts on Matilda at this point would bring down the full force of the United States government upon him. And that was something he simply could not risk. He took a seat behind the desk and pulled up the latest report from his teams across the globe. He expected and found that they had yet again found no trace of Leander and her group.

He growled. How was it possible they could hide *four* aliens? He had men working for him who couldn't hide themselves in a crowd of thousands. And Leander had not only escaped the Drago but had somehow managed to hide four aliens and half a dozen humans from the prying eyes of the world. How the hell was that possible?

But he would find them. It was only a matter of time.

CHAPTER NINE

MAEVE STARED UP AT SAMMY, MARVELING AT HIS MOVEMENTS. He was so incredibly powerful and yet graceful at the same time. She gnawed on her bottom lip, worried that at any moment he might disappear from view.

Iggy, Alvie, Snap, and Luke all ran around following him, smiles on their faces and laughter following their steps, before they sat on the ground to watch. Sammy brought them all joy. But Maeve had no idea how he felt in return. He did not seem bothered by the children being around him, but she had not seen him fully smile either. She knew he was protective of them, especially Luke. But she also knew he could simply disappear into the sky one day. And she didn't know how the kids would handle that.

She stared up at Sammy as he did lazy circles, dropping until he was skimming the treetops. *Please don't leave, Sammy,* she thought again.

As if he heard her, Sammy did one last slow loop over the trees and then landed back in the clearing in front of the kids, taking a few short steps as he touched down. The kids burst into cheers.

He retracted his wings and then walked past Maeve toward the barn. Maeve let out a breath. Thank goodness.

I will not leave them.

Maeve's head jerked up, and her mouth fell open as she stared at Sammy's retreating form. In the last three weeks, he'd never communicated with her or anyone as far as they could tell. She and Greg had hypothesized about telepathic ability. They thought that perhaps it was only Luke who could understand him, due to their similar DNA.

But apparently not.

Luke darted back into the barn after him. And Maeve felt like she needed to take a seat. He'd communicated with her. That was a huge breakthrough. Did it mean he trusted her, at least a little? She felt relief that he knew that they'd been trying to help him this whole time. That had been one of her worries. The inability to communicate with him made her wonder what he thought they were doing with all of their ministrations. But he had understood the whole time. A weight was removed from her.

She smiled as she looked down at Snap, who wrapped her arms around Maeve. "How about if we go get lunch for everybody? Maybe Sammy could join us in eating outside today."

Snap looked up at her with a grin, but it was Iggy who responded. "Ig!" He took off like a shot toward the house.

Maeve shook her head with a smile as she and Snap followed him. Iggy put away more food than anyone Maeve had ever known. She wasn't sure how he wasn't the size of the house at this point. But his metabolism must be so high that he burned off food incredibly fast. Although, she had to admit if there was a human who did the gymnastics and cardio routine that Iggy did regularly, they would probably burn off a ton of calories too. Snap hurried after him, and Maeve was only two steps behind when Luke's voice stopped her.

"Maeve?"

She turned. Luke had really come out of his shell these last few weeks. He still had some nightmares and fears brought on by his time with the Drago in Edmonds, but being near Sammy made him feel safe.

The first few nights, they had all slept near Sammy out of

necessity as they crossed Canada. But once they'd arrived in Norway, Sandra had wanted Luke to sleep in the house with her. His nightmares had woken them all that night. He hadn't had any since Seattle. That was when Sandra realized that it was Sammy's presence keeping the nightmares away. From that point on, she and Luke had slept in the barn with Sammy.

Maeve had to give Sandra a lot of credit. She was definitely scared of Sammy, but she put Luke's peace of mind before her own. And if that meant letting Luke sleep near a seven-foot-tall hybrid alien, then Sandra was going to be right there next to him that whole time.

Luke's brown hair had been cut a little shorter just the other day by Nora, who insisted he needed a more modern cut. Luke squirmed a little under her attention, but he'd seemed pleased by it at the same time. Now they could all see the young man's face. He seemed to have lost a little bit of that little-boy look in the last few weeks. She hoped the reason for the loss was simply due to normal aging and not the stress that he had been under. "Hey, Luke. You want to help with lunch?"

Luke shook his head, darting a look back at the barn. "No. I'm going to stay with Sammy. But there was something he wanted me to give you." He handed her a picture.

Maeve marveled at Luke's skill. He was an incredible artist, but he may have truly outdone himself this time. The page in her hand was a pencil sketch of a young woman. Maeve could almost picture her in her mind's eye—the drawing was that good. She had short hair, incredibly large eyes, and an angled face. If not for the normal ears, she could have been mistaken for an elf.

"Who's this?"

Luke shrugged. "I don't know. But Sammy said you should have the picture."

He disappeared back inside the barn.

Maeve stared down at the picture, confused. While Sammy hadn't communicated with any of them until today, he did regularly communicate with Luke. So it was highly likely that Sammy had indeed made the request. But why would Sammy want her to have this? Was she someone from Area 51? Maybe one of the scientists?

Maeve shook her head, not sure what she was supposed to do with the picture. Maybe she could run it through some sort of facial-recognition program? She'd have to ask Greg, who was their current computer expert. The person she really needed was Penny. With just a drawing, Penny could probably tell her exactly where the woman was at that exact moment. But they would have to make do with what they had.

Folding the picture and slipping it into the back pocket of her jeans, she headed toward the house, wondering why Sammy would be interested in this woman.

"Maeve." Chris appeared from the trees. Maeve turned, a smile breaking across her face at the sight of him. But then her smile faded as she caught the look on his face. She knew that look.

She hated that look.

Chris hurried over to her. "I need to talk to you. Where's everybody else?"

"Most are inside. Why? What happened?"

"Nothing good."

Maeve followed Chris inside. "Is it Pop and Crackle?"

Chris blanched, reaching out to hug Maeve. "No, no. Nothing like that. And there's no indication that anyone knows where we are either."

Maeve took a breath. "Okay, well, that's good. So what is going on?"

Chris gave her a quick rundown on the meteor strike.

Maeve didn't know what to think when he finished. "It was the same location?"

"We need to brief everyone else." Chris took her hand and led her inside.

Greg and Nora were arranging food supplies on the kitchen island. Alvie was laying out bread on the cutting board while Snap slathered each piece with mayonnaise. Iggy vaulted onto the countertop to grab plates.

"That is not sanitary," Greg said, wrapping his arms around Iggy and pulling him from the counter. "How many times have I told you no feet on the counter?"

Iggy dropped his chin. "Ig," he said softly.

"It's okay, buddy. I know you keep forgetting." He placed Iggy on a stool next to Snap. "You can dole out the turkey."

Iggy's head popped up. "Ig!"

Nora wiped down the counter where Iggy had been standing. "All right, I say after lunch we roast some marshmallows. Who's game?"

All the hands around the island went up. "I'm in," Jasper said as he strolled in from down the hall.

Nora raised an eyebrow. "Marshmallows are only for people who help prep lunch."

"Then I volunteer for cleanup duty," Jasper said, snatching a piece of cheese and popping it into his mouth.

Chris opened his mouth to say something, but Maeve reached out and squeezed his hand with a shake of her head. "After lunch. Look at them. They're happy. It can wait until after lunch."

CHAPTER TEN

WHEN LUNCH WAS OVER, JASPER WAS TRUE TO HIS WORD AND cleaned up, along with Mike. Adam and Sandra took all the kids outside to create a fire and roast some marshmallows. Once the kids were out the door, Jasper turned to Maeve and Chris. "Okay, spill it. What's going on?"

"Yeah," Nora said, putting away the last of the dishes. "What's up with you two?"

Maeve and Chris exchanged a look. Maeve was a little disappointed. She'd thought she'd hid her concern pretty well. But they all knew one another rather well by this point, so hiding things from one another was getting more difficult. Chris nodded outside. "Adam already knows, and we can brief Sandra later. It's best if the kids aren't around for this." He took a breath and then succinctly explained about the meteor strike.

By the time he was done, the ramifications lay heavily in the air between them.

"We're sure it's not simply a rehash of the first bombing?" Jasper asked.

Chris shook his head. "No, it was a separate incident. It was a meteorite that struck the same spot."

"Okay," Greg said slowly. "It's a meteorite. Those things

happen. It was just back in 2013 when a large meteor exploded over Chelyabinsk, Russia. The blast was stronger than a nuclear bomb. It was felt all the way in Antarctica. Over a thousand people were injured."

Nora looked around the group. "Am I missing something? Meteorites hit the Earth all the time, don't they?"

"It's true," Maeve said. "The atmosphere is bombarded daily. Most meteors usually burn up in the atmosphere. But large ones, like the Chelyabinsk meteor, do happen, although only every five years or so."

"Yeah," Chris said, slowly drawing out the word. "But I can't help but wonder about it hitting that *exact* spot. That just seems way too coincidental."

"But maybe it *is* just a coincidence," Greg said. "It's unlikely, but you know coincidences do happen."

"Not like this," Jasper said.

"Are we even sure it was a meteorite?" Mike asked.

Chris nodded. "There's some video footage of the meteorite entering the atmosphere. It's definitely a meteorite. It wasn't a missile. Unless, of course, someone is doing some amazing fake video out there."

"Okay, so this is unfortunate but not a major issue. In fact, this is kind of good news, isn't it?" Nora asked. "This will make sure that the Drago are no longer a threat. Shouldn't we be celebrating?"

Maeve exchanged a look with Chris. "I wish that were true. But in our experience, when your gut is telling you that something is happening, you really need to listen to it. Something's going on. And we are completely and totally in the dark."

CHAPTER ELEVEN

SEATTLE, WASHINGTON

Martin hadn't moved for the last five minutes. He sat at his desk, staring at the satellite image. The Drago base in Antarctica had been completely destroyed.

And a meteorite had done it.

He'd known this moment would come. Ever since he'd learned about the Council's existence, he knew it was only a matter of time before they made their move. And this was just the first salvo. They had destroyed the Drago, and now he knew without a doubt humanity would be the next target.

This is the beginning. A cold chill crept up his spine. He jumped to his feet. *I warned them. I warned them all that this day would come.*

He felt only a small sense of satisfaction at having been proven right. That sense of satisfaction was greatly outpaced by his anger. *They should have listened.* He seethed as he paced. *Those cowards.*

The bureaucrats in Washington could not wrap their heads around the possibility of a threat beyond this planet. And now humanity would pay the price for that lack of imagination.

But perhaps it wasn't too late. There were steps they could take. There were steps the leader of R.I.S.E. could take. Better yet, with the MAURC protocol in his hands, Martin would have the power to protect this planet.

He walked over to the window, staring out at the gray Seattle afternoon. The Council would wait; they wouldn't rush, but they would take action. Martin just needed to take action first.

But in order to do that, he needed to be in charge of R.I.S.E. And he needed to make sure there were no "friendly" aliens that could cast doubt on his mission.

He smiled. *Would you look at that? Removing Leander and her people is actually in the best interest of the world.*

He sat back at his desk, pulling up the information on every move R.I.S.E. had made since coming out of the dark. Somewhere in there was the clue to his next step. He just needed to find it.

CHAPTER TWELVE

GEIRANGER, NORWAY

MAEVE TOSSED AND TURNED. SHE COULDN'T SLEEP AT ALL. After they'd discussed the destruction of the Drago base, they'd all agreed that right now, they didn't have enough information. They were debating whether or not to try and contact someone at R.I.S.E., but they couldn't agree on a course of action. Jasper even suggested maybe Martin had a hand in the Antarctica attack and was using it to flush them out.

Maeve wasn't sure how Martin would have managed it, but she couldn't discount it simply because she wanted it to not be true. For the rest of the day, she'd pushed the news to the back of her mind, but now the floodgates were open, and she could think of nothing else. Was Greg right? Was it just a freak coincidence? Like lightning striking the same spot? It was rare, but it happened.

Nora was right too. They *should* be celebrating. This should be a good thing, the Drago home base being destroyed. Then why did she feel in her gut like something was wrong?

Maeve sat up slowly, not wanting to disturb Chris, Snap, or Alvie who lay next to her. She pushed the blankets away just as a hand gently reached out and touched her leg.

"Where are you going?" Chris whispered.

He had his other hand on Snap's back, who was settled on his chest. Maeve smiled at the sight. "Can't sleep. I thought I'd go get some milk."

Chris stared into her eyes before releasing her leg. "Okay. Don't be long."

Maeve leaned over and kissed him and Snap on the forehead. "I won't."

She stood up, and Alvie rolled over into her spot. None of them wanted to sleep alone. And both Chris and Maeve felt better with them all being together.

Maeve stepped out into the living room after putting on her slippers. She pulled one of the blankets off the back of the couch and wrapped it around herself as she walked over to the kitchen island. But instead of heading for the fridge, she took a seat.

She dropped her head into her hands. It all felt like too much. Everything seemed to be spinning out of control. They needed a break. They needed Crackle and Pop back. They needed a normal life, at least for a little while.

Maeve's head jerked up at the sound of a bedroom door closing. She turned around to see Chris heading toward her. She tried to erase the emotion from her face and give him a smile. He stood behind her and wrapped his arms around her. She leaned back into him, drawing on his warmth and his strength.

He leaned down to whisper into her hair. "It's going to be all right. Everything is going to be all right."

His words brought tears to her eyes. Because she wanted more than anything to believe him. At the same time, she knew that she couldn't.

They stayed wrapped together for a few minutes, and Maeve felt the world tilt a little closer to its normal axis at the contact. She'd missed him. They'd been together all throughout this, but they'd had no time alone, no time to connect, just the two of them. These stolen couple of minutes right now meant the world to her.

And just like every other moment lately, it ended way too soon.

Adam jumped down from the loft over the staircase, his whole body tense.

Chris stepped forward, pulling Maeve behind him. "What's wrong?" he asked, immediately on alert. Maeve looked over his shoulder, trying to see what was going on.

"Somebody's here," Adam said quietly.

Chris reached into the kitchen cabinet and pulled out a Glock. He chambered a round and gave Adam a nod. Together, the two of them headed for the front door. Maeve stepped behind the kitchen island and pulled a shotgun from the cabinet. She pocketed a couple of rounds and took a step closer to the hallway, placing herself between the front door and the bedrooms. She wasn't letting anyone get to Alvie or Snap.

Adam and Chris had almost reached the front door when there was a light knock at it.

Maeve frowned. If this was an attack, the attacker was awfully polite. She felt the slightest of stirrings against her brain ease her conscience. She placed the shotgun on the counter, rushed to the front door, and flung it open.

Agaren stood there, highlighted by the moon.

CHAPTER THIRTEEN

SEATTLE, WASHINGTON

MARTIN SLAMMED DOWN THE PHONE. *COWARDS.*

He had been in his office on the phone all morning, trying to get things in place for when he tracked down Leander and her group. He'd just hung up on one of his old contacts in the Marine Corps. The man had refused to provide any military support for Martin.

Martin seethed as he sat behind his desk. He was still in charge of D.E.A.D. He should be able to get something as simple as military support. It was in the charter, for God's sake. But everybody was running scared.

He needed resources. He needed teams on standby so that as soon as he had the location of the first A.L.I.V.E. subject and everybody in that ragtag group, he could eliminate them once and for all. He was done playing nice. There would be no capture options on the table. They all needed to be wiped from the planet.

But Tilda had cut his budget. He no longer had access to military units. He was expected to submit forms and wait for approval.

Approval!

And as if to add insult to injury, he'd just gotten the first report on the location of the abomination.

He stood up, his anger making it impossible to stay seated. He paced along the back of his office. They were helping that thing. After the confusion of the aftermath of the bombing in Edmonds, no one was sure for a few days what had happened to him. But then they'd managed to get their hands on the security recordings for the airport Leander and her group had departed from.

Martin curled his hands into fists. That abomination should have been destroyed years ago. But he'd thought that there were further tests that could have been run on him. He should have been the crown jewel of their research efforts.

But none of those tests had borne fruit. And then in the chaos of Area 51, he had been released. Not by Martin, no, but by a bespectacled ten-year-old computer whiz who was now also working for R.I.S.E.

R.I.S.E. They had been a thorn in his side for decades. *I should have taken out Matilda Watson years ago.*

But even as he thought it, he knew that had never been an option. He'd never been able to find her. He paused. The reason he hadn't been able to find her was because she was in hiding with R.I.S.E. She had kept her location and even their very existence secret from all arms of the U.S. government. But now all their secrets were laid bare for the government to see.

Now she was exposed. He smiled. *So now it may actually be the perfect time to remove that particular thorn from my side.*

So focused was he on finding out the location of the rest of them that he hadn't considered that his old nemesis was now exposed in a different way. She was out of the shadows. She was in the government eye, which meant accountability.

Plus, her guardian was no longer around to help her either. From all reports, he, too, had disappeared with the rest of the group from Edmonds. Matilda was vulnerable, and by extension, so was R.I.S.E. So perhaps now was the time to look into how to remove the scourge of Matilda Watson.

R.I.S.E. had all the power now, but Martin knew that Matilda *was* R.I.S.E. She was the face of the organization. She was the head of the snake. Remove her, and, well …

The desk phone rang. Martin curled his lip as he looked at it. He really didn't want to be disturbed, but he had left some messages for people to get back to him. He crossed the room and looked at the display, then he took a breath, trying to calm the anger racing inside of him before he answered. "Darius, thanks for getting back to me."

"Martin, good to hear from you."

Darius's voice chewed up the phone lines. Darius Higgins was a former four-star general. But he had only retired last month. He still had a lot of sway and influence within the government.

They engaged in small talk for a few minutes. Martin counted them. He hated wasting time on nonessential conversation, but Darius was old school. Only after Martin was nearly bored silly with the adventures of Darius's grandkids did Martin feel it was safe to broach the topic he really wanted to discuss.

"I need some help. I'm running into walls around—"

"Let me stop you right there. I know what's been going on. I might not be in the military any longer, but I'm still around it. I heard about everything that happened at that island off the coast of England." A shudder ran through Darius's voice. "I can't believe those creatures have been on this planet all this time."

"There are still more out there. My agency's in charge of running them down. I need military support to—"

Darius cut him off again as Martin's seethed. "You're not going to get any military support, Martin. No one is going to help you."

Martin was at a loss for words for a moment. He'd never run into this kind of problem before. He always found a way to finagle his way around it. "That can't be true. I have contacts who—"

"Won't do a damn thing. Right now, Matilda Watson is in charge of everything alien related. Every single branch of the U.S. government is hanging on her every word. Her handling of the Drago infestation has made her a legend among the halls of the

Pentagon. No one is going to cross her. No one wants to. As far as they're concerned, what she says goes when it comes to alien life. I'm sorry, but if it is otherworldly, it needs Watson's stamp of approval, or no one is going to help you."

"But I'm in charge of D.E.A.—"

Darius cleared his throat. "She has made it clear that she does not support the mandate of D.E.A.D. There's a Senate committee that will be taking up the issue in two weeks. You should prepare yourself. They are probably going to vote to remove you as head if not disband the agency entirely."

"But the work—"

"R.I.S.E. will take it over."

Martin was stunned into silence. He simply couldn't believe it. *He* had been the one who'd pushed Matilda to finally initiate a strike against the Drago. *He* was the one who was responsible for their destruction, and yet she was the one who was getting all the credit.

"Listen, you still have friends at the Pentagon, so any other missions or situations that you need help with, you just call. We'll be behind you one hundred percent. We just can't help you with this."

Martin wasn't sure what he said after that. It was all kind of a blur. Finally, he sat at his desk, his phone resting on the desk in front of him. He didn't remember putting it down.

No one is going to cross her. She had shut him out completely. He couldn't believe it. After all his careful planning.

And she would never see the threat that the first subject and all of his cohorts posed. She still thought there was such a thing as a good alien. But Martin knew the truth. The only good alien was a dead alien.

He bounded up from his chair, livid. It had actually come to this. He was shut out of government channels that he had worked his entire life to cultivate.

Damn you, Matilda. Whatever happened next, he was going to make sure that Matilda did not see the end of this. If R.I.S.E. was the one who had all the power, then Martin would make sure that he was the one in charge of R.I.S.E.

There was one more card he had to play. He had been hesitating, not wanting to draw attention. But Matilda had forced his hand. If the powers that be thought she had done such an incredible job, he would just have to convince them otherwise.

And if he couldn't use the U.S. military to take them down, well, then he would just have to find another way. He grabbed his phone and looked a number up in the directory. After finding it, he dialed, pacing the room as he waited for someone to pick up.

A gruff voice answered a few seconds later. "Blackjack Security."

Martin smiled. "This is Martin Drummond. I need to speak with Jack Sharp."

Five minutes later, he hung up the phone. Jack Sharp would be here tomorrow. One problem solved. Now it was time to address the larger problem.

He pulled up the files from his laptop. He scanned the titles, remembering and discarding each scenario. Toward the bottom, however, he stopped. Project Resurgence. He'd forgotten about that one. He had planned on using it should his assumption of control at D.E.A.D. be questioned. But he'd slipped easily into the role, and the plan had been scuttled.

But now, with a little tweaking, it might be just the thing he needed. He smiled. *Hope you're enjoying the perks of your position, Tilda, because they won't last much longer.*

CHAPTER FOURTEEN

GEIRANGER, NORWAY

MAEVE CRANED HER NECK TO LOOK BEYOND AGAREN, BUT THE yard was empty. "Pop? Crackle? Where are they?"

"I am sorry. They are not with me."

Maeve's legs felt weak. Chris placed an arm around her to steady her. "Are they ... are they—"

Agaren raised his arms, his voice soothing. "They are well. They have recovered from their injuries."

Tears sprang to Maeve's eyes. She put her hands to her face. The fear she'd been holding on to for the last three weeks rolled through her. Since she'd learned Pop and Crackle had been taken by Agaren, she had been desperate to know whether they were alive or dead. She'd prayed and prayed and prayed, just wanting to know something. Now that she did, it was like all of the emotions of the last few weeks rushed her at once.

Chris held on to her. His arms tightened in response to Agaren's words. "They're okay. They're okay."

Maeve clung to him, nodding her head but not quite ready to speak yet. Chris led her over to the couch, and Agaren followed.

Adam slipped out the door, no doubt to take a tour of the perime-
ter. After she had a seat, she gestured to the other one for Agaren.

"Where are they? When are they coming back?" Chris asked.

"I need to see them," Maeve said at the same time. Chris took
her hand, and Maeve gave him an apologetic smile. "*We* need to see
them."

"And they need to see us," Chris said.

"I will see what I can do. But I cannot make any promises."

Maeve's mouth fell open as the ramifications of his words hit
her. "What?"

Agaren sat uneasily on the seat across from her. "That is part of
what I came to speak with you about." He fell silent.

"You said I could trust their safety with you," Chris said.

"And you can. They are perfectly safe. No one will harm them
within the Council base. I can promise you that." He took a deep
breath. "And that is the problem. Where they are right now, they
are perfectly safe. The Council worries that should they be
returned to you, they will no longer be safe."

Maeve opened her mouth to argue and then shut it. The
Council wasn't wrong. She couldn't guarantee Pop and Crackle's
safety. At the same time, she knew they had no right to keep her
children from her.

"What are you saying?" Chris demanded. "Are you refusing to
give them back?"

Agaren shook his head. "It is not I who is refusing. I know how
much you love the triplets, as you call them. I have no doubt that
your love is a critical component of their development. One that
they will not have with the Council no matter how good the Council's intentions."

"So what do they want? Do they want to do some sort of home
visit, like this is an adoption process?" Maeve asked, trying to jump
ahead in the conversation to the point where she learned what she
needed to do to put her family back together.

"I wish it were that easy. The Council is worried about what
they saw after the Drago's attack."

"What? Humans defending themselves? Of course we'll defend ourselves," Chris said.

"But you were willing to destroy the hybrids in order to defend yourselves."

Maeve's mouth dropped open. "No, we weren't. Chris and the others rushed in, risking their own lives to save all of us before the bombs hit."

"True. But the government had no such reticence. *They* were willing to sacrifice both Alvie and Snap in order to defeat the Drago."

Maeve wasn't sure what to say. The Drago threat to humanity was immense. She knew how the military calculated cost and benefit when it came to those kinds of situations. But how did you explain that to an alien race?

Then she remembered the news that Chris had brought from Antarctica. "The Drago are no longer a threat. There was a meteorite that hit Antarctica. The Drago are gone."

The news did not seem to change Agaren's mood. In fact, if anything, it seemed to make him more somber. "I know. It was the Council who took out the remains of the Drago base."

"What?" Chris asked.

"They deemed the Drago threat too great to be allowed to continue. The Drago attack on the R.I.S.E. base and their endangering of the hybrids was the last straw. The Drago had been given a very long leash. The Council simply cut it."

Maeve sat back, stunned. The Council had intervened. They had destroyed an entire species. *Oh my God.* "If the Drago aren't a threat anymore, then what are they worried about?"

Agaren sighed. "Humanity has had a long and difficult relationship with that which is different. Throughout time, you have all acted as if some humans are less than others based on the color of their skin or their belief system or their country of origin. Yet when you look inside, you humans are all the same. The same blood flows through all of you. The same hearts beat in all of you. Yet you use those alleged differences as an excuse to ostracize, as an excuse to endanger different members of your own species."

Once again, Maeve didn't know how to respond. She wanted to say that humanity had evolved since those times. But the truth was, *Homo sapiens* were an incredibly destructive force. A recent report indicated that humans had wiped out eighty-three percent of all wild mammals and half of all plants. The majority of animals that currently existed were domestic, the large bulk used in food production.

And then when she thought about humanity's impact on global warming, she knew how truly self-destructive humans could be. The oceans were warming, affecting everything from the lives of those who lived in the sea to the humans who lived along its boundaries. Areas of the Earth would soon be so hot as to be unlivable. Drinking water was being polluted, the air was being filled with carbon dioxide, the last of the forests were being destroyed. Yet corporations seemed to be running the show, drowning out the scientists ringing the alarm bell.

But despite that, she did think that humans had evolved. Humans fought against corporations and their dismissal of climate change research. Groups were trying to get the word out. People were leading the fight against racism and prejudice in all its forms. Like the Drago, there *were* humans trying to make a difference.

But she also knew it might not be enough. That the Council could look at humanity in its totality and say that we had simply not evolved enough. After all, it wasn't like she could take Alvie out in public without a huge panic ensuing. But she had to try to make some argument. "Humanity has gotten so much better. We are not what we once were."

Agaren nodded. "I have argued the same thing. The other members of the Council do not see it. They see the ugliness of humanity, not the beauty. They see the wars, not the love. For them, the worry is that humanity is an experiment that has long been on the road to failure as well."

Chris took Maeve's hand, and she was glad for the warmth

because she suddenly felt incredibly cold. *A failed experiment*. She shuddered at the thought. "What happens if they decide the human experiment is no longer worth continuing?"

Agaren stared at her, his dark black eyes somehow conveying a world of meaning. "You are a scientist, Maeve. What do you do when an experiment does not prove fruitful?"

"I would start over with a new one."

Agaren nodded slowly. "Yes."

Maeve sat back, stunned. The Council had already wiped out one species. Now they were looking to wipe out another troublesome species.

Chris gripped Maeve's hand tightly. "There must be something we can do. If we explain the importance of the hybrids, perhaps—"

Agaren cut him off. "It's not just the situation with the triplets. It is the captivity of the Guardian."

"The Guardian? You mean Sammy? He's not a captive. I mean, he was a captive of the Drago. But then we rescued him. We brought him with us to keep him safe. He's in the barn. We're keeping him here just until his wounds heal. If he tries to leave too soon, he'll open up the sutures. But we're not forcing him to stay." Maeve realized what she was saying was true. Sammy was hurt, that was true. But he could still have easily overpowered them. He could have left them at any point. For some reason, he had chosen to stay.

"That is not the Guardian I speak of. This Guardian was taken in 1976. She was removed from her ship by members of the United States space program. She has not been seen since."

Maeve frowned. "1976? NASA didn't do much in 1976. There certainly weren't any manned missions into space."

"Were there any missions?" Chris asked.

"Yes. The *Viking 1* landed on Mars, but it had been launched the year before. The next manned mission wasn't until 1977 when the Space Shuttle *Enterprise* was launched."

"Enterprise?"

Maeve nodded. "It was actually named after its *Star Trek* counterpart."

Chris turned to Agaren. "Are you sure it was 1976?"

Agaren nodded. "Yes."

Chris looked at Maeve. She appeared as bewildered as he felt. "I have no idea. I don't know of any missions. Maybe it was the Russians?"

"No, it was a United States ship that abducted her."

Abducted seems a little strong, Maeve thought but kept to herself. "Where was she when she was taken?"

"She was in cryo-sleep. Her ship crashed on the moon."

"Crashed?" Chris asked.

Agaren nodded.

Maeve sat back again. She knew exactly what Agaren was talking about. The photos had made it out of NASA's hallowed halls and onto the web. Of course, everyone who saw them said that it was nothing more than a hoax. But there were those who believed that it was the truth and that it was NASA's disinformation command system that tried to make it appear unimportant. "She was real?"

Agaren nodded, and Maeve felt the air leave her lungs. *Oh my God.*

"What are you two talking about?" Chris asked.

Maeve tore her gaze from Agaren, her mind reeling. "The Apollo space program began back in 1963. It was supposed to run twenty missions to the moon but stopped after mission 17. However, there are some that say that the program actually continued but that all of the launches and subsequent missions were classified."

"Classified? Why?"

"Because they found something on the moon. Something that they didn't want the public to know about, something that they worried that the public would see and would cause massive panic."

"What was it? A spaceship?" Chris asked.

Maeve shook her head. "No. The remains of an entire civilization."

CHAPTER FIFTEEN

CHRIS CROSSED HIS ARMS OVER HIS CHEST. "A CIVILIZATION? THE moon's never been inhabited."

But Maeve felt light-headed. She'd heard the speculation and seen some of the photos used to support it. But she still couldn't seem to accept it. "It's true? There was a civilization on the moon?"

Agaren nodded. "Yes."

Chris looked between the two of them. "You can't be serious. There is no way that there are remains of a civilization on the moon. It would have been seen, for God's sake."

"Actually, it has been seen. In NASA's very own photos. But once again, the disinformation makes it so that very few are willing to step up and actually say anything. And those who do are ridiculed." She took a deep breath. "There are these incredible, enormous glass structures on the moon."

"Glass?" Chris asked.

Maeve read the skepticism on his face. "Yes. Glass is fragile on Earth because of the pockets of air within it. In space, there is no air. So when glass is created, it's incredibly strong. In fact, it's twice as strong as steel. Using photos from the Apollo missions, different individuals have identified dozens of irregular features on the moon's surface. They contend that the features are not natural and are in fact the remains of a former civilization."

"But that's not possible, right?"

Maeve shrugged. "The evidence is pretty convincing. These structures are enormous, miles high in some cases. One's called the castle, another the worm, there's even what appears to be a crashed ship."

Maeve's head jerked up, and she looked at Agaren. "Was that it?"

He nodded. "Yes. That was the Guardian. And the Council wants her returned." The warning was clear in Agaren's tone, as was the hope that it would be an issue easily resolved.

Maeve swallowed. "And if we can't find her?"

Agaren did not speak for a long moment. "For all your sakes, please do."

CHAPTER SIXTEEN

MAEVE ONCE AGAIN SAT OUTSIDE IN A HEAVY SWEATER ON A wooden Adirondack chair, a thick blanket wrapped around her. The coffee that she'd brought out with her had long gone cold. She hadn't been able to sleep after Agaren left. She'd given up the attempt two hours ago and come outside. It was awfully cold. But even though a chill crept across her skin, she didn't go inside. She stayed and watched as the sun rose over the mountains.

It was stunning.

Every morning she tried to get up to see the sunrise. It was a reminder that they'd made it through another day. It was a silent, optimistic sign of the future she hoped one day they would have.

But today, as glorious as the streaks of pink, orange, and yellow through the sky were, they couldn't touch the ball of fear that had lodged inside her chest.

The Council did not want to return Pop and Crackle. They were worried for their safety. And Maeve couldn't argue that they were wrong. She was worried for the safety of all of them.

And even though the greater issue was the fact that the Council was considering the mass annihilation of the planet, Maeve couldn't help but focus on the triplets and Alvie. On the one hand, the mass annihilation was horrible, but Maeve would be dead. Not much to worry about when you're dead.

But if the Council went through with their plan, they would in all likelihood take the triplets and Alvie off the planet first. They would be the beginning of a new species. But Maeve couldn't imagine how they would handle that. They were such sensitive souls. There was no way they would be able to recover from such an abomination.

And then would the Council decide that they, too, were too flawed? Would they take what they needed from them and start over?

Maeve pulled the sweater tighter around her, but it did little to ward off the chill. She felt like a piece of driftwood being tossed this way and that by the seas without any control, without any power. The Council was all-powerful. They had destroyed the Drago. In one fell swoop, they had eliminated an entire species.

And while she knew that the Drago were evil, warlike creatures, there also had to be some that were good. Look at Adam. He'd helped them every step of the way. Now was he the last of his kind?

Fear ran through Maeve. Did the Council know about Adam? If they didn't, what would happen when they learned of him? Would they come after him too?

The front door opened behind her. Maeve turned as Alvie slipped through the door. She opened up the blanket, and he crawled onto her lap, and then she tucked it over the two of them. He lay his head against her shoulder. She wrapped her arms around him and kissed him on the side of the head. "Good morning."

He snuggled into her, letting out a contented little sigh. The sound of it lifted Maeve's heart. He sounded better this morning. He felt better, emotionally speaking.

An image of Agaren slipped through Maeve's mind.

She nodded. "Yes. He was here last night."

She guessed the next image would be Crackle and Pop, and she wasn't disappointed.

"No. He did not bring them back. But they're healthy. And they're safe." She paused, not sure what to tell him, but she didn't want to lie to him. If things were going to go bad, she needed to start preparing him. She took a deep breath and then spoke. "The Council isn't sure if the Earth is safe for Pop and Crackle right now. They want to keep them until we can guarantee their safety."

Alvie looked up at her, his black eyes so expressive, just like Agaren's had been. They were filled with the same sadness and a little fear. She hugged him tighter. "We'll figure it out. We always do."

Alvie's small hands gripped hers and held her tight.

The two of them sat there, his little body offering her warmth that the blanket and sweater hadn't. Before she knew it, her eyes began to close of their own accord.

And then she was off to a world of dreams.

———

Maeve woke up to Chris gently shaking her shoulder. She opened her eyes slowly, wincing at a crick in her back. The sun was warm on her face, even though the air was cool. She looked down. At some point when she'd been sleeping, Snap had curled under the blanket next to Alvie. She smiled and wished she could wake up like this every morning.

Chris gave her an apologetic smile as he spoke quietly. "Hey. I hate to wake you, but everybody's up in the living room. I thought now would be a good time to have that conversation."

Maeve nodded as Snap let out a little groan and stretched out her arms. Her white-blonde hair had come in a little bit more this last week. Soon Maeve would have to start brushing it. In her mind, she pictured brushing Snap's hair and then pulling it into a ponytail or putting it in braids. She pictured waiting with Snap by the bus stop, holding her hand as they waited for the bus to arrive to take her off to school.

Maeve knew it would never happen, that it was only impossible daydreaming. But at the same time, she loved the idea of it and clung to the memory of those images, even if they would only ever exist in her mind. "Okay. I'll be right in."

Alvie looked up at her. She'd known he was awake, even though he had kept his eyes closed. "Can you take Snap over to Sammy?"

Alvie nodded, stepping onto the ground and helping Snap step down as well. The front door opened, and Iggy bolted out, using his claw hands to move rapidly across the space. When he was five feet away from them, he flung himself into the air to flawlessly initiate a triple somersault and then landed on his two feet. He stopped for a second and then raised his arms up in the air, completing the routine.

Maeve couldn't help but smile as she joined Alvie and Snap in clapping. "Great job, Iggy. A perfect ten."

He gave her a big smile. On the long trip across Canada, Greg had shown Iggy a bunch of gymnastics routines. He'd been trying out the moves ever since. And he got a little disappointed if he didn't get a ten.

Iggy lowered his arms. "Ig."

Snap leaned up and kissed Maeve's cheek before she walked off with Alvie and Iggy toward the barn. Sandra stepped out of the barn and waved at Maeve before disappearing after the three inside.

Maeve stood and stared at the gorgeous landscape. Whatever else was happening around the world, and whatever else would come in the days ahead, she would be grateful for this time she had with her kids. She would be grateful for this beautiful spot. She looked up at the heavens.

And I would be grateful if you allowed us to spend the rest of our days here. And I would be grateful if those days were long, and I would be grateful if those days were many.

Everyone was already inside when Maeve stepped into the cabin. Greg gave her a grin from behind the kitchen island. He walked over and handed her a giant mug of coffee. "Hey there. So I hear we had a visitor last night."

"Oh, I need this." She took it with a grateful smile, taking a deep sip and letting the warmth and caffeine bolster her. "And yes, Agaren was here last night."

Jasper waved to the spot on the couch next to Chris. "Well, don't keep us in suspense. This one hasn't said anything, wanting to wait until everyone was here to have this little conversation. And he wouldn't let me wake you up an hour ago."

Maeve winced. "Sorry about that. It was a rough night."

"Well, that doesn't bode well," Greg mumbled as he took a seat next to her. Nora took a seat across from them. Mike leaned against the back of the seat while Jasper took the other one. Adam settled in against the back wall, where he could listen but also keep an eye out the window for any problems.

Maeve settled in between Greg and Chris on the couch, placing her mug on the coffee table in front of her. No, nothing about that conversation boded well. Maeve nodded to Chris, not wanting to be the one to explain it to everyone.

He squeezed her hand and then turned to the group and explained about Agaren, the Drago, keeping Pop and Crackle, and what the Council said about the future of humanity.

Greg slumped down into the couch once Chris was done. "I knew it was going to be bad news."

Nora leaned forward from where she sat across from them. "Do you think they would really do it? I mean, destroy all of humanity?"

Chris nodded. "According to Agaren, humanity's been an experiment of sorts, one that apparently is not going very well. And the Council has decided that if the experiment's not going well that maybe they need to just stop the whole thing."

"Jesus," Jasper said quietly.

No one spoke for a few moments, each lost in their own thoughts. Neither Maeve nor Chris interrupted them. They'd had a few hours to adapt to what the Council had planned, and even now they were struggling to wrap their heads around it. Everyone else deserved at least a few minutes to take it all in.

Finally, Mike spoke up. "But if they haven't done it yet, it means there's still a chance we can do something to stop it. That humanity can do something to stop it, right?"

"I hope so," Maeve said. "Apparently they were angry that the humans were willing to destroy the hybrids in their quest to rid the world of the Drago. That was a step too far for them."

"They're also angry that some humans have taken a Guardian and kept her hidden away for decades," Chris said.

"A Guardian? Like the one we have in the barn?" Nora asked.

"No, someone else," Maeve said.

"Great," Jasper groaned.

But Greg leaned forward, his eyes lit with curiosity. "They mean a Guardian as in the donor who helped *create* the one we have in the barn."

"Yes, I think that's the case as well." Maeve explained about the rumored secret Apollo missions.

Everyone turned to Jasper, who held up his hands. "Why are you all looking at me?"

"Oh, I don't know, maybe because everything about a secret space program screams R.I.S.E.," Greg said.

Jasper conceded the point with a nod. "Okay, I will admit that it does sound a little bit like us. But I don't know anything about this. I mean, the only one who might know would be someone with access to R.I.S.E.'s databases."

"Then we need to speak with someone at R.I.S.E.," Adam said softly from the side of the room.

Everyone turned to look at him. Adam stepped forward. "I'll contact them."

"Is that safe?" Chris asked.

Adam shook his head. "No. Which is why we can't do it anywhere near here. In fact, it would probably be best to do it face-to-face. I'll find a way to reach out to them safely, and then we'll see what we see."

Jasper shook his head. "No. If anyone is going to contact R.I.S.E., it should be me. You're needed here to protect everybody else. I'll go find a way to contact them. I still have some old spy tricks up my sleeve that I can use."

"Well, I guess that means I'm going too," Mike said.

Jasper opened his mouth to argue, but Mike didn't let him speak. "You know you need somebody to watch your back."

Greg leaned forward, placing his head in his hands. "Ugh, I guess that means I'm going as well."

"Why?" Nora asked.

Greg looked at Jasper and Michael. "How are you guys with computers? Security systems? Getting in and out without leaving a trace?"

Jasper shrugged but did not meet Greg's eyes. "I'm sure we can figure it out."

"And that's why I'm going," Greg said. "Besides, I kind of want to find out about this secretive alien."

"Could they have been at Area 51? Could they have been released with all the other aliens during the experiment?" Chris asked.

Maeve shook her head. "I don't think so. Agaren would have known."

"If she's still alive," Nora grumbled.

"What was that?" Jasper looked over at her.

"Look, I know what Agaren said, but isn't it entirely possible, if she was grabbed decades ago, that she's dead?"

"And probably diced up in a lab somewhere," Jasper muttered.

"Jasper!" Maeve said.

Jasper put up his hands. "What? You know you were all thinking it."

Nora gave him a pointed look. "But if she is dead, then I'm pretty sure our chances of appeasing the Council are dead too."

No one spoke for a few moments before Greg let out a heavy sigh. "Well, that certainly brought down the room."

Nora shrugged. "Sorry, but it seems like a possibility we need to consider."

"She's right," Mike said. "Regardless, we need to find out what happened to her. Maybe if we can provide the Council with information, even if she has passed on, it will be enough."

"It wouldn't be enough for me," Nora said.

"Well, let's work under the assumption that she is still alive and we are not all doomed. Maybe she's still in her cryo-sleep." Greg rubbed his hands together. "So we could have a sleeping beauty. Awesome."

"Yeah, awesome. Except for the fact that us having her is the reason why the Council might destroy the entire world," Nora said.

Greg shrugged. "Fair point. Still, it will be nice to get out in the world again."

Jasper looked at Maeve. "I'm guessing Agaren didn't give you some sort of timeline?"

Maeve shook her head.

He sighed. "Well, then, let's assume it's soon."

Chris looked between the three men. "When will you be leaving?"

Jasper looked at Mike, who gave him a nod before he answered. "Well, it's not like we have a bunch of stuff to pack. We'll leave within the hour."

Maeve looked at the three men, wondering if this might be the last time she saw them. Once again, it felt like things were moving too fast. She simply nodded. "Okay. Be careful."

Jasper stood. "I'm going to get some things together. We'll meet in front in thirty minutes."

Everyone else scattered. Nora and Chris went to go check on the kids. Mike and Adam took off outside to gas up the ATVs. Which left just Greg and Maeve. The two of them sat quietly on the couch for a few minutes before Greg turned to her and gave her a nervous smile. "Into the breach one more time?"

Maeve tried to keep the fear out of her voice as she spoke. "So it seems. Are you sure you're up for this?"

"Yeah. I think this is kind of my role, right? Besides, what I said about those two is right. I mean, I watched Jasper struggle with the TV remote the other day. I might not be good at espionage and strategy, but electronics and computers are definitely *not* his thing."

Maeve reached into her back pocket and pulled out the picture from Luke. "If you get a chance, maybe you could do Sammy a favor."

Greg took the paper from her. "Sammy?"

Maeve nodded. "Luke drew that for him. Said Sammy wanted us to have it. I don't know what that means, but maybe you could give it to whoever you meet from R.I.S.E. See if they can get an ID."

Greg stared down at the paper before he folded it and slipped it into his pocket. "I'll see what I can do."

Maeve gave him a small smile. "We've come a long way, you and I."

Greg jumped up from the couch, his hands out in front of him. "Oh, no. We are not doing the 'introspective look back on our life and the road ahead' speech. Yes, we have come far. We have done some pretty amazing things these last few years. Apparently we just need to add one more amazing thing to that pile. And I plan on doing that. And you need to plan on doing that as well."

Maeve nodded, feeling tears press against her eyes.

Greg sat back down quickly. "Hey, hey, none of that. I'll be fine. And we'll get Pop and Crackle back, and then we'll save the whole world. After all, that's what we do, isn't it?"

Maeve nodded as a tear rolled down her cheek. "Yeah, that's what we do."

Greg hugged her tight. "It's time for Project S.A.V.E."

Maeve frowned as she pulled back to look at him. "S.A.V.E.?"

He grinned. "Save All of us from a Violent End."

Berkeley, California

. . .

Ariana Mitchell felt butterflies race across her stomach as she stepped into the conference room's doorway. Four sets of eyes looked over at her. Professor Sean Tillis, Professor Catherine DeRosa, Professor Mike Hamlin, and Professor John Daly did not offer her a smile. She gave them a tight smile anyway and then walked to the podium set up at the front of the room.

She carefully arranged her notes, trying not to let her nervousness show. She pulled her tablet from her bag, and three tissues dropped out to the ground below. She quickly ducked down to grab them, feeling her cheeks flame high. *Way to make a great impression.*

She stood back up, hoping her cheeks weren't as bright as she thought they were. Hopefully her darker complexion would downplay it. Once again she longed for her long dark-blonde hair. A friend had talked her into getting a cute little pixie cut. And while it was cute, all it seemed to do was accentuate her extremely large blue eyes.

Plus, it made it impossible to hide behind her hair. Until she'd gotten her hair cut, she hadn't realized how much she had relied on her hair as a screen against the world. Now that it was gone, she felt its absence strongly.

Ariana poked around her tablet, quickly opening to the file she needed. She looked out at the four professors when she was done.

Professor Daly gave her a dismissive wave. "Whenever you're ready."

Ariana nodded, glancing back down at her notes. She opened her mouth when the door at the back of the room opened. For a moment, her heart leaped, wondering if he'd come. It crashed down just as quickly. She did not recognize the man in the dark suit who had slipped into the room and taken a seat at the back.

But while she might not know who he was, she knew who had sent him.

Her father.

She supposed she should at least be grateful for that. That he cared enough to make sure that he heard about her dissertation proposal defense.

But she'd hoped that maybe this time he might actually show up. After a lifetime of not showing up, she wasn't sure why she was still so disappointed every time he didn't.

Ariana took another deep breath and began. "Throughout the life course, we know that both the environment and genetics play a role in determining criminal and delinquent behavior. The goal of my dissertation is to highlight the interaction between these two factors, which results in serious behaviors that handcuff an individual to a lifetime of hardship."

———

Ariana stepped out of the room and felt the sweat moistening the back of her blazer. The professors were still inside, talking about her defense. They'd talk among themselves for probably another thirty minutes and then write up a report, although when she'd actually get to see the report was still a question. Her professors were brilliant, but they weren't exactly known for their timeliness.

She walked out of the academic building and took in a lungful of warm California air. She smiled, glancing up at the sun with her eyes closed. *Well, at least it's over. One way or another, I'm hopefully done.*

"Ariana!"

Her eyes flew open, and she looked over where her roommate, Michelle Bonvincino, stood. Michelle had long dark thick hair and dark eyes. She was an Italian girl from the Bronx, and living in California for the last six years had done nothing to take the Bronx out of the girl.

And Michelle would have it no other way.

"So how'd it go?" Michelle linked arms with her.

Ariana groaned. "I don't know. I swear, at one point Daly asked me a question, and my mind went completely blank. I spit something out. I don't even know what it was."

Michelle laughed. "You're always so hard on yourself. You're smarter than anyone I know. I'm sure you aced it."

Ariana ducked her head, uncomfortable with the praise and at the same time warmed by it. Michelle was a godsend. Ariana had spent most of her life with just her mother or governess for company. She hadn't had any real friends until college.

In fact, for a long time, she wasn't even sure she would be able to go to college. Her father was so strict, he rarely let her go anywhere. But finally he'd relented.

Ariana glanced over her shoulder at the familiar black car along the curb—with restrictions. She had a security detail on her at all times. Ariana didn't know any of the new security individuals. They switched every few weeks.

She tried not to think about how it was to make sure that none of them ever got too close to her. But as time went on, and she reviewed her life, it was difficult not to think that he was trying to make sure she was alone in this world.

She shoved down the stirrings of anger and resentment. It was only once she came to Berkeley that she understood how isolated her life had been. Michelle's family had come up that first weekend that she'd been at school. They'd enveloped Ariana into their festivities as if she was a member of the family, a family of the sort that Ariana had never seen and wanted so desperately to belong to. There were hugs and jokes and lots and lots of food. They all just seemed to want to be around one another.

Ariana had had very little contact with anyone her entire childhood. Michelle's overly affectionate ways were a bit startling at first, but now she craved that contact. And she realized how warped her own upbringing had been.

"So, where shall we go to celebrate?" Michelle asked.

"I'm not sure we have anything to celebrate yet."

Michelle waved away her words. "Oh, please. You have As in absolutely every class you've ever taken, with a triple major. You had people recruiting you into their doctoral programs. You passed. Now the question is: what are we going to *eat* to celebrate?"

Ariana said nothing, just grinned at Michelle.

Michelle shuddered. "No, please, no. I beg of you."

"But I like it."

"That is *not* real pizza. You cannot get real pizza outside of New York. Okay, maybe Chicago if you want deep dish."

"But Vito's has tomato pie. It's so good."

Another shudder, this one even more dramatic, ran through Michelle. "No cheese is definitely not pizza. You have had one deprived upbringing, child." Michelle squeezed her arm to take away the sting of her words before she let out a deep sigh. "The things I do for my best friend. All right, Vito's. But you are buying, and then we are going to O'Hannigan's and getting drunk. Seriously, seriously drunk."

Ariana laughed. "Now that is a plan I completely agree with."

CHAPTER SEVENTEEN

THE PLANE RATTLED AS IT FLEW INTO A POCKET OF TURBULENCE. Greg was not comforted by the groan and sway of his chair's movement.

"Always an adventure, isn't it?" Jasper said from the seat across from him.

Greg imagined punching the man in his face. For the last five days, Jasper had been their travel agent. And he was, hands down, the world's worst. They'd taken cars, barely floating ships, hell, at one point they'd even ended up on bicycles. They were going under the radar. They were practically going underneath the earth. Greg was pretty sure that would be the next leg of the trip. Some subterranean caverns that they would trek through to get to their target.

Greg still didn't know who exactly it was that Jasper had arranged for them to meet from R.I.S.E. He said it was safer for everyone if they didn't know. Greg tried not to be angered at being kept in the dark. You'd think at this point he'd be used to it. But he kind of felt like he'd earned a bit of trust. After all, he'd been at this for quite a while, and he thought he'd proven himself on more than one occasion.

The plane touched down with a violent shudder. The engine

backfired. Greg's gaze flew to the window. Smoke billowed out from one of the engines. His eyes grew large as flames appeared.

Jasper leaned past him. "Huh, we should probably get out now."

Greg scrambled to get his seatbelt off and all but lunged for the plane door. Like hell he was about to die in a plane explosion after surviving everything he had. Mike already had the door to the small plane open. He'd been the pilot. He hopped out and headed over to the engine a little too nonchalantly in Greg's opinion, with a fire extinguisher in his hand. He blasted the foam at the small fire while Greg sprinted a safe distance away from the plane.

Jasper slowly strolled over to Greg and joined him, watching Mike eliminate the fire.

"Well, like I say, any landing you can walk away from is a good one, right?" He slapped Greg on the back. If not for the fact that he was pretty sure Jasper could kill him with just his pinky finger, Greg would have decked him right then and there.

"This way." Jasper headed toward a small building. As they walked, Greg finally took the time to look around. They were on the outskirts of some city. Which one, he couldn't even hazard a guess. He wasn't even sure what country they were in. The city looked small.

And next to them was a deserted factory. It looked like an old steel mill that had long since gone out of business. Greg pushed all those thoughts aside as they headed toward a small trailer lined up next to the runway. He glanced back at the runway and realized that it actually wasn't a runway. It was just part of an unfinished road.

Once again, Jasper had shown an incredible knowledge of all things hidden away. He'd taken them to these out-of-the-way outposts that Greg had marveled at. Jasper's encyclopedic knowledge of hard-to-reach places seemed unending. This location seemed to be the closest one to civilization that they'd actually touched down in in the last two days. Greg's hopes rose a little bit as he envisioned the chance of maybe getting a slice of pizza.

He didn't mind being on the run. But the simple food was getting to him. He wanted something that had some spices mixed into it. Hell, at this point he'd fall down to his knees in gratitude if a hamburger from a fast food restaurant was offered to him.

Jasper pulled a key from his pocket and opened up the trailer door. He flicked on the light, illuminating the office beyond it. The trailer held only two large metal desks, a corkboard with a few pieces of paper tacked to it, a bathroom to the left, and a full fridge, sink, and microwave to the right. A couch was pushed up against the wall to the left.

Greg headed for the fridge. He opened the door, then closed it quickly with a wince. Apparently no one had been using the trailer for a while. Whatever was in the fridge looked like it could have been part of an experiment at Area 51. He slumped his shoulders dejectedly.

"It'll be all right, kid. We'll get something good to eat in a little while, okay?"

"Yeah, sure, whatever. When's this contact of yours getting here?"

Jasper glanced at his watch. "They should be here any minute."

The door to the trailer shook as it opened.

Greg glanced up, expecting to see Mike.

Instead, Tilda walked through the door.

CHAPTER EIGHTEEN

FOR A WOMAN WHO'D BEEN NEAR DEATH ONLY A SHORT TIME ago, Greg had to admit that Tilda looked damn good. In fact, she looked even more badass now. Her long gray hair was gone. It had been cut into a very short style. She had a cane as well. For most people, he would think that would make them look a little weaker, but somehow it made it look as if she was even more in command, like she was about to go storm a hill.

Greg took a step toward her to give her a hug, but one look from her made him rethink that action. He crossed his arms behind his back and smiled instead. "It's really good to see you, Tilda."

"And you as well, Dr. Schorn." She gave him a nod. Then she stepped aside to allow Mike in. Except Mike wasn't alone. In his arms was a black-and-white retriever. Hope, who was Alvie and the triplets' dog, wagged her tail at a steady beat as she tried to lick Mike's face.

This time Greg didn't let anything stop him from bounding across the room. "Hope!"

Hope had bandages around her torso, and the back half of her body had been shaved, the fur just starting to regrow. But she still wagged her tail furiously when she caught sight of Greg.

Greg leaned in to her face. She rewarded him with a few good robust licks. "Oh, it's so good to see you. You look so good. Yes, you do. Yes, you do."

Jasper walked over and rubbed Hope on her head before scratching her behind her ears. "Hey there, girl. Good to see you." He looked over at Tilda. "How'd she end up with you?"

"She was brought to a vet clinic in England. When we left for the States, I made sure that she came with us. I figure I can keep an eye on her until Alvie and the triplets are ready for her to return to them."

The mention of Alvie and the triplets caused reality to crash back down on Greg. "I'm not sure if that's going to happen anytime soon ... or ever."

He quickly explained about Agaren's visit and the threat that the Council now held over them. Tilda walked farther into the room and took a seat on the couch. "I was worried that was the case when I saw the footage from Antarctica." She sighed deeply. "Do we have a timeline?"

Jasper shook his head. "Not that we know of. But they moved to eradicate the Drago awfully quickly."

"Yes, they did," Tilda said.

Greg took Hope from Mike's arms and took a seat on the opposite side of the couch from Tilda. He settled Hope in next to him, rubbing her belly as he spoke. "It wasn't just the situation with the Drago that the Council was upset about. They said something about a Guardian being taken. We thought at first they meant Sammy, but they didn't. They meant something that happened years ago."

Tilda nodded her head. "The secret Apollo missions."

"That's what Maeve thought it might be," Mike said.

"I don't remember us making any Apollo missions top secret. Did I miss that somehow?" Jasper asked.

Tilda shook her head. "R.I.S.E. wasn't in charge of those missions."

"It wasn't R.I.S.E.? Who else would have the authority to

secret away a shuttle mission? I mean, isn't that what you guys do?" Greg groaned. "Don't tell me there's another secret space agency. I don't think I could handle that."

"No, nothing like that. You have to understand that back in the seventies, the Cold War was at a fever pitch. The Apollo missions officially stopped right around Watergate, in 1972. All the agencies were fighting one another for resources, both financial and informational. And the public was losing faith in the U.S. government with Nixon coming on the heels of the Vietnam War. At R.I.S.E., we knew how critical space was going to be in the survival of the human race, but we weren't the only ones. The CIA was moving in on R.I.S.E. at the time. They managed to get a large chunk of our funding cut and pushed us out of the line of communication for a number of NASA actions. As a result, we didn't know anything about the secret Apollo missions until years after they'd been conducted."

A pit opened up in Greg's stomach at the mention of the government's premier spook agency. "The CIA? You mean Martin Drummond?"

Tilda's eyes narrowed to slits, her mouth a hard line. "No, it was just before his time, so he wasn't the mastermind behind the secret Apollo missions. That belonged to his predecessor, Robert Buckley."

Jasper shook his head. "Okay, I'm afraid I'm going to need a little background here. How exactly was it possible for the United States government to initiate secret Apollo missions? I mean, the launching of a space shuttle was huge. It's not like people weren't going to notice it shooting off into the sky."

Hope stretched her legs and ambled over to Tilda, laying her head in Tilda's lap. Tilda absentmindedly stroked the dog as she spoke. "Actually, they don't notice. The truth of the matter is that we're sending satellites and resending different probes into space all the time. People get used to seeing it. And they expect the government to announce when there's something important for them to know. So if they see something heading up, they think it's just another satellite being put into position.

"And back then, even with Watergate and Vietnam, there was a lot more trust in the government than there is now, especially with the space program. Some people wouldn't think twice about it. Even after Watergate, it never occurred to the general public that the government would lie to them about something as honored as the space program. So keeping it quiet wasn't difficult."

"But why keep it hidden? What were they up to?" Greg asked.

"To understand that, you have to understand what happened on the Apollo 11 mission. After that first walk on the moon, all missions were quick stop-and-grabs."

"Why?" Greg asked.

"Because Armstrong and Aldrin reported that they were being watched on the edge of a crater by alien ships," Tilda said. "Ships that dwarfed anything on Earth."

Greg remembered hearing about that on some conspiracy sites, but he thought it was nuts. "And nobody thought that was strange?"

Tilda shrugged. "The public was not made aware of it at the time. Like I said, people were much more trusting of the government, especially when it came to the space program. Most don't realize that there were private medical channels where the astronauts could communicate without the public hearing it. They thought the government was completely straightforward about what happened with the moon landing."

Greg grunted. "Yeah, except for the people convinced the moon landing was a hoax."

Tilda continued. "But if you look closely at previous missions, you can see the traces of discoveries on the moon in the press conferences. The astronauts, especially Aldrin, Armstrong, and Michael Collins, were incredibly subdued at their press conference. Not the demeanor you'd expect for the humans who'd just walked on the moon."

Greg had watched a recording of that news conference years

and years ago, but he hadn't picked up on that. But Tilda was right. If it were him, he would have been grinning from ear to ear. That whole press conference, they'd barely smiled. The commentators talking around the astronauts, however, had been so ebullient that it was easy to overlook how reserved the crew had been. He shook his head. Just like everyone else, he'd seen what the government wanted him to see.

"As the years went on," Tilda said, "the astronauts became less inhibited in their conversations. Especially Astronaut Alan Bean, from Apollo 12. But he did it in a very subtle way. I respected him for it."

"How did he relay the information?" Jasper asked.

"Through his art. He took up painting later in life. And he did these landscapes of the moon." Tilda pulled out her phone and quickly brought up one of Bean's paintings, turning it for the group to see.

On the screen was a shot of the moon's surface. It looked like what anyone else would think the moon looked like. Craters marked the predominantly white surface. There was nothing in it that raised any flags, and Greg was looking for flags. He shook his head. "I don't get it. What exactly does this indicate?"

"You see the colors that were used? The pinks, yellows, and oranges? There are colors on the moon."

Greg *knew* that there were no colors on the moon. It was strictly white and gray. Everybody knew that. "Yee-ahh." Greg drew out the word. "But isn't that just some sort of artistic license?"

"It was more than artistic license. It's the colors that you get when you look at the moon through the glass structures."

"What?" Jasper asked. "What glass structures?"

Tilda settled back in the couch. "I think we should order some food. This is going to be a long conversation."

CHAPTER NINETEEN

GEIRANGER, NORWAY

A LIGHT WIND BLEW. NORA LIFTED HER FACE TO THE SKY, enjoying the feel of the cool breeze against her skin. She loved everything about Norway. The air was crisp, the view was unrivaled, and it was safe.

At least as safe as they could get right now. She glanced over as Sandra walked down the path toward her.

But not everybody felt that way. Sandra looked around, her eyes darting from tree to tree before they came to rest on Luke, who was sitting underneath one of the trees with Snap playing checkers.

Sandra's whole body visibly relaxed at the sight of her son. Ever since they had left Washington state, Sandra had been terrified of what might happen to Luke, terrified, Nora knew, of who Luke might become.

Nora didn't know exactly what the connection was between Sammy and Luke, and she was worried about what it could mean. But it was a bit of a double-edged sword. She was terrified of Sammy and all that he represented. At the same time, she knew that he was the one other person on the planet who would protect her son just as strongly as she would.

And probably even more.

Sandra walked over to Nora, nodding toward the spot where Luke and Snap sat. "Any problems?"

Nora shook her head. "Nope. They have been happily playing the whole time."

"That's good. That's real good." Sandra shifted her gaze to Snap, compassion on her face. "I think Snap needed the distraction."

Nora nodded her agreement. Poor Snap had been lost ever since Pop and Crackle had been taken. She seemed just slightly off center. She never smiled the way she used to. Not that Nora was an expert on Snap or anything, but she had gotten to know the little girl some in her dealings with all of them. There had always been an ease to Snap's nature in a way that just defused everyone around her.

Now Snap was so serious. You couldn't help but feel sadness when you were near her. Nora, like everyone else, just wanted to do something to help the little girl feel better. But once again, they were all powerless.

Nora couldn't imagine Iggy being taken away. Even the idea of it made her breath stop and her body go cold. She wasn't sure how Maeve and Chris were handling it. But she supposed being they still had Alvie and Snap to look out for, they had no choice but to carry on. But she'd seen the drawn look on Maeve's face, and Chris's as well, when they thought no one was looking. Not having Pop and Crackle was hurting both of them.

Nora studied Sandra and noted that she looked a little more rested than she had the last few days. "I guess you finally had a good night's sleep."

Sandra nodded. "Yeah, actually, I did." She glanced over at Luke and Snap, then lowered her voice. "What do you think of Sammy? Do you think he's … I mean do you think he's actually on our side?"

Nora didn't answer right away, giving herself time to form her answer. "I don't think Sammy would hurt any of us. And I have the feeling he would do quite a lot to protect us. And with Maeve and Greg helping heal him, I think it's gone quite a ways to instilling some goodwill. So if you're wondering if we have to worry about Sammy being a danger to any of us, I don't think we do."

"Yeah, that's what I was thinking." Sandra's gaze drifted back to Luke, a worried expression on her face.

Nora reached out a hand and squeezed Sandra's. "And Luke most definitely has nothing to worry about from Sammy. I think Sammy's made it clear that he will do everything in his power to keep him safe. Luke is the reason that Sammy found them in Washington. I know the bond between those two makes you nervous. I know you don't understand it. But the reality is that Luke's got one very powerful guardian angel. And while that is difficult to accept, it also makes him very, very lucky."

"I know. It's just ... you know I keep fighting this. I *know* Sammy won't hurt him. And in my gut I know that means Sammy won't hurt me either, but when I look at him ..." Sandra sighed.

"Give yourself a bit of a break. You just learned about all of this recently. The rest of us have known about aliens and the U.S. government's role in all of this for months and years. It's okay that you need a little time to adapt."

Sandra gave her a small grin. "I suppose it hasn't really been that long, has it?"

"No, it definitely hasn't. And your first exposure, well, that wouldn't exactly make you embrace the wonder of it all."

Sandra nodded, her eyes troubled, as she no doubt thought about the Blue Boys that had attacked her and Luke at her home. Sandra had managed to take out one of them. If not for Sammy, though, Luke would not have survived. "Well, I suppose we should just be happy for the peace. And honestly, there are worse places to have to hide out."

"That's for sure." Nora smiled as she looked up into the bright blue sky. It really was ...

Nora frowned, staring upward. A dark object appeared in the sky in the distance.

And it was growing larger.

She stood up, squinting her eyes to get a better view. It seemed to be heading in their direction at an extremely fast pace.

Sandra's head jolted up to the sky, her mouth falling open. "What on earth?"

Nora spoke slowly. "I don't think that's anything from Earth."

Sandra vaulted to her feet and sprinted toward Luke and Snap. "Luke! Snap!"

The two kids paused for a second, looking up to the sky, and then the two of them scrambled to their feet. Sandra reached them and grabbed their hands and raced with them back toward the house.

"Iggy, with me!" Nora yelled as she took off at a run. Iggy leaped down from a tree, running along the ground at Nora's side. Nora darted glances over her shoulder at the ship as it grew closer ... and larger.

So much for peace and quiet.

Without warning, Adam slipped out of the trees and fell in line with her and Iggy. Nora's heart rate spiked, and she glared at him. "Don't *do* that," she said through gritted teeth.

He didn't respond, his gaze locked on the approaching ship. They burst into the clearing in front of the house.

Maeve and Chris were already there, weapons in their hands, even though Nora doubted they'd be very effective against whatever it was that was heading toward them.

Nora noted that Sandra had made a beeline for the barn and for Sammy. Sammy stepped outside, his gaze focused on the ship heading toward them, his arms crossed over his chest. Sandra darted into the barn behind him, pulling Snap and Luke with her.

Alvie was already inside the barn, peeking out. Maeve handed Nora an AR-15. Nora grabbed it and quickly checked to make sure it was in working order. It was good.

The four of them spread out so that each was at a different angle from the incoming ship.

My God, the thing is nearly two stories high. She glanced at the weapon in her hand, knowing that it would be like a peashooter against that thing.

Nora hated this. Throughout this whole process, she'd felt powerless more times than she liked to admit. And right now she was once again feeling like a tiny little nothing being swirled around by fate.

But nonetheless, she gripped her weapon as the ship touched down. Wind blew, kicking up dust and grass. She was forced to turn her head to protect her eyes. But she immediately turned back, the butt of the AR pulled into her shoulder.

"It's okay." Maeve walked to Chris and gently pushed down on the barrel of his weapon. "It's Agaren."

Nora relaxed slightly but not entirely. She knew everybody else trusted Agaren, but she wasn't as convinced about his intentions. After all, he still had Pop and Crackle.

Agaren materialized underneath the ship. For a moment, Nora thought that maybe it had been like a *Star Trek* transporter thing, but then a small ramp opened behind him.

Agaren stepped out, noting the weapons. He paused at the bottom of the ramp, not making any moves.

Maeve strode toward him. "What is it? What happened?"

Agaren looked down at her. "The Council has agreed to let you see them."

CHAPTER TWENTY

FREMONT, CALIFORNIA

GREG BIT INTO HIS FIFTH SLICE OF PIZZA, BUT IT WASN'T getting old. He had missed pizza so much. He licked at the sauce that dribbled down the side of his mouth. Tilda had brought the pizza with her. It was a little cold because they had gotten to talking before Mike brought it in, but Greg was not complaining.

Mike had then stepped outside to keep an eye on things while Tilda, Jasper, and Greg spoke. Greg offered half of the crust of his last slice to Hope. She took it happily with a grateful wag of her tail. "Okay, so there was an actual civilization on the moon?"

"There were rumors about the moon long before there was a space program. According to some Native American tribes, the moon was actually brought here by another civilization, and that civilization lived within the moon."

Jasper laughed. "That's crazy. I mean there's no proof that—" His words died off as Tilda raised an eyebrow at him.

He swallowed noticeably. "Is there proof?"

"Depends on who you ask. There *are* glass structures on the moon that we did not put there."

Greg nodded. He'd read up on the glass structures on the moon on the trip from Norway. It was fascinating. He talked around the pizza in his mouth. "There's also the robot head."

Jasper shot him a glance before turning back to Tilda. "What's he talking about?"

Tilda sighed. "A photo got out that was not supposed to. It clearly depicts a robot's head sitting on the lunar surface."

"But that's not real, right?" Jasper asked.

"It's real," Tilda said.

"And it totally looks like Data," Greg said excitedly.

Jasper frowned. "Huh?"

"Data, from *Star Trek: The Next Generation*. How do you *not* know Data?" Greg asked.

"Because I'm not a geek?" Jasper asked.

Greg gave Hope the rest of his crust. "Your loss."

Jasper rolled his eyes. "Yes, it's very painful. But alleged robot heads aside, no one's lived on the moon. I mean, it's not habitable, right?"

Tilda hedged. "Actually, our scientists' views on that are … evolving. We now know that Mars used to have an atmosphere. We know that something went by and essentially sucked the atmosphere off of Mars. Some say that might have been the moon being put into place."

"Yeah, but that's hypothesizing. That's not proof," Jasper said.

"Well, how about this? Back in 2017, there was an asteroid seen that was not behaving as it should. First off, its shape was unheard of—long and cylindrical, like a cigar. And it spun like a bottle while not emitting either gas or ice. It also failed to follow the projected trajectory. All in all, it wasn't behaving as expected. Scientists hypothesized that it was possible that this was actually an alien probe that was made to look like a meteorite."

"I don't see how." Jasper frowned.

"If they could make a ship look like a meteorite, why not a moon?" Greg said, wondering if George Lucas had heard the legends and that was how he'd come up with the Death Star.

Jasper shook his head. "Yeah, but those scientists had to be some sort of kooks. You know, like some guys who'd been hiding away in the, I don't know, geology lab in the basement for years that no one lets out."

Tilda gave him a small smile. "Actually, they were a research team with the Harvard–Smithsonian Center for Astrophysics, so not kooks."

Greg shook his head. "Okay, so there are structures on the moon. Is that why we haven't gone back since the seventies? I mean, all this hype about getting to the moon, and we haven't been back now in decades."

Tilda nodded her head. "Yes. It was decided that it was too risky to either inflame or panic the world's population by exposing them to alien life. So the decision was made after the Apollo 17 mission not to return to the moon, at least not publicly. In fact, all of the manned and unmanned missions have had, shall we say, a wider audience than was expected."

"Wait, what?" Greg asked.

Tilda winced, stretching out her legs. "Not everything from the moon landing was broadcast. Like I said before, the astronauts had a medical channel. It was supposed to be completely private. Armstrong switched to the medical channel and reported that there were ships, enormous ships, parked on the edge of the crater and watching them. But they weren't the only ones who reported being accompanied on their trips."

"How did that come out anyway, about Armstrong?" Greg asked.

"Believe it or not, HAM radio operators intercepted the signals from the astronauts. But like I said, it wasn't an isolated case. Every trip into space has been monitored by UFOs. Some astronauts have even gone on the record about it."

"But not Armstrong or Aldrich," Jasper said.

Tilda shook her head. "Their families were threatened. They couldn't chance it."

"And later?" Greg asked.

"Buckley died. Martin was pushed out. The threats weren't as strong anymore. But by then, the idea of UFOs was in the realm of the tinfoil-hat people. No one would believe the astronauts, despite their resumes."

Greg shook his head, trying to wrap his mind around it. He wasn't having trouble accepting that astronauts had been eyewitnesses to UFO activity. He was struggling to accept that American heroes had been threatened into silence. Was there no line that Martin and his colleagues wouldn't cross?

Tilda continued. "The government couldn't risk going back to the moon publicly. What if the public saw something they shouldn't see? So it was decided they would go back and investigate the glass structures, but the public would not be told."

"Apollo missions 18 through 20," Greg said.

Tilda nodded. "Yes. And the missions were successful. More so than they ever could have imagined."

"How so?" Greg asked.

"On the last trip, Apollo 20, the astronauts investigated a downed ship on the lunar surface. And they found something." Tilda paused. "Or more accurately, they found *someone*."

CHAPTER TWENTY-ONE

MAEVE DIDN'T LIKE ROLLER COASTERS. HER STOMACH ALWAYS felt like it was trying to escape out her throat. More than that, she hated the pause right before the first drop. The last two seconds always gave her enough time to question whether or not any of this had been a good idea.

Flying in Agaren's ship was even worse than that. It wasn't that it felt worse. In fact, she could admit that it didn't even feel like they were moving. But the large windows in front of her made it clear that they were going much higher than any roller coaster that she had even considered riding.

The ship itself was large, as tall as a two-story building but only as wide as a large swimming pool. It was an unusual color, not exactly silver or white, but somewhere in between. Inside, the walls and floor had a shimmer to them, but there were no noticeable handles or doorways.

In fact, there were no protrusions of any kind. Every surface was smooth and blank.

Not that she'd gotten a tour. The lift that brought them into the ship deposited them right in the cockpit. At first the room had been empty. But with a small movement of his hand, two chairs emerged soundlessly from the floor.

Agaren helped her strap in, although the straps were nothing like regular seatbelts. They barely felt like anything at all. Maeve would have preferred if they felt as if they would protect her, although she knew rationally that if something went wrong, they would either burn up in the atmosphere or they would simply plunge to their deaths. She gripped the chair a little tighter.

"Are you all right?" Agaren asked.

Maeve swallowed. "I'm not really great with heights."

Below her, she could see the oceans of the world. It all looked so different, so small. For a moment, her fear disappeared, giving way to awe. She leaned forward. "It's beautiful."

"I have always thought that the Earth is one of the more beautiful planets. The mix of colors, the mix of people; it is truly an engaging creation."

"How long have you been around Earth?"

"A very, very long time, long before you had the capability or even the dream of flying through the air."

It was hard to imagine being able to watch humanity evolve like that. What must that be like? Was time something that zipped by for him or something that crawled slowly onward? "And Alvie and the triplets? How long will their lifespans be? As long as yours?"

"I do not know. They are part human. I do believe, however, that they will live a longer lifespan than a human but perhaps not as long as a full-blooded Gray."

Maeve sat back, trying to imagine that. Alvie and the triplets could potentially exist for hundreds of years after she was gone. Would they forget about her? Would they be lonely? Would they be able to find people that would make them feel as if they were part of a group, part of a family?

Her heart ached at the idea of them being on their own. At the same time, she was grateful that they would have each other. At least, she hoped they would have each other. If the Council decided not to return Pop and Crackle, she didn't know what she would do. Would Alvie and Snap only have each other at some point?

Or would they all be separated by the Council, each living a cold, lonely existence?

Her thoughts were interrupted as the moon came into sharper relief. Maeve sucked in a breath, watching the white orb grow closer. Her mind reeled. She was actually in space. She was heading to a base on the moon. She'd grown up with Alvie. She'd known that aliens existed. But never in her wildest dreams had she imagined this was possible. A pang of grief tore through her. *My God. Mom, I wish you could see all of this.*

Agaren steered the ship closer to the surface of the moon. They were now flying only a few hundred feet above its surface. Maeve leaned forward even more, trying to get a better view. The surface was much like the pictures she'd seen, pockmarked with lots of craters. It had no way to deflect the meteorites. The Earth was bombarded with hundreds of meteorites every day as well, but most burned up in the atmosphere. It was sitting in cold space, alone and vulnerable.

There were some people who argued that the moon did, in fact, at one point in its existence, have an atmosphere. Recently, research had borne those arguments out, finding that in the distant past, the moon did have a thin atmosphere that had been on the borderline of sustaining life.

Maeve wasn't sure how she felt about that research. It seemed too far-fetched. Yet people thought that about Mars, and now it was known that it, too, had had an atmosphere. Maybe sometime in the future, the moon having an atmosphere would be proven as well.

Still, humans laughed out loud at the thought. Maeve couldn't really blame them. She glanced out again at the surface of the moon. *So thinks the woman being flown to a moon base by an alien to argue to the Council to return her hybrid children.*

Maeve started as a structure appeared on the horizon. It was a tall glass tower of some sort. It looked to be hundreds if not thousands of feet tall. Maeve stared at it in wonder. Who could have created such a monument? She glanced below and saw more glass structures littering the surface.

She'd read about it, but it was something else entirely seeing it. The structures extended miles from the surface. There was nothing even close in size on Earth. "There really was a civilization up here, wasn't there?"

Agaren nodded. "Yes. They have been gone a very long time. They left long before the Council ever took up residence."

"Why did they leave?"

"The same reason everyone leaves: war. There was a war between their race and another. Their buildings were damaged beyond repair. They could no longer sustain life on the moon. And with the losses, they no longer wanted to. So they moved on."

"Where did they go?"

"Some traveled farther into the galaxy. But there weren't many left after the war. And I wonder ..."

"What?" Maeve asked.

"There's a beautiful planet not too far from this site. I wonder if perhaps some of them escaped there."

Maeve turned and looked at the Earth, wondering the same thing. How many species of aliens had visited Earth that humanity had no idea about? On average, there were over 2,000 UFO sightings every year, which Maeve knew was actually down dramatically from 2014, when over 8,000 sightings had been reported.

And those statistics were taken from the official accounts. There was no telling how many people had kept their observations to themselves. Most people are reticent to make any sort of report. *After all, people who believe in aliens are crazy.*

Maeve shifted her thoughts, trying to get her bearings. "Are we heading to the South Pole?"

"Yes. The base is located there, hundreds of feet below the surface."

Maeve sat back, not surprised that was where the base was. A Baylor University team had recently discovered a huge mass underneath the moon's South Pole. The mass was five times the size of the Big Island of Hawaii. Scientists hypothesized that it was perhaps an ancient, even primordial impact on the moon. But apparently the scientists were a little off in their explanation.

But the fact that they found it at all did make her wonder how much longer aliens could remain hidden in the shadows. Humans knew there was something under the surface of the southern pole of the moon. The U.S. government had even recently come out and admitted that released videos of UFOs were real. They stopped short of saying aliens, but they did admit they could not identify the objects in the recordings.

Maeve wondered whether the reduction in UFO sightings in the last few years were the aliens' attempts to put off the inevitable: the acknowledgment of their existence.

"We have never allowed a human onto the base. This is an honor that has been bestowed upon you due to your relationship with the hybrids," Agaren said.

His words pulled her back from her philosophical musings. What the world did or did not acknowledge right now was not a priority. Pop and Crackle were. "I appreciate that. But it doesn't change the fact that the best thing for Pop and Crackle is not to be locked away but to be with their family."

"You do not have to convince me."

But what was left unsaid was that there were beings that Maeve would have to convince. And unless she did, Pop and Crackle would spend their lives on this barren moon without any human contact.

And more importantly, as far as Maeve was concerned, without any love.

CHAPTER TWENTY-TWO

FREMONT, CALIFORNIA

GREG STARED AT TILDA. "THEY REALLY FOUND SOMEONE? You're saying that the U.S. space program actually found someone *living* on the moon?"

Tilda shrugged. "Living might be a bit of a stretch. They found what appeared to be a female humanoid in some sort of suspended animation state. She was attached to lines and being held on a spacecraft."

Greg leaned forward. "What exactly did she look like?"

"She was tall, over six feet, and she had mocha-colored skin, a wide nose, and lips. Her eyes also looked larger than a human's but not by much. Put her in normal clothes, and she could pass for human."

Greg sat back heavily. Hope stirred next to him, and she rearranged herself, all four paws up in the air. Greg absentmindedly rubbed her belly, picturing the woman. She really was a sleeping beauty.

Tilda continued. "The astronauts, of course, were shocked when they found her. They'd been shocked when they had seen the spacecraft, even though they had been briefed on its existence. But actually seeing another living being had been more than they had expected."

"What did they do?" Jasper asked.

Greg had a feeling he knew the answer to that one.

When Tilda spoke, she confirmed it. "The astronauts contacted NASA through a secure channel to ask what they should do. The higher-ups at NASA at the time wanted them to document everything and then leave everything as it was. But they were overruled."

"Buckley," Jasper said.

Tilda nodded. "Yes. He overruled the authorities at NASA. And in this particular situation, he outranked them. He ordered them to retrieve the body and bring it back to the Apollo craft. The astronauts balked at first. It went against their training to so egregiously disturb a site. But Buckley threatened them and their families and ordered them to return with the specimen."

"So they did," Greg said softly.

"You have to understand, Robert Buckley was not someone who made idle threats. Those astronauts knew that if they did not follow through on his orders, their families would pay. The same threats that had been issued to the Apollo 12 crew."

Greg felt sick. Those astronauts had put their lives on the line for the United States, and as a reward, they and their families had been threatened. "That's disgusting."

"*That* was Martin Drummond's mentor," Tilda said.

"What happened to the specimen when she was returned to Earth?" Jasper asked.

"Buckley took control of the specimen as soon as the astronauts touched down. All traces of her and the mission were scrubbed from NASA's files. People were threatened upon pain of death if they revealed any of the contents of the mission. The specimen was never seen again."

"And when did this happen?"

"1976."

Greg sat back, his mind racing. The CIA had removed a female humanoid from the moon decades ago. They had no doubt kept her hidden all this time. But that left him with one nagging question. Jasper asked it.

"Do you know where she is now? Is she the Guardian that the Council is referring to?"

"That makes the most sense. But I have no idea where she is. Buckley had complete control over her. And once he died, I'm assuming that control fell to Martin. And Martin has hidey-holes all over the country, all over the world, that he could stash her in."

Greg's anger spiked. "What's with that guy? I mean, he's evil with a capital E, like one of those villains from the old-timey movies. All that's missing is a long mustache that he can twirl."

A smile threatened to break across Tilda's face. "Oh, I can see Martin strapping someone to a railroad crossing if the need arose. Speaking of Martin, did you know he just disappeared right off RAF Bentwaters before the attack on the Drago holdings, at around the same time you all disappeared?"

Jasper cleared his throat. "Uh, yeah. About that. We kind of kidnapped him."

Tilda's eyebrows rose. "I had a feeling you and Garrigan might have had a hand in his disappearance."

Jasper shrugged. "We needed some information. He had that information."

"Did he escape?" Tilda asked.

Greg shook his head. "Not exactly. We kind of threw him out of an airplane."

Tilda looked between the two of them and then shook her head. "Well, unfortunately, you didn't kill him. He's back in his Seattle office."

Greg stared at Tilda and saw the hard line to her jaw. She really was sorry that they hadn't killed him.

That's cold.

Although Martin had set up the entire world to be attacked by the Drago just so that the United States government could annihilate the Drago, so perhaps it was legitimate to want him dead.

"What's his backstory? There's got to be some way to get to the guy. He knows where the humanoid is. So is there anything that we can use as leverage to get him to help us?" Greg asked.

Tilda gave a bitter laugh. "Help us? Martin doesn't help anyone." She paused. "But there is one way I can think of that we might be able to get him to bend to our will. But it is a very *big* might."

"We'll take anything. We are 'end of the world, destruction is on the horizon' desperate," Jasper said.

Tilda paused, her gaze scanning both of them as if to determine if they were worthy. Greg felt like he'd passed some test when she finally spoke. "Over the years, I've learned that knowing your enemy is the most critical thing you can do. You need to know them better than you know your friends. So I've had my people searching Martin's background over and over and over again. He is constantly under surveillance. His life has been turned inside out. Even with all of that, he kept one thing hidden from me until four years ago, when I uncovered it."

Greg leaned forward. "And? Don't keep us in suspense. What is it?"

"Martin Drummond, the man who arranged for the genocide of an entire race of beings, has a daughter. And she goes to the University of Berkeley."

"A daughter? He procreated?" Greg asked.

Tilda gave a small chuckle as she pulled out her phone. "Yes, although my reports indicate they do not have a very close relationship. This is Ariana Mitchell."

Tilda turned the phone around as Jasper crossed the room to look at it. Greg's mouth fell open as he took in the shot. "Oh my God." He reached for the phone and pulled it out of Tilda's hands.

"What?" she asked.

He looked up at them, his mouth still hanging open. He shook himself and handed Tilda back the phone, then pulled the sketch Maeve had given him from his back pocket. "We're not the only ones who think finding Martin's daughter is a good idea." He uncurled the paper and handed it to Tilda.

She glanced down at it, and her head jerked back up. "Where'd you get this?"

"Luke said Sammy wanted him to draw it. Sammy's looking for her as well."

Jasper grunted. "Well, then, let's not disappoint the man."

CHAPTER TWENTY-THREE

THE COUNCIL BASE

MAEVE HELD HER BREATH AS AGAREN STEERED THEM INTO A cave along the moon's surface. It was dark, but Agaren seemed to have no problem seeing where he needed to go.

"Oh, forgive me."

He touched a spot on the console, and a pale pink light diffused across the windshield, allowing her to see into the dark. Ahead looked like a wall of rock. She sucked in a breath, but then the wall opened up, and their ship slipped through into a tunnel hundreds of feet long.

Maeve closed her eyes, not wanting to watch the rock walls slip by so quickly. When they'd been in space and above the moon, it had been harder to tell that they were moving so fast. But within the close confines of the tunnel walls, it was clear that they were moving at a high rate of speed. Her head began to pound and her stomach began to feel nauseous. Closing her eyes was the best way to keep from getting sick all over Agaren's beautiful spacecraft.

For a moment, she pictured Agaren with a mop and a bucket, trying to clean up her vomit. A smiled tugged at her lips.

This whole situation was surreal.

She felt the craft slow, but she didn't open her eyes right away, wanting to give her stomach a moment to settle.

"We're here."

Maeve cracked open her eyelids and peered out the windshield. The pink light was gone, but the space beyond the windshield exuded light reflecting off the pale white walls of the cave. They were in a hangar, facing an immense glass structure. It towered above the ship and was at least twenty stories from her guesstimate. Inside the glass, she could see figures moving, although she could not make them out clearly.

Agaren unstrapped himself, and Maeve's straps automatically released her. She stood up and then grabbed her seat as her legs wobbled beneath her. She held on for a minute, waiting until the strange light-headedness passed. Agaren waited for her. "We had to add artificial gravity to allow us to walk. It will be more difficult for you. Your legs will feel heavier than they do on Earth."

Maeve nodded and took a step, agreeing that her legs definitely felt heavier. As if there was a five-pound weight attached to each limb. This was going to be a strenuous walk.

Agaren led the way through the craft and down the ramp. A small craft hovered at the base of the ramp. Maeve couldn't see any mechanism that propelled it. There was no exhaust, no noticeable engine. It was a small flat piece of metal with two rows of benches. It looked like a large white toboggan with seating.

Agaren stepped up to it, and after a moment's hesitation, Maeve did the same, carefully taking a seat. The material was odd. It looked like metal, but there was a little give in it. She sat down and braced her hands along the front of the bench, but the sled took off smoothly and kept a sedate pace. She relaxed a little bit, allowing herself a chance to look around.

The sled resembled a toboggan. With the white rock walls surrounding them, it all reminded her of a snow tavern. But it wasn't cold. It was quite warm, but comfortably so. They passed other ships, two of them identical to Agaren's. One was much smaller, looking like it would only hold one or two people. And then beyond that was a massive ship that looked like it was three times the size of an aircraft carrier.

Maeve turned to Agaren. "You only have five ships?"

Agaren shook his head. "No. There are three hangars. This is the smallest one."

"Oh."

Ahead, glass doors slid open, and they rode into a large wide hallway. While the exterior of the building was made entirely of glass, the walls of the interior were made of a silvery white material that sparkled as they passed by. Maeve longed to touch it to figure out what kind of material it was. But before she could ask about it, another door opened to their left, and the sled shifted inside. Maeve's eyes darted to the group of six sitting in chairs at the end of the room. Two of the chairs were empty. Her stomach dropped to her feet. She had no doubt she was in the presence of the Council.

Four were Grays like Agaren, although two of them were much smaller. The other two were strange creatures that Maeve had never seen before, but one bore a striking resemblance to the Blue Boys. It was blue and had a round head and what looked like a beard. She had a feeling that that wasn't hair on his face. The other one was a tall creature that had fins along the back of its head. Its hands were also made of flippers. Maeve wondered at his look. She hadn't seen any water-related aliens at Area 51. Had his kind never been captured?

Agaren stopped the sled ten feet in front of the Council. He stepped off and gave the Council a short bow. "I have brought the Earth creature, Maeve Leander."

Maeve felt a rifling along her brain and got the sense the Council was looking for information. She tried not to blanch at the intrusion, but she felt very much like a powerless lab rat. Apparently she wasn't going to have to provide a speech. The aliens would be able to read all they needed to know entirely by themselves.

Maeve turned to Agaren. "Where are Pop and Crackle?"

Agaren stepped back and waved a hand to his left. One of the white shimmery walls vibrated for a second and then disappeared. Beyond the wall were two small beds with multiple tubes attached to each bed.

And lying on each one was Pop and Crackle.

Maeve let out a gasp and ran toward them. But her legs were so heavy and so slow that it took her longer than she would have liked to reach their side. She reached Pop first, and with a tentative hand, reached out to touch the top of his head. "Pop, I'm here. I'm here."

Pop struggled to open his eyes, only managing it for a split second before they closed again.

Maeve kissed his forehead, placing her hands on either side of his face, and just stared at him. She placed her fingers to his throat to check his pulse, which was beating strongly. She quickly checked his chest, looking for injuries, but he seemed unharmed.

With one last kiss to his forehead, she hurried over to Crackle's bed. She leaned her forehead to his. "I'm here, Crackle. I'm here."

Maeve checked him as well, finding no evidence of injury. "Crackle baby, I'm here. I love you. Chris loves you, so does Alvie, Snap, Greg, and Hope. We all love you. We all miss you."

A single tear rolled down Crackle's cheek.

Maeve struggled to hold her composure at the sight of it. Agaren followed her over.

She turned to him. "What's wrong with them? Why aren't they awake?"

"The Council has decided to keep them in a suspended state while their fate is determined. If they are to remain with the Council, they will remain in this state until a suitable situation can be found for them."

Maeve stared up at Agaren and then looked over at the Council. "You can't do this to them. This is cruel."

The Council stirred, looking among one another, and she once again felt the fingers across her brain. "Stop that. I'm not some toy that you can play with."

"The Council wishes to convey that this is the safest situation for the hybrids until the situation is resolved on Earth."

Maeve shook her head. "This is not the safest situation for them. You'll protect their physical bodies but destroy their psychological ones. They know what is happening around them. They can *feel* what is happening around them."

Agaren shook his head, taking a step forward. "I assure you they cannot—"

His voice cut off as he stared at Pop and Crackle and the tears sliding from the corners of their eyes. "What is this?"

"They are aware. You have left them paralyzed, not oblivious. They know they are alone. They are scared. You cannot leave them here, not like this."

Agaren stared at Pop and Crackle before his gaze met Maeve's. She read the pain there. "I will speak with the Council. You will stay with them?"

Maeve nodded. Agaren turned and stepped from the room, the wall reappearing.

But Maeve didn't mind the wall being there. She wanted the privacy anyway. She stood between the two beds and then found each of their hands. "I'm here, boys. I'm here."

CHAPTER TWENTY-FOUR

FREMONT, CALIFORNIA

GREG WAS TRYING TO WRAP HIS HEAD AROUND TWO THOUGHTS: 1) that Sammy had Luke draw a picture of Martin's daughter and 2) that Martin had procreated. If he had to choose, he'd say the second was more unbelievable. Martin Drummond just did not seem like the kind of guy who got lost in passion. It must've been some sort of artificial insemination thing. "Who's the mother?"

"Martin was actually married at one point," Tilda said, "but she died when the child was six years old. I haven't been able to find out much about the child at all. It was just a fluke that we happened across her."

"How did you find her?" Jasper asked.

"Believe it or not, it was Martin's budget. There was a line for security that our accountants couldn't reconcile. I dispatched a team to investigate it. The security was for Martin's daughter."

Greg shivered. Martin Drummond's offspring. It was bad enough he existed in this world without him adding more Mini Mes to the world. "What do you know about her?"

"Her name is Ariana. From what we can tell, she's a normal girl. Martin doesn't see her very often. In fact, my people have never seen Martin with her. He's never shown up for a parent day at Berkeley. He's never had lunch or dinner with her, even when he's been in the same state. As far as we can tell, he barely has any contact with the girl at all." Tilda paused. "As much as I hate to think it, she may be an innocent in all this. It's why we have monitored her from afar but left her alone. Martin himself has a security detail on her 24/7."

Greg felt guilty just thinking about using the girl if she was nothing more than a pawn in her father's schemes. He knew how that felt. But ... desperate times.

"Okay, so where is she now?"

CHAPTER TWENTY-FIVE

BERKELEY, CALIFORNIA

ARIANA SLID AROUND A GROUP OF FOUR UNDERCLASSMEN standing in the middle of the path, debating the role of the Russian invasion of Afghanistan in the fall of the USSR.

She smiled at the passion in their words. This was what she loved about Berkeley: the students, the variety of views. Each day, when she stepped onto campus, she felt energized.

A dark-suited man entered her peripheral field as she stepped past a coffee kiosk.

Her good mood dimmed. It was her security detail. Their dark suits gave them away.

She'd resented their presence her whole life but especially when she came to college. She'd done nothing to cause anyone harm. There would be no reason for her to be targeted. And if there were, it would only be because of him.

Anger flared up in her as she pictured her father. *I hate him.*

She had for a long time. Ever since she realized that their relationship was not how fathers and daughters were supposed to be. At the same time, she kept hoping that maybe, just maybe, one of these days, he might do something to show that he loved her. Because who didn't want to be loved by their father?

She shook her head, dispelling it of the fanciful notion. Martin Drummond was not a man capable of that. To him, she was a possession. Something to be protected but not something to be loved. Her friend Michelle's family had shown her what a real family was supposed to be like.

Now she lived a life where she was followed around by dark-suited men who kept others away and made her a curiosity, a freak. As if her upbringing didn't do enough to make her feel that way. And right now seeing the personification of her father's control made her feel both angry and helpless.

As a rule, Ariana tried not to feel sorry for herself. She was a believer in doing what you needed to do and focusing on what was ahead of you. She didn't often slip into bouts of self-pity because she knew if she started down that road, she would never stop. After all, her life hadn't exactly been a warm and fuzzy existence. Her mother had died when she was six years old. From that point on, she had been raised by governesses. She'd barely seen her father throughout all of her childhood. And the occasional visit was always cold and official.

She'd had a security detail but no friends. Her father had made sure of that. She'd managed to apply to college without him knowing. And when she'd gotten in, she had put her foot down and demanded that she be allowed to go. Her father had said no.

So she had run away. She ran away ten times over three months. Finally, he agreed to let her go. And she knew it was because, even for him, it was simply too much bother to keep dragging her back.

Berkeley had been eye-opening. She couldn't believe that a world like it existed. As a kid, she had only been allowed to watch documentaries. Her only glimpses of normal life came in car rides to her doctor.

But at Berkeley, she was part of that life. Kids walked around free, chatting and talking to one another. They seemed almost alien.

The first week, she had kept herself separated from everyone. She barely spoke to a single person. She simply watched everyone and everything, soaking it all in, hope blooming in her chest that maybe she could be a normal girl if she just figured out the patterns of her classmates' interactions.

By the second week, though, she began to realize just how different she was from the rest of the kids. She didn't know how to smile and have fun. She didn't even know how to order a sandwich at the cafeteria without studying other kids doing it for thirty minutes. And then the choices were overwhelming. She'd never had to do any of that. She might as well have been living on a deserted island without any human contact for how little she understood how the world worked.

But then one day, she had bumped into Michelle, literally. She had been looking down at a map to see where the biology lab was, and Michelle had come around the corner. They'd practically conked heads.

And the friendship was born. Michelle had led the way. She decided that Ariana was her friend, and there was no talking her out of it. That moment, as far as Ariana was concerned, was when her life had really begun. Now she bristled at the restraints her father had put on her. But not for much longer.

I'm not a child anymore. I'm an adult with rights. She'd been mulling it over for a few weeks, but she knew what she needed to do. She'd contact an attorney. Michelle's brother was a lawyer. He would help her. She needed to make sure she was protected from her father. This had gone on long enough. Her father had done nothing for her the entirety of her life. And she would be damned if he was going to be allowed to control the rest of her life.

"Professor Mitchell?"

Ariana looked up as Maria Hankins, a freshman from her intro class, stood up

from a bench as Ariana passed.

Ariana stopped, forcing a smile to her face. Maria was

extremely shy but incredibly bright. Her speaking to Ariana was a huge effort on her part. "Hi, Maria. How are you?"

"Good. Um, I had a question about the reading, but you're probably busy. It's okay. I'll just—"

Ariana stepped off the path and took a seat on the bench. She patted the spot next to her. "I have a little time. Ask away."

Relief flooded Maria's face as she dropped down next to Ariana.

A sense of purpose filled Ariana. This was what she was meant to do. And this week, she was calling Michelle's brother.

Her father's control of her life had gone on long enough.

CHAPTER TWENTY-SIX

THE COUNCIL BASE

MAEVE HAD MOVED POP FROM HIS BED. NOW HE SAT CURLED UP in Maeve's lap as she sat in Crackle's bed with Crackle tucked into her side. She hated that this was the best she could do for them. She wanted to see their faces, their eyes. But that wasn't an option. Whatever the Council had sedated them with was strong, and Maeve had no idea how to counteract it. At the same time, she knew it would be easier for when she had to leave if they weren't awake. And she hated herself for even thinking it.

She sat with them, telling them about Alvie and Snap. Then she explained about Sammy and how he was still with them. She talked about everything and nothing, wanting to keep the silence at bay and wanting them to at least be able to hear her voice.

She wasn't sure how long she had been in there when the wall fell away again. She looked up as Agaren stepped into the room. If he was surprised by her position, he didn't show it. He nodded to the boys. "How are they?"

Maeve shook her head, trying to hold back the anger she felt at Pop and Crackle's condition. The Council was supposed to be looking after them. This was not the way to do it.

She took a breath to keep calm, but her thoughts were clipped and tinged with anger. She wanted to yell at him, at all of them. *How are they? They're stuck. They're alive but not alive. This is torturous.*

Agaren seemed to understand her mood. "I have spoken with the Council. They share your concern for the emotional state of the hybrids, and they have come up with what they believe is a fair solution."

Maeve's heart lifted. They were going to let Pop and Crackle return to them. It was the only way to ensure their well-being.

Agaren's next words robbed her of that small burst of hope. "They have decided that you or Captain Garrigan can stay here with the hybrids."

Maeve frowned at him, not sure she was understanding him correctly. "Stay?"

Agaren nodded. "Yes. You will live here with them for the remainder of your life."

Maeve's mouth fell open. "You can't be serious."

"I'm afraid I am. They will not agree to the hybrids being returned to Earth. Not while it is so dangerous. And so, in consideration of the hybrids' emotional state, they decided to allow you or Captain Garrigan to stay here."

Maeve stared at him and then looked around the room. Stay *here?* She hadn't even considered that as a possibility. She had thought she would be able to talk the Council into allowing Pop and Crackle to come back home with her. She never imagined that she would be adding more of her family to the base. But as she looked back down at Pop and Crackle, she knew that she would have to take the offer. Either her or Chris would have to agree to move here. They could not abandon Pop and Crackle.

"Will Pop and Crackle remain in the suspended state?"

"Yes, but only until you return here full-time. Then they will be awakened to join you. We will make as many accommodations as we can for you, as well as their comfort and development."

Maeve took a breath. She supposed that was better than nothing, but the idea of it was terrifying. "And I'll be able to visit Earth at times? To see the rest of our family?"

Agaren met her gaze and slowly shook his head. "I'm afraid that that will not be an option."

Maeve frowned. "Why not? I mean, security protocols can be put into place to make sure it could be made safe. Or they could be brought up here to visit."

"It is not a matter of safety; it is a matter of access."

"I don't understand."

"The Council has decided that the human experiment has gone on long enough. In seven days, they will remove the human threat from the Earth."

Maeve's mouth fell open. "Remove the threat? Extinction?"

Agaren nodded. "I tried to argue on behalf of the humans, but I was not successful. In seven days' time, a virus will be released on Earth. It will be lethal to all forms of human life. Across the globe and within two days, all of humanity will be infected. None will survive."

Maeve felt like she had been sucker punched. She couldn't seem to get any air into her lungs. She couldn't form a sentence. All life destroyed. She pictured a field, people lying prone, struggling to breathe. "How can you do this?"

"The Council feels the Drago genes have had too much of an influence. Humans are too selfish in their opinion, and therefore will eventually become like the Drago themselves. As a species, you have already annihilated half of the living species on your world. If left unchecked, they believe that as your technological capabilities grow, you would do the same to other worlds. They cannot allow that to happen."

Maeve stared at him in horror as terror ran through her. "What about Alvie and Snap? What about Sammy and Iggy?"

"Sammy is an aberration, not a purebred. He is of no interest to the Council. Iggy is not the last of his kind. There are more Maldek strewn throughout the galaxy. And the Council feels Pop and Crackle will be more than enough for their needs."

"You'd let them all die too?"

"I do not wish that. I will continue to argue for another approach. I do not wish for any of you to die."

"What if we find this Guardian?"

"It may convince them to spare you. But even with finding her, her treatment at your hands may only reinforce their decision."

Maeve felt like the rug had been pulled out from underneath her. Was there really nothing they could do?

"They have given humanity a week instead of initiating the final solution immediately to allow you to make a decision. Either you or Captain Garrigan will be allowed to stay with Pop and Crackle. You or Captain Garrigan will survive."

"But no one else will," Maeve said softly.

"Yes. You will be the last of your kind. And when you pass, humanity will be gone forever."

CHAPTER TWENTY-SEVEN

FREMONT, CALIFORNIA

In Greg's mind, UC Berkeley would always be the epicenter of the hippie generation. Back in the 1960s, Berkeley seemed to be the center point for the counterculture movement revolving around Free Speech. And even though Berkeley's heyday had been decades ago, Greg had half expected to see wild-haired twentysomethings walking around barefoot and wearing love beads while dozens of Volkswagen vans sat in the parking lot. Instead it was predominantly electric cars and hybrids that were in the parking lot. And rather than hippies, the closest to some sort of counterculture individual he saw were men with man buns.

He had to admit, it was a letdown.

There were, however, a few booths arguing for different causes: environmental protection, LGBTQ protections, voter registration. But even without the virulent protests of his imagination, it seemed a strange choice of schools for Martin's daughter.

Martin has a daughter. Even the thought of it sent a shudder through Greg's body. Martin was the personification of evil as far as Greg was concerned. He had helped spawn the A.L.I.V.E. projects and then let them loose, just to see how the humans would react and how the projects would react to get a better gauge on any future human-alien skirmishes.

The man was a monster. He cared nothing for human life. Greg had very little hope that his daughter was any better. You couldn't be around that kind of evil and remain untouched. She was probably just as cruel as he was, just as immoral.

Generally, Greg wasn't a fan of kidnapping, but in this case, he would most definitely make an exception. He had no compunction with harming someone related to Martin Drummond. After all, Martin Drummond had tried to harm those closest to him on multiple occasions.

"Anything?" Jasper's voice cut into his thoughts through the earpiece that Jasper had given him before he'd let him out of the van. Only Mike and Greg were on campus. Jasper had stayed with the van. He and Mike would contact him once they had eyes on Ariana Mitchell.

Greg reached for his throat and tapped the mic there. "Nothing. But she should be getting out of her class soon."

Ariana was a teaching assistant for introduction to genetics. She'd been a teaching assistant at Berkeley for the last six years. Greg was surprised to learn that she had been made one her junior year. That was not something you normally saw happen. Apparently she was incredibly bright.

So, great, she'll be the evil genius in the family. Wonderful.

He settled back against the wall, taking a bite of a chocolate bar as he searched the crowd for any sign of her.

CHAPTER TWENTY-EIGHT

SAYING GOODBYE TO CRACKLE AND POP WAS THE HARDEST thing Maeve had ever done. She wanted nothing more than to stay with them. At the same time, she knew she needed to go home. She needed to talk to Chris. She needed to talk to Alvie and Snap. They needed to figure out what they were going to do in response to the Council's ultimatum.

She leaned down and kissed Pop on the forehead. She ran her hand over his cheek. "I love you," she said, her voice cracking.

She took a steeling breath, trying to hold back the tears that threatened to fall. She leaned in to Crackle. "I love you too."

She wanted to say that she would be back for them. She wanted to say that everything would be all right. But she couldn't say either of those things. She rested her hands on each of their shoulders, dreading leaving them and yet knowing it had to happen. Finally, she looked up at Agaren, who had been standing silently against the wall as she said goodbye. She nodded.

He stepped out of the room, and she followed. She stopped and glanced back, watching them one more time before the wall shut them off from her. She glanced over at the dais where the Council had sat. It was empty.

Anger boiled through her. They had laid down their ultimatum and left, leaving Maeve feeling angered and overwhelmed.

What am I going to do?

She followed Agaren, trying to keep her breathing even. She wiped at the tears that rolled down her cheeks. This was all so wrong.

She barely remembered the walk back to Agaren's ship. Before she knew it, she was strapped in, and they were once again heading down the long tunnel to the surface of the moon.

She looked at Agaren as he piloted the ship. He looked completely in control.

And completely without emotion.

"Don't you see what you are doing? We're family. You can't split us all up. We belong together."

Agaren said nothing as they burst out of the tunnel and sped across the surface of the moon, this time going much faster than on the trip in.

While Agaren's face showed no emotion, she could hear the depth of them in the timber of his voice. "I know. The Council does not understand things like family. Emotions are not a strong component on our worlds. I argued for you, as did the Agarthans. They, too, exist in family groups. But the overwhelming concern is the survival of the hybrids. And that cannot be guaranteed on your planet. Even now, as you hide away, there are forces moving against you. The Council cannot risk all of the hybrids being lost. The fact that they have allowed two to remain on Earth is a testament to how much they respect the work you have done with them."

Maeve wanted to argue with him. She wanted to say that of course they would protect the hybrids. That they would give every-thing in their power to keep them safe. But the truth was that the powers arrayed against them were much stronger. And alone, they didn't have enough to keep them safe.

Because Agaren was right—there was undeniably a fight in the United States government between those who were on their side and those who were not. Martin had spies everywhere, and it was safe to assume that as soon as he found them, he would do everything in his power to regain control of Alvie and Snap, if not kill them outright.

Maeve watched as they broke free from the surface of the moon and moved out into the darkness of space. This should have been a magical trip. She was in space. But she couldn't take in the beauty of the scenery or the significance of being a human going into space and returning again with an alien of her own free will.

All she could think about was the fact that her family was about to be separated forever. And there was nothing she could do about it.

CHAPTER TWENTY-NINE

SEATTLE, WASHINGTON

Martin's phone beeped. He swatted at it angrily. "What?"

Stacy Mal's voice came back, a nervous tremor in it. "Sorry to disturb you, sir. The latest security report just came in from the California unit."

Martin rolled his eyes. "Just send me the damn file." He disconnected the call.

Stacy had been a pain in his neck ever since he'd returned. She hovered over him like a mother hen. If she kept this up, he was going to have to replace her, and he really didn't want to do that.

Not out of any affection, of course, but because she was damn good at her job. But she was treating him with kid gloves. Yes, he'd been thrown out of a plane. Yes, he'd spent over twenty-four hours being tossed about in the sea. But that was nothing compared to some of the experiences he'd had earlier in life. It was practically a vacation compared to them.

He shoved Stacy from his mind and shifted his focus back to the reports that had piled up in his absence. The search for the remaining escapees from Area 51 continued. They'd recovered or killed half a dozen, but at least two dozen more were still at large.

He spent the next hour going through those reports before assigning special teams and making recommendations for the best way to trap the specimens.

Finally, he pushed back from the desk, rubbing at his eyes. They stung like mad, and he could still smell that damn fish. There was one file left on his hard drive that he needed to review, the one from California, but it could wait until after lunch.

Almost as if she could read his mind, Stacy appeared in his doorway, a large bag from the Mexican place a few miles away in her hand. "Thought you might be hungry. I brought some lunch. There're a couple options, so you can choose."

He wanted to yell at her for being so presumptuous, but his stomach growled. So maybe just this one time, her hovering wasn't such a bad thing. He waved her forward. "Put it on the desk."

She did and then stood, shifting from foot to foot, looking at him. "Is there anything else that you—"

"Don't you have some work to do?"

Stacy paled noticeably. "Yes, of course. I'll leave you to it."

She hurried out of the room, closing the door behind her. He pulled over the bag, and the scent of chili and marinated meat met his nose. He inhaled deeply, grateful for any odor other than fish.

Twenty minutes later, his hunger was satiated, and he pushed the remains of his last taco away from him. He needed a good workout. Maybe he'd hit the treadmill for a couple miles. A long run would help ease some of the tension from his shoulders. His gaze strayed to the computer screen and the file from Berkeley.

Part of him told him to skip it. There was never anything of importance in the reports. But he had not gotten to this position by cutting corners. It was when people started cutting corners that details were missed and control was lost.

And Martin never lost control.

He opened up the file and skimmed through the first page of the report. It was an accounting of Ariana's activities. Nothing out of the ordinary. Classes, time with friends. He curled his lips at that one. She was spending way too much time with that Michelle girl.

I'll have to do something about that.

He skimmed through the photos of the unknowns that had been seen around her. He continued to flick from one face to the next, not really caring about what he was looking at, his mind already shifting to other searches he could do to find Leander and her group.

He flicked to another screen and then went still, his mind taking a moment to catch up to what his eyes had seen. He scrolled back to the prior image. He stared at the profile of a man with glasses and shaggy brown hair. He zoomed in, enlarging the man's face. "What the hell?"

Greg Schorn sat on a bench a few feet away from the building where Ariana taught.

Martin's stomach bottomed out at the same time that his anger boiled. How the hell had they found her? There was no link. There was no trail. There was no possible way they should have been able to find her.

Martin shoved the remains of his lunch to the floor in his haste to grab his phone.

Stacy answered immediately. "Yes?"

"Get me the security detail at Berkeley. Immediately."

"Yes, sir."

Martin waited for five seconds before the call was connected. He paced around his office, waiting for the idiot to pick up. "Carmichael."

"Carmichael, bring her in. Bring the subject in immediately. Get her to a safe house and await further orders."

The agent paused as if he hadn't quite heard Martin correctly before he spoke. "Yes, sir. Right away."

"Call me when you have her secured."

Martin disconnected the call and glared at the image of Greg Schorn on the screen. "How did you find her?" he growled. Then he shook his head. It didn't matter. Because finding Ariana had provided an opportunity.

He grabbed the phone again and quickly dialed the number, this one he knew by heart. "Rapid Response."

James Davidson, formerly Major James Davidson of the Marine Corps, answered almost immediately. "I have a mission for you."

"A bag and tag?"

He stared at the image of Greg Schorn on the screen. "No. An extermination."

CHAPTER THIRTY

BERKELEY, CALIFORNIA

GREG HAD LOOPED ALL OF THE COLLEGE SECURITY CAMERAS TO avoid Martin being able to tag any of them, but they couldn't do anything about all of the cell phones. Tilda had offered to shut all the cell phones down. But if they did that, it would most definitely set off some sort of alarm. So for now, Greg was just trying to make sure his face wasn't caught by any of the cell phones in the area.

Which was proving to be more difficult than he thought. It seemed everybody was on Instagram or had a YouTube account, sharing all of their information with the world. What ever happened to privacy?

Greg took a bite of the ham sandwich he'd picked up from a food truck as he'd made his way on campus. And it was good. Adam's place in Norway was so out of the way that going to the grocery store was a four-hour odyssey—one way. There was no running out if you forgot something.

So he was taking advantage of all the food options he could before he went back. But even with the lack of complicated cuisine, he didn't regret the choices he'd made. He'd do it all over again if given a chance.

But right now as he scanned the crowd of college students, he couldn't help but feel a longing for a different life. Most kids sat alone or were talking in groups, laughing. But all of them looked carefree. Greg shook his head, wanting to yell at all of them that the end was near. But none of them would believe him. He would be that crazy guy that you saw in movies with the sign warning about the end of days.

Now Greg wondered if maybe that crazy guy had been given some inside information that the rest of the human race had not.

Kind of like himself.

"Heads up. Classes are letting out," Mike said through his earpiece. Mike was positioned at the back of the building in case Ariana exited that way.

Greg hastily wrapped up the rest of his sandwich and shoved it into his backpack. He straightened from the wall, rolling his shoulders. He pulled out his phone, even though it wasn't powered up, and pretended to watch the screen while he kept an eye on the door. Streams of students wandered out, most looking like they weren't in a hurry to go anywhere.

Greg scanned them all, searching for Ariana, but didn't see her. The crowd thinned. He began to worry that maybe she hadn't been in class today. They hadn't been able to go into the building and check because her security had been positioned at either end of the hall. They couldn't take the chance of her security recognizing them. Maybe Ariana was taking the day off. Or worse, maybe she had gotten a heads-up from her father and had disappeared somewhere.

Then he saw her step through the door. He'd seen her picture, twice if you included Luke's sketch. But neither did her justice. She was tall, maybe 5'10", and very slim. She had light-brown hair that the sun seemed to be turning blonde. And even from a distance, her eyes were the most incredible blue Greg had ever seen. Her skin was a pale brown, making her eyes look even brighter. Yup, as much as he hated to admit it, Martin's daughter was a knockout.

"Anything?" Jasper asked impatiently.

Greg fumbled for his mic. "Um, yeah. She just left Koshland Hall. She's heading toward the parking lot."

"Which parking lot?"

Greg shook himself, trying to pull himself out of whatever stupor catching sight of Ariana had caused. Greg hitched his backpack higher onto his shoulder and hurried after her. "She's heading to you. She's heading to you."

From the corner of his eye, he saw Mike come around the side of the building. "I see Ariana's security detail. They're moving too. Grab Ariana, and I'll meet you back at the trailer."

"Roger."

Up ahead, Greg saw Jasper in the van going around the row closest to the edge of the parking lot. He moved slowly, as if searching for a parking spot. The van stopped at the entrance of the parking lot, idling by the curb.

Greg was now about twenty feet behind Ariana. Ariana crossed in front of the parking lot, not even looking at the van. Jasper slipped out from it and grabbed her arm. She turned, her eyes going wide in alarm as Jasper put a cloth over her mouth.

Greg sprinted forward and caught Ariana just as her legs buckled. Jasper grabbed her feet, and the two of them hustled into the van. Greg climbed into the back with her as Jasper jumped behind the steering wheel, slamming the car into gear. "We've got company."

Greg glanced out the back windows as Jasper peeled out of the parking lot. Two men sprinted forward, guns raised toward the van, but they didn't shoot.

Greg let out a breath. Well, at least one thing went right.

CHAPTER THIRTY-ONE

GEIRANGER, NORWAY

Maeve stood in the clearing, watching Agaren's ship take off. They hadn't spoken for the remainder of the trip back to Earth. After all, what was there to say?

As they touched down, Maeve had hit the safety harness's release and followed Agaren to the ramp. As it lowered, he handed her a small black box about the size of a key fob. "When you have made your decision, you can contact me through this. I will come right away."

Maeve nodded, a lump in her throat keeping her from speaking. The next time she saw Agaren, it would mean the permanent destruction of her family.

"I am sorry that it has come to this. I know how much you have tried. I had hoped that things would be different, that humanity was ready for the next step. I fear I may have been wrong."

Maeve wanted to argue on humanity's behalf, but she knew how cruel humans could be to one another, never mind to an entirely different species. And besides, it wasn't Agaren she needed to convince. So she took the box and walked silently down the ramp.

She gripped it in her hand, dreading the conversations to come. Her neck ached as she stared up at the sky until Agaren's ship was no longer even a speck in the sky. How was she supposed to make this choice?

"Maeve!"

She turned as Chris ran toward her, Alvie and Snap behind him. Alvie and Snap soon burst past him. Maeve shoved the box into her pocket, dropped to her knees, and held out her arms. Without hesitation, Alvie and Snap flung themselves into them. She gripped them tight, emotions threatening to overwhelm her. She tried to hold them back, knowing that both Alvie and Snap would be able to sense them.

Too soon, Alvie had pulled back and looked into her eyes. *What's wrong?*

She knew she needed to stay strong. It was her job to put on a brave face. But right now it was impossible. And the truth was, she wouldn't be able to keep the truth from either Snap or Alvie for very long. She kissed his forehead. "Crackle and Pop are all right. They're safe. But I'm afraid there is a great deal we need to discuss."

She met Chris's eyes over Alvie and Snap's heads. He slowed his run as he approached, the dawning realization that something was very wrong crossing his face. He stared at her, and she gave him a quick shake of her head.

She stood. Alvie and Snap stepped back. Chris pulled her into his arms. "I've got you."

She clung to him, the tears she had been trying to hold back rolling down her cheeks. The words she needed to say lost in the torrent.

CHAPTER THIRTY-TWO

BERKELEY, CALIFORNIA

ARIANA CAME TO SLOWLY. HER HEAD FELT FUZZY. SHE COULD smell chemicals and practically taste them on her tongue. Unsteady and confused, she opened her eyes cautiously and then reared back. A man she didn't know and had never seen before sat directly across from her.

Her hand touched cool metal behind her. She was sitting on the floor of some sort of panel van. A second man sat behind the wheel. What the hell was going on?

The man in front of her held up his hands. He was around her age, maybe a year or two older. He had tousled brown hair and dark-rimmed glasses. He wore a black T-shirt and jeans, which showed off a surprisingly toned body, because everything else about the guy gave off a nerdy vibe. "Hey, hey. It's okay. There's nothing to worry about. You're okay."

Ariana stared at him in shock. Nothing to worry about? She was in a van with two men she didn't know. That seemed like plenty to worry about. She shrank a little farther back. "Who are you?"

"I'm Greg Schorn, and this is—"

"Jesus, Greg," the driver said. "No names."

Greg cringed. "What? Well, her dad's going to know who we are once we contact him."

"My father? You grabbed me because of my father?"

Greg nodded. "Yes. Your father... He's holding someone that we need to get back. And so we need to trade you for her. It will be fine," he said quickly. "We won't hurt you. I mean, I know this is like, emotionally painful, maybe, but you won't be physically harmed." He took a breath. "I'm sorry. I've never kidnapped someone before, and I wouldn't have kidnapped you if it weren't really important, like end-of-the-world important."

Ariana studied the man in front of her. He didn't really give off a soldier-of-fortune vibe, although the man in front definitely seemed to have a better idea of what he was doing. Greg, if that was really his name, seemed more of the geeky type. Honestly, he kind of looked like a TA from her economics class.

As she was studying him, his words finally resonated with her. "Wait, end of the world?"

Greg nodded, looking completely serious.

Great, you're crazy.

"I'm not crazy."

Ariana's head jerked up, and she stared at him. "Did I say that out loud?"

Greg nodded. "Uh, yeah. And I know it *sounds* crazy, but trust me, in the last few years, I have seen and heard crazier. But we just need to trade you for—"

Ariana shook her head, wanting to laugh or bang her head against the side of the van in frustration. "I'm not close with my dad. I don't even think—"

"We know you guys aren't close."

"You do?" She shook her head, reevaluating the guy in front of her. "I think you've made a mistake. I mean, my dad wouldn't kidnap someone."

Greg must have read the doubt in her voice. "Actually, he did, or more accurately, someone else did, and then he took her from him. It's kind of complicated. But to make a long story short, your father is holding somebody, and we need to get her back. And it is not an exaggeration to say that there will be worldwide ramifications if we don't."

Ariana stared at the man in front of her and then over at the driver, who met her gaze in the rearview mirror. "You guys haven't really done anything too bad yet. Why don't you just let me go? You can just pull over, and I'll get out. And I won't tell anybody about you."

The driver scoffed. "Yeah, like I haven't heard that before."

The words did not exactly bring Ariana comfort. She turned her attention back to the guy in front of her. He actually seemed like a decent sort of guy, or at least as decent as a guy could seem in this kind of situation. "Okay, I don't know what's going on, but it has nothing to do with me. I haven't talked to my father in months. He's not going to help you because you have me."

Greg shook his head. "Of course he will. You're his daughter. I mean, all parents love their kids. It's like a biological imperative."

Ariana had to hold in her snort. Her father did *not* have that biological imperative. Maybe he'd missed out on the compassion gene when it was being handed out, because she knew for a fact that her father had not an ounce of empathy in him. At least not for her. He'd made that abundantly clear over and over again throughout her life.

"You're wrong."

Greg opened his mouth to speak again, but the driver spoke before he could. "Do you know what your father does?"

Ariana looked between Greg and the back of the driver's head. "He works for the government."

"What part of the government?" the driver asked.

"I actually don't know. But I know he's important. He has agents and people that work for him. And he's very busy."

"Well, you've got that right," Greg mumbled.

Ariana looked between the two men. "I don't know what's going on, but I'm telling you, my father won't trade for me. He will send people for me, though. You guys are in danger. You really should let me out."

Greg shook his head. "Yeah, well, thanks to your father, we've been in danger for a good long while. I'm kind of getting used to it."

CHAPTER THIRTY-THREE

SEATTLE, WASHINGTON

MARTIN PACED HIS OFFICE, WAITING FOR CARMICHAEL TO CALL him back, but there was nothing coming from California. He reached for the phone just as it rang.

"Report."

Carmichael stuttered as he began to speak. "Uh, sir, we, um, we've had a problem."

"Where is my daughter?"

"Uh, she was grabbed by a three-man team. One took out the agents directly on her and then escaped through the campus. The other two loaded her into a van and took off."

"Do you have any leads?"

"Um, one guy had glasses."

I'm surrounded by incompetence. They had abducted his daughter from under the nose of her security detail. Martin pulled his phone away from his ear, wishing he could reach through it and strangle the man on the other end.

"Find. My. Daughter." He slammed the phone back down. Taking a breath, he dialed again.

His commander answered. "Yes, sir?"

"How far out are you?"

"Fifteen minutes, sir."

Martin checked his watch. "Let me know when you are in position."

"Yes, sir."

Martin hung up the phone. R.I.S.E. had her. He had no doubt about that. But how had Matilda even known she existed?

A knock sounded at his door. He took a few deep breaths and then sat back behind his desk. "Come in."

He looked up as Stacy stepped in, ushering in a tall muscular man. Damn it. Sharp. He'd forgotten about him. He'd need to make this quick.

Sharp wore a blue jacket with a crisp white Oxford shirt that contrasted sharply with his tan skin and white-blonde hair.

Martin stood as the man crossed the room to shake his hand. "It's good to meet you, Director Drummond. I'm Jack Sharp."

Martin shook Jack's hand, noting the calloused grip. Sharp might look like a trust-fund baby, but his hands gave away the real story. Jack Sharp had been a Green Beret. He'd served five tours in Afghanistan and another two in Iraq. When he'd gotten out, he'd started Blackjack Security, a private military operation that the U.S. government often hired when they were running low on troops.

The Blackjacks had gotten into trouble over time in both Afghanistan and Iraq. The code of conduct that governed military behavior did not extend to the private military. And their abuses had caught the attention of the brass and the media on more than one occasion.

But Martin didn't care about any of that. War was hell, as the saying went. And whatever these guys needed to do to protect America was fine with him.

"Take a seat."

"Thanks," Jack said as he seated himself across from Martin. "How can I help you, Director Drummond?"

Martin studied the man in front of him. He'd read the reports.

He knew Sharp was a serious soldier and also not one given to fits of fancy. He had his feet firmly planted on the ground, which meant that getting him to understand and even believe what the problem was might be a bit of an issue. "What do you know about what we do here?"

Jack met his gaze, unflinching. "The D.E.A.D. tracks down the escapees from Area 51. So far you have tracked down more than a few dozen types of alien hybrids. Although at least a couple dozen more are still at large."

Martin raised an eyebrow, surprised. "And where did you hear that?"

Jack shrugged. "I have friends in high places."

"So you are aware that there is an alien presence on the planet?"

Jack nodded. "And that the incident at the Arizona mall was also alien related. My understanding is that the alien presence was entirely contained at Area 51 until recently."

Martin folded his hands in front of him on the desk. "That's not entirely true. Have you ever heard of an island called Hy-Brasil?"

Fifteen minutes later, Martin finished telling Jack about the incident at Hy-Brasil. Jack had taken it well, although Martin could see the shock on the man's face.

"The individuals responsible for bringing the Drago out of hiding are still on the loose, along with the very first experiment from the A.L.I.V.E. Project. *That* is where you come in. Do you think your men will have a problem with that?"

Sharp shook his head. "My men don't ask questions. I give them a target, they take out the target. It's a simple and efficient arrangement. Besides, I think they'll very much be on board with taking down some aliens and traitors to the United States of America."

Martin nodded. "Good. As soon as I have a target, I want your men ready to go. They will be taking out everyone on sight. No captures, only kills."

"Understood. When will you have a target for us?"

"Any day now. Have your men on standby. I want them on the eastern coast. I have a feeling our targets are somewhere in Europe. The East Coast will give you a faster reaction time."

Sharp stood. "Yes, sir. I'll have everybody ready to go in an hour, and we'll make our way to our airfield outside Baltimore."

Martin smiled. "I look forward to doing business with you."

Sharp returned the smile. "And I you, sir."

Martin hit the button on the bottom of his desk, and Stacy appeared at the door to escort Sharp out. As soon as the door was closed, he looked at his watch. Two minutes.

Right on schedule, Davidson sent a text. *On site.*

Martin sat at his desk and brought up the program. In twenty-two years, he'd never had call to use it. But the current situation demanded it. All those precautions he'd put in place had now borne themselves out.

He called Davidson, putting the call on speakerphone so his hands were free.

"Yes, sir?"

"Protocol Alpha Charlie Zebra."

"Yes, sir. Alpha Charlie Zebra. Ready, sir."

"Signal up in three, two, one." Martin punched the enter key on his keyboard. The red light on his monitor turned green.

"I have the signal, sir. They are forty-five minutes away, heading west."

"Get my property back."

"Yes, sir."

CHAPTER THIRTY-FOUR

FREMONT, CALIFORNIA

ARIANA HAD BEEN COUNTING THE TIME. THEY'D DRIVEN FOR about an hour before they pulled onto an uneven road. A few minutes later, they stopped, and a third man opened the door from the outside. "Everything okay?" he asked.

"Yeah, we're good." Greg slid out of the van. He reached back in for Ariana.

She pulled her arms out of his reach. "I don't need help."

Greg snatched his hand back. "Sorry," he mumbled.

And Ariana had the strangest urge to tell him it was all right. He looked like a kicked puppy. But it wasn't all right. He'd kidnapped her. She shouldn't feel anything for him but anger.

As Ariana stepped out of the van, her hopes plummeted. She'd thought maybe there might be a chance for her to escape, or maybe yell for help, once they stopped. But they were in the middle of nowhere. There was an abandoned factory behind her and some crappy old trailer in front of her.

Greg waved toward the trailer. The other man had already moved off. Ariana noted the weapon at his waist. She noted for the first time the weapon at Greg's waist as well. "Um, we need you to go in there."

She met Greg's eyes for a moment before looking away with a sigh and heading for the trailer. The driver stood at the trailer door and held it open for her. "This way, please."

Ariana stepped inside, and the man pointed to the couch along the wall. "Take a seat. This will probably take a while."

Ariana sat down. Greg stepped in a minute later, followed by the other man.

"Any problems?" the driver asked.

The other man shook his head. "Nah. I lost her security pretty easily."

Ariana bit her lip. Apparently her dad had been right about her needing security.

Of course, a fat lot of help it had done her. And if not for her father, she wouldn't be in this situation to begin with.

Greg walked over to the fridge and pulled out two bottles of water. He placed one on the side table next to Ariana. "Uh, here you go. Um, there's some really old magazines in that drawer next to you, if you want to read or something. Are you hungry?"

She shook her head.

"Well, that's probably good, because all we have left is cold pizza."

"Greg," the driver called from the other side of the room.

Greg glanced over at him before turning back to Ariana. "Uh, sorry. I'll be right back." He crossed the room to the other two.

Ariana studied the men across from her. As much as she wanted to hate them, they didn't seem like cruel men. They seemed like men who had been pushed to the edge. She had no doubt her father had been the one doing the pushing.

She sighed, trying to figure out a way to resolve this that didn't involve her life getting completely derailed. But she didn't think that was an option.

Ariana looked at the ceiling and prayed to God, whom she had never believed in. *If you exist, I could really use a little help.*

CHAPTER THIRTY-FIVE

ARIANA MITCHELL WAS NOT WHO GREG HAD EXPECTED. SHE wasn't arrogant or whiny. She had just accepted that this was her situation, and honestly, that kind of made him a little sad. Because he had the feeling having her movements restricted was not something new to her.

He joined Mike and Jasper on the side of the trailer opposite from Ariana. He lowered his voice. "So what are we going to do with her?"

"Take her to another secure location. And then when the time is right, we'll trade her," Jasper said.

"He won't trade anyone for me."

They all turned to Ariana. She shrugged. "It's not exactly a big room. I can hear you pretty easily."

Mike shook his head. "Of course he'll trade for you. You're his daughter."

Ariana let out a scoff. "I have little to no relationship with my father. He's certainly not going to give up something that he wants for *me*."

Mike shook his head, his arms crossed over his chest. "He has a security detail on you. Of course he'll want to get you back."

Ariana shook her head. "You don't understand my father. He will *not* trade for me. That's not how he works."

"Then how does he work?" Greg asked.

Ariana looked at all of them and then just looked away, shaking her head.

Greg stared at Ariana. He didn't get the feeling that she was lying to them. She honestly didn't think that her father would trade for her release. She thought her father would keep whatever he had rather than try to get Ariana to safety.

And as much as he didn't want to, he felt bad for Ariana. Greg had a tough relationship with his family. Saying it was strained was an understatement. They didn't talk on a day-to-day basis, but at the same time he knew each of them would take a bullet for him, and he'd do the same for them. What must it be like to think that family didn't have your back? To believe that at the end of the day, they weren't the ones who were going to be there for you?

It must be a pretty lonely existence.

Jasper stood. "Okay, I'll go check the plane and contact the boss. She should have the safe house ready, and then we need to get moving. I don't like being here this long."

Jasper opened the door to the trailer and then stopped still. Mike was instantly on his feet behind him. "What?"

"We have company."

CHAPTER THIRTY-SIX

GEIRANGER, NORWAY

MAEVE SENT ALVIE AND SNAP OFF WITH SANDRA AND NORA. The two women promised to keep them entertained. Maeve was thankful. She knew that she needed to tell them, but she needed to tell Chris first. She was going to break down when she did, and she'd rather that neither Alvie nor Snap saw that.

Once Maeve and Chris had walked a good mile from the cabin, she stopped. She took a seat on a downed tree and leaned her elbows on her thighs, her face in her hands. Chris crouched in front of her. "Tell me," he said softly.

She took a stuttering breath and then told him everything that had happened.

By the time she was done, the tears that had been raining down her cheeks had stopped. She felt drained, exhausted.

Chris paced in front of her, his hand continually going to his mouth and wiping it as if somehow he could wipe the horror away. "How can they do this? They can't just keep them."

"They can." Maeve sighed, picturing the emotionless Council. "We're essentially animals to them in many ways. We're the lion parents demanding that the zoo return our cubs. But just like them, we have no power here. We're completely at their mercy ... or lack thereof."

"We're not animals. We have feelings. We have emotions, so do Pop and Crackle."

Maeve nodded slowly. "They understand that, at least on an academic level. Which is why they made the offer. One of us can stay with them. One of us can help make sure that their emotional needs are met. Beyond that ..." She shook her head.

Chris looked like he had been punched in the stomach. Maeve knew how he felt. It was as if her insides had been clawed out. How was she supposed to make this choice? How were *they* supposed to make this choice? No matter what they chose, she would be separated from people she loved.

And even beyond that, what kind of life were Pop and Crackle going to have on that base? There was no laughter. There was no fun. There was no joy. What kind of an existence would that be for any of them?

At the same time, she knew that she could not abandon them to that existence on their own. But how could she leave Alvie? Even the thought of it made her want to throw up. They had always been with one another. How could she possibly leave him behind?

"What are we going to do?" Chris asked quietly.

Maeve shook her head. "I don't know."

Chris took a seat on the log next to her.

Maeve gripped his hand. "There's something else I need to tell you." She took a deep breath and told him about the Council's deadline.

"A week?" Chris asked softly. "We only have a week?"

Maeve nodded. She didn't know what else to say. She didn't even know what to think. It was too much information. So if either she or Chris went to the ship to stay with Pop and Crackle, everyone else would die. Alvie and Snap would die, unless by some miracle they found the Guardian and she hadn't been treated horribly. "I can't do this. I can't make this decision."

"You don't have to," Chris said softly. "I'll make it. You go. You take care of Crackle and Pop. You live."

Maeve shook her head "No. That's not going to happen. I'm not leaving you behind to—" Her words cut off, not able to say the truth of what was going to happen. "There has to be another way. There has to be something we can do."

Chris just shook his head, his gaze straying out over the woods. Squirrels darted up a tree. Nearby, birds flew overhead. It was a peaceful scene. "We need to get them to take Alvie and Snap."

Maeve turned to look at him. "What?"

"If the worst comes to pass, we need to get them to take Alvie and Snap as well. If they stay here, they'll die. But if they're up there, they'll get to live ... and so will you."

Maeve shook her head. "No. We'll all go together."

"Getting them to take just Alvie and Snap will be a long shot. Another human? They won't want that." Chris squeezed her hand.

"Then we'll come up with another option."

He leaned over and kissed her gently on the lips. "But if things turn badly, then you need to go join Crackle and Pop."

"What about you?"

"I'll stay here, loving you to my last breath."

The tears Maeve thought she had finished crying rolled down her cheeks. "How has it come to this?"

Chris pulled her into his shoulder without answering.

But much like the trip from the moon with Agaren, there was nothing to say. Right now, there were no scenarios that either of them could come up with that would not rip their family apart. Whoever made it to the Council's base would forever feel guilty for going.

And whoever was left behind, well, after a time, they wouldn't feel anything at all.

CHAPTER THIRTY-SEVEN

GREG BOUNDED UP FROM HIS SEAT. "WHAT DO YOU MEAN WE have company?"

Mike and Jasper ignored him as Mike grabbed the bag from the desk and unzipped it. He started handing out equipment.

Jasper pulled on a bulletproof vest as he talked. "Get Ariana out of here. We'll cover your escape."

Mike handed Greg two bulletproof vests. Greg struggled into one and then hurried over to Ariana. "Put this on."

Ariana shook her head, her mouth falling open. "I'm not wearing that."

"Ariana, there are people coming. I know they are probably your father's men. That means they're all going to be armed. Please put this on."

Ariana hesitated and then grabbed it, pulling it over her head.

Greg took her hand. "Come on, we need to go."

Ariana followed behind him quietly.

Jasper kicked open the door and then dropped to a knee, lining up his weapon with the incoming cars. "Go."

Greg hurried out the door, pulling Ariana behind him. Mike moved ahead of them, scanning the area as he went.

"Oh no." Ariana stumbled behind him and fell heavily to the ground.

Greg turned around. "Are you all right?"

She nodded, her head down. "Yeah. I'm okay."

Her head jerked up, and her eyes went wide. "Oh my God, what's that?"

Greg whirled around, scanning the area but not seeing what had caused Ariana's alarm. "What's what?"

But Ariana's only answer was the two-by-four she had grabbed from the ground and swung at the back of Greg's head.

CHAPTER THIRTY-EIGHT

GREG HIT THE GROUND HARD. STARS DANCED AT THE EDGES OF his vision as the back of his head screamed in agony. He looked up in time to see Ariana sprinting away. "Mike," he groaned.

Mike turned around, his gaze quickly shifting from Greg to Ariana's retreating frame.

Greg got to his knees and waved an arm toward Ariana. "Go get her."

Jasper sprinted down the stairs toward them. "No time."

Greg looked over his shoulder as three SUVs bore down on them. "Damn it."

One of the SUVs broke off from the group and headed toward Ariana, but Ariana was moving incredibly fast. She reached the factory gate and slipped inside.

Mike latched on to Greg's bicep and hauled him to his feet. "You good?"

Greg blinked a few times to chase the stars away as the pain in the back of his head made him long to lie down. But instead, he pulled his Glock from its holster. "Yeah. I'll just shoot the guys in the middle," he said with a wince.

Jasper nodded as he reached the two of them. "That's the spirit."

The three of them hustled around to the side of the trailer. There was no other coverage nearby except for the factory, but the other SUV was already there, blocking the way. Even Greg knew that these were bad odds. Three SUVs meant at least twelve guys versus the three of them.

He swallowed. He wasn't exactly trained in urban warfare. He could hit the side of a barn as long as the barn wasn't moving. But he wasn't so great with smaller targets. The two SUVs screeched to a halt, and men poured from the car. Jasper and Mike lined up their shots. Greg did the same, noting his hands were not quite as steady as those of the other two.

Next to him, Jasper counted down quietly. "Three, two, one."

Each of them took their shot. Jasper and Mike's men hit the ground. Greg's guy just moved to the side. A hail of gunfire was redirected at them. They all ducked behind the trailer, crouching low. Greg said a little prayer of desperation.

Then the gunfire shifted direction. Greg frowned, looking at Jasper. But before he could ask a question, a scream sounded from the SUVs.

Greg scrambled over to the edge of the trailer and peeked his head out. Sammy swiped one of his wings, sending a man crashing into the side of one of the SUVs. The glass exploded with the impact.

Jasper peeked his head around the corner as well, his head just above Greg's. "Where the hell did he come from?"

CHAPTER THIRTY-NINE

Ariana still couldn't believe she had done that. She couldn't even remember consciously making a plan. She'd seen the long piece of wood and grabbed it, swinging it before she could stop herself.

She cringed, picturing Greg pitching forward. She really hoped she hadn't done any permanent damage.

But she hadn't stayed hovering above him, checking to see his condition. No, she took off like a shot for the old factory. Her father's men were on the way. And as much as she didn't like her father, she certainly wasn't going to let herself be used as a pawn by Greg and his friends. Her father had done that for long enough. She figured if she got lost in the factory, it would at least give her time to figure out a way out of this. Maybe she could even slip out a side door and avoid all of them. She sprinted forward, her legs carrying her incredibly fast. And energy seemed to flow through her that she hadn't felt before.

Probably adrenaline.

A screech of brakes sounded behind her. She glanced over her shoulder, and this time she nearly fell for real. A creature—that was the only way to describe it—swooped down from the sky. His arms were extended, or rather, his wings were. He was maroon and giant sized.

Ariana's mouth dropped open. She picked up her pace. *Oh my God. Oh my God. Oh my God.*

She bolted through the open gate of the factory and leaped over a piece of discarded metal. What was that thing? And who the hell's side was it on? Her whole body shook as she darted into the first building. It was some sort of office building. This was not going to do. She sprinted through it, crashing into the back door and spilling onto the dirt outside. She scrambled back to her feet, aiming for the tall silent factory. It was open along the bottom level, with no walls. She sprinted toward it, her blood pounding too loud in her ears to make out if anyone was giving chase.

Tall columns of machinery that she couldn't identify lined the path in front of her. More cylinders and rectangular tubes ran about ten feet off the ground. At the far end of the space, she could make out a metal staircase. Beyond that was more open ground that led to another factory. *God, this place is immense.* It hadn't looked that big from the trailer. But that was good. Big meant it would be tougher for anyone to find her.

She sprinted through the columns of machines, bypassing a long silent conveyor belt. Behind her, gunfire broke out, and she swallowed hard. She pictured Greg lying on the ground, and she hoped that he was okay. She might not want to be their pawn, but she also didn't want them dead.

Ariana sprinted forward and then ducked behind a tall column of steel, stopping to catch her breath. But in reality, she didn't need to catch her breath. Her breathing was actually pretty good, all things considered. And that was pretty amazing.

It was her mind that needed a moment to catch up. That thing hadn't been human. But how was that possible? What the hell had her father gotten her into?

Somewhere behind her, she heard the scrape of metal. She tensed, not knowing what or who was now in the factory with her. Peeking around the column of steel, she searched for the source but didn't see anything. She leaned back, not sure what she should do.

Maybe there was no one in here yet. Maybe she had just dislodged some piece of metal when she'd run by.

She peeked out again and still didn't see anybody. She counted to three and then sprinted into the factory.

"Hey!"

She cringed but didn't stop.

"Ariana! Stop!"

She didn't know who was behind her, but she had no intention of following their orders. Gunshots burst out around her, pinging off the metal to her right and to her left.

She screeched to a halt, her hands up, her shoulders hunched. She turned slowly, expecting to see one of Greg's friends.

But it wasn't them. The man pointing a gun at her was dressed in all black. Ariana knew without a doubt that he was one of her father's men.

One of her father's men had *shot* at her.

The man kept his gun trained on her as he walked slowly toward her. "That's right. Stay there. I have orders not to kill you. But I will hurt you if you run, do you understand?"

Ariana nodded, despair racing through her. Her first shot at true freedom, and it had lasted less than five minutes.

A shadow crossed over Ariana from above. Her head jerked up as the creature from before raced toward them at a mind-boggling speed.

Ariana gasped, stumbling back. The creature ignored her. He grabbed the gunman and had him up into the air before Ariana could do more than blink. He soared into the air at least fifty feet and then let the man go. The man screamed all the way down until, with a sickening thud, he went silent.

The creature hovered in the air and then slowly started to fly toward Ariana. Ariana backed away and then started to run.

Ariana's breath came out in pants now. Fear tore at her. That creature had just killed a man. Of course, it was the man who had been trying to abduct her, but still.

She reached the stairwell and ducked underneath. She glanced around but didn't see any sign of anyone. She scanned the air, looking for any indication of the flying creature, but she saw nothing. The slight vibration of metal was the only thing that told her she wasn't alone. Her nerves danced along her skin. Slowly, she turned.

The flying creature stood only ten feet away. It had landed on a catwalk five feet above her. With a grace she didn't expect, it dropped down to the ground. She backed up, hitting her head on the edge of the stairwell. It made no move toward her. It just stared at her. The creature was incredibly muscular and humanoid. It had a human face, but those wings and its color definitely weren't. The whole time she studied it, it didn't move a muscle, as if it understood she was scared.

Ariana's fear began to recede. She felt the strangest sense of connection. As if somehow she had met the creature before.

Which was not possible, because she was pretty sure she would remember a seven-foot red-colored humanoid with wings. Yet despite the wicked talons at the points of its wings, she had the strangest feeling that it wasn't there to hurt her.

The creature took a small step toward her. Her breath hitched. She reached back, her hand grabbing the stairwell railing for support.

The creature paused, waiting. Then it slowly raised a hand, reaching it out toward her.

Ariana looked at the hand and then at the face. She took a step forward, and almost without thinking, raised her own hand.

Gunfire burst out from behind the creature. It raised its wings as if to shield her before turning and sweeping with one of its massive wings at the gunman who had approached unnoticed. The man slammed into the side of the factory wall.

A hand slipped around her mouth, yanking her to the side as an arm wrapped around her body, trapping her arms against her. She was dragged away as a group of twelve men in black advanced on the creature.

It flew up into the air, hovering only ten feet away, its eyes focused on Ariana as it attempted to dive toward her. But a net of some sort was launched at it. It caught on one of his wings. Lights sparked along the net. The creature's back arched, its mouth opening in pain before it plummeted to the ground.

The man holding Ariana dug into Ariana's ribs, but with his arm trapping both of hers there was nothing she could do. He pulled her away from the fight. The winged creature was crumpled on the ground as the men approached. *Oh God, no.* She knew without a doubt they were going to kill him.

Gunfire burst out from somewhere to her right. Ariana's head jerked to the side. Greg and the driver moved in and kept the men away from the winged creature.

Ariana frowned. Were they protecting him? Did they know him?

But she didn't have time to see anything beyond that as she was grabbed and thrown into an SUV.

She hit the floor of the vehicle. A door slammed shut behind her after the man who grabbed her hopped in. "Go, go, go!"

The SUV took off. She rolled, her back crashing painfully into the back of the seats. She was lying on her side on the floor behind the driver seat and the passenger seat. The driver picked up his speed and seemed to be swerving. His erratic driving made it impossible for Ariana to right herself. She was rolling from side to side and repeatedly slammed into the back of the seat.

Pain rolled through her back as she tried to right herself, but with the movement of the car, it was impossible. Tears sprang to her eyes.

Why is this happening to me?

CHAPTER FORTY

SEATTLE, WASHINGTON

WAITING WAS NOT MARTIN'S STRONG SUIT. HE HAD ARRANGED his life so he rarely had to wait. People jumped to do his bidding. But now, he was waiting. Waiting to find out if they had recovered his daughter.

He paced his office, clenching and unclenching his fists. *Where is she?* He growled, picturing Greg Schorn. He was a stupid little lab rat, and yet somehow that stupid little lab rat had caused him a mountain of problems. *If I ever get the chance, I will shoot that man myself.*

His phone rang, and he leaped for it. "Report."

"We have her, sir. Cut the signal."

Martin immediately hit the enter key on his computer. The green light on the screen shifted to red. Martin lowered the phone to the desk and then himself to the chair. His legs were shaking. That had been too close.

He punched up the cameras for his Rapid Response Team. It looked like they were still in the thick of it. He frowned, switching from camera to camera, then his hand stilled. He rewound back to the beginning and fast forwarded until the SUVs arrived.

S.A.V.E. 153

And a giant creature landed on them from the air.

Sweat broke out along his forehead. He'd gotten there so *fast*. Martin had known he would, but to see it was something altogether different. He watched the fight, trying to keep up with the abomination, but the creature kept taking down his men, forcing Martin to switch from camera to camera.

"He is powerful," he murmured grudgingly.

With disappointment, he watched his daughter cower by the stairs before one of his men grabbed her. Such a disappointment.

His phone rang again. He grabbed it. "Yes?"

"It's Gabbard, sir. Project Resurgence is operational. We're just waiting on your go."

Martin narrowed his eyes, staring at the screen. R.I.S.E had dared to come after what was his. Now it was time to show them how foolish that action had been. "You have a green light."

"Yes, sir."

CHAPTER FORTY-ONE

THE DRIVER DIDN'T SAY ANYTHING BUT CONTINUED HIS aggressive evasive driving. Ariana's neck and back ached as she was tossed this way and that. She gritted her teeth as tears of pain sprang to her eyes.

After ten minutes, the driver finally eased up on the accelerator. "Okay. We got the all-clear. She can get up."

The man who'd grabbed her reached down and pulled her up by the shoulders. She winced as her back screamed in protest. "Stop it."

The man let her go immediately. Ariana hauled herself up onto the seat and looked at the two men. "Who are you?"

"Director Drummond sent us. We're taking you to a safe location."

Great, another safe location. She stared out the window, looking up at the sky, but there was no telltale sign of wings. "What was that back there?"

The man next to her shook his head. "I'm afraid you don't have clearance for that."

Ariana glared at him. "Well, then you should tell the things that I don't have clearance for that they shouldn't attack me."

The man said nothing in response, just turned his gaze to the window as he scanned the sky.

Ariana found herself doing the same from her side of the car. She pictured the creature again, analyzing it now with a scientific eye. She didn't believe in monsters, demons, or aliens, which meant that someone had created that thing. There was no chance a creature like that could hide out without being seen. Immediately stories of the Jersey Devil and Mothman filled her mind. Was it possible that was who the creature was?

Even so, it didn't explain where the creature had come from. It seemed to be a cross between a human and a bat. But neither of those species would account for its size. Maybe a growth hormone had been added?

As the landscape whipped by, her mind churned over the mystery of the creature. But those ruminations couldn't displace the fear that was slowly building in her.

And it wasn't a fear of the creature.

She glanced at the two men.

Her father's men.

He would take this situation and use it to lock her away again, like he had done her whole childhood. With each mile they traveled, she knew she was getting closer and closer to the loss of her freedom. And with each mile, she felt more and more powerless.

CHAPTER FORTY-TWO

FREMONT, CALIFORNIA

Greg took aim at one of the men moving in on Sammy. He pulled the trigger over and over again, not letting up. He caught the man in the shoulder and then in the leg. He took aim for a second man, and by some miracle, actually managed to catch the guy in the thigh while he was running. Greg had been aiming for the guy's chest, but he'd take the win.

Jasper and Mike took out the remaining men and walked through the group, kicking weapons out of reach. Greg walked slowly toward Sammy, scanning the area. He glanced over at where he'd last seen Ariana. But from the corner of his eye, he had seen the SUV arrive. He'd seen the man who'd grabbed her throw her in and take off. They had lost her. They'd had her for all of an hour before she'd been recovered. He wanted to think that she was safe now, but from what Ariana had said, he wasn't sure that was true either.

Greg carefully approached Sammy, ignoring the groans and cries of the injured men around them. He yanked off his fleece and, keeping it over his hands, touched the netting. A sharp spark ran up his arm. He yanked his hands back.

Okay, this is going to hurt.

Bracing himself, he grabbed the net and yanked it off Sammy. Pain darted up his arms, and the echo of the pain remained even as he tossed the net aside. He hopped from foot to foot as the tingles receded. "Ow, ow, ow, ow."

He stepped closer to Sammy. Burns dotted the surface of his wings, but it didn't look like any of them were too bad. "Sammy? Are you all right?"

Sammy opened his eyes and stared into Greg's face. Then, without warning, he bolted into the air. Wind blew against Greg's hair, making him stumble back. *Man, that guy is powerful.*

Sammy hovered in the air, his head turning from side to side. Greg knew he was looking for Ariana. Greg stared at him, trying to figure out how the hell Sammy was even here. Sammy flew off, staying about fifty feet above the ground, moving at a fast pace. Greg watched until he could no longer see him.

As he pulled his fleece back on, Jasper tugged on his sleeve. "We need to get going. Someone's no doubt heard the gunfire."

Greg spared a glance at the men lying on the ground around them. Jasper and Mike had put zip ties around the wrists of those less injured. They wouldn't be following them anytime soon, but Jasper was right. The spot was isolated, but the gunfire had been loud. And with Sammy flying around, it was only a matter of time before someone called the cops.

Greg watched Jasper from the corner of his eye as they ran back toward the trailer. "Any idea how Sammy showed up? How'd he know where we were?"

Jasper shook his head. Greg could tell he was worried. "I have no idea. No one should've known where we were."

"Did you see how he seemed to be going for Ariana? It was like he was protecting her, or at least trying to, the way he did Luke."

"Why would he do that?" Mike asked.

Jasper shook his head. "I don't know. I mean, if anything, Drummond was responsible for Sammy's captivity. Do you think he was trying to get Ariana to get back at Drummond?"

"No, I don't think it was that. He could've killed her."

Even from a distance, Greg had seen Sammy lower himself and then stand in front of Ariana. Then he'd extended a hand. Greg had never seen him do that with anyone, not in the whole time they'd been in Norway. He was interactive, but everyone else had to make the first overture when interacting with him. He'd never seen Sammy actually make an overture to another person.

Greg had spoken with Luke, though, about his first meetings with Sammy, and he had described a very similar first interaction. Sammy had arrived in the barn quietly and had stayed perfectly still, allowing Luke time to examine him. Then he had extended a single hand.

Greg frowned. What made Luke and Ariana so different? Or maybe he should be asking what made them so similar? There had to be a link between those two, a reason why Sammy had the same reaction to both of them. And why Sammy somehow sought them both out.

That led to the next question: How exactly *did* Sammy seek them out? Sammy was fast. That was true. But he would have had to fly for days to get here. So how was he in the United States right now? Something didn't add up.

Mike sprinted ahead to the SUV. Jasper and Greg clambered in as he pulled the SUV alongside them with a small shower of gravel. Without a word, Mike took off. Pulling his Glock from its holster, Greg glanced out the window but didn't see any sign of anyone giving chase. He let out a sigh of relief.

Mike slammed on the brakes.

Greg jolted forward, barely managing to get a hand in front of him to keep from going face first into the back of the driver's seat. "What the—"

His voice broke off as he looked through the front windshield. Sammy straightened from a crouch in the road.

"He dropped down right in front of me," Mike said.

Greg put his hand on the handle of the door. "Well, let's see what he wants."

"Yeah, *that* sounds like a good idea," Jasper mumbled, but he got out of the car as well.

Greg holstered his Glock and walked toward Sammy with his hands up. "Sammy? Are you okay? Do you need something?"

Sammy said nothing, just looked at Greg before he bolted forward, wrapped Greg in his arm, and rocketed up into the air.

Greg screamed. Then his ears popped, and the strangest feeling came over him, almost like he was being sucked through a small opening. His head felt heavy and his thoughts got muddled.

Then another pop, and he felt cold air once again rushing at him. Sammy touched down on the ground. Greg was half convinced that his brain was now leaking out of his ears.

He tumbled to the cold ground, feeling grass underneath his hands. He managed to lift his head, blinking rapidly at the image in front of him.

No, this can't be right.

CHAPTER FORTY-THREE

GEIRANGER, NORWAY

MAEVE AND CHRIS STAYED OUT IN THE WOODS FOR ANOTHER hour before they walked slowly back to the cabin. They still weren't sure how they were going to tell Alvie and Snap.

So for right now, they weren't going to.

Maeve knew that keeping it from them was going to be all but impossible, but she just didn't know how to have this conversation with them. She kept hoping that some sort of miracle would spring up, and maybe she would never have to. And if these were their last few days together, Maeve didn't want unhappiness marring it.

On the walk back, they intentionally switched to another topic to try and get their emotions under control. They focused on the drawing Luke had done for Sammy.

"But what I don't get is how would he even meet someone?" Chris asked. "I mean, he was kept in isolation, right?"

"During his time with the U.S. government, yes, undeniably. But maybe she was someone he saw when he was out."

But that was just a guess. Maeve had no idea why Sammy was interested in the woman. But the fact that he was was intriguing. At the same time, she couldn't help but wonder how he had found

Luke. They had never been able to discern that. He had flown across state after state to arrive at the Gillibrands' home. That was intentional. He'd sought him out, and neither Luke nor Sandra had any idea that Sammy even existed prior to his showing up. So maybe this other woman was connected in a similar way.

They were a little ways away from the cabin when Alvie came running up. He looked and felt anxious.

Maeve was immediately on alert. "What's going on?"

In her mind, she saw an image of Sammy bursting into the sky and then disappearing. "Oh my God."

She looked over at Chris, and from his shocked expression, she knew that he had seen the same thing that she had. Immediately, Maeve's mind whirled.

Sammy had been able to avoid capture, unlike a lot of the other creatures from Area 51. Was that because he had some sort of invisibility? Could he make himself somehow untraceable to the human eye?

But the bigger question was: What had spurred this action? What was going on? And why hadn't he returned? At the same time, she felt the fear from Alvie. And she couldn't help but be angry at Sammy. He'd said he wouldn't leave them.

Nora hurried over to them as Alvie took Chris's hand to show him where Sammy had disappeared from.

"He just disappeared?" Maeve asked.

Nora nodded. "He was in the air one second, and then he was completely gone."

"Do you think he disappeared or just went invisible?"

Nora hesitated. "I don't think he was invisible. There was a strange noise, kind of like a small sonic boom. And then he was gone."

"How long ago?"

"About thirty minutes, give or take."

Maeve wasn't sure what to say. She had no idea what was going on with Sammy. But she hoped for the kids' sake he came back soon.

A noise sounded from the sky above. Nora's and Maeve's heads jerked up as a puff of smoke appeared, and then Sammy appeared out of thin air. This time, though, he wasn't alone. He was carrying someone. He dove to the ground and stopped, gently placing his passenger on the forest floor.

Greg stood for a minute and then wobbled, dropping to his knees. He looked up for a minute, a frown on his face. "Maeve?"

Then he emptied the contents of his stomach to the ground below him.

CHAPTER FORTY-FOUR

WASHINGTON, D.C.

THE HEADACHE WAS BEGINNING TO BUILD JUST BEHIND TILDA'S eyes. She walked down the hall of the Pentagon toward her office. Almost everyone she passed acknowledged her with a slight flare of their eyebrows and a nod. She had become an unwilling celebrity within the ranks of the military industrial complex and the intelligence agencies thanks to the events of the last few weeks.

She keyed into her office and closed the door behind her, leaning heavily against it. *God save me from any more useless meetings.*

She pushed off the door and made her way to her desk. Tilda had been a part of R.I.S.E. for fifty years. She'd been in charge of it for the last few decades. With that role came a large degree of autonomy. She'd been able to make decisions for people and do whatever needed to be done without consulting a committee.

But now that she was fully embraced within the hallowed halls of America's military forces, all that had changed. All of a sudden she found herself sitting in on committees and meetings about other people's activities. She never understood why people felt the need to call a meeting when an email would be just as effective and much less time-consuming.

She sank into the chair behind her desk, leaned back, closed her eyes, and wished not for the first time that Adam was with her. They had met fifty years ago, when she'd first joined R.I.S.E. He'd worked for Wernher von Braun. She had been just out of college, and no one would hire her because no one wanted a girl with a science degree.

But Wernher von Braun had seen something in her and brought her on. As the years had gone on, Adam had remained unchanged. He was still the most incredible-looking man she had ever seen. She, however, like everyone else, had been affected by the sands of time.

Oftentimes, she felt like she had been *run over* by the sands of time. But Adam never once indicated that he wanted anything other than her. They had spent all of that time side by side. He'd been a constant soothing presence no matter how chaotic their world got. It had been the two of them facing every challenge together.

And now for the first time, they weren't. She understood why he needed to go with Maeve and the others. She approved of him going with them. But she truly had not realized how difficult it would be without him. She prided herself on being a tough, no-nonsense, not overly emotional woman.

But she'd caught herself wishing she could see his face, wishing she could feel his hand in hers. She sighed. There was nothing to be done for it. Not right now.

Hope wagged her tail from the dog bed in the corner of Tilda's office and gave a big stretch. Tilda smiled over at her as Hope carefully got to her feet, still a little unsteady at times. But she was healing well. Hope nestled into Tilda's side. Tilda reached down and petted her, rubbing her hand through her not-quite-there-yet fur. "Well, at least I've got you, girl."

Hope wagged her tail harder in response.

The office door shot open. Tilda's head jerked up, her arm reflexively going for the desk drawer where she kept her Browning. Pearl hustled in, her eyes wild. "There's been an attack."

She didn't wait for Tilda's response. She bustled over to the screens on the side of Tilda's office. She quickly brought up the footage. By the time Tilda was next to her, she had it ready to go. "Where?"

"Phoenix, Arizona. At an outlet mall."

Tilda held on to her other questions as the footage began to play. At first it looked like any other day in a shopping mall, with people wandering by in twos or threes. A few kids here and there running. Some people pushing strollers. Everything looked normal, peaceful.

The first sign of something amiss was a man and a woman running, a child clasped in the man's arms as they sprinted across the screen.

Tilda narrowed her eyes, looking for the perpetrator as more and more people began to sprint for the exits. Without sound, she could only imagine the screaming as people desperately fled.

One hurried forward, constantly glancing over her shoulder. She was in her fifties, maybe a little older. Her stride was shorter, her pace much slower than the rest. She was halfway across the screen when something leaped at her from behind. It pounced onto her back, and the woman was down. The creature tore at her. The woman's light top became a dark shredded mess. Then the creature was up and running again, sprinting for another target.

"Freeze it."

Pearl did, zooming in without having to be told.

A cold chill fell over Tilda as she looked at the face of the Drago. "How many dead?"

"Eighteen. It would have been more, but by pure luck, one of our teams was just ten minutes away. There's maybe another dozen or more wounded. Some people fled the scene before first responders arrived. It's possible they'll go to hospitals on their own."

"How many Drago?"

"Two. Both were killed."

Tilda nodded her head, imagining the chaos that the appearance of two Drago caused.

"What was the temperature in Phoenix today?"

If Pearl thought the question was unusual, she didn't show it. She tapped on her tablet for a few seconds before answering. "A hundred and two."

Tilda's gaze went back to the screen, her mind whirling. The Drago had many strengths. They could withstand cold, their skin was practically impervious, but one of their weaknesses was heat. So why would two Drago be in Phoenix of all places?

She turned to Pearl. "I need all the video footage coming out of Phoenix. I want to know every car that's been in and out of that city in the last twenty-four hours. I want everything—ATMs, traffic cams, cell phone footage. Get everything to Penny and get her whatever else she needs."

Pearl's hands didn't stop moving over her tablet as she spoke. "What are you thinking?"

Tilda looked back at the screen. "I don't know what I'm thinking yet, but something's not right. And I want to know how two Drago got to that mall. They certainly didn't take the bus. They certainly didn't walk there. There is no Drago outpost anywhere near Phoenix."

Pearl's hands hesitated over her screen as she looked up at Tilda . "Do you think ... Is it possible this is the beginning of them taking revenge?"

Tilda shook her head and spoke without hesitation. "No. If the Drago survived in large enough groups to seek revenge, they would have waited. They would have created a much more damaging response. For them, this is nothing. No, this is something else. This is *someone* else. And I think we both know whose fingerprints are all over this attack."

"Martin Drummond."

Tilda nodded. "Yes. So find me Martin's fingerprints. This

attack was actually sloppy, which is not like him. Which means he's made other mistakes. I need those mistakes."

Pearl's tablet beeped. She glanced at it, a stricken look on her face before she looked up. "The Joint Chiefs want to speak with you."

Tilda nodded. She had been expecting that. "When?"

"An hour."

"Then let's see what we can find out in an hour."

CHAPTER FORTY-FIVE

GEIRANGER, NORWAY

GREG FELT LIKE HIS INSIDES HAD BEEN WHIRLED AROUND AND then put back in their place. Everything ached. He was on his hands and knees, losing the contents of his stomach. Even without the stomach purge, there was no way he could stand. He was pretty sure that he was about five seconds away from collapsing on the ground and curling up in the fetal position, praying to whatever god would make all of this horribleness just go away.

A hand landed on his shoulder and began rubbing his back softly. "Greg?"

Greg turned his head, looking at Maeve through slitted eyes. She hadn't been a hallucination. "Maeve? What are you doing here?"

She gave him a confused smile. "I think the better question is what are you doing here? You're back in Norway."

Greg's mouth fell open, and he stared up at her. The flight with Sammy must have messed with his hearing too. "What did you say?"

"You're back in Norway. Where'd you come from?"

Greg's mouth fell open, his thoughts moving slowly. He was

back in Norway? Seconds ago he was in ... "California, I was in California about ten seconds ago."

"Seconds?"

Greg fell onto his butt. He pulled his knees up to his chest, knowing that was as close as he was getting to standing anytime soon. "Yeah. Jasper, Mike, and I found Martin's daughter. Martin's men found us, and then Sammy appeared out of nowhere. Or I guess here."

"Martin has a daughter?"

Greg nodded. "Yeah, he has a daughter. It's the woman that Luke drew. There's a lot that's been going on."

"You don't know the half of it."

For the first time, Greg took a close look at his friend. Her face was drawn, her eyes rimmed red. *Oh no.* "I'll tell you mine if you tell me yours."

Maeve nodded. "Deal."

Maeve and Nora helped Greg over to one of the Adirondack chairs. Maeve and Nora stayed with him while Chris kept an eye on the kids. Greg spoke first, telling them about leaving Norway and ending with Sammy appearing and trying to grab Ariana before Martin's men did.

"What's she like?" Maeve asked.

"She's ..." Greg paused, picturing Ariana. "She's nothing like her father. She's smart, resilient, kind, I think. She doesn't even know what her father does for a living besides knowing he works for the government. He kept her sheltered, *seriously* sheltered, her whole life. I actually feel sorry for her."

"And you're sure that's who Sammy was looking for?" Nora asked.

"Even if we doubted that after finding her, Sammy made a beeline for her when he arrived. He was looking for her all right."

"Why?" Nora asked.

"No idea." Greg turned to Maeve. "Now your turn."

Maeve took a deep breath. She glanced between Nora and

Greg and then turned her gaze to her hands clasped in her lap. "I took a little trip with Agaren."

Greg listened in amazement as Maeve described where she had been for the last few hours. Even after everything Tilda had said, he still thought that a civilization on the moon was crazy. He should have known better.

At the same time, he couldn't help but be a little jealous. While he left on a fishing trolley with Mike and Jasper, Maeve had taken a trip to the moon. The moon!

But as awed as he was by a former civilization having existed on the moon, it didn't overshadow the pain he felt when she described Pop and Crackle's existence in some sort of suspended animation. That sympathy shifted to rage when she explained the Council's ultimatum for Maeve and for the rest of the human race.

"So that's where we're at. We haven't told Snap or Alvie. They know something's up. And I know I have to tell them, but I just … I don't even know how to start. They'll want to know why the Council is forcing this choice. And I don't have a good explanation for that."

"What are you going to do?" Nora asked.

Maeve shook her head. "I really don't know. I can't leave Pop and Crackle up there on their own. They can tell what's going on around them. That's not a life."

"But if you stay here, you won't have a life," Nora said softly.

Maeve nodded. "I know. But it seems wrong that I can escape all that. And do I really want to? The last human? And all of you …" Maeve shook her head, her chin trembling as she looked away.

No one said anything for a moment. With everything that had happened, it was hard to accept the looming destruction of humanity was only a few days away. Greg couldn't really wrap his head around that. But he knew what Maeve meant. She'd be the only human left to mourn the rest of her race. He felt guilty enough about what Ariana was going through right now; he couldn't imagine the survivor's guilt Maeve would feel.

He forced a lightness to his tone as he spoke. "Well, I'm definitely jealous of your mode of transportation. By the way, Tilda has Hope. I warned her to keep an eye on her shoes."

A small smile broke out on Maeve's face. "Well, at least that's some good news."

"Well, we know Martin has the Guardian, so that's something. Although Tilda has zero ideas where she might be. But she's rallying her forces to see what she can find."

Nora looked at him with raised eyebrows. "What were you guys planning on doing with Martin's daughter?"

Greg shook his head. "I don't know. Originally the plan was to trade her for the Guardian, but now, well, one, we don't have her anymore. And two, it's obvious she's somehow tied to all of this. There's some sort of link between her and Sammy."

All three of them looked toward the barn where Sammy had disappeared after he'd returned. He'd closed the door behind him, and no one had been willing to knock yet. Even the kids were outside the barn for a change.

"So Sammy just somehow magically appeared over California in seconds," Maeve said softly.

"Well, I can attest that he was definitely here until about thirty minutes before Greg arrived. And there's no way he could make it there no matter how fast he flew," Nora said.

Maeve looked at Greg. "What about you? What did you feel and see when you traveled with him?"

Greg struggled to remember. "It was strange. We were leaving the factory, as we figured Martin would be sending more people back for us or the cops would be showing up. Sammy landed in front of the car. We got out, and then Sammy grabbed me and took off into the air." Greg swallowed, his stomach once again reliving the incredibly fast acceleration.

"Anyway, we went up and up and up, and then all of a sudden it felt almost like we were being squeezed through something. I shut my eyes, and my head felt like it was being held in a vise. I waited for it to pop. But it didn't, and the next thing I knew, we were here."

"So what are you talking about, some sort of *Star Trek* transporter kind of thing?" Nora asked.

Greg shook his head. "No. This is something that Sammy can *do*. This isn't some sort of technology that's been created."

"I wonder ..." Maeve said softly.

Nora and Greg turned toward her. "You wonder what?" Greg asked.

"It's been theorized that we exist on multiple dimensions that overlap one another, but we can only see the dimension that we are actually in."

Greg nodded, realizing where she was going with this line of thought. "You think Sammy can travel between dimensions."

"It's just a theory, of course, but it would explain how he managed to get across the United States without anyone reporting him. And it would explain how he was able to grab you and then get back here in just minutes."

"But is that even possible? I mean—" Nora cut herself off and shook her head. "Sorry, for a second there, I forgot where I was and what I was talking about. Cross-dimensional travel, of course it's possible."

"That's a subject for another time," Maeve said. "I'm more curious as to why Sammy was so interested in Martin's daughter. You really don't think it was some sort of revenge?"

Greg shook his head, the image of Sammy reaching an arm out for Ariana slipping into his mind. "No, I don't think he wanted to hurt her. In fact, I got the impression he was trying to help her."

"Like he helped Luke?"

Greg nodded. "Yeah, he did track him down to Washington state, and before that he tracked him to Kansas and protected him from the Blue Boys. So maybe he's also protecting Ariana?"

"But how?" Nora asked. "There's what, over seven billion people on the planet? How did he find her? And why couldn't he find her after Martin's men took her?"

"Or before," Greg said.

"Is there any indication that Ariana interacted with Sammy before? That maybe she knew him?" Maeve asked.

Greg shook his head, picturing Ariana's face. "No. She looked completely shocked by his appearance. And after speaking with her, I got the impression she didn't know anything about aliens, her father's work, or absolutely anything along those lines. Plus, it seems like she and her father didn't have a close relationship."

"That's not exactly a shock," Nora muttered.

Maeve narrowed her eyes. "So why would Sammy want to find her? Why go all that way?"

"And again, how did he find her?" Nora asked. "The world is a rather large place. How did he know *exactly* where she would be?"

Maeve looked over at Nora. "These are all really good questions. And there's only one person who can answer them for us."

They all looked toward the barn. Maeve spoke first. "We need to have Adam get in touch with Tilda. And then we need to go have a chat with Sammy."

CHAPTER FORTY-SIX

BERKELEY, CALIFORNIA

HER FATHER'S MEN RUSHED ARIANA THROUGH THE CITY STREETS. Before she knew it, they were leaving the city of Berkeley behind and racing down the highway.

"Where are we going?" Ariana asked.

"That's classified," the man next to her said.

And that's how it went for the next two hours. Every time she asked a question, the response she was given was that it was classified. After a while, she just gave up asking and stared at the landscape rushing by, noticing the shift from lush green California to a more desert landscape.

Finally the driver pulled off onto a dirt road. The car bumped and shook as he hurried across the uneven terrain. Ariana kept glancing at the sky and the road behind them, looking for their pursuer. But there was no one. So why were these guys in such a rush?

The driver pulled to a halt in front of a square utility shed. Ariana stared at it in confusion. They drove all this way for this? Even with only the three of them, it would be a bit crowded.

The heavy metal door opened up as soon as the SUV stopped.

Another man in black fatigues stepped out, a serious-looking weapon slung over his shoulder. He gazed at the SUV before scanning the sky. Two other men stepped out behind him, going through the same process.

Ariana couldn't help but look up as well. The sky was bright blue with a few dotted clouds. And absolutely no sign of a giant winged creature.

Before she could make any comment, the man who had grabbed her back at the factory opened his door, and with one arm clasped around Ariana's bicep, pulled her from the car.

Ariana stumbled, her feet not landing squarely on the uneven ground.

The man didn't slow. He pulled her forward.

"Ow! That hurts." Ariana tried to pull herself from the man's grip, but he was too strong.

He hustled her into the shed.

Ariana wasn't sure what she had expected, but it certainly wasn't another heavy door only four feet in. The driver walked up to the door and placed a keycard on the faceplate next to the doorframe. White light outlined the plate, and then the light above the door blinked green. The door opened with a puff of air.

The driver moved through quickly, and Ariana was once again hustled through unceremoniously behind him. Being the shed wasn't very big, she was unsurprised to see that she was on a small landing only three feet wide before it emptied into a stairwell heading down. The driver hurried down without pause. The man next to her still gripped her arm, pulling her down.

Ariana grabbed onto the railing to keep from being plunged forward. "Will you let go of me? Where do you think I'm going to go?"

The man released her arm. Ariana shook out her bicep, knowing that she was going to have a bruise.

"Keep going," the man said.

With a glare, she continued down the stairs. She had no idea where they were, and yet somehow, once again, she had a sense of déjà vu. Yet she was pretty sure she would remember if she had been in some sort of underground secret base.

The farther they traveled down the stairwell, however, the deeper the sense that she *had* been here before stole over her. Had she maybe seen something like this in a movie? When Michelle realized Ariana hadn't seen any movies, she'd made them binge movies every weekend for a month straight. But Ariana didn't remember any that looked like this.

She couldn't figure out why this feeling was creeping over her. The deeper they went, though, the more certain she became that she had been here before or at least someplace exactly like it. But when on earth had that been?

It took at least fifteen minutes to reach the bottom of the stairwell. Ariana felt a little light-headed, and her legs were wobbly. Whatever strength she felt earlier when running was well and truly gone.

As the driver flashed his keycard at the panel next to the metal door at the base of the stairs, Ariana glanced back up. They were twenty stories below the surface. Ariana had been counting. She did not look forward to the climb back out. Why wasn't there an elevator?

At the bottom of the stairs, the landing led to a wide hallway that continued on for another hundred feet before splitting off into four more hallways, all at an angle from the original main hallway. The driver hurried forward and took the second hallway on the right. Ariana followed, looking around. She'd seen a few doors, but the faceplates next to them provided no descriptive information. The only designations were letters and numbers.

She turned to look back at the man who had grabbed her. "I need to speak with my father. You need to call him now."

"Your father is aware of where you are. He has been notified of your condition."

Ariana wanted to scream in frustration. Notified of her condition? What the hell did that mean?

The driver stopped at another heavy metal door similar to the one that had been on the surface. And once again, he used his keycard to access it. When the door slid open, he stepped through and waved Ariana in. She paused, a feeling of dread coming over her. She did not want to step through that doorway.

The man behind her, however, must have read her hesitation. He grabbed her on either side of her arms and pushed her through. He didn't let go as they stepped through. The driver turned to a small room on the left with a glass wall.

Ariana backed up. "No. No, no."

The driver opened up the glass wall using another faceplate. The man behind Ariana shoved her through. It took her legs a moment to catch up with her torso. She managed to get her hands out in front of her before she hit the opposite wall.

By the time she whirled around, the glass wall had slammed shut. She stared at it in shock. Neither man said a word to her. They just disappeared back through the heavy metal door, which slammed closed with a deafening thud.

Ariana stood in silence for a moment, looking around, trying to accept what had just happened. She was a prisoner. Her father had instructed these men to imprison her in a cell. She slid down along the wall and sat with her knees pulled up to her chest.

I was better off with the other three.

A vision of the winged creature floated through her mind. *I might've been better off with him as well.*

Washington, D.C.

Tilda headed down the hallway. The sound of her footsteps was lost in the carpet underneath her feet. She was heading to the Situation Room to brief the Joint Chiefs of Staff.

The president had been briefed on the situation in Arizona, and now he wanted answers. Apparently he was angry that the Drago had reappeared, under the belief that the threat had been nullified. Tilda had warned them that it was possible that there would be individual Drago attacks, but apparently that had gone right over the president's head.

The aide that accompanied her paused in front of the Situation Room. She turned to Pearl. "You'll have to wait out here."

Tilda handed Pearl her cell phone. No phones were allowed inside. Pearl stepped back, taking a seat at one of the chairs across the hall. The aide opened up the door, and Tilda stepped through.

Tilda had been working in government for decades. She had protected Earth from multiple alien events, and yet she had only been to the White House three times. Two of those times had been decades ago.

Tilda hadn't been in the Situation Room since before its renovation in 2006 and 2007. Back then, it had been a mahogany dinosaur with unreliable audio-visual encryption that occasionally blacked out. Most people who worked in it regularly referred to it as a low-tech dungeon.

But the renovations had gone a long way to bringing it into the new age. There were now sensors in the ceiling to detect cellular signals, along with a lead-lined box for the depositing of cell phones for all of the room's occupants.

In addition, there were several clear booths for making private phone calls. Two tiers of curved computer terminals were also added that could be fed both classified and unclassified data from around the country and the world for watch officers. In addition, there were six flat-panel displays for secure video conferencing.

As Tilda stepped in, the seven men who made up the Joint Chiefs looked over at her. Tilda had met each of the individuals in varying capacities during her time with the government. But in the last few weeks, she had met with them twice to discuss the alien threat. She found them to be intelligent, capable men. But she also knew that they weren't individuals interested in small talk. They wanted answers. And they wanted them quickly.

She strode toward the head of the table, not waiting for someone to offer her a chair. "Gentlemen." She took a seat and gestured for all of them to do the same. She would be the one running this meeting, even though they had been the ones who called her. "I have the latest information on the attack in Phoenix."

The chairman, General Matt White from the Army, cut in as he took a seat. "We were under the impression that these kinds of attacks would not be happening again."

"Then you weren't listening," Tilda responded, her voice just as cold. "I warned you that there was the possibility of reprisals."

Matt's eyebrows raised, apparently not used to people speaking to him in such a way. Tilda didn't have time to massage the man's ego. "But this was not a retaliatory attack."

General Scott Troppler, commandant of the Marine Corps, leaned forward. Tilda had always found him to be on the more intellectual side of the military officers she had met. At one point, she had even attempted to recruit him to R.I.S.E. But his heart belonged with the Marines.

"If not a retaliatory attack, then what?" Scott asked.

"They were a weapon. They were sent to the mall to cause disruption."

"Sent? By who?" asked General Joseph Sally, chief of staff of the Air Force.

"Martin Drummond."

Her announcement created a stir around the table. Each of the men knew who Drummond was. Most of them had not met him in person, but they knew of his work.

"That's a very serious charge. I'm assuming you have something to back it up?" asked Mitchell Robbins, chief of staff of the Army.

Tilda nodded to the aide who had accompanied her. She handed out the information packets that she had created just for this meeting. "After I found out about the attack, I immediately began questioning why the Drago would attack in that particular spot. Their one weakness, if you can call it that, is that the Drago do not do well in warm weather. It won't kill them, but in time, it tends to weaken them. So they generally prefer to stay in colder climates or at least more moderate climates. Phoenix was over 100 today. There is no chance they would voluntarily choose that location to initiate an attack. "

"But aren't you putting too much faith in their reasoning? These things are animals," the chairman said.

"Don't let their appearance fool you. They are highly intelligent, just as intelligent as humans. What they lack is a conscience. They would never intentionally put themselves in a situation where they would be weakened. But someone who is trying to use them would."

"You seem sure of that," Vice Chairman General Lee Raider said.

"I am. By placing them in that situation, Martin would be able to contain the fallout. If my team had not been able to get to the mall as quickly as they had, the Drago no doubt would have moved on from the mall to other targets. They would have headed to the heart of the city of Phoenix. But with the heat, within an hour they would have been seriously weakened, making them easier to catch and kill. I believe that was Martin's plan all along. Moreover, the outlet is located on the outskirts of Phoenix. It is not in the middle of the city."

"Which would also reduce the casualty count," Troppler said.

Tilda nodded. "If the Drago had planned the attack, they would have gone to a city center. They'd be aiming for massive casualties. There was no benefit to them in this attack."

"I know that there is antagonism between R.I.S.E. and D.E.A.D., but we need more than theories," Raider said.

"And that's why I provided you with these packets. As you can see, based on the Drago's origin, they were transported to the outlet in a maroon panel van. It was seen driving into Phoenix at six a.m. this morning. It stayed outside the outlet for an hour before it drove to the loading dock. The cameras were conveniently malfunctioning at the loading dock at that time. From the video footage inside, we know that the Drago appeared from that area. That's where they were dropped off."

Troppler leaned forward, peering at the third page of the packet. "You found the van?"

"The van was seen driving off. We got a partial license plate, and my team was able to intercept it. It took some digging, but we were able to link it to a holding company that Drummond often uses for some of his more illicit activities."

"So Martin Drummond is connected to this," the chairman said.

Tilda shook her head. "No, not just connected. I'm saying Martin Drummond released those Drago."

"Why would he do that?" asked General David Gallagher, chief of staff of the National Guard Bureau.

Tilda sat back, studying the men in the room. This would be the part that they would have the most resistance to accepting. "Martin Drummond has been on the edges of the fight against alien life practically from its inception. He was brought on by Buckley a couple of decades after R.I.S.E. was created. But he has a single solitary goal: to destroy all alien life."

"Isn't that R.I.S.E.'s goal as well?" Raider asked.

"No. R.I.S.E.'s goal is to maintain the safety of Earth. Maintaining the safety of Earth means allowing certain alien life to go unencumbered. Not all aliens are militaristic or warlike. Some are incredibly peaceful. But should they be pushed, they could become warlike, which would endanger the planet Earth. Because remember: We are well behind the technology of every single species we have come in contact with. It requires a careful balance between creatures who, if not our allies, are at least not a threat versus those who would do us harm. Martin does not understand this balance. He sees all of them as a threat, and therefore his goal is to destroy all of them."

"I can understand that mindset," Robbins grunted.

"I can as well. However, the job of R.I.S.E. is to look beyond irrational fear and see the facts as they are. Martin wants to be in charge of R.I.S.E. I am sure that he is not happy with my recent exalted status within the hallowed halls of the U.S. government.

And if he pushes me out, then he believes he would be the natural person that the government would turn to in order to replace me. And he would make the case for it."

Tilda looked around the table, making eye contact with each individual. "And I'm sure he's already contacted some of you to make such an argument."

Raider looked away, but Troppler nodded. "He's been in touch with some of my people, suggesting that you were too soft in your approach."

"Look, I understand that this is a new front for the U.S. government. But we do not have the luxury of making mistakes. We have learned that when it comes to engaging in war, winning the hearts and minds of the people is oftentimes the key to success. When it comes to alien forces, the situation is no less complex. We cannot simply go in there, guns blazing. Besides the fact that technologically they are light-years ahead of us, all the 'violence only' approach will accomplish is the annihilation of the human race."

Robbins scoffed. "Annihilation? That seems like hyperbole."

"I wish it were. We are an ant farm, gentlemen. Whatever hubris and arrogance you think has led us to this pinnacle of technological ability, we are cavemen compared to the forces arrayed against us. We can throw our wooden spears at them if we like, but they can just stomp us under their boot. We need to be smarter about this. And this kind of attack"—Tilda waved her hand toward the information sheets on the table—"only further weakens us. Martin Drummond is a danger to the U.S. government, to the people of the United States, and to the world. He needs to be shut down. His resources need to be cut off."

"That's a rather large ask," White said.

"It is not an ask. It's a necessity." Tilda took a breath. "You gentlemen may not like where we are at. You may have reservations about what the next step is. I do not. I have understood this threat for decades. Martin Drummond is a threat to the stability of not just the country but the world. He needs to be restrained. And there is one more issue, one even more pressing."

Tilda took a deep breath. She knew that so far, she'd covered the easy part of the conversation. Now she had to convince them that a threat they'd just learned about posed an extinction-level threat to all of them. Picturing Adam from the video call this morning, she straightened her shoulders and told the Joint Chiefs about the Council's threat. It did not go over well.

"They can't be serious," Raider said.

"They are. The destruction of the Drago makes that clear. We need to find the Guardian, and Martin Drummond has hidden her. We need to lock down every single one of his sites and interrogate all of his people. We need to find her. It is not hyperbole to say that the fate of the world rests on us finding her."

Tilda spoke with the Joint Chiefs for another hour. It was a constant back and forth, with them questioning and her pushing back. Finally, they asked her to step outside.

Pearl was still waiting for her. Tilda went with her down to the cafeteria and got a bite to eat. They were just finishing up when the aide returned to them. "The Joint Chiefs are ready to see you again."

Five minutes later, she was back in the Situation Room, facing the chiefs. The Joint Chiefs had stood up as she entered. She didn't bother sitting down. "Well?"

The chairman nodded, his voice grave. "Martin Drummond has been sidelined. All government resources have been cut off from him. You have the full weight of the United States government behind you. But I hope you understand he will still have other resources that he can utilize."

"I am aware. But this is the first step in securing our future. Let's hope it's enough."

CHAPTER FORTY-SEVEN

GEIRANGER, NORWAY

Only Maeve and Nora went to have a conversation with Sammy. Greg looked like he was about to fall over, so Maeve told him he needed to go lie down. After helping him into the house, Nora and Maeve walked toward the barn.

Nora reached the door first but hesitated before opening it, looking back at Maeve. "Are you ready for this?"

Maeve nodded, even though she wasn't sure she was. "No. But let's go."

Nora slid the barn door open. The space with the beds was empty. Maeve frowned, looking around. Had he disappeared again? Could he simply disappear at will? She'd been working under the assumption that he needed to build up some sort of speed to make it happen.

Nora tapped Maeve on the shoulder and pointed to the loft. Sammy stood braced against the railing, staring down at them.

Maeve cleared her throat. "Sammy, we'd like to speak with you."

With a short leap, Sammy jumped over the railing and landed in a crouch in front of Maeve and Nora before straightening.

Maeve took a step back once again. His size really was intimidating.

Nora stayed where she was, her arms crossed over her chest. "You need to answer some questions. Tell us about Martin's daughter."

Sammy nodded. "I've been looking for her a long time."

Maeve's mouth fell open at the sound of Sammy's voice. "You can speak?"

Sammy gave her what was the most human baleful look she'd ever seen.

Nora snorted in response. "Guess so. Now, what's with the focus on Martin's daughter? Why have you been looking for her?"

"Because she's one of my kind."

Maeve frowned. "One of your kind? She's like you?"

Sammy nodded. "We have the same parents."

Same parents. Maeve's mind whirled.

Nora looked between Maeve and Sammy, the crease between her eyes deepening. "But I thought she was Martin's daughter?"

Sammy nodded. "She is. Martin is my father."

CHAPTER FORTY-EIGHT

SEATTLE, WASHINGTON

ARIANA CURLED UP ON THE COT AGAIN. MARTIN WATCHED HER with disgust. She was so weak.

He shook his head, turning from the monitor. He never should have let her reach this stage. The experiment had provided everything it was going to. He should have had her exterminated years ago.

But sentimentality, something he was not known for, had gripped him at the idea. And he had allowed her to live.

It was her mother that brought it on. Ariana was a mix of the two of them, and Martin couldn't quite bring himself to destroy her. He would never have a life with her mother, but knowing that a small piece of her existed in this world and was alive and walking around, well, that made everything better. But now that sentimentality may have just provided an opportunity, an opportunity for Ariana to make up for her weaknesses.

He glanced up as one of his men appeared in the doorway. "Your transportation is here."

"I'll be there momentarily."

The man disappeared from the doorway.

Martin shut down the computer. He needed to move. He'd just received the call from the Pentagon. Tilda was out for his blood. Somehow she had convinced the powers that be that he was behind the Drago mall attack. He shoved his laptop into his bag. How had she figured it out? He'd known she would suspect it, but actually being able to prove it? He shook his head. How had she done it?

From the few friends he had left in the intelligence circles, he knew plans were in motion to target all of his safehouses, at least all of his known ones. Lucky for him, he kept more than a few hidden from any prying eyes.

Stacy appeared in the doorway, wringing her hands. "Everything's been put into position."

"And the angel?"

"She has been safely moved onto the truck."

"Any problems with the preparations?"

Stacy shook her head. "No, sir. She wasn't harmed in any way. There was no stop in any of her monitoring or her functions. She's stable."

"Good." Martin stood up from the desk and pulled on his jacket, then he looped his bag over his shoulders and headed for the door. His analysts were still working busily at their terminals. They didn't know that government agents would be raiding the office within the hour. He needed them not to know. It would take the government time to interview all of them. Time Martin needed to make his own escape.

He strode for the exit. As he pushed open the door, the damp, cool air rolled over him. A nondescript white panel truck stood idling in the parking lot. Next to it was a Honda Accord, five years old. It was one of the most common cars on the road. He'd drive it most of the way to Arizona. No one would expect him in it.

He nodded at the men at the back of the truck. They quickly rolled up the cargo door. Martin hauled himself into the back. A series of cardboard boxes greeted him, a small path between the ones on the right. He squeezed past them and was faced with another wall of boxes. He moved to the left to the other path. Past the boxes, a room had been constructed. The top could not be seen over the boxes. He placed his hand on the template to the right. The gray door slid open.

A technician in a white coat looked up from her position at the back of the room. The side of the room was lined with gray cabinets filled with medical supplies. "Director Martin."

He stepped inside. "How is she?"

"All her levels are normal. No changes, even with the move. I expect a smooth transition to the new site."

"Good. Now get out."

The technician placed her tablet on the counter next to her and walked past Martin without a word. The door slid closed behind her.

Martin turned his attention to the left-hand side of the room, which was filled with a large hospital bed and monitoring equipment.

And lying on the bed was his angel.

She had dark skin, wide lips, and her hair was long and braided. She looked a great deal like the woman that Ariana called mother. But Rochelle Mitchell wasn't Ariana's biological mother.

Martin stepped forward, looking at the angel that had been found in a spacecraft on the moon. No, Ariana's mother was someone much more grand. Which was why Ariana was such a disappointment. She had been the culmination of the merging of Martin's DNA and one of the angels. She had been the second creation. They had worked out some of the kinks that had gone wrong with the first evolution. She should've been perfect. But she was weak, not the warrior queen that her mother was.

Martin leaned down and ran a hand over his love's head. "It's okay, my love. Our daughter will be safe from them. And I think it's perhaps time she gave us a grandchild."

CHAPTER FORTY-NINE

MARCH 13, 1997

Six-year-old Ariana sat cross-legged on her living room floor, singing along with the opening refrain of *Sesame Street*.

"Sunny days, chasing the clouds away ..."

Her mother ran in from the backyard, her eyes wide, her whole body trembling. She leaned down to Ariana after turning off the TV.

"Mom," Ariana whined. "You promised."

"I know, Ariana, but we have to go. We have to go now." Her mother's dark eyes looked into Ariana's. Her skin looked even darker in the dim light of the living room.

She grabbed Ariana and ran to the front door. She pulled it open, and two men stood waiting for them on the front stoop. An SUV idled by the curb. Without a word, they hustled Ariana and her mother into the waiting SUV's back seat.

Ariana's mother strapped her into the booster seat and then

strapped herself in next to her. She gripped Ariana's hand, holding her tightly. "It'll be okay, sweetheart. It'll be okay."

Ariana didn't understand what was going on, but she knew her mom was worried. She reached up a hand and touched her mom's face. "Okay, Mama."

Her mom gave her a nervous smile and kissed her forehead. "There's my brave girl."

"What *is* that?" one of the men from the front seat said, his voice sounding strange.

Ariana glanced at the windshield and saw the strange lights up in the sky. They were so pretty. "Look, Mama. Planes."

"Those aren't planes," the driver said in a gruff voice.

His partner slapped him on the arm. "Quiet."

Ariana looked between the two men and then up at the sky. "What are they?"

Ariana's mother leaned over and pushed her hair back from her forehead, giving her another kiss. "Nothing, honey. Just planes. Like you said."

But Ariana knew her mother was lying. She stared up at the sky as the SUV raced down the street. More and more people stood along the edge of the road, staring up at the lights in the sky.

Ariana's gaze was pulled back to them time and time again. They were strange planes. They were all flying in a row. It almost looked like a triangle, except it was missing the bottom line. She'd never seen planes do that. They must be really good pilots.

"They're heading this way," the man in the passenger seat said quietly. The driver gave an abrupt nod and pressed down on the accelerator a little more.

Slowly, the city gave way to brush and desert. The driver slammed to a stop in front of a small squat square metal building in the middle of nowhere. Ariana's mother quickly undid her seatbelt and Ariana's as well. She pulled Ariana into her arms and stepped out of the car.

Her father stood in the open doorway of the metal building. Ariana called out to him. "Dad."

Her father didn't smile at her. He never smiled at her. But he did reach for her as soon as Ariana's mother reached the side. "Hurry," her father said before stepping into the building.

Ariana's father hurried down the steps. Ariana bounced with each step he took. At first it was fun being jostled around. But then it began to hurt her neck a little bit. "Daddy, slow down."

Her father ignored her, continuing down the stairs. Ariana leaned her head against his chest for a moment before pulling away. Leaning on his chest only caused her to slam her head into his chest over and over again.

"Martin, slow down. You're hurting her." Ariana's mother reached for her.

Her father ignored her. He picked up his pace, moving even faster down the stairs.

"Martin!" Ariana's mother called out behind them, fear in her voice.

Finally, they reached the bottom. Ariana felt dizzy, her head swimming. Her father hurried with her through a big heavy door and into the hallway. All Ariana saw were glimpses of lights. This time she did rest her head on her father's shoulder, needing something steady. She was so dizzy.

Her father stepped into a separate hallway. Ariana glanced up as he stopped. They were standing in front of the glass wall. It was pretty. Ariana reached out a hand and touched it. As soon as she did, the glass gave way. She jerked her hand back in surprise.

Her father strode into the cell and placed her on the cot at the back of it. She was so dizzy she nearly fell over. She reached for her father, but he was already striding back to the hallway. As soon as he stepped into the hallway, the glass wall slid shut behind him.

Ariana stared at it in shock. Then she jumped off the cot and ran to the glass wall, beating her hands against it. "Daddy! Daddy, let me out!"

Her mother stepped to the doorway, her face red, her chest heaving. She looked from Ariana beating her little fists against the glass wall to Ariana's father. She stepped toward him, her hands curled into fists. "What are you doing? Get her out of there!"

Her father's voice was too low for Ariana to hear all of his response. She only caught snippets here and there. "Dangerous ... safety ... good."

Ariana's mother faced her father, her hands on her hips. She reached up and shoved her father in the chest. "I said let her out of there now!"

Ariana had no trouble hearing her mom.

Her father gripped her mother's arm and pulled her down the hallway. Ariana couldn't hear anything they were saying now, but her mother glanced over her shoulder, tears tracking down her cheeks.

Ariana went still, staring at her mother's terror-stricken face. Then her mother let her father lead her over by the arm. He placed his hand on the screen next to the door.

The glass wall shot up again. Ariana smiled and took a step forward, but her father simply shoved her mother into the cell as well. Ariana's mother grabbed Ariana, pulling her back as the glass wall slammed shut behind her. Her mother turned, holding Ariana's hand, and stared at her father as he disappeared into the other hallway. He didn't look back.

Ariana tugged on her mother's hand. "Mama? Where's Daddy going?"

"To hell," her mother whispered, although Ariana wasn't sure if she heard her correctly because her mother would never say a bad word like that.

Her mother took a trembling breath and wiped the tears from her eyes. She leaned down and picked Ariana up, hugging her closely to her. "I don't know. But it's all right. As long as the two of us are together, everything will be all right."

Ariana's mother carried her to the cot at the back of the cell. She sat down and placed Ariana in her lap. Her mother wrapped her arms around her and snuggled her tight.

Ariana closed her eyes. She loved when her mom did this. It

was as if the two of them were one person. Ariana knew that her mother loved her more than anyone in the world. And she also knew that she was the most important person in her mother's world, even more important than her father.

Her mother started singing softly. "Hush, little baby, don't say a word, Mama's going to buy you a mockingbird. And if that mockingbird don't sing, Mama's going to buy you a diamond ring ..."

Ariana closed her eyes, feeling safe. She knew that no matter what happened, her mother would keep her that way.

———

Ariana's eyes flew open, and for just a moment, she felt traces of her mother's arms wrapped around her. She wiped away the tears at the edge of her eyes.

She had forgotten all about that. Her mother had died a short time later. It couldn't have been long, maybe just a week. A car accident.

Ariana sat up, leaning her chin on her knees. She had forgotten her mother's warm embraces. She'd forgotten the songs she used to sing to her. She had forgotten how safe she felt with her. Tears threatened to fall. *I'm sorry, Mama.*

Over the years, it had been difficult to even pull up her mother's face in her memory. Her father didn't have any pictures of her. For the first couple years, Ariana would draw her. But then those drawings began to supplant the memories. Her mother now became represented by a crayon vision of a woman with cocoa-colored skin and a halo of black hair.

Loss and grief pierced her chest. Her mama had loved her. Ariana knew that. But somewhere along the way, she had forgotten it.

Ariana examined her cell and knew this was the exact same cell she had been in with her mother.

The cell her father had put them in.

Ariana glanced around, not sure what to make of any of this.

Her life was nothing like that of any other kids. It had been lonely and without love after her mother had passed. The last couple of years had been freeing in a way that she never thought possible. It had reminded her how full her life could be.

Her watch beeped, and she looked around, but her bag hadn't been thrown in here with her. She stepped up to the glass wall and banged on it. "I need my medicine!"

No one responded. No one approached. She glanced around the cell and caught sight of the camera in the corner. She walked up to it. "I need my medicine," she repeated.

She waited, but no one came. She sat down heavily on the cot, bringing her knees to her chest once again. She'd been put on the medicine shortly after her mother died. She had a serious autoimmune disorder. Her medicine kept her healthy. She took it twice a day. She wasn't sure what would happen if she missed a dose. She never had before.

But she had a horrible feeling that she might be about to find out.

CHAPTER FIFTY

GEIRANGER, NORWAY

MAEVE COULD HAVE BEEN KNOCKED OVER WITH A FEATHER. Whatever she had expected Sammy to say, it certainly wasn't that.

"What?" Nora asked, shock splayed across her features as well.

"The woman called Ariana has the same biological parents that I do. The male is Martin Drummond."

Maeve was beyond words. Martin must have used his own DNA in one of the experiments. It was the only answer. But Greg hadn't mentioned Ariana looking anything other than human.

Nora finally found her voice. "Luke, what about Luke? How is he related to you?"

"His DNA is more diluted. We have the same ancestors. He would be the equivalent in your world to a distant cousin."

Maeve stumbled back and took a seat on the edge of one of the beds. This was not how she had expected this conversation to go. "So Martin Drummond, the head CIA spook who's made it his lifetime goal to prepare for an alien threat, has a son who's ..." She paused, looking for a diplomatic way to phrase it. "You?"

Sammy nodded. "He created me from his own DNA and that of my mother."

"Your mother? Where is she?" Nora asked.

"She is sleeping. My father has kept her sleeping since she was brought to this planet."

"How do you know that? Have you seen her? Have you met her?" Nora asked.

Sammy shook his head. "No, but I can feel her. I can communicate with her."

Maeve just stared at him, not sure how any of this could get more surreal.

Nora frowned. "Wasn't everyone released from Area 51?"

Maeve shook her head, thinking of the first time she had seen Agaren. "Most were. But Martin had certain beings moved." She looked at Sammy. "I'm guessing your mother was one of the ones moved."

Sammy nodded. "He keeps her close."

Maeve shuddered.

"Creepy," Nora mumbled.

"What kind of ..." Once again, Maeve struggled to try and find the right words. "What species is she?"

"She's a Guardian. She is one of the eternal beings. She was in her hibernation when she was taken from her ship and brought to Earth. They kept her in this state, experimenting on her for years before they used her to create me."

"Bastard," Nora cursed softly.

Sammy continued. "My father was not happy with his first-generation offspring. Years later, he had them use her again to create my sister. After that, they stopped attempting to create more, at least in that way. Instead, they used parts of my mother's DNA in an experiment on soldiers. They hoped it would strengthen them. It did not work the way it was intended. It did not do anything to the soldiers who were exposed. But one soldier impregnated his wife during that time, and the child has some of her DNA."

"Luke?" Nora said.

Sammy nodded. "Yes."

"How are you able to find your sister?" Maeve asked.

"I have not felt her signal for years. I knew she was alive, but I could never sense where she was. Finally, I felt her and then went to go find her, but I did not succeed."

"And now? Can you sense her now?" Maeve asked.

Sammy shook his head. "No. Something is blocking her from me. I don't know what it is. But it has blocked me from finding her all these years."

Maeve's mind was blown. Martin had used his own DNA to create an alien hybrid. *My God, the absolute ego.* The man had so little concern for the lives that he had created.

"Have you met your father?" Nora asked.

Sammy curled his lip in disgust. "Yes. He tried to use me as a weapon. I refused. He tortured me in an attempt to get me to do what he wanted. Still I refused. So he had me locked away."

"My God, that's horrible," Nora said.

And Maeve knew that those words weren't enough to cover exactly what Sammy had just shared. Even his own DNA within Sammy hadn't stopped Martin from torturing him.

Which meant that there was no reason to think it would stop him from torturing his daughter as well.

Sammy looked at her and nodded as if reading her mind. "She is not safe with him. I need to find her. I need to get her to safety. Will you help me?"

There were so many things on Maeve's plate right now that she couldn't even imagine how she could add another thing. But her heart wouldn't let her say no. "Yes, we'll do whatever we can."

CHAPTER FIFTY-ONE

CAVE CREEK, ARIZONA

THEY HADN'T TURNED OFF THE LIGHTS. ARIANA HAD BEEN awake now for over forty-eight hours. In all that time, they hadn't turned off the lights or even dimmed them. Ariana had also been by herself the entire time.

She had tried to sleep, but the lights made it impossible. They seemed to pierce through her eyelids. She lay on a cot that extended from the wall, her face turned into the wall, her arm over her eyes. But still, it didn't help much. She dozed for maybe an hour or two, not nearly enough, and it felt as if her brain had been wide awake the whole time. At best, all she'd managed was to rest her eyelids.

Sitting up, she rubbed her stinging eyes. She didn't understand any of this. For hours, she had tried to figure out what was going on. But as the hours went on, she found it harder and harder to think clearly.

She didn't understand why her father was doing this to her. How could he let them treat her this way? He couldn't know. That was the only explanation she could come up with. He knew they'd taken her but not how she was being treated. Even he wouldn't allow that ... right?

An image of the creature extending his hand toward her flashed through her mind. She hadn't been able to figure out the look on his face when he'd done that.

But even as she thought it, she knew that wasn't true. She *did* understand that look. He had wanted her to reach out for him. He wanted her to take his hand, to choose him.

She wondered what would've happened if she had just reached out. If her fingers had clasped his. Where would she be now? Would she be in a worse situation?

Looking around her cell, she tried to imagine what a worse situation would be. And she realized that in all likelihood, she would have been better off had she taken the strange creature's offer.

But who was he? And where had he come from?

Standing up, she stretched out her back. Everything ached. She reached for the ceiling and then for her toes. God, she felt stiff.

Ariana checked her watch again. She'd missed two days' worth of her meds. Fear crawled up her throat. The medicine had been a constant in her life since she was a kid. She never missed a dose. Now she'd missed four. It made her hyperaware of her body, waiting for the inevitable moment when the symptoms appeared. So far she'd been lucky, but she knew that it was only a matter of time before things took a turn for the worse.

A few more stretches eased the aches and reduced some of the worry. Everything felt fine. In fact, she felt strangely strong. And she really didn't know what to make of that.

She walked over to the small sink in the corner, turned the faucet on, and took a long drink. Wiping her mouth with the back of her hand, she glared up at the camera. There was no privacy in this cell. They watched everything she did.

She hoped that when her father found out that he would raise hell with all of them. But there was a small part in the back of her brain that wondered if maybe her father already knew. If maybe he knew and didn't care.

But she shut down that thought almost immediately. No. Her father was a cold man. That was true. But he had always protected her, in his own way. He wouldn't sanction her being treated like this. No, when he found out where she was, and she had no doubt he would, he would make sure she was released. And he would hold those who had done this to her accountable.

Ariana stepped away from the sink, looking around and wondering what exactly she was supposed to do. The idea of another day looming out in front of her with nothing but her thoughts made her light-headed. She didn't even have her phone to keep her company. She was going more than a little stir crazy.

The hallway door opened. Her head jerked up. Two guards appeared in their black uniforms. One flashed a keycard at the panel next to the door. The door slid open.

And as much as Ariana wanted to get out of the cell, she took a step away from the two of them.

"You need to come with us."

Ariana took another step back. "Why? Where are you taking me?"

"You need to come with us," the man repeated before waving the other guard forward. Ariana looked between the two men, trying to figure out what was going on.

The one who hadn't spoken pulled out a Taser. Two prongs buried themselves into Ariana's chest. Her back arched as volts of electricity rolled through her. Her jaw and legs locked up. She didn't scream, at least out loud. The pain was too much for her to even manage that. In her brain, though, she screamed and screamed again.

She was vaguely aware that the men had grabbed her. Her arms were yanked behind her back and plastic cuffs were slipped around them. The strength that she had felt just a few minutes ago had completely disappeared. Now all she felt was weak. The guards each grabbed her under an arm and dragged her down the hallway.

Ariana's head fell forward, and all she could see was tiles. It took some effort, but eventually she was able to lift her head. They'd stopped in front of a door that she didn't recognize. She hadn't been down this hallway before. It was a different color than the other one. It was a pale blue.

In front of her, the door slid open. The men immediately dragged her through. Four individuals in white lab coats stood waiting. Ariana's gaze turned to the stretcher in the middle of the room. "No, no, no," she moaned, trying to get her feet under her.

But the men had the momentum, and her limbs still weren't completely under her control yet. They pulled her forward, and with a practiced move, had her on top of the stretcher in one lift. Two more guards grabbed her legs and attached restraints around her ankles.

She was rolled onto her side, her back stretching painfully with her feet already shackled, and got one arm restrained before they removed the zip ties around her wrist. The guards snapped them off and then quickly yanked her other arm into the other restraint.

Ariana panted, feeling exhausted and terrified. Why were they treating her like this? Each guard outweighed her by a hundred pounds. She was no threat. She wasn't Hannibal Lecter. She was a grad student.

But they were acting like she was the greatest threat they'd ever come across.

When she was secured, the guards stepped back, and the doctors moved in. But the guards didn't leave the room. They stood around the stretcher, allowing the doctors enough room to maneuver but keeping themselves close in case they were needed.

Ariana looked at the woman who stepped up to the table. The bottom half of her face was covered with a medical mask so all she could see was the top of her nose and her eyes. But that was enough. "Dr. Thompson?"

The woman didn't respond. She just gripped Ariana's arm and put a rubber tie around it, then patted the crease of her arm for a vein.

"Dr. Thompson, what are you doing? Why are you doing this?"

The doctor she'd had since she was a child didn't respond at all. She gave no indication of knowing Ariana.

But Ariana knew it was her. She'd been her doctor since she was four years old. She was the one who diagnosed her autoimmune disease. She was the one who Ariana had seen every month for the last twenty-two years.

Even when Ariana had gone to California, Dr. Thompson had moved offices so that Ariana could continue to see her when she was at Berkeley. Ariana couldn't wrap her head around the fact that the doctor whom she had known her whole life, the doctor who smiled at her and looked after her, was a part of this.

Maybe she was a captive too. Maybe they were holding something over her and she had to do this. Ariana clung to that idea. She looked away as Dr. Thompson plunged the needle into her arm and began to draw blood. Ariana watched the guards around the table for the first time, taking a good look at their faces.

Her gaze snapped back to the second and third one. *I know you.* The thought chilled her to the bone. Both guards had been her protection at Berkeley last year. They had followed her for about three months.

She swallowed and looked back at Dr. Thompson. Her hands were completely steady. Not an ounce of fear showed on the woman's face. She filled six vials with blood and handed them to one of the white-coated doctors. "Send this to the lab. This is the priority. The director wants answers quickly."

The director? Ariana's heart started to pound. No, no, he couldn't know. He could not know she was here. He couldn't have okayed this.

Dr. Thompson leaned down and whispered in Ariana's ear. For a moment, Ariana felt hope, thinking that she was right. That the doctor was doing this under duress. But her cold tone robbed her of those hopes.

"You need to behave yourself, or it will get worse. This is for your own good." Dr. Thompson stood and waved at one of the other doctors.

A gas mask was fitted over her mouth. She struggled, turning her head to avoid it. One of the guards stepped up. He gripped her on either side of the head, holding her in place. Tears sprang to her eyes and slipped down her cheeks. But no one noticed, or more likely, they noticed but didn't care.

She held her breath for as long as she could manage, even though she knew she was only putting off the inevitable.

Stars dotted her vision. Her mouth burst open. She sucked in the chemical-tainted air. Faces in the room began to blur, and then dots in her vision began to grow larger and coalesce.

She fought the darkness pulling at her. But then in a moment of complete clarity, she gave up the fight. She didn't want to be awake for whatever they were going to do. And she didn't have the strength to fight them anyway. She closed her eyes and prayed that whatever they were about to do, she was completely unconscious for all of it.

CHAPTER FIFTY-TWO

GEIRANGER, NORWAY

GREG OPENED HIS EYES AND STARED AT THE CEILING. THE LAST few nights, he'd slept like the dead. Apparently being transported across dimensions did that to you. He still struggled with accepting what happened. He'd thought he was beyond the ability to be surprised. He thought after everything he had been through, there was no more impossible in his world.

Nice to know he was wrong.

He stood up and headed to the shower. The hot water beating down on him woke him a little more fully and eased the ache in his shoulders and back.

Water rained down upon him as he mulled over what Maeve had stopped by to tell him right after he'd come back. He'd barely been conscious, on the edge of sleep when she told him that Ariana was Sammy's sister. And Sammy was somehow Martin's son.

Yet another thing Greg was having trouble getting his head around.

But he had a feeling he now knew who Sammy and Ariana's mother was. His subconscious had actually worked it out while he slept last night. He'd dreamt of the Guardians who'd appeared to the Russian cosmonauts back in the 1980s. They'd surrounded their ship with their large wings and warnings about humanity's future unless we changed our ways.

That sounded an awful lot like the way Sammy had interceded first for Chris back in Area 51, and then for Luke and for the rest of them, keeping them safe. And there was something other-worldly about him, unlike the other hybrids that he had run into.

Of course, there was nothing otherworldly about Ariana. She was gorgeous, true, but more in a supermodel kind of way than in an alien-from-another-planet kind of way.

Greg shut off the water and quickly toweled off before throwing on his clothes. He leaned his hands on the edge of the sink and stared at his reflection in the mirror. He shifted his wet brown hair away from his eyes. With a start, he realized his face had changed a lot in the last couple months. He actually hadn't spent much time staring in a mirror during that time. The man that looked back at him now actually looked like a man.

Usually Greg thought he looked like a slightly advanced high school student whenever he caught a glimpse of himself in the mirror. Right now, though, his cheekbones stood out, and there were even a few wrinkles at the corner of his eyes.

He supposed it was all the responsibilities that the last few months had pushed down upon him.

And he had a feeling those responsibilities were only going to increase. *Of course, if we don't get the angel back, aging won't be a problem for me or anyone else.*

But even if they somehow managed that feat, Maeve was still in an unenviable position. He couldn't believe the Council was actu-ally making Maeve choose between her family on Earth and the welfare of Pop and Crackle on their base. It was beyond cruel. This Council had messed with humanity years ago, and now humanity was paying the price. But they weren't holding the Drago responsible—they were holding humanity responsible. Setting them up for some sort of test, a test which Greg could tell they were pretty sure humanity was going to fail.

And speaking of failure ... His thoughts turned back to Ariana. He couldn't help but feel guilty about what had happened to her. Was it possible her father had actually locked her away? Normally he would say that was impossible. But this was Martin. No evil seemed out of bounds for him. But with the fate of the world on the line, what else could they have done but grab her?

We could have left her alone.

And that was the thought that had dogged him the last few days. If they had let her be, would she be continuing her life completely oblivious to all of this craziness? He had done this, dragged her into this mess, and he couldn't help but feel guilty about the result.

And she was Sammy's sister, for God's sake. How messed up was that? Sammy had sensed her in California, but shortly after she'd been grabbed by Martin's men, whatever Sammy had been tuning into was gone again. And he had not been able to sense her since.

Greg didn't know what to make of that. There were animals that could sense one another, but not over thousands of miles. Without Sammy being able to sense her, what chance did they have at finding her? And did they even really need to? Maybe he was worrying over nothing. She was probably fine.

But try as he might, he couldn't seem to convince himself of that.

Greg bowed his head, feeling the stress building up in his chest. He needed to do something. It was all so completely overwhelming. At this point, he'd actually lost count of how many gunfights he'd been in. Five years ago, the closest he'd gotten to a gunfight was watching one in a darkened movie theater. Now he could disassemble a Glock and put it back together just as quickly. He couldn't even hazard a guess at how many people he'd seen get shot.

He didn't regret anything he had done these last few years. Helping humanity, helping his friends, he would do it all over again in a split second.

But that didn't change the fact that he could really use a vacation.

Greg opened the bathroom door and headed out to the main living area. No one was around. He stopped short in surprise. He'd thought everybody would be up. Then he glanced at the clock above the stove. It was just coming up on five a.m. He'd gone to bed extremely early last night. Everybody else would probably be asleep for another few hours.

Quietly, he made his way into the kitchen and started the coffee brewing. He rummaged through the cabinets and found a can of oatmeal. Setting some water to boil, he got himself a bowl and a spoon, keeping his mind blank as he focused only on his breakfast. Breakfast was enough right at this moment.

He grabbed some blueberries from the fridge and put them into a little bowl.

A few minutes later he had a cup of coffee, his bowl of oatmeal with blueberries, and he headed outside. Taking a seat on one of the Adirondack chairs that faced the fjord, he took his first bite of oatmeal, staring at the crystal-blue waters. It was very easy when sitting here, everything peaceful, to think that he was actually on vacation. He ate his oatmeal in silence, not letting any thoughts drift into his mind, just taking in the tranquility of the morning.

When he was finished with his oatmeal, he set the bowl aside and pulled out his phone. They'd picked up phones when they had been on the run. His had a small little camera.

He flicked through the pictures he'd taken of the places they had been. He'd taken one of Jasper crawling out of a tent really early one morning. Another of Mike riding on the back of a bike. A few of them on that incredibly smelly fishing boat. Chaotic as it was, the trip had actually been a lot of fun.

Until the gunfire.

The door opened behind him. Greg glanced over his shoulder as Iggy walked slowly out of the cabin.

Greg smiled at him. "Hey, Iggy."

"Ig!" Iggy tore over to him with a giant grin on his face. He jumped when he was about six feet away and landed in Greg's lap.

Greg winced, sucking in a breath. *That's going to leave a mark.* But Iggy didn't seem to notice the pain he had caused his friend as he happily chattered away. "Ig, ig, ig."

Greg settled back in his chair, patting Iggy on the back. "Good to see you too, Iggy."

Iggy leaned back against Greg and let out a little sigh.

Greg still couldn't get how anyone could think Iggy was a threat. He paused, remembering Iggy saving his life at Martin's base in New Mexico. Okay, in that situation he could see how someone could think that Iggy was a threat, but when he wasn't protecting the people around him, he was the sweetest little guy ever created.

Iggy pointed at Greg's phone. "Ig?"

Greg nodded. "Yeah, those are the pictures from when Jasper, Mike, and I went on our trip. You want to see them?"

Iggy nodded, staring intently at Greg's phone. "Ig."

Greg flipped back to the beginning of the photos. "Okay, let's see. So this here is Hans. He was a fisherman that took us over to Iceland. Really nice guy. He cooked us a really good salmon dinner that first night." Greg continued flipping through the pictures, sharing a little anecdote with each one.

"And this was the fishing shack of a small little town that we—"

Iggy sat straight up, staring intently at the photo. "Ig."

Greg frowned. He'd thought he was beginning to understand Iggy's vocalizations. But he'd never heard him sound so serious. "What's wrong?"

Iggy pointed to the photo. "Ig! Ig! Ig!"

Greg stared at the picture, not sure what was making Iggy so excited. The picture was of a wharf in Narsaq, Greenland. There was a small shack where an older couple sold bait and a small fishing boat that was tied up to the dock. The sun was setting in the background, leaving the sky with lines of dark blue, pinks, yellows, and reds.

"Ig-ig?" Iggy pointed at the photo.

Greg thought he might be indicating the bait shack, so he examined it more closely but didn't see anything that would make anyone excited. It was an old wooden shack that had been there for decades. It was practically white from the sun and the salt. A small window was shuttered from where they sold the bait. That was about it.

Iggy pointed at the screen again. "Ig. Ig."

Greg frowned as Iggy pointed and realized it was the fishing boat that Iggy seemed to be focused on. He zoomed in, bringing the picture into higher relief. But that didn't help either. It looked like any other fishing boat. The name Claude was on the side of it.

Greg shrugged. "I don't understand, Iggy. What's got you so upset?"

"Ig. Ig." Iggy pointed at the stern of the ship.

Greg zoomed in on the back half of the boat. There was a small little symbol on the edge of it.

Greg frowned, trying to make it out and wondering how the heck Iggy had even seen it. Apparently Iggy's eyesight was a lot better than any of them had realized.

Squinting, Greg could just make out the small symbol. It was a circle with something that almost looked like an Egyptian hiero-glyph in it. "Is this what you're looking at?"

Iggy jumped up and down on the edge of the chair. "Ig. Ig!"

Greg stared at the symbol. He'd never seen anything like it before. Then again, hieroglyphs weren't really his thing. Why on earth would this be on a little fishing boat in the middle of nowhere? He ran a finger slowly over the symbol.

"Ig." Iggy sounded so forlorn.

Greg stared at the symbol and then shook his head. He had no idea what it was. But it seemed important to Iggy. And if he couldn't take a vacation, maybe the least he could do was some-thing to make Iggy happy. He stood up. "Okay. Let's go wake up Adam. Apparently we need to take a hike to the top of the mountain."

CHAPTER FIFTY-THREE

CAVE CREEK, ARIZONA

Ariana blinked at the bright lights glaring down at her from the ceiling. She closed her eyes to block out their harshness. Her mouth felt dry, and her thoughts were fuzzy. She squinted her eyes open again, not recognizing where she was for a moment.

Then it all hit her.

Ariana's eyes flew open as she sat up quickly. Her back slammed into the cool tile wall behind her. She crushed her eyes shut, the light painful. She put a hand over them as she squinted. Her vision wavered, and her eyes ached. She turned her head toward the wall, trying to give her eyes time to adjust. Finally, she could open them fully, although they stung painfully. She wiped away the tears that rolled down her cheeks.

She was back in her cell. Visions of Dr. Thompson, the guards, and that room swam through her mind. She gripped the edge of the bed, feeling dizzy. Her stomach rolled.

They had knocked her out. *What did they do to me?*

She rolled onto her side, vaguely aware of an ache in her stomach, although she couldn't tell if it was from what had been done to her or from a combination of fear and hunger. But that was as much attention as she could give to it. She wasn't ready to investigate it more fully. She needed a minute, or maybe a lifetime, to be ready to accept what had happened to her.

She stared up at the glass wall, taking slow, measured breaths. Her breathing wasn't impacted. So whatever they had done hadn't been to her lungs or her chest. She lay there for a few minutes more before she managed to work up the courage to stand. When she did, her head swam.

She took a couple more deep breaths, willing that light-headedness away. A tray had been set on the table next to the cot. A sandwich, PB&J from the look of it, sat there along with a tall glass of water. Both had been placed on plastic containers. She reached for the water first and downed the contents quickly.

She wiped her mouth with the back of her hand when she was done. How long had she been out? Her throat was so dry. It must've been hours. The water was lukewarm but refreshing nonetheless.

But it didn't quite quench her thirst. She walked over to the sink and refilled her glass, downing its contents quickly. She filled the glass again and drained it. She leaned heavily against the sink. Her legs felt shaky. Her whole body felt shaky. Gripping the cup, she slowly made her way back to the cot and sat down. She wasn't hungry, even though she knew she should eat.

Instead, she looked at her arm. A small bandage had been placed over the injection point. She scanned the rest of her arm, but there was no further sign of violation. She glanced under her hospital gown, but there was nothing there either. She frowned, looking at her legs again. There was no sign of any injection site or any incision. Finally, she looked at her other arm.

And that was when she found it. Near her shoulder, under her arm, was a small bandage. She pulled the bandage off and saw just a few small stitches. Someone had cut her. But why?

She replaced the bandage and slowly searched her body again. But that was the only site she could see. She stared at its location, trying to figure out what could possibly be there that they wanted to examine.

But her knowledge of anatomy was rudimentary at best. And as far as she knew, nothing of critical importance was located there.

Maybe it wasn't something they wanted to examine, maybe it was something they wanted removed.

She shook her head. Now that was impossible. But she couldn't help but think that the incision had been made in the same location as her birth-control implant.

She'd had it inserted years ago. In fact, she'd had birth-control implants since she was thirteen years old. Dr. Thompson said that the effects of her menstrual cycle could weaken her already weakened immune system, so she had started Ariana on birth control at a very young age.

Ariana stared at the incision. But now Dr. Thompson had removed it. Why? She struggled to come up with an answer, but none were forthcoming. None of this made any kind of sense. She was at a complete loss. She didn't know why any of this was happening. She didn't know what was going on. A vision of that strange creature wafted through her brain again. And now at least she knew the answer to the question she had asked earlier.

No, she would not have been in a worse situation if she had gone with him. She had a feeling that not going with him was the worst decision she had ever made in her life.

CHAPTER FIFTY-FOUR

GEIRANGER, NORWAY

GREG MANAGED TO TALK THE OTHERS INTO LETTING HIM DO A search for the symbol Iggy was interested in at the top of the mountain. He could tell from the way Maeve and Chris responded that they didn't think there was anything to it, but they had their minds preoccupied with other things at the moment, so they didn't put up too much of an argument. Adam had given him a long look and said he was all right with Greg going so long as he took Nora with him.

Greg tried not to be annoyed that Adam insisted he bring security. At the same time, he knew it was a good precaution. He had a tendency to get lost in his work. And even if he wasn't lost in his work, he definitely wasn't the soldier that Nora was.

The two of them hiked up the trail toward the summit. Iggy had wanted to go with them, but Nora had promised that she would spend some time, just the two of them, when she returned. He seemed satisfied with that, at least for the moment. Greg kept glancing around, expecting Iggy to pop up behind a tree or gallop down at them from somewhere along the trail. He wasn't very good at staying where he didn't want to be.

"Do you really think this is anything?" Nora asked.

Greg shrugged. "I don't know, to be honest. I've never seen Iggy get so excited about something, though, have you?"

"Well, he does act that way when he sees a Snickers bar, but that's about the only thing I've seen get him that excited."

Greg watch Nora from the corner of his eye. "Are you worried?"

Nora didn't answer for a long while, and then she sighed. "Yes. I'm always worried about Iggy. He obviously doesn't belong here. But he's here with us now, and I can't imagine my life without him."

"You know he loves you just as much as you love him, don't you?"

"I know. But he's a Maldek. He's not from this planet. We don't know anything about him really. I mean, he's sweet, he's kind, he's incredibly loyal and protective." Nora paused. "But whatever this symbol is, is it something *else* that he's equally loyal to? What if we find something that changes him or—" She cut off her words, shaking her head.

"What if he becomes more attached to something else?" Greg asked quietly.

Nora nodded without looking at him. "I know it's selfish and stupid. It's probably nothing. But I just have this feeling ..."

Greg shook his head. "It's not selfish. You love him. You want what's best for him. But you *also* want what's best for him to be to stay with you. I get that. I'm jealous of the relationship you two have. Because he is loyal beyond anything I've ever seen. And he's so ridiculously cute and funny. Who wouldn't want him in their lives?"

"Yeah, that's what I'm afraid of," Nora said quietly.

"Hey, look, we don't even know if this is anything. Like you said, he gets just as excited over a Snickers bar. So this could just be something like that. Maybe it's an ancient symbol for food or something."

But even as Greg said it, he didn't believe it. Iggy's reaction had been much more serious than the reaction he'd shown later when showing Nora the symbol. He had never seen Iggy that serious. Greg hadn't mentioned that to Nora. She had enough worries on her mind. He didn't need to add some unfounded concerns of his own to her pile.

"Here we are."

Greg spied the tarp that hid the large array. He walked over and pulled it off then grinned, excitement building inside of him. He didn't know what the symbol stood for, but it was nice to have something that wasn't a matter of life and death to investigate for a change.

CHAPTER FIFTY-FIVE

CAVE CREEK, ARIZONA

INSTEAD OF HEADING STRAIGHT TO ARIZONA, MARTIN HAD taken a side trip through South Dakota. He wanted to make sure he was not being followed. He holed up in a shack he rented for cash for a few days to take in the scope of R.I.S.E.'s efforts against him.

They had pulled out all the stops. He'd gotten reports that a dozen of his sites had been shut down and the staff taken in for questioning. And she had found a few more of the accounts he thought he'd hidden well. All in all, Matilda was proving to be a serious pain in his ass.

The only positive was that Martin had all his agents ready to act at a moment's notice. He had the rest of his forces on standby as well. This would be a full court press. He was not holding anyone back. As soon as he had a location for Subject One and the rest of his group, he could send them all out immediately.

But he had absolutely no inkling as to where they'd gone.

He'd had no more sightings of Greg Schorn after Berkeley. His men couldn't even swear if Greg had been at the factory with Ariana.

There had been two men with Schorn, but his men hadn't gotten a good look at either of them. And neither had appeared on the Rapid Response teams' cameras. He had a feeling that the two men were probably Tilda's people, but he had absolutely no intel on their identities. Tilda kept her people's identities close to her chest. And she often had them working in different branches of government, where no one knew they were affiliated with R.I.S.E. Looking for them would be like looking for a needle in a haystack.

But dammit, he needed something.

The car stopped, and his driver turned around to look at him. "We're here, sir."

Martin looked up in surprise. The driver had picked him up from South Dakota this morning. The trip had flown by. Apparently being annoyed and frustrated helped the time pass quickly.

He stepped out of the car, and a wall of heat surrounded him. He gritted his teeth, all too familiar with this kind of heat.

He glanced to the south. He'd grown up not too far from here. Summers had been brutal. There was nothing you could do to cool down that trailer home he'd shared with his mother.

Not that his mother had ever tried.

Martin shook off the thought. He didn't need old baggage dogging him today. And for the most part, he'd done a pretty good job of keeping any thoughts of his upbringing away from his adult life.

He supposed it was only reasonable that he would be thinking about his own childhood today.

After all, he was here to see his daughter.

He opened the heavy steel door by placing his hand on the screen next to it. The door opened only a few inches with a small release of air. All the doors were attuned to his handprint and his alone. Anyone else entering or exiting needed to use a keycard.

He pulled the door open the rest of the way. He slipped inside and shut the door behind him. The interior of the small square building was a good twenty degrees cooler than the exterior. He rolled his shoulders, shaking off the heat and his maudlin thoughts at the same time. Then he jogged down the steps, focused on the task at hand.

His daughter had been here for five days. They'd done all the testing, but he wanted to see the results himself, and he didn't want any of it sent electronically. Besides, this was as good a place to hide out as any. Tilda's reach had only widened in the last few months. Martin had a feeling he was going to have to isolate his cells of agents from one another even more than he already had. If Tilda got wind of one, he didn't want anyone being able to tie it to the others.

Anger churned through his gut. Damn her. Martin was the reason that they had been able to destroy the Drago, and yet Matilda was the one reaping all the benefits. Martin had been the one who had rid the world of the alien threat.

But did he get any credit for it? Of course not. And now he'd been tossed aside like yesterday's news.

He knew, though, that fighting Matilda was a losing battle. She had the U.S. government on her side at this point. And Martin was in no place to take them on.

But Martin could make good on his original intention. He could remove the alien presence from the planet, at least the independent ones.

He had been tracking down the escapees from Area 51, and by his count, he'd gotten at least ninety-five percent at this point. But Subject One remained out of his grasp.

And he was the one that Martin needed to see destroyed. Subject One was an abomination in more ways than one. These aliens were not here to make human lives easier. They were here to destroy humans. And once Martin had rid the world of the subjects he had created, then he would be able to convince the U.S. government that Martin and Martin alone was the one who could truly defend the world against the coming alien threat.

Because he knew in his gut that it was coming. The aliens were much stronger and much more powerful than any country on Earth. They had shown amazing restraint up to this point. But there would come a time when that restraint broke. And he truly believed that Antarctica was the first sign of that.

If they hadn't reached the point of no return yet, they would soon. And they would decide that humans no longer deserved to be the masters of their own destiny. Then they would destroy it all. Martin had no doubt about that.

He was humanity's last line of defense.

He reached the bottom of the stairs and headed down the hall. He passed the hallway leading to his daughter's cell without pause or hesitation. His office was down the hallway to the left, and he quickly turned to it. He stopped in, dropped his bag, and then headed to the conference room down the hall.

The room was large, with an oval-shaped table that could seat ten. His science team currently sat around it silently, reviewing files on their tablets as they waited for him. They all stood up as Martin entered. Stacy stood next to the door and handed him a coffee along with a tablet. Martin took both and headed to his seat at the head of the table. Everyone else was already seated.

Martin skimmed through the file open on his tablet. He looked up when he was done. "She'll be fertile within the next twenty-four hours?"

Dr. Thompson nodded. "Yes. We can begin egg harvesting at that time."

Martin nodded. "Excellent. And how many eggs do you think you'll be able to harvest?"

"Normally it would be fifteen, but she has just come off the suppressant. It will most likely be a smaller yield this month, maybe six or even less. But beginning next month, we should be able to get a normal batch."

He didn't reply as the possible applications rolled through his mind. The yield wasn't as high as he would like, but it would have to do. The possibilities were intriguing, though. What DNA should he mix with hers? Or should he strip hers down first to its purest parts?

He had to admit he was excited. For Ariana and her brother's birth, they had been forced to use a human host.

But now they had Ariana.

Would her unique biology make a difference? Would she help usher in a new legion of Guardians dedicated to protecting Earth?

Perhaps you aren't so useless after all, daughter.

Dr. Thompson misread his silence. "She won't be in any pain, if that's what you're worried about. We'll make sure that the harvesting is smooth and without any unnecessary discomfort."

Martin waved away her concerns. "That is not an issue. Just make sure that there are no complications."

The doctors then provided a rundown on Ariana's physical state. He was surprised to learn that she was a lot stronger than he had realized. The effects of the drugs that he'd had her on and the implants had been diminishing her strength since she was a child. Now that she was older and free of interventions, it was coming back quickly. "The guards have taken the proper precautions?"

Dr. Thompson nodded. "I took the liberty of doubling her guard whenever she was being moved."

Martin nodded. "That's good."

Although he doubted that Ariana would make an escape attempt. She wasn't violent. She never had been in her life. She was a mouse, really. No, he didn't worry about her overpowering the guards, even though from these reports it was obvious that she could do exactly that.

He stood up when he had finished his questions. He strode from the room without another word and headed down the hall to his office.

Stacy hurried behind him. "I just wanted to update you that our teams have been unable to find any trace of the group in England. The child that they were following turned out to be false."

Martin growled. There'd been a report of a child matching Luke Gillibrand's description in London. But of course it wasn't him. Every lead they'd gotten so far had been false.

He stepped into his office. "Fine. Keep me updated."

He closed the door almost in Stacy's face. Martin headed to his desk and sat down, flipping his computer on. He tried to focus on the files he'd prepared in anticipation of R.I.S.E.'s next moves, but he couldn't seem to focus. He finally switched to a map of the globe, zooming in and out on different regions.

Where are you hiding?

Martin had been in the spy business for nearly forty years. He had never failed in his professional life.

Until now.

The inability to capture or kill Subject One was his greatest and only failure. He'd never exerted so much energy and focus on one particular job, and still the subject had eluded him.

And now his *son* was eluding him as well.

He drummed his fingers on the desk and then stood up, pacing through the office. He took some deep breaths, stilling his thoughts.

I'm thinking about this wrong. I'm approaching this the way I normally do. Obviously that is not working. I need to think outside the box, come at this from a different angle.

In his mind, he conjured and discarded dozens of ideas before he stopped still.

He walked over to his monitor and flicked on the security camera for Ariana's cell. She sat in the corner of the room, writing on a piece of paper. Martin studied her, playing the pros and cons. It would be a risk, but if it paid off, it would solve all of his problems at once.

He smiled. *Ariana, you are going to get what you want, at least for a little while. And then I am going to get something I have wanted for quite some time.*

CHAPTER FIFTY-SIX

GEIRANGER, NORWAY

IT TOOK AN HOUR TO TRACK DOWN A SYMBOL ALMOST IDENTICAL to one that Greg had seen on the ship. But as Greg looked at it, he tried and failed to figure out what the link was.

And at the same time, he didn't like where his search had taken him.

The first forty-five minutes, he'd had absolutely no luck. He'd tried a generalized Google image search, followed by a search of a few government databases. Tilda had helpfully left them with a back door into some government servers.

But Greg kept running into walls, finding symbols similar but not quite right. The closest had been hieroglyphs from an ancient tomb in the Valley of the Kings. But the angle was wrong, the dimensions not accurate. It just plain didn't fit. About to give up, knowing that they couldn't stay on the link for much longer, he did a Hail Mary search of UFO sites, figuring what the heck. It couldn't hurt.

And that was when he hit pay dirt.

The symbol on the ship was the same as one of the symbols that Sergeant Jim Penniston had reported being on the UFO in the

Rendelsham Forest incident. According to Penniston, a series of symbols similar to hieroglyphics had been etched into the side of the ship he'd seen land outside RAF Bentwaters back in 1980. After the encounter, Penniston had written them down as best he could remember them.

Greg stared at the screen, not believing his eyes. He knew he shouldn't be surprised that there was a UFO link, and yet somehow he was.

He'd expected the search to turn up nothing. And for the first forty-five minutes, he felt relief flowing through him. It was nothing. Just Iggy getting excited about something they didn't quite understand.

But now he was staring at the same symbol that was allegedly on the alien ship that had touched down outside a British military base.

Nora stepped back into view, having just completed her patrol. "We need to get going soon. We can't stay on that much longer."

Greg nodded. "Yeah. I'm just going to check one last thing."

He uploaded the photo of the boat, running a search along with the name of the boat through one of Tilda's databases.

And he got a hit. It was registered to a Dane Lansky of Svente, Norway. A quick internet search revealed that although the town belonged to Norway, it was actually located on the northern tip of the main island of Svalbard, which was part of a group of islands halfway between Norway and the Arctic.

Greg jotted down the name in his notebook and the town. The ship had been registered back in 1973. He frowned. That was years before Rendelsham. Maybe someone had added the symbol later. Maybe it was just a coincidence that it looked like one of the markings on the Rendelsham UFO. Recording the info in his notebook, he closed the laptop and covered the equipment with the tarp.

"Did you find anything?" Nora asked as he walked up to him.

What should he say? He wasn't sure what any of it meant. And while for him it was a curiosity, for Nora it meant a lot more. He needed to speak with Maeve. Maybe together they could figure out if the symbol was of any real import. So he shook his head. "No, nothing yet."

Maeve stood outside the cabin, watching as Snap climbed a tree with Iggy. Her balance was now as good as Alvie's. She was only two years old chronologically, but intellectually she was light-years ahead of most adults.

Emotionally, though, she was still a child. She still needed the comfort and support a parental figure could offer. She climbed, sure of her steps, but she continually glanced over to make sure that Maeve was still watching. Maeve smiled, encouraging her on, and Snap would return the smile before continuing on her journey.

Alvie climbed behind Snap, ready to grab her should she fall, even though he knew it was unlikely. He, too, kept glancing over at Maeve. But he wasn't looking for the same sort of support that Snap was. He knew something was wrong, and he was looking to check Maeve's emotions, to see how she was doing. So Maeve kept a tight lid on the fear that had been crawling through her ever since she had seen Pop and Crackle. She wanted Alvie and Snap to have as carefree a time these next few days as she could manage.

Iggy let out a little squeal from the branch he was swinging on. He launched himself to another branch ten feet lower on the opposite tree before doing a somersault and landing on the ground.

Maeve's heart leaped into her throat. She stumbled forward, ready to do something, even though she knew she wouldn't make it in time. But he just stood up, landing on his feet, and took off at his crablike run to the path leading from the house.

Nora and Greg appeared over the rise, and Iggy's exuberant display finally made sense. Maeve watched with a smile as he leaped into the air. Nora caught him in her arms with practiced ease. He then snuggled into her shoulder.

Those two were no less attached then Maeve was to her gang.

She knew that the other woman understood how difficult this choice was.

And that helped, knowing that she wasn't the only one feeling as if this was a Sophie's choice that she had to make.

But for both of them, the other issue was more daunting. They had less than a week to figure out a way to change the Council's mind. Mere days to save the human race. They had spent hours going over ideas and possibilities. But none of them were of substance. What they needed was the location of the woman Martin had hidden away, but they weren't going to be able to discern that from here.

They knew Tilda was searching all his known hideouts. But that would take time. And Maeve and her group were too far away to do anything to help. It was beyond frustrating.

With a wave, Nora and Iggy headed back to the cabin. Greg headed over to Maeve. He gave her a distracted smile. "Got a few minutes?"

Maeve studied him, not liking the seriousness in his face. "Is this about the R.I.S.E. search? Did you hear from Tilda?"

"No, no. Sorry, it's not that. It's something else."

She nodded to some chairs that had been set up a little farther away from where the kids were climbing. "Back there?"

"That's good," Greg said. They walked over to the chairs in silence.

Maeve gave Alvie and Snap a little wave before she took her seat. "I'm guessing you found something."

Greg nodded as he sat. "Yes, but I don't know what to make of it."

Maeve listened as Greg explained about the search, finding the symbol, and its uncanny resemblance to one of the hieroglyphs on the side of the Rendelsham ship. She felt no shock at the revelation. She was beyond shock at this point.

When Greg fell silent, she looked at him. "What are you going to do?"

He shrugged, his gaze on Alvie and Snap. "I don't know. I

didn't tell Nora because I wasn't sure what to say. I mean, this could be nothing."

"No, it's not."

Greg sighed. "Yeah, I know. But I hope it's nothing."

"So what do you *want* to do?"

Greg lowered his head into his hands. "God, I don't know." He began to massage his temple. "It's crazy, isn't it? Every day it seems like there's some new revelation that pulls the rug out from underneath our feet."

"Yeah, I know what you mean."

"Have you made a decision?"

Maeve nodded. "Yes."

She and Chris had talked late into the night. As much as they danced around it, Maeve knew that one of them had to go. Abandoning Pop and Crackle wasn't an option. She understood Pop and Crackle better than anyone. And if there was some sort of medical issue, she'd be the one in the best position to deal with it. Back here, assuming the world didn't end, Chris would have the help of Greg and all of Matilda's resources to help Alvie and Snap. There, Chris would be on his own and out of his depth.

"It's you. You're going, aren't you?" Greg asked softly.

Maeve nodded, not able to speak as tears sprang to her eyes. At that moment, Alvie's head jerked up. He looked over, but she gave him a wave with a bright smile, shoving the feeling of loss that had already enveloped her away. "It has to be me."

"When? When are you going?" Greg asked, a tremor in his voice.

Maeve shook her head. "I don't know. Not until I absolutely have to."

Greg looked over at Alvie and Snap. "Do they know?"

"No. I'm not going to tell them until I have to. You know how sensitive they are. They wouldn't be able to focus on anything else. And I want the memories of their last days with me filled with happiness, not sorrow, especially if ..." She shrugged, not able to say the words.

Greg nodded, his chin trembling as he looked away from her. "I'll miss you."

Maeve reached over and took his hand, squeezing it in hers. "And I you. But I'm counting on you to help Chris. I need you to get in contact with John and have him send over all my files on Alvie's development from Wright-Pat. I need you to know everything about Alvie. With me gone, you're going to have to be in charge of their care."

"I'll take care of them."

"I know you will. Thank you."

They sat there with their hands clasped, neither of them speaking. Maeve was so thankful to have a friend like Greg. With her unusual upbringing, it was rather strange that two of them had ever even met, never mind hit it off. She didn't take that for granted. She never had.

Greg cleared his throat, releasing Maeve's hand. "Do you think Tilda will be able to find the woman? Do you think Earth will survive?"

"R.I.S.E. has done some pretty amazing things." Maeve said, knowing she wasn't directly answering his question. But she didn't know how to answer that question.

Maeve gave herself a mental shake. She would not spend these last few precious days mourning. She would mourn when she had to. "So when are you leaving?"

Greg looked over at her, his brow furrowed. "Leaving?"

She gave a small laugh. "Oh, come on, Greg, I know you. You want to find out what the deal is with the symbol. You want to figure out why Iggy reacted the way he did."

"I do, but it seems silly to take off on that kind of trip when we're in the middle of everything."

"Greg, we're always in the middle of everything. There's never going to be a good time. And soon, well ... don't you want something to distract you a little bit? God knows, I'm looking for things to distract me. Since you want to find out what's going on with the symbol, just go."

Greg shook his head. "You understand how much it took just to get us to the States? I mean, to get to Svalbard without Jasper and Mike, I don't know how I would manage it."

Maeve raised an eyebrow. "Really? Because I do believe we have a teleporter living in our barn."

Shock flashed across Greg's face before he smiled. "You know what? I do believe you're right."

CHAPTER FIFTY-SEVEN

CAVE CREEK, ARIZONA

ARIANA'S EYES OPENED SLOWLY. SHE STARED UP AT THE CEILING, an image she was all too familiar with. From what she could tell, she had been in her cell for at least four days. Her father hadn't come to see her even once. And she knew he had been here. She had heard him. She wasn't sure how, and part of her wondered if she was hallucinating. She felt as if she could hear through the walls. She could have sworn she'd heard the doctors talking yesterday before she had been brought into the room.

You can't trust any of them, Ariana. You have to trust yourself.

Ariana ignored the voice. She had heard it on and off for the last few hours. She didn't want to think about where the voice originated. Because she was pretty sure it meant she was going crazy.

At the same time, there was a comfort in the voice. It felt warm and loving.

Which, as far as she could tell, only meant she really *was* going crazy. Because nothing about this situation should make her feel good.

Ariana stood up as the two guards appeared outside her glass wall. Neither smiled. Taylor, who had once been security at Berkeley, nodded at her. "Time to go."

Ariana swallowed. "Where am I going?"

The glass wall slid away as Taylor stepped in, a set of cuffs in his hands. "To see the docs. Don't cause any trouble."

Ariana just stared at him. Her, cause trouble? She hadn't complained. She hadn't fought them. She'd done everything they asked, and now he was talking as if she was the one causing problems. She shoved down her resentment and just held out her arms.

Taylor snapped the cuffs around them. "Good girl."

He gripped her by the arm and led her outside the cell. Two more guards stood waiting. One took the lead while the other one fell in on her other side, gripping her arm. The fourth took up position behind her.

She looked back at the other guard and then straight ahead. Four guards? Why on earth did they think she needed four guards? She looked over at Taylor. "What's going on?"

He didn't say anything, just pulled her forward.

Ariana felt a chill, then heat flashed over her.

You need to run. You need to fight.

The voice was urgent now. Something was wrong. Something was very wrong.

She tried to keep her breathing even, not letting the guards around her know that she was upset as she strained to see down the hallway to figure out what was coming. She could hear voices, and she realized it was two guards in the room that she had just passed. They were laughing at some TV show. She looked back at the door. How had she heard that? The door was closed. She started to shake, not sure if she was hearing things or truly going insane.

She wasn't sure what to hope for. Being insane might be preferable to accepting the reality of her current situation. Up ahead, she saw the medical suite. She strained to listen.

"... harvesting. Make sure everything is ready. The subject will be here shortly."

"How many dishes should I prepare?"

"Twenty. It's possible we could get at least fifteen eggs from her, maybe more," Dr. Thompson said.

They're going to harvest my eggs? Ariana slammed to a stop. Taylor, who held her arm, jerked back, nearly flying off his feet. The guard on the other side did the same. "What the—"

Ariana stepped back, shaking her head. "I'm not going in there. I'm not."

Taylor gripped her arm again to move her forward. He spoke through gritted teeth as he squeezed her arm. "Let's. Go."

The guy behind her stepped forward. Without thinking, Ariana shook herself loose from Taylor and backed up, her head hitting the chin of the guy behind her. He let out a scream and dropped to the ground, blood pouring from his mouth.

Ariana stared at him in shock. How had she—

Taylor lunged at her, his Taser in front of him. Pained arched through Ariana's body. Then more pain arched from the other side as the other guard used his Taser as well. Ariana dropped to her knees.

Taylor leaned down and looked into her face. "Freak," he said, more electricity shooting through her. The last thing she saw was his leering face before the punch that knocked her out.

CHAPTER FIFTY-EIGHT

GEIRANGER, NORWAY

Nora looked at Greg, worry, fear, and suspicion warring for dominance across her face. "You really think it's the same symbol?"

Greg had just explained to Nora about the symbol and what he had found. He also told her how he'd found the address of the boat owner.

"Yeah, it's the same symbol. I was going to go out there and just see what I could see. I mean, it may just be a wild goose chase. Maybe someone just thought it was cool and painted it on the back of the ship. It could be nothing. But I thought it might be worth checking out."

"I'm going with you."

Greg gave her a smile. "I was hoping you'd say that."

Adam had a storage bin of winter gear in the basement. They loaded up, and then they each filled a backpack with some food, a phone, extra thermals, and a few odds and ends. A few minutes later, they were standing in front of Sammy after having explained what they had found and asking whether or not he would be able to take them there. Sammy gave them a nod, and Greg let out a breath. He wasn't really sure if Sammy could manage it. "Okay. Well, we're ready. Nora?"

She glanced around. "Yeah, I left Iggy with Sandra and Luke. Hopefully they'll keep him busy, and he won't even notice that I've left."

Greg thought that was highly unlikely, but he figured if Nora was going for optimism, he'd give it a shot too.

"Okay, then." He stepped up to Sammy. "I'm ready."

Sammy didn't hesitate. He wrapped his arms around Greg and launched himself into the air. Even knowing what was going to happen, Greg's stomach rolled. He slammed his eyes shut and took shallow breaths. *Please don't let me throw up. Please don't let me throw up. Please don't let me throw up.*

He felt the same strange pulling sensation and then the sense of being hurtled at a high rate of speed through an enclosed area before the pop.

He kept his eyes closed this time, until he felt Sammy touch down. He wobbled for a minute and then sank down to the snow-covered ground. Sammy didn't wait. He darted back into the air and disappeared. Greg lay on the ground, then rolled onto his side, praying the light-headedness would go away. He didn't even try to sit up. He'd learned his lesson last time.

He heard another pop, and then Nora collapsed to the ground next to him. "Oh my God, that's awful," she groaned.

Sammy didn't wait around. He was gone as soon as he deposited Nora.

Greg didn't say anything in response, but he thought he might've groaned. A few minutes later, the light-headedness had passed. He gingerly sat up, ready to sit back down if his stomach started to roll. But happily, it stayed settled. He looked over at Nora, who sat up as well, her face abnormally pale.

"That was the worst thing that has ever happened to me," she said. "I think we should take a boat back."

"What? The boat ride alone would be about sixteen hours, and then about the same traveling by car."

"Worth it," she groaned as she got to her feet.

Greg did the same, and for the first time, he looked around. They were on the outskirts of the town, hidden away in the mountaintop. There weren't regular blocks. Each house seem to be propped up on its own little portion of the hill. The colors of the houses—reds, blues, and yellows—stood out against the snowy backdrop.

"Wow, this is really cute," Nora said.

Greg nodded his agreement. Even if they didn't find anything, at least they'd get to hang out in a cute little town for a few hours.

He pulled his phone out of his pocket and saw that it wasn't damaged by the trip. He'd call Maeve to let Sammy know that they needed to be picked up whenever they were ready. He slipped it back into his pocket. It was about lunchtime, but some of the lights were starting to come on in the homes closer to the top of the mountain. This close to the Arctic, the days were very short. "Well, shall we?"

Nora smiled. "I'm actually kind of looking forward to this now."

They both had just taken a step when a small boom from above caused them both to look up toward the sky.

Sammy reappeared, moving lightning fast for the ground. He touched down lightly, stopping at the very last second. The move made Greg cringe with the memory of Sammy doing the same to him. Sammy had his back to them so they couldn't see exactly what he was doing, and two seconds later, he took off back into the sky. Greg stared back to where Sammy had landed.

Smiling back at them was Iggy.

CHAPTER FIFTY-NINE

SVENTE, SVALBARD ISLAND, NORWAY

GREG STARTED TO BACK AWAY, SHAKING HIS HEAD. "No, no, no, no, no."

Iggy wasn't even slightly put off by the greeting. He vaulted over to them and leaped into Nora's arms. He quickly climbed up to her shoulder and rested his head on the top of hers, his arms curling around the side of her face. He gave a little sigh. "Ig."

Greg just stared at him in shock. This was not good. This was definitely not good. What the hell had Sammy been thinking bringing him here?

Greg looked at Nora, who stood with her mouth hanging open. He knew he had the same dumbstruck look on his own face.

"What are we supposed to do now?" Greg asked.

"I don't know. I'm not the one who brought him."

"Ig?" Iggy asked. His voice had a little tremor in it.

Nora reached out and patted his leg. "Of course I'm happy to see you, buddy. We just have to be stealthy. And it's kind of hard to sneak into town with, well, you."

He paused and then clambered down from Nora's shoulder, pulling her backpack off as he did.

"Hey," Nora said as she was spun around. Iggy ignored her and opened up the backpack, pulling out different materials. Then he dove into the backpack and peeked his head back out, a skullcap on his head. "Ig."

Greg could tell Nora was trying hard not to smile. "Yeah, I don't think that's going to do it, buddy. I think the, you know, green cast of your skin might suggest that you're not a human baby."

Iggy ducked down until he was all but lost inside the backpack. "Ig," came the muffled reply.

Greg looked over at Nora, who had given up the fight against smiling. "You're not actually going along with this, are you?"

Nora shrugged. "Look, he can stay hidden if he wants to."

"Yeah, but the question is, how long will he want to?"

Nora grabbed the stuff that Iggy had tossed out of the backpack and shoved it into Greg's. Then she carefully pulled her backpack onto her shoulders and tightened the straps. "I guess we're about to find out."

CHAPTER SIXTY

THIS IS INSANE, GREG THOUGHT AS HE, NORA, AND IGGY walked toward the town of Svente. Iggy was in Nora's backpack with just his little head popping out. His ears had worked their way free from the skullcap. He kept sticking out his tongue, trying to catch snowflakes.

Greg shook his head. There was zero chance this was going to work. Everyone in town was going to know that Iggy was with them. He was not exactly inconspicuous. He seemed to embrace life, which was a wonderful thing, but right now they needed someone who didn't get distracted by things like butterflies or snowflakes.

They were a few hundred yards away from the edge of town when Nora stopped. She looked back at Iggy. "Okay, buddy. You need to go quiet. Not a peep, understand?"

"Ig." He slowly lowered himself into the bag. Greg pressed the flap over him, not locking it because he didn't want to freak Iggy out.

Nora adjusted the straps and then nodded. "Okay. Let's go."

Greg shook his head but said nothing. In his mind, he tried to figure out how exactly they were going to be able to get out of town quickly once Iggy was discovered. The town looked pretty spread out. There were homes all over the place. This was not going to end well.

Nora and Greg walked the next ten minutes in silence, just observing as they made their way into the business area of the town. They passed about half a dozen homes. Most of them were set pretty far off from the road. They were simple houses with two windows in the front and small peaked roofs. They all looked like Cape Cods. And each one was either blue, red, or yellow.

It was a striking color combination against the snowy back-drop. Perhaps that was the point, to make sure that the homes could be seen. There was already three feet of snow down. He could imagine as they entered winter, it only got worse.

After another few minutes, they made their way to the center of town. Although "town" seemed a rather euphemistic label for this series of buildings. There was a large general store and a medical clinic that, according to the sign on the door, was only open one week a month. A bookstore/coffee shop/post office. And one small restaurant, which according to the large sign on the side of the building, served only breakfast and lunch, except for Wednesdays, when they also served dinner. Greg and Nora stopped across the street from it.

"I think we should check it out. But maybe we should leave Iggy somewhere while we go in," Greg said.

"Ig," Iggy protested from the bag. Greg gave Nora an exasper-ated look and raised his hands mouthing, *See?*

Nora nodded. "Iggy, you have to stay out here while we go inside."

They walked to the back of the restaurant and found a small shed. It was unlocked. Nora slipped off her backpack and placed it inside. "You need to stay quiet, Iggy, okay? We'll be back in just a little bit."

"Ig," came the muffled reply.

Greg took off his scarf and opened the backpack. He carefully wound it around Iggy's neck. "Just stay quiet, okay, little buddy?"

Iggy leaned his head into Greg's palm. He gave a soft little purr.

Greg smiled and then rubbed his head. "We'll be back soon." He stood, then carefully closed the shed door before they worked their way back to the front of the diner.

They passed the diner windows as they made their way to the front door. Greg tried to peer in, but it had iced over, making it impossible to detect much more than some dark-colored shapes. But hopefully that meant it was also difficult to see outside, and no one had noticed them wandering around to the back.

Nora reached for the door, and after a quick nod from Greg, she pulled it open and stepped inside.

The diner was actually a converted shipping container. It was extremely long and narrow. On one side of the container, windows had been cut out. Booths lined that wall. The other side was counters, and in the back was the kitchen. Everybody stopped what they were doing when Greg and Nora stepped in.

Greg looked around nervously. "Should we just sit anywhere?"

The guy behind the counter nodded at them. "Just grab whatever booth you want. I'll be over in a minute."

Greg and Nora took a booth near the kitchen in the back, where it thankfully was a little bit warmer. Nora slid into one side of the booth while Greg took the other. She grabbed two menus from the back of the booth and handed one of them to Greg. He scanned it, making his decision quickly. "Hey, they have Impossible burgers here."

Nora shook her head but didn't have a chance to say anything before the tall bald muscular guy behind the counter appeared at the edge of the table. He placed two coffee mugs on the table, and without even asking, began to fill them. "What can I get you two?"

"An Impossible burger and fries, please," Greg said. The man nodded and looked at Nora.

Nora nodded to the board by the front door. "I'll take the special."

"Sure thing." The man left the coffee pot on the table and headed back to the counter.

Greg took a sip of the coffee and gave a small wince. If this was an indication of the meal to come, he was not going to enjoy it.

Nora took a sip of hers and barely grimaced. "Heads-up," she said quietly.

Greg turned as three men from a booth by the front door walked toward them. They stopped at the edge of the table in a semicircle, boxing Nora and Greg in.

They each had ruddy complexions from a life spent outdoors. Two looked to be in their thirties while one had to be pushing sixty. Each wore a thick wool sweater and heavy wool pants. But they each wore a different color skullcap—red, yellow, and blue. For a moment, Greg wondered if they matched the color of their homes to their caps and how extensive the matching went. Did the yellow guy have only yellow furniture?

"So where did you two come in from?" Red Cap asked.

"Nowhere special. We're just passing through," Greg said.

"Funny thing is, there weren't any flights today. So how did you two get here?" Blue Cap asked.

Greg looked at Nora, who spoke with confidence. "We took snowmobiles. We came over from Daneborg. We're scientists with the U.S. Geological Survey. We're doing a survey of the area."

Blue Cap nodded. "I see. Did the storm the other day catch you guys off guard?"

"We haven't really had too much trouble," Nora said without blinking and, Greg noted, without truly answering.

Red Cap on the left grunted. "You planning on staying in Svente?"

Nora shrugged. "We're hoping to stock up on some supplies, have a few hot meals, and we'll head back out first thing in the morning."

"Well, safe travels, then," Yellow Cap said before nodding to the other two. They headed back to their table.

"That was definitely a 'you're not welcome in these parts' kind of conversation," Greg said dryly.

Nora nodded, her eyes narrowed. "Yeah, and they're keeping an eye on us too."

Greg started to turn.

"Don't look," Nora hissed. "Seriously, Greg."

He winced. "Sorry. I've never been very good at that 'people are looking at me and I shouldn't look back at them' thing."

Nora shook her head. "Let's eat, and then we'll take a tour of the town, and hopefully that coffee shop will be open. Then we can maybe see if there are any newspapers for the town or something that might tell us why that symbol was on that boat or who Dane is."

"Okay," Greg said, not feeling a lot of optimism that anything was going to come of this little search. If that was the welcome wagon, he didn't think they were going to have much luck with anybody else.

But really, what had he expected? They'd basically leaped at the chance to check out a symbol because it made Iggy excited. Talk about clutching at straws. This was going to be a complete waste of time.

The waiter returned, placing their plates on the table. "Ketchup's along the back," he said before heading back to the counter.

Greg loaded his burger with ketchup and took a bite. He nodded. They actually now made a pretty good facsimile of hamburger with plant protein. He supposed he shouldn't be too surprised. After all, decades ago they had figured out how to recreate an alien from DNA. A decent-tasting plant burger shouldn't be beyond the scope of human capability.

Greg glanced out the window, noting the sun was starting to dim outside. He ate a little faster, picturing Iggy in the shed. He wasn't sure if Iggy would be warm enough or not. He didn't seem to be bothered by any temperature fluctuations, but they couldn't count on it. And they also couldn't count on him not being discovered.

Across from him, Nora apparently had the same idea, because

she was practically finished with her meal. It only took them another five minutes to finish. Greg poured himself another cup of coffee and downed it before they headed to the counter to pay the bill. Two minutes later, they were out the door again. They'd been in the diner for all of twenty minutes.

On the street, a yellow pickup truck passed slowly, but it wasn't a cause for concern. With how snow-packed the street was, going fast was just a really bad idea.

Nevertheless, they waited until the truck was gone before they started to head around the side of the building. They got to the shed and opened it up. Nora reached down for the backpack and then stopped short. She stood up abruptly, looking around, her head swinging wildly.

"What's wrong?" Greg asked, even though in his heart he knew. He just really, really hoped he was wrong.

"Iggy. He's gone."

CHAPTER SIXTY-ONE

GREG STARED INTO THE BACKPACK IN DISBELIEF. HE PICKED IT up and rifled through it, thinking that if he just moved a couple of protein bars, he'd find Iggy hiding inside. Next to him, Nora scanned the area. "Dammit. The snow's too hard," she said softly.

Greg stared at the snow-covered ground. But she was right: the snow was packed too tightly to leave any tracks from Iggy. "What are we going to do?"

"We have to find him. We can't just let him wander around here."

"Nora, if he's found ..."

"I know. I *know*. But there aren't a lot of people in this place. There's a chance he won't be seen, or if he is seen, people will just assume he's some dog that they didn't get a good look at."

Greg knew that was probably true. At the same time, he couldn't imagine Iggy being mistaken for a dog or cat. And there wasn't a lot of wildlife around in this part of the world.

Nora strode toward the street. "We need to split up. I'll head south and you head north."

In Greg's head, he pictured the map of the area. North of them were a few warehouses, and then the Arctic Ocean. There was nothing else along the coast. He prayed that there was someplace for Iggy to hide. And that Iggy had the sense to hide when someone showed up.

He nodded. "Okay. If you don't find Iggy in an hour, we regroup at the coffee shop and then figure out where we need to go next."

Nora just gave him an abrupt nod and took a sharp left at the street, her head scanning back and forth for any sign of Iggy.

Greg watched her for a moment before heading north and scanning the area in the same way. *Iggy, I love you, but right now, I could kill you.*

————

There were two large warehouses on the dock of Svente. Greg hurried toward them, his face feeling frozen stiff. He'd been searching for thirty minutes and had seen no signs of Iggy.

His heart raced, and that was only partly from the cold. What if they couldn't find him? It wasn't like they could put out some sort of APB and get the locals in on the search. Plus, they were quite literally in the Arctic. Even with his crab walk, Iggy could cover a lot of ground pretty quickly. He wouldn't wander out of the city limits, though, would he? Greg couldn't imagine how they would find him if that were the case.

What the hell had he been thinking taking off like that? Greg never should have let Iggy come with them. As soon as Sammy had shown up with him, he should have called Maeve and had Sammy come back. They should have aborted the whole trip right then and there.

Besides, he didn't think they were going to find anything anyway. Obviously there were only a couple dozen people in town. The likelihood of them knowing anything about the symbol or it having any connection to Iggy was beyond slim.

This was a stupid decision. A couple of days left to live, and was he living it up on a beach somewhere with cocktails and a pretty girl? Nooo. He was bundled up in seven layers, trudging through the arctic cold, looking for a misbehaving alien. *Oh yeah, I know how to live.*

As angry as he was at Iggy, he was also awfully concerned. Iggy was, in many ways, like a child. And he really didn't have any malice in him, unless of course, you were trying to hurt somebody he cared about. So he could see Iggy walking up to someone in an offer of friendship.

And Greg knew that interaction could go very, very wrong.

Greg rubbed his hands together, feeling the cold slip through his gloves. Why would anyone live here? It was like living in an ice box.

Ahead, the lights were on in both of the warehouses. Greg hustled toward the first one and tried the door. He gave a small prayer of thanks when the handle moved under his grip. He slipped inside, quickly closing the door behind him. He leaned against the door, closing his eyes, and just let himself enjoy the warmth for a moment.

He opened his eyes and glanced around. The place was silent. There didn't seem to be anyone there. But lights were on, so Greg couldn't count on that being the case. He quietly moved along the aisle. The warehouse had four large rows of crates piled ten feet high.

He quietly walked down the first row, searching between the crates, on top of them, and in the rafters as he walked. But there was no movement.

The warehouse was quiet without a sound, and Greg was beginning to lose hope. Iggy wasn't exactly the quiet sort. But the lack of noise made him feel a little more confident that he was in fact truly alone. "Iggy?"

No response. He hurried down the row, checking all the nooks and crannies and calling softly for Iggy. But no little green head appeared.

He rounded the final corner, his hopes plummeting. He

thought that the lights in the warehouse might have drawn Iggy in. But this place was a loss as well. "Iggy?"

Movement at the end of the row pulled Greg's attention.

A man with white hair and a matching white beard stepped into view. "Can I help you?"

CHAPTER SIXTY-TWO

CAVE CREEK, ARIZONA

ARIANA'S EYES FLUTTERED OPEN. SHE STARED AT THE CEILING, recognizing it immediately. She had counted all of the ceiling tiles dozens of times. In her mind, she had rearranged them, making different shapes and patterns.

The right side of her face throbbed. She reached up a hand and then yanked it away with a hiss as she felt the swollen skin underneath her right eye.

Then it all came flooding back. The walk to the medical suite, hearing the doctor talk about harvesting, and then being attacked by the guards. She reached her hand down to her stomach, feeling hollow. *They took my eggs.*

Ariana had never really thought about having children. Right now it was all she could do to keep up with her work at school. The future wasn't really something she considered. In the back of her mind, though, she knew that one day she would have a family, husband, kids. She would be the kind of mom that her mom had been, and her husband would be the kind of dad her father could never be. That thought had been nestled away in the corner of her mind, like the finish line of a race. She just had to make it through school, and then she'd have the means to escape her father's control and live her life the way she wanted to.

God, I was so naïve. She knew now that he would never let her go. She was his, bought and paid for like some slave.

Her hand rested on her stomach, feeling the violation. What were they going to do with her eggs? Why would they even want them?

This was wrong in so many ways. She didn't understand any of this. Why was this happening to her? She'd been a good girl. Her whole life, she'd never made trouble. She'd done everything that had been expected of her. Mostly because she hoped that maybe, just maybe, her father might actually show her a little love.

That had been a wasted effort. He was never going to be a father to her. He was never going to love her. She was well and truly on her own.

Tears pressed against Ariana's eyes. Was this going to be her existence? Were they going to keep her in the cell forever? She knew in her gut that there was no way they would let her out.

And even if she did manage to get out and tell people, there was no guarantee that people would believe her. She thought of the Jamelske case in upstate New York. That man had held women captive in his dungeon basement for months at a time, but instead of killing them, he would set them free.

But when the women told people what had happened to them, no one believed them, not their family, and not the police. So Jamelske was able to continue grabbing girls off the street, and when the girls were released, they continued living in the nightmare because they were still on their own.

But Ariana knew she wasn't alone. Michelle would believe her. Michelle's family would believe her as well. They would help her.

As soon as the thought went through her mind, though, she knew she could never drag them into this. They had too much to lose. She would never be able to forgive herself if something happened to them.

She almost laughed out loud at the ridiculousness of her

thoughts. There was no need to worry about that. Because she knew down deep that she was not getting out of here. They were testing her. They were probing her. They wouldn't let the test subject go until the experiment was complete and successful. That could take years. And then, once the test was completed? Would they let her go then, or would they kill her to ensure no one knew what had happened to her?

Ariana rolled over to her side, curling her legs up into her chest. Was that her future? Would she be tested and probed for years, only to end up dead when she was of no more use to them?

Tears rolled down her cheeks, but she didn't wipe them away. As a child, she had always kept her tears hidden from her father. He viewed them as weakness. She'd seen the disgust in his eyes. But she didn't care who saw her tears now. She didn't care what they thought. And she needed to cry.

She lay there for she didn't know how long, feeling sorry for herself and powerless. Michelle always said you should let yourself wallow, at least for a little while. Denying your feelings did nothing but help them grow.

Sure enough, after a while, the tears were spent. And Ariana felt a little lighter. She'd needed the release. As she sat up, she noticed a stack of clothes carefully folded on the table next to her cot. With a start, she realized they were her clothes.

What were they playing at now?

She didn't know, but she wanted to feel her own clothes on her. She glanced up at the camera for a moment before ignoring it. Whoever was watching her had no doubt seen everything already. Nonetheless, she turned her back to the camera as she slipped off the paper slippers and pulled her jeans on beneath her hospital gown.

Just the feel of them brought her comfort. They made her feel slightly more in

control. She yanked off the hospital gown and finished dressing. She pulled on her boots, shoving her feet into them, and quickly tied them. She felt stronger with them on. The slippers that she had been wearing were little more than fabric, leaving her feeling vulnerable.

And she had no doubt that that was partly their intent.

She'd had a lifetime of people trying to make her feel vulnerable, so she could recognize the strategy when she saw it.

She frowned as she sat at the edge of her cot, staring down at her feet. This particular game she didn't understand. Why would they return her clothes to her?

The glass wall in front of her slid open. Ariana stood slowly, staring at it. There were no guards on the other side. The door to the hallway stood open. She frowned, trying to figure out what was going on, what new derivation of the game someone had thought up.

She waited for the guard to appear, but no one did. She took a cautious step forward, and then another. No one appeared. There were no sounds beyond the cell. She strained, listening for anything. In the distance, she could hear a few guards talking low. But it was coming from the medical suite area, not near the exit.

Her pulse raced in a combination of fear and hope. This was her chance. She paused at the edge of her cell, debating what to do. If she stepped out of this room, she knew for sure that she was going against the rules. There would be no coming back.

Following the rules hasn't gotten you anywhere, though, has it? It wasn't the voice she was hearing but her own mind mocking her.

She reached up and touched her swollen cheek. Following the rules had gotten her thrown in here.

Go, Ariana, run. This time she recognized the voice, and that small urging was all she needed.

She straightened her shoulders. She was getting out of here, or she was going to die trying, because this was not a life she was going to live. She hurried out of the cell, hugging the edge of the hallway. She peeked around the corner but didn't see anyone. Her heart pounded. A bead of sweat rolled down her back. *Now or never.*

She sprinted toward the exit the way she had come. Ahead, she could see the door leading to the stairwell. It was closed.

Dammit. She slid to a halt in front of it. The control panel next to it glowed red. She hadn't thought of that. She needed someone with authority to allow her out.

The light above the door flicked green a second before it opened toward her. Two guards stepped through.

Ariana hesitated for only a second before she grabbed one of the guards and flung him across the hall. She wasn't sure who was more shocked, the guard or herself, as he slammed into the wall and then crumpled to the floor.

The other guard advanced on her. She kicked him right between the legs. His knees bowed before he crashed to the ground, a look of extreme pain on his face.

Ariana sprinted through the open doorway and up the stairs. Adrenaline surged through her, which was the only reason she could think of why the twenty flights of stairs didn't turn her legs to jelly.

She reached the top of the stairwell in mere minutes, which she was sure was too fast, but she didn't take any time to think about that. She needed to move. The door at the top of the stairs didn't require a security code to open, at least from the inside.

She said a quick thanks and flung the door open, not bothering to look first. If anyone was coming, she had nowhere to hide anyway. She sprinted outside.

A wall of heat slammed into her. She ignored it and sprinted down the road. She scanned the area, looking for any sign of life. But they were in the middle of the desert. Immediately she imagined being stuck in the desert with no water and no shelter. It would be a death sentence.

But so is staying in that cell, the little voice inside her mind reminded her. She burst down the road as an alarm rang out behind her.

An SUV came into view down the dirt road, spitting gravel as it charged toward her.

She bolted off the road and across the uneven terrain. The SUV gave chase, the body of the car slamming up and down as it tried to take on the rutted landscape.

Ariana didn't slow. She just continued her sprint across the desert, praying that somehow, some way, she'd figure a way out of this.

CHAPTER SIXTY-THREE

SVENTE, SVALBARD ISLAND, NORWAY

GREG'S MIND WHIRLED AS HE TRIED TO REMEMBER WHAT NORA had told the men at the diner. "Um, hey. Um, hi. I'm Greg. I'm a geologist with the U.S. government."

The man raised a bushy white brow. "And you think there are rocks in my warehouse?"

Greg gave a small laugh. "Ha hha. No, no, of course not. My dog wandered off. And I was just looking for him."

"You brought a dog with you?"

"Technically it's my partner's dog. I told her it was a bad idea."

A small boy darted out from behind the crates and hid behind the legs of the man questioning Greg.

Greg stared at the little boy, watching him from behind Sven's legs. The boy looked like he was about three years old. He had big blue eyes and shockingly white-blond hair. His skin was incredibly pale, and there was a small tremor in his body that Greg assumed was from fear. Perhaps he wasn't used to strangers in his town. It didn't look like they got very many of them.

Greg gave the boy a small smile. "Hi there."

The boy gave a little squeak and ducked back behind the man. The man reached behind him and patted him gently on the head.

"Your son's cute. What's his name?"

The man shook his head. "He's not my son. But I'm looking after him this week."

Greg found that a strange choice of words. The boy peeked out at him again. His large eyes focused on Greg from behind the fringe of blond hair. The boy blinked, and for just a split second, his irises changed shape, elongating.

Greg sucked in a breath, his gaze going from the child up to the man. Behind him, he heard the unmistakable sound of a round being chambered.

Greg put up his hands, the hairs on his neck rising. "Hey, there's no reason for that."

The person behind him with the shotgun stepped into his field of vision. It was a tall woman who had brown hair worked into a thick braid. She kept her gun aimed at Greg as she spoke. "Yeah, I don't think that's true."

She blinked, and her irises elongated as well. Greg's mouth fell open. "Drago."

The woman stilled, and then her eyes narrowed. "Where'd you hear that name?"

Greg stared between the woman, the boy, and the man, trying to come up with an answer that did not end up with him getting shot. He couldn't think of any. He had never been very good with lying on demand, so he decided to go with the truth. "I've met Drago. A lot of them, in fact. I even met their queen."

The woman's grip tightened on her weapon. "You're an ally of the Drago?"

There was no emotion in the woman's question, yet Greg had a feeling that his answer was going to be very important not just to her but also to his future. He nodded slowly. "I wouldn't exactly call us allies. The queen took myself and some friends hostage."

The woman frowned. "Why would she do that?"

While Greg wasn't a good liar, he knew enough to realize he didn't want to reveal anything about Alvie or the triplets. So he gave them a half-truth, hoping they didn't probe too hard. "My friend and I are scientists with a special agency within the Department of Defense."

The man cut him off. "I thought you were a geologist."

Greg winced. "Um, no, sorry. That wasn't actually true."

"Then why are you here?" he demanded.

"Did the queen send you?" the woman asked. "Are you a spy for the Drago?"

"What? No, no. We definitely don't work for her or with her. It is safe to say we don't get along."

"You said you knew her."

Greg spoke quickly. "No, I said we were *kidnapped* by her. That was not voluntary, not by any stretch. We have a special knowledge of alien anatomy. The queen wanted us to help her create more hybrids." He looked at the woman in front of him. "More that look like you, human looking."

"And did you? Did you help her?" she asked.

Greg shook his head. "No. We were lucky. Some friends of ours rescued us, and we've been on the run ever since."

"Do you understand Drago anatomy?" the man cut in.

The man looked awfully tense, making Greg even more tense. "I, um, I understand it a little bit. My specialty was in a different branch of anatomy."

"What branch?" the man asked.

"Uh, well, I specialized in a different hybrid species."

"What species?" the woman asked.

"Um, I believe it was part Drago and part alligator."

Horror slashed across the woman's face. "Why on earth would someone do that?"

Greg shook his head. "I don't know. You'd have to ask the United States government."

The woman tightened her grip, pulling the rifle a little more snugly into her shoulder.

The man looked at her, speaking intently. "Sylvia, he's familiar with hybrid anatomy. We need him."

"We can't trust him. We've stayed safe this long because we haven't trusted anyone."

"If I could maybe just interject," Greg said. "I promise that I am very good at keeping secrets. Really, really good."

Sylvia raised an eyebrow with a scoff. "Really? Because you just told us that the United States government has been secretly creating alien hybrids."

Greg's mouth fell open. Holy crap, she was right. "Um, well, you see—"

The door behind him burst open, and the woman's rifle turned toward it. Nora rolled through the door, taking cover behind some crates, her weapon aimed at the woman. "Drop it."

The woman shook her head. "I wouldn't do that if I were you. You drop yours."

Nora scoffed. "Not sure you get how this works. You're out in the open. I have you dead to rights. You need to drop that. If you turn toward my friend, I will drop you."

A growl drifted down from the ceiling. Greg's head jerked up, and he saw movement in the corner, but he couldn't make it out in the dark. Then the movement clarified. Iggy swung into view, landing on the woman's rifle. He yanked it from her grip as he slipped away from her. The woman's mouth fell open. "Claude?"

Greg reared back. "Claude? Who the heck is—"

A second figure vaulted in from the left and leaped at Iggy. Iggy rolled out of the way, bouncing to his feet and then up on top of the crate.

He glared down at his mirror image, who was staring up at him with its teeth bared.

CHAPTER SIXTY-FOUR

CAVE CREEK, ARIZONA

ARIANA HAD NEVER RUN SO FAST IN HER LIFE. SHE BOLTED across the desert landscape, looking for an escape route. But there was nothing. It was just sand and scrub brush.

She glanced over her shoulder. Behind her, the SUV had turned off the road and was bouncing along the uneven terrain after her. It was only a few dozen yards away.

And closing fast.

Her heart was in her throat as she struggled to come up with something she could do. She was not going back to that cell. She *couldn't* go back to that cell.

That was a death sentence, as sure as standing up in front of a firing squad. She couldn't let them take her back there, no matter what. *Please, somebody help me. Please, somebody help me.*

But she held out little hope that her prayer would be answered. There was absolutely nothing around. She saw no telephone wires. There were no planes flying overhead. And she certainly didn't see a road ahead of her or any cars. And if she did, would she only put those people in danger by running to them?

She was pretty sure the men in the SUV were heavily armed.

And the men who had taken her back at the factory had shown no reservation at using force to take her. She didn't think an innocent family traveling through the desert would stand a chance against them.

She hadn't thought through this escape. But then again, there hadn't been time to. The cell had been open, and she'd bolted. She knew in her gut that this was the only chance she was going to get. A now-or-never moment. But right now, even though she was technically free for these couple of minutes, she knew they would catch her soon.

I won't let them take me back there. I'm not going to spend my life in a cell. They'll have to kill me.

The thought didn't shock her as much as it should have. Spending those days alone in the cell had convinced her that that was no life. She had no interaction beyond the guards taking her back and forth to the medical suite. Even when they delivered food, there was no conversation, no smiles, no interaction. She was essentially in solitary confinement.

And she knew enough about the research on solitary confinement to know that she would slowly start losing her mind within a short window. She was already thinking she could hear through walls and that a kind, benevolent spirit was speaking to her.

And she was *not* going to let that be her legacy.

Resolved, she straightened her spine and lengthened her stride. She would run as long as she could. She would make them tear after her across the desert. She would take the most difficult route possible and shake their SUV to dust.

Ahead, as if in answer to her plans, the terrain began to rise. She vaulted forward over a small bush and sprinted between some tall towering rocks.

She wound her way up, feeling a small sense of relief when she was hidden from view by the rocks. She knew it was only a temporary reprieve, but being these were probably her last few minutes alive, she would take whatever relief she could get.

She wound her way up and followed the small path that had

been created by some form of wildlife. She sprinted, her thigh muscles straining while her breaths came out in pants.

And then she slammed to a stop.

There was a fifty-foot drop in front of her. She stared down at it and gasped. *No, no. It can't end like this.*

Behind her, she could hear the SUV slam to a stop. Doors opened, and men shouted instructions to one another. They would be on her any minute.

Below her, she saw the remains of the hill. It was a tangle of rocks. She wasn't sure what had happened. Maybe a lightning strike or some sort of rockslide. But this part of the hill was gone. She couldn't climb down the cliff; it was sheer in long spots. Jumping down was certain death. She glanced over her shoulder, hearing the footfalls of her pursuers.

But waiting for them would be death as well. Ahead, a shape appeared in the sky. She squinted, trying to make it out. Large wings beat back the air. Hope sprouted in her chest.

Behind her, her pursuers came that much closer. Ariana looked at the shape racing toward her in the sky. She took a couple of steps back.

One of the men from the SUV appeared around the rock, his weapon trained on her. "Stay where you are!"

Ariana faced the creature as he soared closer. She closed her eyes for just a second. "Now," she breathed. Then she took off at a sprint and leaped off the side of the cliff.

"No!" the guard behind her yelled.

But Ariana was already airborne. She leaped out for what only felt like a second before she began to plunge down. She closed her eyes, her stomach in her throat, preparing herself for the pain about to come.

CHAPTER SIXTY-FIVE

SVENTE, NORWAY

IGGY'S SHOULDERS WERE HUNCHED UP, HIS GAZE LOCKED ON THE other Maldek. His teeth bared, a low growl came from his throat. The other Maldek's stance was no less aggressive.

Greg stared between the two of them in absolute shock. They were the same size, with the same pointy ears and shock of white hair on the very top of their heads. Both were green, although Iggy's green was more vibrant than the other, who had an almost chalky cast to his skin.

But his lobster-like claws looked just as deadly as Iggy's. "You ... you have a Maldek."

The woman looked equally shocked as she stared at Iggy. "How ..."

All of the adults stood staring at the two Maldeks, no one seeming able to form a complete sentence.

But the young boy behind the man didn't seem nearly as paralyzed. He darted around the man and in between the two Maldeks. He held up a hand to Claude. "No."

All the hackles along Claude's shoulders and back immediately dropped. He gave the young boy a bashful look and then stepped forward. The boy patted him on the head. "Good boy."

The boy turned and looked up at Iggy. Iggy tilted his head this way and that, getting a read on the boy before his hackles disappeared as well. Iggy leaped off the crate with a somersault, making the boy smile wider. Iggy leaned forward and rubbed his head against the boy's chest.

The boy giggled. "Good boy."

The woman looked between Greg and Nora, her eyes almost as large as Iggy's. "I think we need to talk."

CHAPTER SIXTY-SIX

CAVE CREEK, ARIZONA

ARIANA JOLTED AS TWO ARMS WRAPPED AROUND HER. HER CHEST heaved as she looked up into the face of the creature. It didn't look down at her but stared straight ahead as it swung its heavy wings away from the cliff face.

Gunfire burst out behind her. She winced, but it was too far away to reach them. The creature picked up speed. Ariana closed her eyes, tucking her head into its chest. She felt the strangest squeezing sensation before her ears popped and wind rushed against her face once again.

She opened her eyes. Her brain seemed to falter for a moment. She couldn't quite grasp what was in front of her. There were rolling green hills with little homes dotted among them.

The creature made a slow looping circle and then dropped gently to the ground. It released her. She stepped down, her feet firmly planted on the ground. The creature took a step back, making no move toward her.

Ariana stared up at him, taking in the strong contours of his face. She was convinced now that it was a male. It looked human except for the color of its skin, and of course those large leathery wings.

"Are you all right?"

Ariana's mouth fell open at the words from the creature's lips. "I-I think so."

He nodded. "I have been looking for you for a very long time."

Ariana took another step back. She knew she should be afraid, but for some reason logic wasn't dictating her actions. "What do you mean you've been looking for me?"

He just stared at her for a long minute. Ariana should've felt unnerved by his attention, and yet she didn't. She felt strangely comforted by it.

"Who are you?"

"I am called Sammy."

Sammy? It seemed such a normal name, a cute name for such an intimidating creature. "I-I'm Ariana."

He nodded.

"Why ... why did you save me?"

Even as she asked him, she wasn't sure that was what he had done. He might have taken her from the men following her, but was she safer here? The truth was, though, she felt no threat from him. She wasn't scared of him.

Part of her reeled at that realization. After all, his size, his appearance, everything about him, should have sent her running. And yet she wasn't running. She was waiting. She wanted an answer to her question.

"We are family, you and I."

Shock rippled through Ariana. At the same time, she recognized the truth in his words. They were connected somehow, the two of them. But on the other hand, her brain recoiled from his words. He was a monster.

So even though she felt his words to be true, she couldn't reconcile how that could be. She took another step back. "No, that's not possible."

He reached out a hand for her, and she cringed away from it.

Sammy's face went expressionless, but she caught the flash of sadness as his hand dropped. "We are. And you know it to be true."

He gave her one last look before he launched himself into the air. Ariana watched him go.

"You are, you know. Family."

Ariana whirled around at the voice.

The woman standing there didn't appear to be a threat. She was about five foot six with long brown hair pulled into a ponytail. She wore boots, jeans, and a dark-blue fleece. She looked normal, no threat.

But the man next to her, who was dressed similarly, had the build of a soldier, and the comfortable way he held the large gun in his hands reinforced that image.

The woman took a step forward, her hands up. "I'm sure you have a lot of questions. My name is Maeve. Perhaps I can answer some of them for you."

CHAPTER SIXTY-SEVEN

CAVE CREEK, ARIZONA

Martin sat at his desk watching his daughter's progress across the desert on the monitor. The entire area surrounding the base was completely under surveillance for five miles. Beyond that, he had electronic surveillance that indicated when cars were heading this way that would automatically notify his security forces.

Ariana ran across the desert amazingly fast. She'd been subsisting on a very low calorie diet. She should be weak from fatigue and drained of energy. Instead, she looked like she was trying out for the Olympics.

Martin grunted. Apparently she was her mother's daughter after all. He'd seen no sign of it in her upbringing. She had been horribly, uncomfortably normal. It seemed she was just a late bloomer.

She veered to the left and sprinted up over a hill between some towering rocks. He switched to drone footage and caught sight of her again only a few seconds later. She was nearing the top. He noted the rock fall that his security team had notified him of last week.

Now what will you do?

His security team reached the beginning of the path that she had taken and started up after her. She sprinted to the top and then came to a screeching halt at the cliff face.

He scanned the area around his daughter. Nothing. This was a waste. The security would have her in just a—

Martin leaned forward, noticing a dark object in the sky. He smiled. "It's about time."

The object moved closer. He switched the images to a split screen, watching his daughter's reaction as the abomination approached. She stared up at it, her mouth hanging open. Then she looked over her shoulder, backing up toward the security detail.

She was going to give herself up. Martin shook his head. Always such a disappointment.

But then she took off in a sprint and leaped from the edge of the cliff. The abomination swooped down and caught her as she began to plunge to the rocks below. Shock tremored through Martin.

Ariana had jumped off a cliff. She had never done anything even remotely that risky her entire life. *Well, well, you have some surprises up your sleeves after all, daughter.*

The abomination burst into the air with Ariana wrapped in his arms, then within moments, he disappeared.

Martin watched the empty space, a smile growing wider across his face. *I have surprises too, daughter.*

He grabbed his phone and immediately called Jack Sharp. He didn't bother with niceties as the man answered the phone. "Do you have him?"

"It's just coming online now. Hold."

Martin drummed his fingers on the desk, waiting for a response.

"Okay. Got the signal. Solid. It's coming from Norway. Geiranger, Norway to be specific."

"How long will it take you to get there?"

"I have the engine already idling. We'll be in the air in five minutes, and then it will take us approximately another ten hours to arrive. We'll have to stop in Greenland to refuel."

Martin nodded. "Excellent. Keep me updated."

"Will do."

Martin brought up the tracker he'd hidden in Ariana's boots on his computer monitor. It blinked away. He sat back, feeling a sense of contentment. Finally.

CHAPTER SIXTY-EIGHT

SVENTE, NORWAY

GREG SAT AT A SMALL WOODEN TABLE OUTSIDE AN OFFICE AT THE back of the warehouse next to a small kitchen area. The woman who introduced herself as Sylvia took a seat across from him. Nora sat next to him while the man, whose name was Richard, sat across from him.

The young boy, Sebastian, sat on the ground playing with Iggy and Claude. Nora could barely tear her eyes away from Claude. It was so strange to see another one of them. After some initial hesitation and that slight hint of violence, Claude and Iggy took to each other like ducks to water. Now they were clambering over crates together while Sebastian watched, clapping.

Sylvia indicated Iggy, who leaped from a crate up to the rafters and was swinging and giving one of his best uneven bars routines. "How did you end up with him?"

Nora smiled up at Iggy, who glanced down at her with a giant grin on his face. "He found me."

Nora explained about being part of the Department of Extraterrestrial and Alien Defense and being sent to retrieve Iggy. Then she recounted finding him and deciding he wasn't as dangerous as she had been led to believe. She gave a shortened version of how she ended up linking up with Maeve, Greg, and the rest, leaving out Alvie and the triplets like Greg had done.

Richard and Sylvia looked at each other and then at Greg. "Are there more Maldeks out there?"

Greg shook his head. "I can't say for sure, but I doubt it. Iggy's a pure breed, not one of the hybrids."

Nora nodded toward Claude, who Greg had noted moved a little slower than Iggy. "How did you find him?"

Richard smiled at Nora. "I didn't. He found me like Iggy found you. I was living in England at the time, right next to RAF Bentwaters. There was an incident on the base back in 1980—"

"The Rendelsham Forest incident," Greg said.

Richard nodded. "Yes. Strange lights appeared in the sky for a few days around Christmas. We all thought it was some sort of experimental aircraft that they were working on. I went out to my shed a few days later, looking for some ice salt for the driveway. And there was Claude, curled up asleep in the back of my shed. One of my sheepdogs was curled up with him. At first I thought maybe it was a dog with mange. But when Claude woke up, I knew that he was no dog."

"How come you didn't turn him in to the authorities?" Nora asked.

Richard shifted in his chair, placing his large hands on the table. "My initial thought, of course, was that I should do just that. But a snowstorm hit, and the roads were pretty ugly. I decided to wait until the storm passed. But once I got to know him, I couldn't see him being caged for the rest of his life. I'd been in the military for a long time. I knew what they would do to him once they got him."

"But then how did you end up here with ..." Greg's words failed him as he looked over at Sylvia.

"With someone like me?" Sylvia raised an eyebrow.

Greg nodded. "Yeah. You are Drago, aren't you?"

The woman shook her head. "Not pure Drago. My mother was human. My father was Drago."

Greg's mouth gaped. He knew he probably looked like a fish thrown on dry land, but he couldn't quite seem to close his mouth.

Nora looked at Greg and then Sylvia. "You mean you're not the result of an experiment?"

Sylvia clasped her hands in front of her on the table. "I don't know anything about that. My father, he lived in Svente since he was about Sebastian's age. He met my mother years later. And then they had me."

"Where is your father?" Greg asked, thinking about how Adam had been alive for hundreds of years.

Sylvia's mouth tightened. "It was a fishing accident. He was out with his crew when the weather turned. None of them made it back."

"I'm sorry," Nora said.

"So how did you end up here?" Greg asked Richard again.

"Dumb luck. After I decided to keep Claude, I knew I couldn't stay in England, especially not right next to a military base. So I started researching out-of-the-way locations where I could live. I stumbled over an old post about Svente, I don't even remember how. They talked about everyone keeping to themselves and also how they needed someone to help bring supplies in. My family's been in shipping for years. It seemed like a good place to hide out. I didn't learn that Claude wasn't the only unusual resident until I'd been here a few years."

Greg looked over his shoulder at Sebastian, who followed Iggy and Claude's exploits across the warehouse. "So Sebastian's your son?"

Richard shook his head. "No. We don't know who his parents are. He was found, just a few weeks ago."

"Just like my father was," Sylvia said.

"What do you mean?" Nora asked.

"When my father was younger, about Sebastian's age, he was found by some hunters in the snow and brought back here.

There've been legends about children being found in the ice for hundreds of years in the village. My father was the second child the town documented having retrieved from the snow. Sebastian's the third. He was found a month ago. We don't know anything about him. We don't even know where he came from. He's been living with different families as we try to figure out who exactly would be the best match for him, but there have been some complications. We haven't been able to take him to the doctor because, well, you know."

Greg studied the small boy. He was cute. He looked a lot like what he imagined Adam probably looked like as a child. "What are the complications?"

As if in answer to her question, the ball Sebastian was holding tumbled out of his hands. He stared straight ahead, and then his whole body began to shake.

Greg was out of his chair in a flash as the seizure took hold of the boy. Greg reached him before he fell back onto the hard concrete floor. He caught him in his arms, holding his head gently in his lap as he cradled him on the ground.

Sebastian shook and shook. But there was nothing Greg could do without medical supplies. A shot of benzodiazepines could help calm the seizures. He'd have to see if they had any in the medical office that he'd seen.

Greg looked at his watch, keeping track of the time. The seizure lasted a full two minutes, but it felt so much longer. When it was finally finished, all the adults let out a breath.

"That was longer than his last one." Sylvia crouched next to Greg and pushed Sebastian's hair back carefully.

"How often does he have these?" Nora asked.

"He's had three since he arrived. This one makes four." Richard stood by the table, wringing his hands, his brow furrowed with concern.

"Is there a place I can lay him down?" Greg asked.

It took Richard a moment to pull his gaze from Sebastian. He nodded, pointing to the office. "There's a couch in there."

Sylvia had the couch cleared off and stood waiting with a blanket as Greg laid the small boy down. Sylvia covered him with the blanket, pulling it up to his chin.

Greg stepped back, giving her room as Nora stepped up next to him. "Do you know what's causing that?"

He shook his head. This was way beyond his skill set. He and Maeve had done an autopsy on a Drago, but that was just basic anatomy they were looking at. It was a huge jump to go from that to understanding the cause of a seizure.

Greg knew that seizures were essentially the brain short-circuiting. In kids, seizures were sometimes a condition that children simply aged out of. But he also knew there were much more serious cases where the prognosis was much more dire. He needed help.

"No. We need to get Maeve and Adam. Now."

CHAPTER SIXTY-NINE

GEIRANGER, NORWAY

Maeve wasn't sure what exactly to say to the woman across from her. Ariana Mitchell looked like she was ready to bolt. Maeve couldn't exactly blame her. She had Chris move a little farther away to give them some room. She knew he was making her nervous.

Maeve kept her hands up as she stepped forward. "I know this is a lot to take in. But we really don't mean you any harm."

Ariana looked around, her eyes wild. "Where am I?"

Maeve winced, knowing that knowledge was not going to help calm the woman down. "You're in Geiranger, Norway."

Ariana's mouth fell open. "No, really, where am I?"

Maeve sighed. "You *are* actually in Norway. Greg showed up a few days ago the same way you did, and it took us all a while to accept that Sammy can travel that way."

Maeve frowned, studying Ariana. She looked frightened and bewildered but not sick. "How are you feeling, by the way?"

"Feeling? Confused, annoyed, I just ..." Ariana shook her head.

"But physically, are you okay?"

"Yeah, I'm fine, I guess."

Huh. So apparently she can handle the trip a lot better than Greg. Was that because she shared Sammy's DNA?

A shiver ran through Ariana. She was only wearing a lightweight T-shirt and jeans. She was not prepared for this weather.

"Look, I know you have no reason to trust me, but our cabin's not far from here, just a few hundred feet. Maybe we could head there and you could warm up?"

Ariana looked around. Maeve didn't think telling her there was no other cabin for miles would put her at ease. "Did you say Greg before?"

"Yeah, Sammy brought him back here after they lost you. Greg's been really torn up, worried about you."

"He has?"

Maeve nodded. Then she felt the presence at the back of her mind. *No, Alvie, don't*—

It was too late. Alvie and Snap stepped out of the trees with Sammy.

Ariana's jaw dropped, her eyes bulging. "Are they ... are they ..." She couldn't seem to finish her sentence.

Maeve took a breath. "The bigger one is Alvie, and the smaller one is Snap. They're part human."

"Like me," Sammy said. "And you."

"I'm not like them." Ariana took a step back.

"No, not exactly. They're part Gray. You, from what we can tell, are part Guardian. A different ..." Maeve stumbled over the word species, worried it would alienate the woman. "... type."

Surprise flashed across Ariana's face, and then she looked at Snap. "Did they just—"

"Yes, that's how they communicate."

Ariana nodded, casting another glance at Alvie and Snap. But it wasn't fear this time. It looked more like wonder. Maeve let out a breath. Maybe this would be all right after all.

CHAPTER SEVENTY

SVENTE, NORWAY

Greg stepped outside of the warehouse. The air chilled him almost immediately. It couldn't be more than twenty degrees.

He stamped his feet in place as he pulled out his phone. He tugged off one glove, holding it in his mouth as he dialed. Then he quickly placed the glove back on his hand and began to walk to try and keep his blood moving.

Come on, pick up. Pick up. He needed Maeve's input. Maybe more than that, he needed Adam's.

Maeve picked up on the other side of the call. "Hello?"

Greg forced cheerfulness into his voice. "Hey, Kathy. It's Jeff."

"Jeff, good to hear you. How are you doing?"

Before Greg had left, they agreed that they needed to take the extra precaution of not using their names if he had to make a call back, just in case Martin somehow tapped into their phone lines.

It was probably an unnecessary precaution, but nothing seemed off the table when it came to that man. For a moment, his chest clenched as he thought of Ariana. He wondered if she was safe. And he wished there was a way he could find out.

"How's the trip? Do you need to get back?" Maeve asked, consistent with their prearranged script.

"No," Greg said. "Actually I was thinking that maybe you and ..." He paused. They hadn't come up with a code name for Adam, so he had to hope Maeve figured it out. "I was hoping you and Andy could come here."

"Andy?"

"Yeah, believe it or not, I found some people who might be his cousins. And I thought it might be a good thing if they met."

Maeve was quiet for a long moment. "I really didn't want to leave the kids right now."

"Well, you know I wouldn't ask if I didn't think it was important. And I really, really think you should come. I could really use your help with something."

Maeve hesitated. "Okay. Well, let me just get my stuff together, and Andy and I will head on over."

Greg smiled. "Great. See you soon."

He disconnected the call. He reviewed it in his mind, looking for any sort of indication that he might have given away either his or Maeve's identity, but he didn't see any red flags. And he had to really hope that she understood he was talking about Adam. He supposed it was possible that she thought he was talking about Sammy. He really hoped she didn't show up with Sammy. He could imagine, even with a small town like this, what kind of a commotion Sammy just popping up in the middle of it would cause.

He walked quickly back to the warehouse and slipped in the door, shutting it firmly behind him. The heat made his skin tingle almost painfully. But he still closed his eyes, leaning against the door inside. It was so much better than out there.

He pushed himself off the door, and Richard looked up from the kitchen area. "Just brewed some coffee. Sylvia went to the medical clinic to grab some supplies the doctor suggested when she called him about Sebastian's seizures. Any luck reaching your friends?"

Greg nodded. "Yes. Although I'm not sure how long it will take them to get here."

Richard looked back toward the door. "Well, we're pretty isolated out here. And the next flight's not due till morning."

"Yeah, uh, my people will, um ... Well, we have a different, more efficient way of traveling."

Richard tilted his head. "Is that so?"

Greg just nodded and then ducked into the office.

Nora looked up from where she sat next to Sebastian's bed. Claude was curled up at Sebastian's feet while Iggy sat in Nora's lap. "Any problems?"

Greg pushed away from the door, keeping his voice low. "I don't think so. But being I couldn't say Adam's name, I kind of have to hope that she knows who I was talking about."

"I'm sure she will. She's pretty smart."

Greg nodded toward Sebastian. "How's he doing?"

Nora glanced at Claude, who kept a watchful eye on him. "He hasn't regained consciousness. Is that normal for a seizure?"

"It can be. It might take his brain a bit to reset. A seizure is essentially a burst of abnormal electric activity in the brain. The brain basically shuts down all but basic functions as the body locks up."

Nora shuddered. "He's had one every week since he arrived. That can't be good for a growing boy."

"It's not," Greg said, his voice grave.

"What happens if you and Maeve can't figure out how to stop the seizures?"

Greg looked at the small boy. "It's possible he could live his life just having them once a week, and it'll just be his existence. It's also possible that they'll increase in frequency. And if that happens ..." He shook his head. "Well, let's just hope that doesn't happen."

CHAPTER SEVENTY-ONE

MAEVE FELT LIKE SHE WAS BEING SQUEEZED THROUGH A VISE. IT only lasted for a few seconds, but it was an awful feeling. Cold air stung her cheeks, which told her she had arrived. But she kept her eyes shut, heeding Greg's advice.

Sammy touched down gently, so gently that Maeve hadn't even realized they had stopped. He lowered her to the ground. "We are here."

Maeve cracked her eyes open, waiting for the overwhelming sensation that had enveloped Greg when he had first gone through.

But she didn't feel that bad. She was a little light-headed and held on to Sammy until she felt like her legs could maintain her weight, but other than that, she felt fine. She released him and took a tentative step. "I'm good, I think."

Sammy looked around, not making any move to go until he saw Adam step out of the trees. Sammy had brought him over before he had taken Maeve. At Adam's nod, Sammy looked down at Maeve. "I will go back to Norway. But I will check in on you in an hour. If there are no problems, I will return again. But call Chris if you need me to come get you sooner."

Maeve looked up at the strange man. She reached out and squeezed his forearm. "Thank you, Sammy."

Surprise floated across his face, and he reached over and patted her hand on his arm before he launched himself into the sky. Maeve watched him go until he disappeared. He was truly amazing.

She tore her gaze away and turned to Adam, another amazing man. Although, she guessed technically neither of them really fit that category.

Adam walked toward her and then nodded toward the path. "The town is that way. I took a quick look, and everything appears quiet. There don't seem to be any out-of-towners here except for Greg and Nora. And Iggy."

Maeve nodded. "Then lead the way."

Adam turned on his heel and headed into the woods.

Maeve stayed right behind him, following in his tracks. Adam hadn't said much since they'd arrived in Norway. It must be surreal to be back at the home his family had taken him to hundreds of years earlier. She couldn't even imagine all the things he must've seen in that time.

But she still got a sense of loneliness from Adam. She'd never felt that when she had been with him at other times. That, of course, had been because Tilda had been around. He truly loved her. And he wasn't fully himself when she wasn't with him.

She felt guilty keeping him with them, although it wasn't actually her decision. He'd made the choice himself. She still felt as if she should encourage him to go back to Tilda. It was obvious that he missed her terribly. But she was selfish enough not to say anything. If Martin found them, if anyone found them, they'd need Adam. And she simply couldn't risk it.

"It's just up ahead."

Maeve's head jerked up, and she looked through the trees, spying a small little town. It looked like what she imagined an Alaskan town would look like. Covered in snow with not much decoration.

Serviceable. The word that came to mind was serviceable. It looked like the town functioned for what it was. It provided supplies to help keep people alive, but there was no extra decoration or ornamentation to the place.

"Do you know where they are?"

Adam nodded. "Yes."

She didn't question how he knew. She didn't really understand much about the Drago. She understood their anatomy, although Adam's was somewhat different than the reptilian version. She did wonder at what Greg had said about there being a cousin here. Was it another Drago?

Greg hadn't sounded concerned or scared, so what exactly had he and Nora stumbled on?

Maeve followed Adam as he led her along the back of the town, past the shops to a small warehouse that sat on the edge near the water. On either side, there were no lights, no signs of any civilization. Just lots and lots of open ground covered in snow. A light wind came in over the water, dropping the temperature another ten degrees. Maeve shivered in response, despite the warm clothing she wore.

"Wait here," Adam said to Maeve. Shifting from foot to foot to keep warm, she stayed where he left her, trusting him to check if it was safe. He disappeared around the side of the building and then reappeared a few minutes later. "All good."

Maeve nodded, heading for the door at the back of the warehouse. It opened before either she or Adam could knock. Nora stood highlighted in the doorway. She gave them a smile. "That was fast."

"Thanks to Adam's storage of winter gear, we were able to get situated pretty quickly."

Adam took the door from Nora and allowed the two women to step in first before he followed. He pulled the door tight behind him. Standing at the door, he scanned the warehouse.

A tall brunette woman appeared from a small office that seemed to be tucked in the back of the warehouse. She and Adam stared at one another for an interminable amount of time before she nodded. "This way."

Maeve looked between Adam and the woman. The woman appeared human, but then so too did Adam. She followed Nora back to the office, and as the woman disappeared inside, she followed.

Greg bounded up from his spot by a couch where he'd been taking a pulse. Relief flooded his features. "Thank God. This is Sebastian."

Maeve moved quickly to the couch, inhaling sharply at the sight of the small pale boy. She glanced for only a moment at Iggy, who lay curled up next to him.

Nora stepped over to the desk, and Iggy climbed onto her shoulders. Maeve's gaze shot back to "Iggy" on the couch again. Her mouth fell open, and she jerked her head toward Greg. "That's not Iggy."

Greg nodded. "There's a lot we need to tell you. This is Claude."

Maeve didn't know what to say. There were *two* Maldeks. Claude appeared to be much older than Iggy, and he seemed to be awfully attached to the young boy who looked way too small tucked under a thick gray blanket on the couch. Maeve knelt down. She felt the boy's neck, feeling a steady pulse that was a little on the fast side, much like the Drago's heart rate.

"He's been having seizures every week for the last month," Greg said.

Sylvia nodded. "Yes. He's usually awake by now, though."

Maeve turned to Adam, who stood as if frozen in the doorway. "Adam, have you heard of anything like this? Some sort of seizures among the Drago?"

Adam slowly pulled his gaze from the boy. The two of them look so much alike. It was uncanny. "Looks like Adam's got his own little mini me," Greg mumbled next to her.

Maeve nodded her agreement. She looked back at Adam, who still hadn't answered her. "Adam?"

Adam tore his gaze away from the young boy. "I don't ... it was so long ago. I remember them saying something about an illness. But I don't remember anything more than that. I was only about four when I was last with the Drago."

Sylvia started, staring at Adam. "Are you one of them?"

Adam nodded slowly. "Yes."

Sylvia paled noticeably. "I ... I had heard that they looked fully human, but I didn't believe it. I mean, I look fully human, but I'm only part Drago, and my dad, he did too. But in my mind, from the way he described them, I thought he was really rare. Are you saying that Sebastian's *fully* Drago?"

Adam nodded, looking back at the bed. His voice was soft as he answered. "Yes. And he's my nephew."

CHAPTER SEVENTY-TWO

GREG STARED BETWEEN ADAM AND SEBASTIAN. THEY REALLY did look like they could be father and son. "Are you sure?"

Adam nodded, his gaze on the boy while he stayed firmly in the doorway. "Yes, he is Tatiana's son."

Maeve's mouth fell open. "How do you know that?"

"I just do. It's a sense, an understanding."

Sylvia cleared her throat. "I think I have a little bit of that. I can feel my children, wherever they are. I just know."

Maeve looked at Adam. "But he's not your son."

"No, but Tatiana was my sister. I can feel the connection with him." Adam's words spoke about connection, but physically Adam looked like he would need to be pried from the doorway to bring him closer to the boy.

No one said anything for a long moment. Claude was the one who broke the silence. He picked up his head, his gaze on Sebastian's face. "Ig?"

Sebastian's eyes flickered open. Maeve was still kneeling by the bed. She smiled. "Hi, Sebastian. I'm Maeve," she said softly.

Sebastian looked up at her, and then his eyes scanned the group until his gaze found Adam. He pulled his little hand from under the blanket and stretched it toward Adam.

CHAPTER SEVENTY-THREE

GREG HAD SEEN ADAM FACE DOWN KILLER ALIEN HYBRIDS, machine-gun-toting humans, and never once had he looked scared.

Right now, though, he looked downright terrified.

Adam's eyes grew wide, and he looked like he was going to bolt. Nora walked over to him and nudged his arm. "Go on."

Adam took a short step and then another. Sebastian held out his hand the entire time.

Maeve moved out of the way, and Adam took his place. He cautiously placed his hand around Sebastian's. Sebastian closed his eyes again, a smile on his face.

Maeve nudged her head toward the doorway. Nora and Greg followed.

"Wow," Greg said. "I can't believe that happened. Man, I've never seen Adam look scared."

"It's a whole new world for him," Nora said.

"Speaking of whole new worlds, we had a visitor. Sammy brought Ariana back."

Greg's heart rate spiked. "Ariana? Is she okay?"

"She's … adjusting. I spoke with her for a little bit and I'm not sure what was done to her, but it's left her a little haunted."

Greg's stomach dropped. "I should have done more. I should have found her. I should have—"

Nora linked her arm through his. "Hey, stop that. You didn't know any of this would happen. And if Sammy couldn't protect her or find her, then there's nothing you could have done."

"But I agreed to grabbing her. If I hadn't—"

Nora cut him off. "She still would have had Martin for a father."

Maeve nodded. "Whatever Martin did to her was always part of the plan. Grabbing her may have sped up the timetable, but it didn't cause this. Don't take on that blame. Place it where it belongs: with Martin."

Greg knew they were both right, but he still felt so guilty. "I-I need to get back."

"Call Chris. Sammy will come for you."

Greg pulled out his phone and looked back at the office. "What about Sebastian?"

"I'm going to take some blood. We'll see if Sammy can get us to a lab. If not, I'll have to have it sent somewhere for testing."

"There's a med clinic in town. They probably left some equipment," Nora said.

"I'll check there first."

"You have an idea, don't you?" Greg asked.

Maeve nodded. "More like a hope. But if it pans out, then Sebastian should be fine."

"I hate that I'm pulling you away from Alvie and Snap," Greg said.

"It's okay. This is important too. I'll get the samples and then head back as well. Maybe you could have Sammy come back for me in about thirty minutes?"

Greg nodded. "Okay."

"And Iggy and I will stay for a while," said Nora. "Plus, I think it's a good idea if Adam stays. I think Sebastian might be good for him."

Maeve looked back toward the office. "Yeah, I agree. Now go."

Greg didn't waste any time. He sprinted for the door. Ariana was back.

CHAPTER SEVENTY-FOUR

WASHINGTON, D.C.

THE R.I.S.E. WING OF THE PENTAGON WAS A BUZZ OF ACTIVITY. Tilda had seen the concerned looks from other branches of the military that had passed, but as of right now, she was keeping the search on a need-to-know basis. The last thing she needed was someone who Martin knew keying him in.

Although being she had found no sign of him in Seattle, she had a feeling that cat was already out of the bag.

She walked out of the control center trying to keep the fear from her face.

They had only a few days left. She had marshaled all the resources of R.I.S.E. and scavenged some from other branches of the U.S. military and intelligence agencies to search all of Martin's safe houses, all his haunts, and all his homes. She had people investigating all of them. But they were extensive. The operations were taking time.

As Tilda made her way down the hall, people scurried past her, all of them giving her a wide berth as she walked. She had always known that Martin was a dangerous man. She'd always known that he was someone who needed to be contained. Yet even she had never imagined that he would be the reason for the destruction of the human race. *God damn you, Martin.*

Years ago, she had contemplated taking him out. He had caused the death of six of her team members and had interfered in another dozen R.I.S.E. operations. The goal of R.I.S.E. was to enhance and protect the inhabitants of Earth. She worried that if they went down the road toward assassination, even for someone like Martin, that it would be a very slippery slope. So she had held off.

Now that restraint was coming back to bite her. *I should've killed him.*

All of it, the Drago rising up, the Area 51 debacle, and now the ultimatum from the Council, would all have been avoided had she taken him out decades ago. Her foolish need to protect the inhabitants of this planet had unwisely extended to Martin. And she should not have let that be the case.

She stepped into her office. Pearl sat behind her desk and started to stand. Tilda waved her back down and took a seat on the couch. "No, no. Stay. What do you have?"

"Nothing good. Our teams have checked twenty-six of his locations. Four of them were completely empty. The other twenty-two had a skeleton staff. They all claim not to know where Martin is."

"Wonderful. What have we got on deck?"

"There're another twenty-three sites that are in the process of being searched as we speak. Some of them are CIA sites that are used jointly with other agents, but Martin has used them in the past."

Tilda rubbed her brow. God, this was getting messy. Now they were overlapping with other agencies. People were going to get hurt. People who were not the target of this manhunt. There was no avoiding it. She didn't know who she could trust in the CIA. And they needed to find Martin.

Even as she thought it, she knew that this was like looking for a needle in a haystack. That bastard. He had literally brought them to the brink of destruction, and now he was hiding away like some sewer rat.

Martin, whenever we find you, I hope that your death is slow and painful, she thought. But what she said was, "Okay. Expand the search. I want all CIA locations under surveillance. Anybody who ever talked to him, I want them under surveillance. Finding him is priority one."

"We'll need additional resources for that."

Tilda nodded. "I've got them."

Pearl grabbed her tablet and headed out of the office, closing the door behind her.

Tilda closed her eyes and leaned her head back on the couch. The Joint Chiefs had already okayed a huge influx of resources. Tilda once again had the resources of the U.S. government at her fingertips. And even with that, she knew that they would have to be very lucky to find Martin in time.

Please let us be lucky.

A knock on the door pulled her attention. "Come in," she said, even though she wanted to tell whoever it was to get lost.

A familiar face stepped through the door. Hope stood up from her dog bed and hurried over, her tail wagging like mad. Jasper knelt down with a smile and rubbed her behind the ears. "How you doing, girl?" His smile dropped as he looked up at Tilda. "We have a problem."

"Just one?"

This time Jasper offered her half a smile. "Well, just one more that I know of."

Tilda steeled herself. "Okay. What is it?"

"Martin Drummond has found himself an army."

CHAPTER SEVENTY-FIVE

GEIRANGER, NORWAY

Last night, Greg had hurried back, leaving Maeve, who was trying to spend her last few days with Snap and Alvie. And when he'd gotten here, Ariana had been asleep.

He'd had Sammy take him back to Maeve. She'd been wrapping up, but she had been right about Sebastian's condition. She'd left instructions with Sylvia and Adam, and then the two of them had left.

When they returned, Maeve had immediately gone to check on Alvie and Snap. He'd heard the opening refrain of *Frozen* a few minutes later and knew Maeve was in for the night.

Greg still wanted to see Ariana, so he'd waited up on the couch for as long as he could before he fell asleep as well. A rustling in the hall woke him, and he shot up from the couch. "What? Huh?"

Ariana jumped back from where she stood at the edge of the kitchen. Her gaze caught his, and she frowned. "Greg?"

"Hey, uh, hi." He wiped his mouth, hoping he hadn't been drooling.

"Um, I'm sorry I woke you. I was just going to make myself some coffee."

"No, no problem." Greg wrestled with his blanket, finally freeing his feet. He pulled on his boots. "I was just about to get up too."

Ariana raised an eyebrow but didn't say anything else. Greg felt his cheeks flame. *Smooth, Greg, really smooth.*

Ariana filled the coffeepot with water while Greg got out the coffee grounds and filter. "Sorry, no Keurig. Adam's kind of old school."

"I haven't met him."

"No, he's, um, visiting family."

Neither of them spoke as the coffee slowly brewed. Greg scrambled for something to say, but his mind was blank. Finally, he just grabbed some bagels from the freezer and popped them in the microwave. When it beeped, he asked, "Uh, cream cheese?"

"Butter, if you have it."

He nodded, pulling it from the fridge. He loaded up both bagels while Ariana poured coffee into two mugs.

"How about if we eat outside? Just so we don't wake anyone else up."

Greg grabbed them both thick jackets, and Ariana followed him outside. He headed to the Adirondack chairs, hoping the view might put her at ease.

For a few minutes, they both just sat and ate quietly. Finally, Ariana broke the silence. "It's really beautiful here."

"Yeah, it's hard to believe there's any evil in the world when you look at this," Greg said, then winced. *Stupid word choice, Greg.*

"But there is," Ariana said softly.

"I'm sorry," he said in a rush. "I'm so sorry. I never should have let you get pulled into all of this. I just—"

Ariana shook her head. "It's not your fault. You didn't pull me into this. My father did."

Greg studied her, seeing the downturn in her mouth and the haunted look in her eyes. "Do you want to talk about it? About what happened?"

Ariana shook her head and then stopped. "Yeah, actually, I think I do."

————

Greg and Ariana spoke for the next two hours. She told him all about what she had gone through, and anger boiled up inside of Greg. Then she asked how he had ended up with Maeve, Alvie, and Snap. So he'd explained about all of them and what they had been through. He tried to keep Martin out of his explanation, but he must not have done a very good job because when he finished, she said, "My father's a really horrible man, isn't he?"

Greg opened his mouth to answer when the barn door slid open. Sammy stepped out, his face turned to the sun before he walked over toward them.

Ariana put her mug down and stood up. Greg quickly did the same, not wanting the two of them towering over him.

"How did you sleep?" Sammy asked.

"Good, um, good," Ariana said. "Thanks."

Sammy nodded and seemed content to simply stare at her.

Maeve stepped out from the house. "Oh, good, you're up."

Greg glanced over with a frown. "What are you doing up so early?"

"I wanted to go check on Sebastian before the kids woke up. But, of course, they're already up, so that didn't work. But I'm just going to go quickly and see how he's doing."

"I could go," Greg said quickly.

"I was hoping you might go back and check on him this afternoon."

"Sure, no problem. Whatever you need."

"Thanks." Maeve smiled at Ariana. "My gang's helping make eggs and pancakes. They should be ready in about twenty minutes, if you're hungry."

"Uh, thanks. That, um, sounds good," Ariana said.

Maeve looked at Sammy. "Are you ready?"

He nodded and opened his arms. Maeve stepped into them. In a blink, they were in the air, and then they were gone.

Ariana stared up at where they had been. "That ... She trusts him?"

Greg nodded. "Yeah, we all do. I mean, it was kind of a slow road to get there, but it was how he looked that was the big stumbling block. If we looked just at his actions, it became a lot easier."

Ariana took a seat. "Could you tell me about him?"

Greg sat back down as well. "I'd be happy to."

CHAPTER SEVENTY-SIX

SVENTE, NORWAY

IT HAD BEEN AN UNUSUAL TWENTY-FOUR HOURS. MAEVE HAD managed to get into the medical clinic in Svente. There was enough equipment for the tests she needed. And luckily, it was a relatively easy fix. Sebastian had a protein deficiency. In humans, protein deficiency was also linked to seizures. So as long as they increased his protein intake enough, Sebastian's seizures should stop.

She'd left after the discovery, with Sylvia promising to get protein into him at every meal. Adam had elected to stay behind. Now as she walked toward the warehouse after Sammy had dropped her off, she was wondering how he was doing. He'd seemed a little lost last night, but at the same time, she and everyone else could see the connection between him and Sebastian.

Of course, if they didn't find the Guardian, it didn't matter how protective Adam was of the boy. He wouldn't be able to save them. They still didn't know if Tilda had had any luck tracking the Guardian down. Maeve had to think that if they had, Tilda would have reached out to them. In this case, no news was definitely not good news.

Now she was hoping she could check in on Sebastian and get back quickly. Sammy was waiting behind the warehouse for her. She didn't like being away from Chris and the kids, especially not if these were their last few days together.

Richard opened the warehouse door before Maeve knocked. She smiled at the man. "Morning."

He smiled. "Morning to you."

Maeve stepped past him into the welcoming warmth of the warehouse. "How's Sebastian?"

"He had a good night. He played a little with Claude this morning, which he normally doesn't do so soon after a seizure. He ate well both last night and this morning. Your friend hasn't left his side. They seemed to have taken to one another. He was putting him down for a nap." Richard nodded his head toward the back of the warehouse. "I'm happy to see the boy finding his place. We all need our place."

Claude galloped down the path between the boxes. "Ig."

Richard sighed. "Yes, yes, I know." Richard looked at Maeve. "I promised Claude a trip to the coffee shop. He's a little stubborn when things have been promised to him."

"Iggy's the same way."

"Will you be all right for a little while?"

"I'm sure we'll be fine. I'm just here for a quick visit anyway."

Richard tilted his head. "None of you have explained exactly how you're appearing and disappearing so quickly."

Maeve glanced down at Claude. "Well, I think that's maybe a story for a different time."

"Fair enough. Will I see you again later?"

Maeve swallowed, guilt weighing her down. Should she tell the man about the looming danger? Would it help to know, or was ignorance bliss at this moment in time? She shook her head. "No, if everything goes all right, Greg will come by later and check on him."

Richard extended his hand. "Thank you for all you're doing for Sebastian. I hope to see you soon."

"I hope so too."

Richard and Claude slipped out the door, barely letting any cold air in.

Maeve unwrapped her scarf as she moved through the pallets of goods and toward the office at the back. The scent of coffee was in the air. Maeve was tempted to pour herself a mug, but first she wanted to see how Sebastian was doing.

She stepped into the office. Adam sat next to the bed, reading Sebastian a book about three little ducklings. Maeve smiled at the sight. One of Adam's hands was wrapped in the boy's, and he struggled to turn the pages one handed. But he did not let go of the boy's hand.

Maeve didn't interrupt, just waited until Adam was finished. Sebastian's eyes were closed, and his breaths were moving softly in and out.

Maeve moved from her perch, and Adam turned around.

"Hey," she said softly as she leaned down to check on the boy. His pulse was within normal ranges, and more importantly his color was up. She nodded at Adam. "He's asleep."

Adam didn't release his hand right away. He stayed there, looking uncertain. Maeve waited, and eventually Adam released the little boy's hand. He stared down at the young child, a look of confusion on his face.

"Are you all right?" Maeve asked.

Adam shook his head. "I don't understand any of this."

"Understand what?"

"Why would he want me?"

Maeve smiled, pulling the blankets up to Sebastian's chin and then smoothing them down. "Why wouldn't he?"

"Because I'm one of them."

"Perhaps it makes him feel more comfortable."

"But he would be better off with a human family. He would be better off with people who could teach him how to love and exist in this world."

Maeve stood up, studying the man in front of her. He looked completely bewildered as to why Sebastian would find comfort in his presence. But Maeve wasn't. There was a strength in Adam that made you feel safe. Her children felt it, even the adults felt it. She wasn't a bit surprised that Sebastian felt it too.

"Adam, you have one of the biggest hearts of anyone I know."

Shock splashed across Adam's face. "But I'm..."

"What? A Drago? What you are doesn't determine who you are. You've demonstrated who you are over and over again. You've risked your life, your happiness to protect us. And you have an instinctive grasp of what children in particular need. You have demonstrated that time and again. So no, I'm not surprised that Sebastian is drawn to you. I would be surprised if he wasn't."

"I can't take care of him. I wouldn't be a good—" He cut himself off, struggling to even say the word.

"What, a father? Well, I know a little something about becoming a parent in a nontraditional way. It's definitely an adjustment. But some things are just meant to be. I was meant to be a mom to Pop, Crackle, and Snap." Her heart ached at the mention of Pop and Crackle, but she shoved it aside for the moment. "And maybe, just maybe, you were meant to play a larger role in this little boy's life."

"I don't know how to do that. And I don't know if we have the time to ..."

Maeve nodded. "You might not. But you can stay by his side to the end. So that he knows he's not alone."

"I don't know how to do that."

"Yes, you do. It sounds like your family was pretty amazing. Just do what they did."

"They tried to kill me."

"No. The Drago weren't your family. Family are not always the ones that bring you into this world. Family are the ones who love you, who want what's best for you, and who show you how to get by in this world. And your family seems to have done a pretty amazing job."

Adam stared at her and then Sebastian. And Maeve noted a small little emotion she didn't think she'd ever seen on Adam's face before: hope.

She smiled. "Well, it looks like everything is going well here. I need to get back. Sebastian's going to be all right. Later, when he wakes up and Greg's here, we'll get some more samples and check his levels. But I think we're on the right track. Are you going to stay for a while?"

Adam nodded. "Yes. Unless you need me back ..."

Maeve cut him off. "No, we're okay for now. Stay. He needs you."

Adam glanced down at the little boy and nodded before looking back at Maeve. "Okay. I'll see you soon."

Maeve patted him on the shoulder as she left. But she couldn't help but stop in the doorway and watch as Adam sat next to the bed. This time he was the one who took Sebastian's hand.

She smiled. Adam needed this. He'd been a soldier for too long. He needed to play a different role. And it looked like Sebastian had decided that role was going to be father.

Maeve grabbed her coat from on top of the crates and wrapped her scarf back around her neck.

Sammy said he would keep watch from the back of the warehouse for when Maeve was ready. She stepped outside after making sure no one was around. She headed for the woods without seeing anyone and then slipped inside. She'd only been walking for a few seconds when Sammy appeared. He dropped silently to the ground twenty feet to her left. Maeve gasped, her heart tripping over itself in fright. "Maybe a little warning next time."

He smiled. "Sorry."

Maeve raised an eyebrow. "You did that on purpose."

Sammy shrugged. Maeve laughed out loud at the gesture. It looked so human. Maybe they were all rubbing off on him. Maybe he was simply less stressed knowing that she was near. "How's Ariana?"

"Better. She seems connected to Greg. He puts her at ease."

"He does have a tendency to do that. It's difficult not to be disarmed when he's around. But he usually trips over something, which makes most people laugh out loud."

"He is a bit clumsy."

"Well, I'm ready to go back."

Sammy opened his arms, and Maeve walked into them. She closed her eyes as he wrapped his arms around her. She felt the pressure change as they took off into the air, and then once again they slipped through dimensions. The squeeze felt no less onerous this time. And then the pop, and she knew they were through.

But it wasn't the calm peace of Norway that greeted her.

It was gunfire.

CHAPTER SEVENTY-SEVEN

BREAKFAST HAD GONE PRETTY WELL. ARIANA HAD BEEN A LITTLE shocked at first when she and Greg had stepped back into the cabin. Greg couldn't really blame her. Iggy was using the railing along the loft like a balance beam while Snap, Alvie, and Luke cheered him on from below.

But once they all sat down to eat, he noticed her relax. It was like any other family sitting down for a meal. They joked and laughed. Everyone made a point of including Ariana but not pressing her about where she had been or her father. All in all, Greg didn't think it could have gone better.

Afterward, he and Ariana volunteered to clean up while everyone else trooped outside. They didn't talk while they cleaned, but it was a comfortable silence. As Ariana placed the last of the plates in the cabinet, she asked, "You all really look out for each other, don't you?"

Greg leaned against the counter. "Yeah. I mean, I've laid my life on the line for just about each of them, and they've done the same for me." He paused. "You can stay here too."

"What?"

"We kind of take people in. And you need a place to hide out from, well, your dad, might as well hide here."

"But you guys would be in danger."

He smiled. "Yeah, we're kind of already there."

"I couldn't do that. I mean, they wouldn't want—"

"Let me stop you right there. I know these guys better than anyone. And yes, they would want to help you."

Ariana glanced out the window. "It is beautiful here."

"And you'd get a chance to get to know your brother. That's good."

Ariana looked like she really wanted to say yes. But he could tell she worried about the danger she might put them in. "I don't know. I think I need to think about it. I'm going to take a little walk."

"Okay. Uh, just grab a jacket. It gets cold."

She gave him a smile, and after grabbing a flannel by the door, slipped outside.

Greg waited a few minutes, putting the last of the silverware away before heading outside himself. He smiled at the bright blue sky. He looked around but didn't see anyone. They were probably up at the clearing. The kids liked the space.

He noted the barn door was open. He walked over and started to close it. Gunfire screamed from the direction of the clearing.

CHAPTER SEVENTY-EIGHT

THE SOUND OF GUNFIRE BURST THROUGH THE SKY. SAMMY turned, abruptly picking up speed and shifting to an erratic flying pattern. Maeve's eyes flew open. The ground went by at a dizzying speed, but she searched anyway, looking for any sign of where the shooting was coming from and where exactly her family was.

But she couldn't see any of them. And from what she could tell, Sammy was heading away from the cabin and into the trees.

Sammy dove into the coverage of the trees, flying low as the gunfire cut off. Maeve tapped on Sammy's arm, needing to yell to be heard over the sound of the wind rushing by. "Sammy, I need to find Alvie and Snap. Do you know where they are?"

"They were at the cabin when I left."

Maeve's heart sunk. The gunfire was undeniably coming from Martin's men. Who else could it be? The cabin would be their first stop.

"Sammy, put me down. Go find them. Please go find them."

Sammy looked down at her and then quickly touched down on the ground. Maeve grabbed on to the base of a tree to keep her balance as he launched himself into the sky. But instead of heading to the cabin, he launched himself straight up into the sky and disappeared.

CHAPTER SEVENTY-NINE

GREG STOOD AT THE SIDE OF THE BARN, HIS HEART POUNDING. Martin had found them. How the hell had he found them?

A man in black jogged past the far side of the barn. Greg flattened himself against the wall. *Please don't have seen me.*

He waited for the man to return, but the space remained empty. Greg let out a breath before he sucked in a chestful of oxygen, his head feeling light. He had no weapon. He didn't know where anybody else was. And he felt completely and totally blindsided. The last couple of times he'd been in one of these situations, he had someone with him who was skilled in the art of war. And they'd intentionally gone into those situations. This time, they'd been caught completely by surprise.

And he tried not to think about the fact that neither Sammy nor Adam was here. Which meant that their defense right now consisted of Nora, Sandra, Iggy, and Chris. Not that they weren't talented, because they were. But he didn't think three humans and one alien were going to be able to stop whatever forces Martin had sent after them.

Greg slowly backed up around the side of the barn, away from the direction he'd seen the man walking. He stepped around the side, still looking toward the front of the barn when he felt the press of a muzzle between his shoulder blades. "Hands up."

Greg closed his eyes. "Dammit."

"Turn around."

Greg slowly turned, his hands raised in the air. The man behind him was dressed entirely in tactical black. And he held an AR-15 in his arms. The man shook his head, talking into the mic on his collar. "No, sir. The scientist, Schorn." He paused. "Yes, sir."

The man met Greg's gaze and shrugged. "Sorry, buddy."

Greg tensed.

A small shadow dropped from the roof of the barn. The man's head jolted up, and he raised the weapon's muzzle to follow, but he was too slow. Iggy landed on the man's shoulders and impaled his talons in either side of his neck. The man's eyes widened. His blood sprayed across the side of the barn and across Greg's face. Greg slammed his mouth shut and wrenched the weapon from the guy's hands as he fell.

Greg wiped off his face with the back of his sleeve. "Thanks, Iggy," he said, quietly trying not to be sick. *And please don't let this guy have had any communicable diseases.* "Where is everybody?"

"Ig, ig." Iggy scampered off the man and hurried toward the back of the barn with his loping gait. Greg followed, checking out the AR-15. He'd never actually used one of them. But he was nothing if not a quick learner. It had a giant drum that easily held ninety rounds. And while he didn't know exactly how many rounds it could shoot per second, he knew it was a lot. These things definitely should not be available to the average citizen.

Gunfire rang out from Greg's left. He flattened himself against the side of the barn, peeking around the corner. He watched in horror as Alvie and Snap sprinted across the field with a group of five men in black giving chase.

Without hesitation, Greg opened fire. He managed to catch two of the guys in the leg. The other three scattered, taking cover. From the corner of his eye, he watched Alvie and Snap disappear into the trees. Greg said a small thank-you that they were safe.

But then gunfire was being directed at him. Iggy scampered up the side of the barn and disappeared over the roof. Greg wasn't Spider-Man, so he didn't follow. Instead, he sprinted into the woods.

He might not have planned on this fight. But it looked like he was definitely in it.

CHAPTER EIGHTY

MAEVE WALKED THROUGH THE WOODS, FEELING COMPLETELY exposed. Like a crazy person, she was heading toward the gunfire. But her family was there. What else could she do?

She hated not knowing where everybody was. She could be walking in the completely wrong direction. They could've escaped going a different way, and here she was heading straight into danger.

It had to be Martin. What was wrong with that man? Why was he causing such misery?

A burst of gunfire sounded from somewhere far to her left. She paused midstep but then continued on, her whole body one exposed nerve. She shifted from tree to tree, which on the one hand made her feel ridiculous. But on the other hand, the only time she felt even remotely safe was when she was hiding behind one of the thick trunks.

Her heart raced, and her breathing came out in pants. It was so loud she was pretty sure it would give away exactly where she was. The one good thing was that she didn't have to use her voice to find Alvie and Snap out here.

Alvie? Snap? Where are you? She mentally called out to them every few feet, praying that they were still all right. A shadow flew overhead. Maeve's head jerked up. She spied Sammy's wings as he flew by. He was moving too fast for her to see his face. She was glad he was back. Maybe he had just jumped to the cabin?

The telltale flutter of a consciousness rippled against her mind. Maeve grabbed on to it like it was a lifeline. *Alvie? Snap?*

Here.

Maeve's knees barely gave out in relief. *Are you safe?*

Men with guns everywhere.

Stay hidden. Where are you?

Near the falls.

Is Chris with you?

No. He was with Luke and Sandra. We haven't seen him.

Maeve's heart plunged. They were separated. That was her worst fear.

Okay, I'm coming to you. Tell me if you need to move, okay?

Okay. Careful.

You too.

Maeve shifted to her right. The falls were a former waterfall that had dried up decades ago, according to Adam. It was a series of rocks built into the hillside. There were lots of good places to hide there, especially for people the size of Alvie and Snap.

She picked up her pace, wanting to all-out sprint but knowing she still needed to take care. She needed to be aware of her surroundings. She wouldn't do Alvie and Snap any good if she got herself killed.

But if somewhere along the way, she spied Martin, she was going to kill him. Unlike her death, his would bring a lot of good to a lot of people.

CHAPTER EIGHTY-ONE

GREG WALKED THROUGH THE TREES, HIS SKIN CRAWLING. HE hated this. He hated not knowing where everybody was. He hated not knowing where the guys with the guns were.

When he was a kid, his family spent a lot of time with his cousins. There were twelve of them. And they would play a game called Bloody Murder.

He hated it.

One person would go and hide in the dark, and then the other eleven would sit on the swing set and count to a hundred by fives. When they reached a hundred, the cousins would split off, disappearing into the yard to look for the one person who was hiding. When they found them, someone would yell "Bloody murder!" and then they would all sprint back to the base. The person who was "it" would try to tag as many as possible before they could reach the base.

Then those who had been tagged would hide, along with the first person. And so eventually there was only one poor soul left on the playset counting to one hundred.

The person left was almost always Greg. He hated to venture very far from the base, wanting the safety of the base at his back.

Which meant he would be the one who would have to walk out into the dark yard where eleven other kids waited to pounce.

Greg felt like his last couple years he'd been playing a nonstop grown-up version of Bloody Murder.

His hands shook, and he wiped the sweat from his brow. He gripped the AR-15 tightly, swinging it this way and that as he moved. He didn't know how soldiers did this on a regular basis. He felt like he was about to have a heart attack.

Gunfire picked up behind him and hit the tree next to him. Greg dove for the ground, rolling as he did. He came up behind a tree and peeked out.

But more gunfire sent him back.

Without looking, he reached around and sent off a spray of cover fire. The gunfire stopped at least for a few seconds. That's all Greg wanted. He took off at a sprint through the trees.

Gunfire rang out behind him, but it was aimed at where he'd been.

Greg glanced behind him. No one appeared to be giving chase. His head turned forward just as he slammed into another warm body.

CHAPTER EIGHTY-TWO

GREG LAY ON THE GROUND STUNNED, THE AIR HAVING BEEN punched from his stomach. He gasped like a fish on land.

Ariana crouched down next to him. "Greg! Greg, are you all right?"

Greg nodded as he finally was able to take a breath. "Yeah. You?"

Ariana shook her head, looking around wildly. "No. I most definitely am not."

Greg got to his feet. "We need to keep moving."

He grabbed her hand and pulled her farther into the trees.

"It's my father's men, isn't it?"

Greg nodded. "Yes."

Ariana was silent for a moment and then pulled her hand from Greg's hand. "I should go turn myself in. If I give myself up, the rest of you will be safe."

Greg shook his head and took Ariana's hand again to get her moving. "No, that won't work. We all have a long history with your father. And what he's doing right now has been a goal of his for a long time."

"What?"

"He wants Alvie and Snap in his control or dead. And Luke

too. And of course he wants the rest of us dead because, well, we've been messing up his plans a lot lately. And Sammy? I'm pretty sure he want Sammy dead."

"But he's my brother."

Greg glanced over at her stricken face. He spoke quietly. "I don't think family relations mean a lot to Martin."

Ariana nodded her head slowly. "Yeah. That's true."

Gunfire burst out behind them. Bark from the tree next to Greg exploded, sending slivers of wood into his arm.

He cursed even as he yanked Ariana forward. They tore through the trees, but then they reached a wall of rock. It looked like an old landslide. Water trickled through the rocks, leaving the rocks slick. They'd never be able to climb it in time. Above, the mountain soared, the sun shining. Just a short distance away, everything looked peaceful.

Ariana looked at Greg. "What are we supposed to do?"

Greg shook his head, hearing the footfalls approaching quickly. There were at least three of them, maybe more.

He swallowed. There was no cover for either of them. And there was a wall of rock behind them. Ariana looked up at him. He gripped her hand tighter. "I'm glad I got the chance to know you."

Ariana squeezed his hand back. Then Greg raised his AR-15.

CHAPTER EIGHTY-THREE

MAEVE HEARD THE SOUND OF FOOTFALLS HEADING TOWARD HER. She ducked behind a series of bushes and said a small prayer that they did not look this way. The soldiers didn't come anywhere near her, and soon the footfalls retreated. Letting out a sigh of relief, Maeve hurried toward the falls. She walked up quietly, scanning the ground, but saw no sign of Alvie or Snap.

Alvie? Snap? I'm here.

Alvie's small head popped out from behind a rock a couple dozen feet away. Snap's popped out a second later. Emotions threatened to overwhelm Maeve as she stared at those two little faces. They'd been through so much, and all they wanted was a little love.

Maeve clambered over the rocks, scraping her knees and hands but not caring. She crouched down in front of them and yanked both of them into a giant hug. Pulling back, she cupped their faces in her hands, staring into their eyes. *Are you both all right?*

They nodded back at her, but there was a scratch along Snap's cheek and abrasions along Alvie's arms.

How could those men do this to them? To anyone. Maybe the Council was right. Maybe we don't deserve this planet anymore.

She shoved the dark thought away. Now was not the time. Maeve stood. *Okay, we need to go.*

As she had been making her way through the forest, she had come up with a plan of sorts. They would head down the trail to where the ATVs were. If they were lucky, they might be able to grab one and take off. It wasn't a great plan. But she had absolutely no other idea where to take them.

Maeve reached her hands for them. Alvie grabbed hers and stood just as gunfire sounded.

Maeve dove for the ground, pulling Alvie down as well. He crashed into her chest. She rolled him onto the ground and then grabbed Snap, shoving her underneath her as well. She lay on top of them as gunfire destroyed the rocks in front of them. Slivers of rock cut into Maeve's skin, but she refused to move.

At the same time, she knew that this was a temporary measure. She could protect them for these next few seconds, but soon whoever was firing would come around the rock toward them, and there would be nothing she could do.

She tensed, waiting for that moment. *I love you. I love you both.*

The gunfire was cut off as a man screamed. Maeve bit her lip and peeked around the boulder in time to see Adam grab the gunman and fling him into the side of a tree.

Maeve wanted to weep with relief at the sight of him. He was scratched and bruised, and one of his sleeves even seemed to be a bit scorched, but he never looked so damn good to her in her entire life.

Maeve scrambled to her feet, ignoring the stings in her back, and grabbed Snap and Alvie's hands. "Come on."

Maeve had Snap climb onto her shoulders to make it easier. Alvie scampered ahead to reach Adam's side. Adam scanned them, no doubt checking for any serious injuries.

"We're good," Maeve said.

"Stay behind me." Without another word, he took off at a quick pace down the path. Maeve kept Snap on her back, but Alvie stayed by her side. Maeve's heart felt like it had taken up residence in her throat as her head moved from side to side, waiting for someone to appear or gunfire to break out.

Then it happened. Two men in black appeared in the path in front of them, their weapons raised.

Maeve glanced behind her as another two stepped up behind. "Adam."

Adam took aim at the two in front. Maeve turned her back to Adam, facing the men behind her. She yanked Alvie behind her, covering Alvie and Snap the best she could, and closed her eyes.

Then she heard the first shot.

CHAPTER EIGHTY-FOUR

ARIANA GRIPPED GREG'S ARM AS HE SAW THE SHADOWS OF THE men moving toward them. He swallowed, taking aim.

Then his vision wavered, shifting to a tunnel, and a fast-moving rainbow surrounded him. *Oh no.*

He dropped the AR and latched on to Ariana as he slammed his eyes closed.

Fear pulsed through him as he grabbed harder onto Ariana's arm, not sure what would happen if he released her while he was in between spaces. With a pop, he knew he was through. He felt warm air on his face and solid ground underneath his feet.

He cracked his eyes open and took a peek. Desert surrounded them.

For the first time, he didn't feel like he wanted to throw up. He wasn't sure if that was because his body was getting used to traveling through dimensions or because somehow Ariana hadn't traveled through the air, but either way, he was grateful.

He released his grip on Ariana and took a look at her face. She stared around them in shock. Her mouth hung open. "What just happened?"

"Well, if you still have any doubts about being related to

Sammy, you can put them to rest. You seem to have inherited the family's ability to jump between spaces."

Ariana shook her head. "But I couldn't have."

"Well, it sure wasn't me. Although I can't really say I like your choice of venues. Where are we?"

Ariana pointed to a small utility shed in the distance. "That's where my father held me."

Greg's eyes widened in alarm. "You need to jump us back right now."

Ariana shook her head. "I don't even know how I got us here!"

"Just do whatever you did then. We were running, about to be shot, and then poof," Greg said.

"I can't!"

"Okay, okay, just really wish you weren't here anymore." Greg took her arm again. He slammed his eyes shut, waiting for the telltale feel of the shift.

But nothing happened.

He peeked carefully through his lids. Ariana had her eyes closed as well, her brow furrowed.

"Nothing?" he asked.

Ariana's shoulders drooped. "I don't know what I did. I mean, in my life I've wished I wasn't a lot of places. I never disappeared from them!"

"Damn it," he growled, and then despair rolled through him. "We ran out on them."

Even though it was unintentional, he needed to get back. Anything could be happening to them right now. But it looked like in order to get back, he was going to have to do it the old-fashioned way.

Ariana stared at the shed. "I can't believe I brought us here. Why here?"

"Maybe it's just the first place that popped into your mind. I'm not really sure how that works, but maybe you need to picture it."

"Maybe. As we were running, I was thinking that I was safer here than at the cabin with you guys."

"Well, at least you know where we are."

"Not really. I mean, I ran that way." Ariana pointed to a rock formation in the distance. "And then Sammy came. When he arrived, we disappeared. I never really got a chance to see what was around here."

"Okay, well, we can't stay here. Let's just—"

The door behind them flew open. Two guards stepped through with their weapons aimed at Ariana and Greg. "Hands up."

Greg's shoulders sagged. Stupid, stupid. Of course they had surveillance. He should have made them get out of there as soon as he realized where they were.

But his mind had still been blown away by the fact that they were actually here. He never imagined that Ariana was capable of that kind of jump. From the look on her face, it was clear she hadn't either.

He wondered if maybe as time went on, more and more of her abilities would evolve. Perhaps some of the experiments they had conducted on her involved removing whatever it was that had been blocking their development. If that were true, then there was a chance that others were going to pop up as well.

He took a peek at her back but saw no indication that wings were about to sprout from underneath. He had to admit that would be really cool. Her skin tone also remained the same human color, so there was no way to tell how her abilities would manifest compared to Sammy's.

Sammy was essentially the first generation, Ariana the second. They had to have made improvements, although he blanched at the idea of "improvements," as if sentient beings could be so easily modified or should be. Her father had a lot of explaining to do.

Greg raised his hands automatically. "Hey, hey, hey. No need for that. We're not here to fight you."

One of the guards sneered, suggesting the idea of them fighting was laughable. "Keep your hands up."

Greg nodded at the man, hunching his shoulders a little more. Fear flashed across Ariana's face as the men approached.

"Ariana, remember you're not the weak little girl you were when you first showed up here. Things have changed," Greg whispered.

"Walk toward us," one of the guards ordered.

"Of course, coming." Greg stepped in front of one of the guards.

The man gave Greg a look that said he knew he was in charge. Greg had seen that look from a lot of guys in high school.

He hated that look.

Greg smiled back at him and then kicked him right between the legs. The man's knees buckled as his mouth made a silent O.

Greg stepped forward and slammed his elbow into the man's chin. The man collapsed to the ground. It all happened so fast that even Greg was struggling to believe he'd just done that.

The second guard turned.

Ariana grabbed a hold of the muzzle of his rifle and slammed her open palm into his face. Blood burst from the man's nose before Ariana grabbed him by the front of his shirt and threw him across the space. He slammed into the side of the shed and then crumpled down in a heap.

Greg smiled. "Not bad for a couple of geeks."

Ariana grinned at him in return. "I didn't know I could do that."

"I have a feeling there's a lot of things you don't know you can do."

Ariana glanced behind her.

Greg gave a small chuckle. "Not yet. I already looked."

Ariana sighed in relief. "I'm all good with the strength and the transportation benefits, but I'm really hoping that my skin color doesn't change, and I definitely don't want wings."

"Huh. I was just thinking they'd look pretty cool." Greg picked up the weapon his man had dropped and then scanned the area around them. He checked his guy's pockets, but there were no car keys, unfortunately. He did, however, find a keycard that he slipped into his pocket. He wasn't planning on going inside, but he also didn't want these guys to get back inside too easily either.

He stood up. "Okay. Let's follow the road. We'll have to come across some sort of major road eventually, and I guess we'll just follow that until we find some sort of civilization. Okay?"

Ariana nodded absentmindedly, her gaze on the open doorway.

Greg hurried over to the door and grabbed the back of it. "Let's just close this up, shall we?"

Ariana put up a hand. "No."

Greg looked up at her in surprise. "No? Why not?"

Ariana took a step toward the bunker. "Because I think I need to go down there."

CHAPTER EIGHTY-FIVE

MAEVE STOOD WITH HER ARMS SPREAD WIDE, TRYING TO MAKE herself a bigger target and hopefully block Alvie and Snap from the gunfire. She waited for the impact as the gunfire rang out.

But it never came.

She cracked open her eye as the sound of the shots died away. The two men down the path lay on the ground. She glanced over her shoulder. The other two men were down as well. Two familiar figures stepped from the trees. Jasper and Mike, along with six other commandos in R.I.S.E. uniforms, stepped forward.

Jasper grinned. "Sorry we're late. We've been tracking Martin's men. We didn't want to tip anyone off by heading here directly with reinforcements. We had to wait until we were sure they knew where you were."

Maeve walked toward him and hugged him tight. "I love you, Jasper."

He chuckled, patting her on the back. "All the girls do."

Chris ran up the path, and Maeve stepped away from Jasper, soaking in the sight of him. He looked no worse for wear, but his eyes were haunted. The look didn't disappear until he took in the sight of Maeve, Alvie, and Snap. He hurried forward. Alvie and

Snap sprinted toward him, leaping up to hurl themselves into his arms. Chris hugged them tight, looking over them to Maeve.

She nodded. "We're okay. What about Nora and Iggy?"

"They're good," Chris said.

"Greg, Ariana, and Sammy?"

Chris shook his head. "I saw Sammy fly overhead, but I haven't caught sight of either Greg or Ariana."

"But we'll find them."

Maeve looked over as Tilda stepped out of the woods. Adam made a small choking sound and then was a blur as he sprinted toward her. He grabbed her and hugged her tight. Then, in full view of everyone, kissed her like a soldier returning from war.

Which Maeve supposed he was.

"Well, I guess that cat's out of the bag," Jasper mumbled.

"I think it's about time they had their day in the sun, don't you?" Maeve asked.

Jasper grinned. "That I do."

They all headed back to the cabin. Maeve tried not to look at the bodies that littered the path. Technically she knew she should probably help in case any of them were still alive. But being they had all come here to kill her family, she couldn't quite bring herself to do it.

She'd just reached the cabin when Sammy dropped down in front of her.

A few of the R.I.S.E. soldiers who hadn't seen him before jumped back in fright, but no one raised their weapons. Apparently Tilda had done a good job of briefing her people.

Maeve walked over to him. "Thank you for bringing Adam. It made all the difference."

"I need your help."

Maeve stared at his face, noting stress lines around his eyes. "What is it?"

"My sister."

Chris stood at her shoulder. "I've got ours. Go."

Maeve hugged him tight, then stepped toward Sammy. "Let's go."

CHAPTER EIGHTY-SIX

ARIANA WASN'T SURE WHAT CAME OVER HER. SHE AND GREG were now walking down the dark stairwell to the place that she had been held captive. What the heck was she doing? She did not want to be here.

And yet there was something that pulled her forward. She couldn't explain it, and she decided that she wasn't going to try. She just needed to listen to the voice inside her head telling her that she needed to go downstairs, that there was something she needed to see.

They reached the bottom of the stairwell and stopped. She frowned at the door lock. She didn't have a key. How were they supposed to

Greg held up a keycard he pulled from his pocket.

Ariana looked at it in surprise. "Where'd you get that?"

"I took it off one of the guys up top. You ready?" Greg held the gun that he'd taken from one of the guards. Ariana was surprised at how comfortable it looked in his arms. He struck her as a serious nerd. But apparently the serious nerd had held a machine gun once or twice in his life.

She nodded. "Okay, I'm ready."

Greg waved the card over the door lock. It flashed green before the door popped open slightly. Greg peeked out into the hallway. "Empty."

Ariana nodded, stepping through. "Follow me."

Her cell had been down the hall into the right. But she had a feeling she was supposed to go farther into the facility. She headed down the hall, bypassing the hallway that led to her cell and turned to the left just past it.

"Where is everybody?" Greg whispered. "I mean, not that I'm complaining. I'm glad we're not running into people, but shouldn't we be?"

"I don't know. Maybe they're all back with your—" Ariana winced, cutting off her words.

Greg's face became a mask. "Yeah, you're probably right."

"But your friends seem pretty capable. And with Sammy, not exactly easy to defeat."

Greg nodded. "Yeah, and Maeve, Chris, and Nora have been through a couple of pretty dicey situations. And I know he doesn't look it, but Alvie's a really good person to have in a fight."

"Seriously?" Ariana was trying to picture it, but she couldn't. He was so sweet.

"Seriously. And Iggy, man, you should see that guy in a fight. He's like a one-man army. So I'm sure they'll be fine."

Greg was rambling. Ariana knew he was trying to convince himself that his friends would be all right. And yet again, Ariana felt guilty for having taken him away, unintentional though it may have been.

At the same time, she knew that there was a good chance that his friends wouldn't survive what they were facing back home. After all, they were massively outnumbered. They had some weapons, but nothing compared to the force arrayed against them.

And the thought made her sick. They had been nothing but kind to her. They had taken her in and helped her. Her own father had turned his back on her. He'd been the reason she'd been on the run. Strangers had shown her more compassion than—

She cut off that line of thought. She couldn't think like that.

Greg was right. They needed to get back. She straightened her shoulders. Okay, she'd investigate whatever it was that was calling her on, and then they'd find a way to get back to Greg's friends. It might be too late by then, but maybe they could still do something to help.

Ariana reached the end of the hall. She could go left or right now. Without pause, she headed left. She could feel in her bones that this was the right direction. She ignored all the doors they passed, focused on the one facing them at the end of the hall.

There. She needed to go there.

She picked up her pace, comforted by Greg's steady presence beside her. She stopped in front of the door. It looked no different than any of the others they'd passed.

"Is this it?" Greg asked.

"There's something on the other side I need to see." She looked at Greg.

He met her gaze before he handed her the keycard. "Then open it up."

I'm here.

The words stole Ariana's breath. With a shaking hand, she reached for the handle.

"Ariana!" Greg shoved her into the wall as a gunshot cut through the hallway.

Greg let out a grunt and fell to the ground. Blood seeped from a wound in his side.

Ariana looked at Greg and then down the hall. Her father stood there, his gun pointed directly at her.

CHAPTER EIGHTY-SEVEN

GREG LAY ON THE GROUND, NOT MOVING. BLOOD SEEPED FROM his wound onto the gray tile floor. Ariana stared down at him in horror and shock. *He saved me.*

She glared down the hall at her father. "What are you doing?"

"Removing a threat."

"He's not a threat. He's a good man. He's a—"

Martin tilted his head. "Is that *interest* I hear in your voice, daughter?"

Ariana slammed her mouth shut, wishing that laser eyes were one of her abilities.

He walked toward her, his gun leveled at her. "I have to say, I *am* impressed at what you've accomplished. I didn't think you were capable of the jumps. We didn't even know the abomination could do it until he'd been released."

"His *name* is Sammy."

Martin carried on as if she hadn't even spoken. "You're the weaker of the two, but apparently not by much. It's fascinating. You are going to provide us with lots of data in the years to come."

"I am *not* going with you."

"Oh, you have no choice."

Three men appeared in the hallway behind her father, all of their weapons aimed at Ariana.

"What is this?" she demanded.

"You didn't actually think the base was empty, did you? I wanted to see what brought you back down here. You had a chance to run on the surface, and yet you intentionally came back down here. I wanted to see why." He nudged his chin toward the door behind her. "Now I know."

"What's behind there?"

Martin smiled. "You'll never know."

He waved his men forward. Ariana felt all her muscles tighten. Her back ached. But in a good way. She rolled her hands into fists as the men approached her. She was not going back in that cell. She narrowed her eyes, her vision sharpening.

The men were five feet away when she launched herself at the first one. She placed one hand on the gun muzzle and shoved it to the wall as she slammed her fist into his face. His head jerked back, his eyes going wide as his neck snapped.

She twirled, slamming a back fist into the face of another. His nose exploded in a burst of cartilage. Sickened but not stopping, she kicked him into the third guard. The two guards crashed into the wall with the force of the kick. Blood smeared the wall from the back of the third guard's head as he slid down before crumpling to the tile floor, the second guard on top of him. Neither stirred.

Ariana turned toward her father. He'd taken a few steps back. Surprise flashed across his face. She stormed toward him. He turned and fled down the hall. She shot a quick glance at Greg. He was bleeding, but it wasn't too bad. If she attended to him, though, her father would no doubt be back with reinforcements. And then they'd be in even worse shape.

"I'll be back," she promised before she sprinted down the hall after her father.

As she dashed down the hall, she caught sight of her father turning down a separate hall. She put on a burst of speed, worried she'd lose him. But then she saw him duck into the hall where her cell had been.

Which made no sense. It was a dead end. There was no exit that way.

She sprinted after him, stopping short as he stepped inside one of the cells. The glass wall slid down between them. He smiled at her. "You can't get me in here."

She stared at him, wondering if he'd gone mad. "But you can't get out."

He held up a small remote. "Of course I can. This facility is mine. I control everything in it."

"You don't control me."

"Not yet. But I will."

A door at the end of the hall slid open. Ariana stared as goose-bumps broke out across her skin. A strange clacking sounded, like someone drumming fingernails on a window. Then the creature that was making the noise stepped into the hall. It was over six feet tall, and it looked like an alligator standing upright, except its snout was much shorter.

She stared at it in horror as the talons on its feet clacked along the ground as it walked toward her. Two more cells opened, and another two creatures joined the first. Saliva dripped from the edges of their mouths as they eyed her.

Martin smiled. "My pets."

Ariana took one last look at her father and ran.

CHAPTER EIGHTY-EIGHT

THE WOUND IN GREG'S SIDE BURNED. HE FELT LIKE SOMEONE had run him through with a sword. He saw Ariana take off after her father, and he'd wanted to yell at her not to go. Martin no doubt had a backup plan.

But he didn't have time.

With trembling hands, he reached down and felt the wound. He reached along his back and found where the bullet had exited. A through and through. That was good. And it got him in the side. Another few inches, and it would have missed him altogether. In fact, if he had to get shot, it was probably the best he could wish for.

Which only goes to show how much my wishes have changed in the last few years.

He got to his hands and knees and then, using the wall, got to his feet. He winced as pain lanced through his side. He pulled off his fleece, wrapping it tightly around the wound. It would hopefully slow the bleeding down a little bit, at least until he could get some actual first aid.

He made his way slowly down the hall, using the wall for support. He reached the end of the hall when a shriek echoed down the hall.

Greg went cold, all the hairs on his body rose up. He knew that sound. He had nightmares about that sound.

No, no, no, no, no. There was no possible way they could have a Hank. Even as he thought it, though, he knew that in all likelihood Martin had kept a few just for himself. After all, they had covered his escape at the Dulce base, and they had proven to be incredibly formidable, so why wouldn't that raging psychopath make sure that he had a couple of extras on hand?

Greg glanced back toward the hall were the M4 he'd taken from the guard lay. Focused on his injury, he'd forgotten to grab it.

Footsteps pounded down a hall near him. He ducked back, peering around the corner. Ariana sprinted out of the hallway to his left and headed down the hall at an incredible speed.

A Hank sprinted after her. It slid on the tile floor and slammed into the wall before catching its feet and taking off after her. Two more followed. The first one made the turn a little more adeptly than its predecessor and took off after Ariana as well.

The second one, though, slipped on the tile floor and hit the wall. It flipped onto its back with the force of the fall but instead of getting up, it went still.

Then its head turned slowly toward Greg.

Greg stared into the Hank's face. Fear and terror stole over him. He didn't wait. He ran, his hand holding his side. He heard the Hank giving chase and pictured it getting closer and closer. He waited until he felt it was right behind him and then dove for the tiles.

As expected, the Hank jumped over him with a swipe of its talons. They liked to disembowel their prey first. That meant they had to leap up and use the talons on their feet.

Expecting the target to stay on course, the Hank had swung hard. Without a target, the force caused it to spin and stumble and trip over its feet. Greg switched directions and then dove into the empty office that he had seen when Ariana ran past.

He slammed the door shut behind him, and the locks automatically engaged. The Hank slammed itself over and over again at the steel door, but the door held. Greg backed away from the door as it trembled under the Hank's assault.

There were no other doors in the room. He wasn't getting out of here anytime soon.

He walked over to the desk, which had three monitors set up on it. Security camera footage from the facility was displayed. He watched Ariana sprint down a hallway with the two Hanks after her. Then he noticed movement on another feed. His heart nearly dropped into his chest when he saw Maeve in the stairwell. What the hell was she doing here?

In the next second, he knew that answer, as Sammy stepped into the frame. He glanced at the other frames as the banging on the door near him stopped. The Hank that had been outside his door now sniffed the air and then darted down the hall. Greg tried to follow its trail, but he knew in his gut where it was heading.

It had new prey to chase down.

It was going for Maeve.

Greg hit the mouse, and the monitor flared to life. By some miracle of God, there was no password on it. Martin must have been in a rush.

Greg searched the files, looking for something that would help him. There were files for every single system within the base. Martin was an evil genius. His mind whirled, imagining all the atrocities Martin had inflicted upon them.

And then he went still. *This is Martin's office.* An idea began to form in the back of his mind.

He quickly searched the computer for the files on the Hanks. *Come on, come on, come on.*

Yes. He quickly hit the file labeled Kecksburg AG-4, the fourth generation of Hanks. He scanned the file and found the codes Martin used to control them. "Okay, okay."

He reached for the drawer next to him and rummaged through before slamming it shut and moving on to the next one. He went through all of them, but it wasn't here.

He moved to the bookcase by the wall. And on the second

shelf, he saw the controller. He grabbed it and scrambled back to the desk. He placed the controller on the desk and got to work.

CHAPTER EIGHTY-NINE

MAEVE WALKED SLOWLY AND FOLLOWED SAMMY DOWN THE darkened stairwell, flashbacks of a similar stairwell at Area 51 racing through her mind. She swallowed but didn't let up her pace. "You're sure they're down here?"

"Yes," Sammy said. "Along with our mother."

Maeve stopped on the stairwell, excitement swirling through her. "Your mother? She's alive?"

Sammy frowned. "Yes. But she's contained. I do not know how to free her. But I think you will. I will keep you safe. And my mother, she's the one the Council is looking for."

Maeve took a breath and straightened her shoulders. "Okay. Let's go get her."

They walked down the remaining steps in silence. At the bottom, a steel door had been left ajar. *Well, that's not a good sign,* Maeve thought.

But Sammy didn't even hesitate at the door. He pulled it fully open and ducked under the doorframe. She supposed being an incredibly powerful seven-foot-tall human/alien hybrid left one fearful of very little.

Maeve followed him a little more cautiously, glancing into the hallway first. But there was no one around. The door behind her swung shut. The red light above the door flashed on, telling her it was locked.

The fear that had been rising through her as they descended into the base now reached a fever pitch. "Sammy."

He glanced over at her, but before she could respond, a voice came over the PA system. "Dr. Leander, how nice of you to join us."

Maeve shivered. She knew that voice. Martin.

"And you've brought my son. Thank you for that. I've brought some friends with me as well. They will be joining you shortly."

Maeve's heart began to race.

She could hear the scrabbling of nails on the tile floor. *Oh no.* She didn't know which creature was heading toward them, but she knew it was one of Martin's creations. "Sammy, we need to get out of here."

Sammy grabbed her hand and hurried down the hallway. Before they'd gotten more than halfway down, a Hank stepped into view at the end of the hall. It let out a ferocious screech and charged.

CHAPTER NINETY

Ariana sprinted down the hallway. The base was much larger than she had realized. There were hallways upon hallways tucked in the back, and they all seem to loop around.

She darted a glance over her shoulder. The creatures were only about five feet behind her. The only thing that had kept her out of reach of these things so far was her speed and the slick tile floors. Every time she turned a corner, they slid, helping her increase the distance between them.

So she turned another corner, crashed into the opposite wall, and bounced off it before continuing her run. Behind her, she heard the scrabble of nails and a thud as each of the creatures hit the wall, losing their footing. She lengthened her stride just a little bit more.

I know this hallway. It was blue. The medical wing. An idea took shape in her mind. She headed for the room where they had operated on her.

She said a quick prayer as she picked up her pace and barreled toward the door. The door flew open as she crashed into it, the doorframe cracking. She tripped and rolled, slamming into the back of a stretcher, but quickly got to her feet.

She raced around the stretcher and yanked out the drawers on the other side of the room, looking for something that would help her against these creatures. *Come on. Come on.* She rifled through the drawers, looking for some sort of sedative.

She grabbed a syringe but didn't see any medicines she recognized. But she did catch sight of something just under the counter.

A screech sounded behind her. Ariana whirled around as the creatures stepped into the room. They spread out, one going right and one going left.

Smart. These things were not some basic creatures. They were planning. *My God, Dad, what did you create?*

Ariana lunged for the bottle of bleach. Ripping the plastic off the syringe, she tilted the bottle and filled the syringe with the noxious chemical. One of the creatures edged toward her. She sprang to her feet and threw the open bottle of bleach at it. It leaped back with a roar, its nose sniffing the air.

The other one took advantage of her distraction and leaped for her. She barely managed to get out of the way of the talons. One caught the edge of her shirt and ripped a long gash in the material. Ariana slipped under as it leaped again, and she rolled to her feet. Not stopping to let herself doubt, she jumped onto its back. Cringing, she wrapped one arm around its throat and her legs around its torso to keep her balance. Then she plunged the syringe into its eyeball.

The creature reared back, and its head slammed into Ariana's forehead. She flew back, feeling dazed. The creature let out a scream. It shook, stumbling from side to side, white foam spraying from its mouth.

Ariana scrambled back, hitting the cabinets in her haste. The creature clawed at its eyes, then stopped moving and dropped straight to the floor.

The other creature had stayed on the other side of the room, its gaze locked on its partner.

Now it pulled its gaze from its dead compatriot and met Ariana's eyes. Saliva dripped from the right side of its mouth as it let out a roar and leaped.

CHAPTER NINETY-ONE

THE HANK CHARGED DOWN THE HALL TOWARD MAEVE AND Sammy. Sammy pulled Maeve to a stop. He slammed his foot into one of the doors, and it swung open. Maeve dashed inside. It was a lounge of some sort, with a couch and two sets of bunk beds along the walls.

Sammy followed Maeve in quickly. He slammed the door shut behind him and stood braced against it.

The Hank slammed into the door. Sammy jolted forward only a fraction. Maeve ran over to add her weight to the door, knowing that it was not going to work for long.

The Hank slammed into the door over and over again, its attempt growing more frantic. Sweat coated Maeve's body, which trembled.

This was it. She'd thought she'd have more time. She thought she would be able to spend time with Alvie and Snap. My God, now what would Chris do? Would he have to choose between taking care of Alvie and Snap on Earth and Pop and Crackle at the Council's base? Worse, would Martin be able to escape with the Guardian, forcing Chris to choose between staying and dying with two of their children or leaving them behind to live with the other two?

No, no, it could not end this way. They had come too far. Sammy was right, they were so close.

The Hank let out a screech and slammed into the door again. Maeve flew across the room, hitting the couch.

Sammy was shoved nearly as far as her, which was enough for the Hank to get inside.

It stood in the doorway, letting out a ferocious screech. Maeve couldn't tear her eyes away from it. It stared at each of them, its chest heaving. Its head tilted to the side. Then it tilted it the other way as if not sure what it was seeing. Maeve was too scared to even move. It let out a low growl, and then almost as if against its will, it turned and ran out of the room.

Maeve stared at the empty doorway, trying to figure out what had just happened. That was not a natural behavior. It wasn't as if it had sensed prey. It simply left. Maeve stepped away from the couch, her legs feeling like Jell-O.

Sammy stepped into the hallway. "It's gone."

Maeve peered out the doorway. She swallowed, glancing back the way they had come, wanting more than anything to go back up those stairs and leave whatever other horrors were hidden in here behind. But she knew this was the only chance for them to find the Guardian. She could not leave her here with Martin.

And besides, Greg and Ariana were somewhere down here as well, so she stepped into the hall. She and Sammy made their way slowly forward. Maeve's nerves were stretched thin. Her heart pounded in her ears. She kept waiting for one of the Hanks to leap out at them.

Sammy put up a hand. "Someone is coming."

Maeve went still, staring at the end of the hall, her body braced to run.

But it wasn't a Hank that stepped into view. Greg's side was soaked in blood, but he smiled, a small device in his hands. "Hi, guys."

CHAPTER NINETY-TWO

GREG'S HEART WAS IN HIS THROAT AS HE TOOK IN THE SIGHT OF Sammy and Maeve. They looked no worse for wear. He thought for sure he'd be too late. It took him precious minutes to figure out how to control the Hanks. But he'd had to go for the one on Ariana first, as she seemed in greater danger. When he turned back to check on Maeve and Sammy, his breath had left his lungs when he'd seen the Hank crash into their hiding spot.

He leaned against the wall now as they walked down the hall toward him. "Greg, are you all right?" Maeve asked.

He nodded slowly. "I found the Hank controls. The two remaining ones are in the cells next to Martin."

"Martin's in a cell?"

Greg nodded, suddenly feeling really, really tired. "Yeah. He locked himself in and then released the Hanks."

"And Ariana? Is she all right?" Sammy asked.

"I am." Ariana hurried down the hall toward them. "I don't know what happened. One of those things was poised to kill me, and then it just turned away."

Maeve smiled. "Greg did that."

Ariana looked at him in surprise. "How?"

He waved away her question. "One of Martin's toys. I'll explain later. Right now, I'd really just like to get out of here."

Sammy shook his head. "Not quite yet." He started down the hall. Ariana followed him.

Greg struggled to keep in his groan. *Of course. Why leave now when all the dangers are locked up? Let's just stay and see if Martin has more tricks up his sleeves.*

"Guess were not leaving quite yet." Maeve grabbed Greg's arm. "You sure you're okay?"

"Yeah, but Martin shot me."

"Did you shoot him back?"

"No, I was too busy bleeding on the ground."

Maeve choked back a laugh. "Can he get out?"

"No, but he thinks he can. I overrode his controls. He's stuck in there until we decide what to do with him."

Up ahead, Ariana and Sammy turned left. Greg and Maeve followed them. Greg was unsurprised when they stopped at the door where he and Ariana had stopped earlier. He blanched as he caught sight of his blood on the ground. Sammy and Ariana hesitated outside the door.

"Is that where she is?" Maeve asked.

Ariana nodded. "Yes."

Neither of them seemed like they were going to move.

Greg leaned against the wall. "Well, not to rush anybody, but there is kind of the whole impending end of the human race on the horizon. Maybe we should see what's behind the door?"

Sammy nodded. He reached out his hand, grasped the handle, and turned. Nothing happened.

Greg fumbled into his pockets and pulled out a keycard. "Okay, I think you might need this." He flashed the keycard over the plate on the right-hand side of the door. The light flashed green.

Sammy turned the handle again, and this time the door swung open. After only a moment's hesitation, he stepped into the room.

CHAPTER NINETY-THREE

THE ROOM LOOKED LIKE A HOSPITAL ROOM, COMPLETE WITH A patient. Now, Maeve stood over the bed studying the woman that lay before her as her mind reeled from the possibilities. Was she really the mother of both Ariana and Sammy? Had she truly been taken from the moon during one of the Apollo missions?

Was this who the Council was looking for? As she studied the quiet form in front of her, doubts and worries plagued her mind. Would the Council be appeased simply by them returning her, or would her state be the final nail in humanity's coffin?

She no longer doubted that what they had officially been told about the space program was only the tip of the iceberg. But even so, it was hard to accept that this woman, who looked so human, wasn't from Earth.

She was tall, easily at least six feet. She had dark-brown hair that was arranged in braids. Her lips were full and her nose wide. Her skin was a light brown. Nothing about her suggested she was anything other than human. Her eyes were a little larger than perhaps most humans, as were Ariana's. But they weren't so far afield that anyone would think she was an entirely different species.

Nothing about her suggested that she was one of the

Guardians mentioned in the Russian cosmonauts' reports. From what Maeve recalled, those Guardians were more of an ethereal kind of being, almost as if they didn't even have a substance. But the woman in front of her was very real.

Ariana moved closer to the other side of the bed, staring down at the woman. "Is she alive?"

Maeve scanned the monitors that were lined up along the head of the bed. She nodded. "Yes, she's alive. She's being kept in some sort of suspended state. It's possible she's in a coma."

"Can we just unplug her?" Ariana asked. "Will that wake her up?"

Greg shook his head, pulling up the notes at the end of the bed. "I wouldn't advise that. Not until we know for sure what's going on with her."

Maeve looked at the machines and realized that most of them were actually just monitoring her. She didn't have oxygen that was being fed into her or anything that was maintaining her beyond a saline drip. "I'm not so sure that's true."

According to what Maeve knew, which granted wasn't much, when the Apollo astronauts found her, she was already in some sort of suspended state. They brought all the machines with them, still attached to her, keeping her in the same state. Martin's people must have done the same thing, although it seemed they shifted her to their own equipment.

"So it *is* possible you could just remove her from the machines?" Ariana asked.

Maeve and Greg exchanged a glance. Neither of them wanted to be responsible for making that decision. This woman had been kept in a vegetative state for decades. Even if she could breathe on her own, the reality was, her brain could be gone. It was possible for someone's heart to still pump but for there to be no brain activity. Nothing indicated anything about brain activity.

Plus, unless she had been receiving physical therapy, her muscles would have wasted away from lack of use. Yet she looked healthy. Maeve reached out and felt along the woman's arm, surprised to feel muscle there.

And the fact was, if she was the Guardian the Council was looking for, the sooner they woke her, the better.

Sammy spoke quietly from the foot of the bed. "It's all right. You can remove her from the machines."

Maeve studied Sammy, noting the confidence in his voice. "What makes you say that?"

"She told me. It's okay." Sammy nodded toward the bed.

Maeve's gaze darted to the woman on the bed, then back to Sammy. "Are you sure?"

This time it was Ariana who answered. "Yes. She says it's all right."

Greg and Maeve exchanged a glance. Greg placed the clipboard on the table next to the bed. "Well, I'm game if you are."

Maeve swallowed. She knew how they could detach her, and in what order, but she still wasn't sure it was the right decision.

But she supposed technically both Ariana and Sammy were next of kin. It was their decision to make, not hers and Greg's. She wished she had a little more time to study the woman to make sure they understood the risks.

Greg reached over toward the heart monitor and flipped it off. "It's okay, Maeve. It's what they want."

Maeve nodded and then got to work. As they went through the process of removing her, Maeve realized it was only a single sedative keeping her under.

Maeve wasn't sure how long it would take them to see a change once they disconnected it. "I need to ask you two again, are you sure this is what you want? We could wait until we've had a chance to—"

"She's waited long enough. It will be all right," Sammy said.

Maeve and Greg exchanged a glance before Maeve removed the line from the woman's arm. Greg took it from her and handed her a bandage, which she placed over the wound. Then Greg and Maeve stepped back from the bed.

Ariana took a step forward. "Is that it?"

Greg nodded. "Yes. But we can't know for sure how long it will take her to come to. She's been under for a long time. You have to prepare yourselves for the possibility that she might not ever regain consciousness."

Maeve watched the woman on the bed as Greg spoke, explaining potential problems with coming back to consciousness after being in a vegetative state for an extended period of time. The woman's hand twitched. It was a slight movement that Maeve wasn't sure that she had even seen.

The side of the woman's mouth turned down for just a second. Her eyeballs started to move rapidly behind her eyelids. "Greg."

He whirled around, looking down at the bed. Ariana let out a little gasp as the woman opened her eyes.

Blue eyes peered up at them, the same blue color as both Ariana's and Sammy's.

———

Greg checked the woman's pulse and responses. She was able to respond to commands, which Maeve was completely shocked by. Not only because of her vegetative state but also: how had she learned English?

But that wasn't really the biggest concern at this moment in time. During the entire exam, the woman never said a word, but she also never took her eyes off of Ariana and Sammy. Finally, Maeve and Greg stepped out of the room, giving them a little privacy. Now they sat on the floor in the hallway outside. Neither of them had said a word for the last few minutes.

Finally Greg spoke. "Is everyone okay back home? How did you get here?"

Maeve gave him a rundown of the attack and R.I.S.E.'s timely arrival.

"I swear, Tilda needs to be canonized. I mean, how many medals do you think they could give her? Maybe they should just give her her own country as a big thank-you from the world." Greg smiled and then winced.

Maeve reached for him, pulling up the side of his shirt. Blood had started to seep through his hastily constructed bandage. "We really need to take care of this."

Greg waved her away. "It's fine."

"It's not." Maeve stood and then pulled Greg to his feet. Using the keycard Greg had, Maeve opened the medical suite next to the room the Guardian was in.

"On the stretcher," she ordered Greg as she gathered supplies. After washing her hands and pulling on gloves, she pushed the small metal tray closer to Greg.

Flipping on the light, she pulled off the bandage and examined the wound. "It's not too bad. But I'm going to put in a few stitches for now until we can get it looked at at a hospital."

Greg sighed, leaning his head back. "My first bullet wound."

"Think of the bragging rights you've earned." Maeve cleaned the area, making Greg wince. "Sorry," she mumbled. "Numbing agent."

Greg nodded, looking away as she swabbed the area. "So what do you think they're talking about?" Greg asked.

"I have no idea." And she really didn't. This was the mother and children's first meeting. And they had all been through so much. What *were* they saying to one another? How did you capture everything that had happened in a lifetime in a few moments? Where did you even start?

"I just hope she's nothing like Martin," Greg said.

Maeve shuddered. "Amen to that."

CHAPTER NINETY-FOUR

As soon as Greg and Maeve left the room, Ariana wanted to call them back. With the two of them there, it was easy to allow herself to be distracted from the reality of what had just happened: Their mother had awoken. A woman that neither she nor Sammy knew at all.

Ariana looked at Sammy staring down at their mother intently. She didn't know Sammy much either. She had met him less than a week ago, although her time with him could be counted in hours or even minutes.

Now she'd found out the woman who'd raised her, who'd loved her, wasn't her biological mother. And that the woman who was her biological mother was not even from this planet. She took a step back from the bed. This was all happening too fast. She needed to get out of here. She needed to—

"It's all right."

Her mother's voice was soft, almost musical. The sound of it stopped Ariana in her tracks. She felt like she had heard that voice before. Like somehow deep down she'd always known that voice.

Her mother sat up in bed. "You have found one another. I am happy for that."

"I am sorry we were not able to get to you sooner," Sammy said.

"You found me as soon as you could. That is all that matters." She swung her legs over the bed.

Ariana's eyes widened. "How are you doing that?"

Comas weren't her area of expertise, but she was pretty sure most patients required more than a few minutes to recuperate.

Her mother's blue eyes trapped Ariana's. "I am not human."

The words, though said softly, slammed into Ariana. Her mother was not human. *And neither am I.* The true impact of that hadn't hit Ariana until this moment. Her chest seized up and her throat tightened. *She's not human and neither am I. I don't belong here. None of us belong here.*

Before Ariana could flee the room, her mother took her arm with a gentle squeeze. "You belong here, child. This planet is your home, and you will do great things here."

Her mother inched toward the edge of the bed. Sammy moved forward to help her stand.

Ariana was struck at the similarity in their facial expressions. Both were focused, both intent. *I'm nothing like either of them.*

"Yes, you are, my dear. More than you realize."

That was the second time her mother had guessed at what she was thinking ... which meant it wasn't a guess. "You can read my thoughts?"

"I apologize for the intrusion. I do not normally engage in such behaviors without permission. I am a little out of practice. I know this will take some time. Perhaps it would help if you were to call me by my name, Ethera."

"Ethera," Ariana said.

Her mother smiled. "It is good to finally meet you both. I knew of your existence but could only see glimpses of you now and then through other's minds. It was not enough."

Ariana felt the longing in her words. She bit her bottom lip. Her mother had been a victim in all of this as much and perhaps more than either Sammy or she had been.

"Well, we have time now," Sammy said.

"Yes, we do." Her mother looked down at the shift she was wearing with a grimace. "Can you help me find something to wear? There is somewhere we must go first."

"Where?" Ariana asked.

Her mother's voice, which Ariana had thought musical only a few seconds ago, took on a sharp, hard edge. "To see Martin Drummond."

CHAPTER NINETY-FIVE

G REG HAD FOUND A JUMPSUIT AND SOME BOOTS THAT FIT
Ethera and brought them for her to wear. She looked so human in
her tan jumpsuit that it was hard to imagine that she was anything
but that.

But she was. She was an alien being. And Ariana was her
daughter.

Even with everything Maeve had seen and experienced, she
struggled with this one. Ariana and her mother both looked so
human. The Russian cosmonauts spoke of the Guardians as creatures of light. Neither Sammy, Ariana, nor Ethera looked like what
the cosmonauts had described.

And Maeve knew if she was struggling, Ariana had to be reeling. She knew it was going to take her months, if not years to truly
understand everything that had happened in the last few days.

Once Ethera had gotten changed, she stood up, her energy
seeming fully restored. Another marvel. People in long-term comas
did not bounce back that quickly. It was a slow, painful slog. Maeve
supposed her remarkable recovery was evidence enough that the
woman was not fully human.

Now Ethera strode down the hall with the rest of them
following in her wake. Maeve wasn't sure what exactly Ethera had

planned, but she moved with determination. Without any guidance, she headed to the containment cells.

Ethera didn't even spare a glance for the Hanks that flung themselves against the glass walls, trying to escape. She headed to the cell where Martin was held. She stepped in front of the glass wall, her arms behind her back. Maeve, Sammy, Ariana, and Greg fanned out behind her.

Maeve stared at the man who had created all of this. He had been the boogeyman in the back of her mind ever since all of this had begun. And yet now as she looked at him, she saw him for what he was: just another human. One that had been given too much power.

Martin jolted to his feet from the cot. His mouth hung open. He moved toward the glass wall as if he couldn't help himself. He reached out a hand toward Ethera. "My love."

Ethera looked at him without expression. "Open the cell."

Martin hurried to the panel behind the wall. The wall retracted. Martin smiled as Ethera stepped into the cell. "You are even more beautiful now."

Ethera said nothing as she stepped toward Martin. She placed her hands on either side of his face. Martin smiled, his face looking downright blissful.

Ethera slipped one hand around the back of his head and the other around his chin. She twisted hard.

The unmistakable snap of Martin's neck breaking rang out through the cell block.

Martin's eyes flew open. He stared in shock, and then all the light disappeared from his eyes.

Ethera released him, stepping back. His body crumpled to the ground in a lifeless heap.

Ariana gasped. Maeve stumbled back.

But Sammy nodded. "Good."

Greg nodded as well, seconding his words.

Ethera stepped out of the cell and looked at Ariana with concern. She reached for Ariana, but Ariana took a step back. Her mother pulled her hands back slowly. "I could see into his heart. It was too damaged to be repaired. The darkness had festered over the years. Had he been allowed to live, he would have led to the downfall of everyone and everything he touched. He would have led to the end of this planet. Ending his life saved the lives of others. But I took no pleasure in it."

Ariana nodded but didn't seem to know what to say. Her mother seemed to understand. She shifted her gaze to encompass all of them. "Now, we must speak with the Council."

CHAPTER NINETY-SIX

THE DRY HEAT AND BRIGHT LIGHT WERE A WELCOME CHANGE from the controlled temperature of Martin's lair. Maeve stepped outside, grateful to feel the sun on her face. She glanced back at the open doorway. They had set off fires across Martin's base. The Hanks couldn't be discovered, or worse, recreated. And Ariana wanted her samples destroyed. They decided to torch the entire base.

And it felt good. It felt like a catharsis, like they were finally able to put Martin behind them. Maeve felt no compassion for the man whose corpse now burned in the cell below. If anything, his death had been too easy.

Greg stepped out next to her, stretching and then wincing. "Oof, remind me not to do that again." He paused, his gaze turned to the sky. "Uh, Maeve, what is that?"

Maeve followed Greg's gaze, seeing the dark shape growing larger in the sky.

"Is that what I think it is?" Greg asked.

Maeve nodded. "That's Agaren's ship."

Sammy, Ariana, and Ethera stepped out of the bunker. Ethera stepped away from the group, looking toward the approaching ship. She turned back to each of them. "I will meet you at the

Council's base. We have much to discuss."

Her gaze lingered on Ariana and Sammy for a moment longer before she was engulfed in a bright-orange light. The light stretched until it was ten feet tall with wings that were clearly outlined in the light before it shot straight up into the sky.

"I guess she really is a Guardian," Greg said.

Maeve couldn't tear her gaze away from the orange light. "So it seems."

"What do you think she's going to tell the Council?" he asked.

Maeve shook her head, hoping that her reappearance might be enough to stay the Council's hand. But when Ethera recounted her experiences at the hands of Martin, perhaps their fates would be sealed. She swallowed a ball of cold fear taking lodge in her stomach. "I don't know. But I guess we're going to find out."

———

The ride to the moon seemed to take longer this time, perhaps because Maeve was anxious to see Pop and Crackle and to find out what the Council had decided. This time there were five seats that appeared on the deck of Agaren's ship.

Sammy seemed the most uneasy inside the ship. But then again, for someone who could fly, she supposed it would feel unnatural to allow something else to fly for him. And while the trip did seem long, she luckily was sitting next to Greg, who stared in wonder at everything he saw. Which definitely helped distract her from the meeting to come.

Soon she found herself stepping onto one of the sled vehicles and moving through the Council's base. She ignored Greg's nervous rambling. She couldn't seem to speak. Ariana and Sammy were similarly silent. Even Agaren only spoke when necessary.

Greg's chatter died off as the doors to the Council's meeting room slid open. Once again, the Council was waiting. But this time, Ethera had taken her rightful place in the chair in the middle. Maeve glanced over to where Pop and Crackle were. The wall was still up, giving her no view of them.

They exited the sled. Agaren took his place on the dais with the others. Greg, Maeve, Ariana, and Sammy lined up in front of them. Greg slipped his hand into Maeve's, and she squeezed it, thankful for the comfort. Then they waited.

Ethera stood. "Humans are complex creatures. You have the capacity for great love, sacrifice, but also great evil and selfishness. There is a war within each of you between these forces of good and evil, and too often the good loses out."

Maeve felt sick. After all they had been through, the Council was still going to rule against them. Her chest felt tight, and her eyes began to burn with unshed tears.

"But there are sparks of hope. I have seen through my daughter and my son the capacity for kindness in the human race." Ethera focused her gaze on Maeve. "And through you, we have seen the lengths a human would go to protect the ones they love. It is heartening to see such efforts."

Greg squeezed her hand, but Maeve couldn't tear her gaze away from Ethera as hope began to bloom in her chest. "The human experiment has been a long one. I do not believe that it is complete yet. There is still time for humanity to find the goodness within. And we have seen great hope. Humanity will not be ended. The experiment may continue."

Maeve's shoulders sagged in relief. But then she glanced over to where Pop and Crackle were. "And Pop and Crackle? What is to become of them?"

Ethera shook her head. "I am afraid that while humanity shows promise, we cannot risk the lives of the hybrids. The choice remains the same. You may join them or remain on Earth. But they cannot be returned to Earth unless a true safe haven for them can be established."

Maeve's world crumbled again. She would still have to choose. Pop and Crackle versus Alvie, Snap, Chris, and all of her friends on

Earth. Grief threatened to overwhelm her. How was she going to do this?

"What about us?" Ariana asked, a tremor in her voice.

Ethera smiled at her children. "You belong on Earth. It is home for both of you. And you have found people there to care for you."

"But ... but what about you?" Ariana asked.

"We will have time. I will visit you, and I will enable you to visit me here when you wish. I would like to get to know my children. That is, if you would like that."

"I would," Sammy said.

After only a moment's hesitation, Ariana nodded as well. "I would as well."

Maeve stared at the three of them, her heart breaking. Ethera's family was now whole. But Maeve's had been torn apart. Next to her, Greg raised his hand. "Um, Your Highnesses or Royalships? I'm really not sure how to address you guys."

Ethera turned to Greg. "Titles are unnecessary. What is it you wish to say, Dr. Schorn?"

He took a deep breath. "You said that Pop and Crackle could not be returned to Earth unless they could be given a safe haven."

Ethera nodded. "Yes, that is true."

Greg smiled. "Well, I think I have just the place. Let me tell you about a little town called Svente."

EPILOGUE

SVENTE, NORWAY

SIX MONTHS LATER

THE VILLAGE OF SVENTE WAS CALM AS MAEVE STEPPED OUT OF the small house. The snow had finally stopped falling, although there was still about four feet on the ground. But it had warmed all the way up to 32, and it was strange how warm 32° could feel after temperatures had been stuck in the single digits for a few months.

Snap, Crackle, and Pop burst out the door behind her. Each wore a heavy winter coat, hats, gloves, and had a backpack. They sprinted down the path. Hope bounded out of the door behind them, barking and jumping, sensing their excitement and being part of it as well.

"Hey, hey, did you guys forget something?"

Each of the triplets stopped on a dime and then whirled around and sprinted back for Maeve. Pop reached her first, giving a leap. Maeve caught him in her arms with a laugh. He hugged her tight. *Bye, Mama.*

Maeve's chest tightened at the thought. She kissed him on the cheek. "Have a good day today."

Crackle and Snap each gave her the same treatment before they sprinted down the path, waiting anxiously at the edge of it. Chris stepped out of the house with a cup of coffee in an insulated travel mug. Steam seeped from the small hole in the lid. He kissed Maeve on the cheek. "I'm going to stop by Bill's. He should have fresh bread. Any requests?"

Maeve nodded. "You mind stopping in at the post office? I ordered a few things from Amazon."

Chris laughed. "What is it this time? A cappuccino maker?"

Maeve shook her head. "No, that was on backorder. It will take an extra week."

Chris smiled as he shook his head and headed toward the triplets. "Okay, my little gang of ruffians. Who's going to have a good day at school today?"

Each of the triplets raised their hand as they clambered around Chris. They could barely contain themselves as they walked next to him down the road. Hope trotted along next to them, looking completely satisfied with the world. Alvie had already left to help Bill, the town's baker, make bread this morning. Apparently he had a real flair for baking.

Maeve watched them go, her heart bursting at the sight. This was what she had wanted for all of them. She had wanted them to have a normal life. The triplets had started at the school four months ago. The people of Svente had paused for a moment at the sight of them, but then they had simply accepted them into the fold. They were already keeping the secrets of their other village members. They saw no problem with adding a few more secrets to the pile.

Maeve's biggest complaint was how cold it was, but she could get used to that. Putting up with frigid temperatures if it meant her kids got to have a semblance of a normal life? No problem.

Maeve's computer beeped behind her. She quickly closed the door and wrapped her arms around herself as she made her way to the kitchen table. She clicked on FaceTime and smiled as Greg's face popped up. "Hey, Greg. How's it going?"

"Pretty good. Ariana is all settled in. And I've got the latest batch of escapees that D.E.A.D. was able to track down."

Maeve groaned. "You really need to stop calling it that."

"Well, then, they really need to come up with a different name."

"When are you coming by?"

"Ariana said she'd have us up there for dinner. And she wants to see how Sammy's doing."

"He's kind of good."

In Martin's lab, Greg and Maeve had discovered the suppressant that had been used on Ariana all those years. With Sammy's permission, they had used it on him just to see what the effect might be. And it was startling. His wings had disappeared, and his skin had taken on a normal cast. He now could pass for human.

But with the right dosage, they figured out how he could pass as human but pull out the wings when he needed them. He could now slip between different modes, almost like a superhero. If he wanted to be Sammy the flying avenging angel, he could be. But otherwise he could pass for anybody else. He worked at the docks, loading and unloading ships. He lived in a house just two doors down from Maeve. Nora and Iggy lived at the house in between. And Luke and Sandra lived in the house on the other side.

And as far as Maeve could tell, Sammy seemed to be happy. Maeve was shocked by all of it. She was shocked that her kids finally had a normal life. She was shocked that Sammy was able to slip into human society so easily. She was shocked that they had all managed to find a life up here.

Of course, Tilda had put security protocols in place for the town. Now it was a R.I.S.E. offshoot. They had more people but also more protection than they ever had before. And they were decidedly off the grid. Tilda had even had them removed from Google Maps. Any mention of the town had all but disappeared. Jasper and Mike lived in town, and a R.I.S.E. base was being constructed a few miles away. Maeve would work at the base once it was up and running, as would Chris, Nora, and Sandra.

And so would Alvie. His mind was light-years ahead of the rest of them, so when it came to the question of space exploration, Tilda knew there was no one better than Alvie to be in charge of the science for that program.

But Tilda herself had surprised everyone by going into semiretirement. She would never be fully retired. It was Tilda, after all. But she had handed most of the day-to-day activities over to Pearl and John Forrester, who had moved here from Wright-Pat.

"Everything set up for tonight?" Greg asked.

"Just a few last-minute details and we're good to go. You'll be here in time for the party?"

Greg grinned. "You couldn't keep me away."

———

Hours later, Maeve could finally relax. The party had started, and she was officially off duty and on party relaxation mode, at least until cleanup.

Richard had agreed to allow them to hold the party in his warehouse. They'd pushed aside the pallets, and with a lot of help from Sammy, Iggy, and Claude, they'd strung streamers and balloons all over the place. Two eight-foot tables were covered in red tablecloths and loaded down with food. Another held a giant birthday cake, already reduced to half its size, and a stack of brightly wrapped gifts. Now dozens of R.I.S.E. and Svente townspeople milled about, eating and talking.

Tilda stepped into view through the crowd, Sebastian's hand firmly held within her own. Adam stepped next to them. As he passed them, his hand rested for just a second on the back of Sebastian's head.

Maeve smiled at the sight. Tilda and Adam had adopted Sebastian. Sebastian brought out an affection in Adam that none of them had seen before, except perhaps Tilda. She seemed completely unsurprised at how good a father Adam was. And Tilda was a downright doting mother. They made an adorable little family.

They got lost in the crowd, and Maeve looked around, trying to find the birthday boy in the midst of this group of about fifty people. Iggy and Claude were playing in the corner with Snap, Crackle, Pop, Luke, and a few of the town's kids. Nora and Sandra stood nearby chatting, with only occasional glances over at the kids.

Sammy stood in a corner speaking with Greg and Ariana, while Jasper loaded up a plate from the buffet. Mike stood nearby, shaking his head at him. Even Ethera had come to town for the party. She stood talking to John Forrester.

Maeve smiled at the sight of all of them. Somehow, they had made it through this. Somehow they had survived Martin and the Council and everything. And now, they had an actual community where all of them could live. It was beyond her wildest dreams.

She scanned the group, frowning, unable to spot Alvie. Then she saw him sitting at the top of the stairs of the warehouse. Maeve walked over to him, wondering what was on his mind. He'd been shielding his thoughts from her more and more. She knew that was a good thing. It was part of him growing up. But she still wished he'd let her in a little bit more.

She climbed the stairs and sat next to him. He leaned his head into her shoulder, and she wrapped her arm around him. "Happy?"

A feeling of contentment wafted through her, making her smile. *Happy.*

And that was all that Maeve wanted. She wanted her family and friends happy. And if, after all the horrors they had been through, they could manage that, even if it meant living at the very edge of the world in an ice box, well, then she considered herself pretty damn lucky.

The End

FACT OR FICTION?

Thank you for reading *S.A.V.E.*! I hope you enjoyed it. If you did, please consider leaving a review.

It's always sad when a series comes to an end. The characters become like family. But with this series, at least I was able to leave them in a good place ... and Martin in a very warm, uncomfortable one.

The prequel to the A.L.I.V.E. Series, *B.E.G.I.N.* is exclusively available to my mailing list. If you haven't signed up yet, you can sign up for my mailing list here.

Now on to the facts ... and some of the fictions.

Geiranger and Svente, Norway. Geiranger Norway is a real place. My description is as accurate as I could make. From the pictures I saw, it looks amazing! It has a small population of only around 200 in its slow season. But in the peak season it balloons to one million. Do yourself a favor and google it just for the images or click here.

Svente, however, is a not a real town. The island where I placed the town however does exist. The Svalbard Islands are located in the Arctic Ocean between Norway and the Arctic and is very sparsely populated.

Alien Base Under the Surface of the Moon. There is a

huge mass underneath the moon's surface. It is five times the size of the Big Island of Hawaii and is located under the moon's South Pole. In fact, the mass is so large, that the South Pole actually experiences higher levels of gravity. Plus, the weight of the mass pulls the crater floor down by more than a kilometer.

No one is saying it is an alien base. Most scientists briefed on it believe it to be the result of a massive collision between the moon and an asteroid. For more information Google mass under the moon's surface or click here.

Interstellar Object. There was a mysterious cigar-shaped object spotted tumbling through the solar system in 2017. It was named Oumuamua, meaning "a messenger that reaches out from the distant past" in Hawaiian.

And who declared it might be an interstellar alien space probe? Harvard Smithsonian Center for Astrophysics. Click here for more information.

Meteorites. Thousands of meteorites hit the earth every day. The bulk of them burn up in the atmosphere. Occasionally however, a few slip through. Some of them causing incredible damage

The Chelyabinsk meteor was a small chunk of space rock the size of a six story building. It exploded over the Russian city of Chelyabinsk back in 2013. The blast was stronger than a nuclear explosion, triggering detections from monitoring stations in Antarctica. Over 1200 people were injured. For more information, google Russian meteorite or click here.

Meteorites and the Moon. The moon similar to the Earth is bombarded by meteorites daily. Unlike the Earth, however, the moon does not have an atmosphere to protect it. Its surface takes the impact of all these incursions.

Which relates to another issue: did the moon ever have an atmosphere that could support life? Believe it or not, the answer is getting closer to yes. Scientists now acknowledge that the moon did at one point have an atmosphere, although they believe it was just shy of being capable of sustaining life. But who knows what further research will bring?

For more information, click here or google the moon's atmosphere.

Glass Structures on the Moon. The existence of glass structures on the moon is firmly in the conspiracy theory camp. Having said that, I read a fascinating book on the topic: *Dark Mission* by Richard Hoagland. It was truly fascinating. So are there glass structures on the moon? I have no idea. But it is intriguing.

Secret Apollo Missions. Seventeen Apollo missions were launched between 1963 and 1972. (The first one resulted in a tragic fire on the launching pad.) But the Apollo missions were supposed to extend beyond 17. Apollo Missions 18,19, and 20 were all intended to be lunar missions. They were cancelled due to budgetary constraints. Once again, in the conspiracy world, there are those who contend that the either: 1) the missions were cancelled because the astronauts were warned off the moon, or 2) the missions were completed in secret.

Astronauts and UFOs. According to reports, Aldrin and Armstrong reported over a medical channel that they were being watched while they were on the moon. The information on the news conference following their return is also accurate. They were very subdued. It is entirely plausible however that this was due to the fact that they were tired or overwhelmed from the space flight.

Other astronauts years later came out and said that they believed UFOs were real. And that they saw them while on their NASA missions.

Astronaut Alan Bean, who passed away in 2018, did take up art later in life. He painted landscapes of the moon. And those landscapes, rather than just being monotone, incorporated color. And here's he said about these paintings: "But I'm the only one who can paint the moon, because I'm the only one who knows whether that's right or not."

You can see some of his paintings here.

Annual UFO Sightings. There has been a decrease in

reported UFO sightings. Which is interesting given that US military just recently announced that they cannot explain all of the flying objects they have come across.

Thank you for taking this journey with me, Alvie, Maeve, Greg, the triplets, Chris and all the rest!

I hope your next reading adventure fills your heart and stimulates your mind!

Until next time,

RD

P.S. And please consider leaving a review. Thank you. :)

ABOUT THE AUTHOR

R.D. Brady is an American writer who grew up on Long Island, NY but has made her home in both the South and Midwest before settling in upstate New York. On her way to becoming a full-time writer, R.D. received a Ph.D. in Criminology and taught for ten years at a small liberal arts college.

R.D. left the glamorous life of grading papers behind in 2013 with the publication of her first novel, the supernatural action adventure, *The Belial Stone*. Over ten novels later and hundreds of thousands of books sold, and she hasn't looked back. Her novels tap into her criminological background, her years spent studying martial arts, and the unexplained aspects of our history. Join her on her next adventure!

To learn about her upcoming publications, sign up for her newsletter here or on her website (rdbradybooks.com).

BOOKS BY R.D. BRADY

Hominid

The Belial Series (in order)
The Belial Stone
The Belial Library
The Belial Ring
Recruit: A Belial Series Novella
The Belial Children
The Belial Origins
The Belial Search
The Belial Guard
The Belial Warrior
The Belial Plan
The Belial Witches
The Belial War
The Belial Fall
The Belial Sacrifice

The A.L.I.V.E. Series
B.E.G.I.N.
A.L.I.V.E.

D.E.A.D.
R.I.S.E.
S.A.V.E.

The Steve Kane Series
Runs Deep
Runs Deeper

The Unwelcome Series
Protect
Seek
Proxy

The Nola James Series
Surrender the Fear
Escape the Fear

Published as Riley D. Brady
The Key of Apollo
The Curse of Hecate

Be sure to sign up for R.D.'s mailing list to be the first to hear when she has a new release!

Made in the USA
Coppell, TX
28 November 2019